SECTOR EIGHT

A NOVEL
BY MICHAEL ATAMANOV

Wishing you safe travels on your fantasy journey,

Michael Atamanov

PERIMETER DEFENSE
BOOK# 1

MAGIC DOME BOOKS

Sector Eight
Perimeter Defense, Book # 1
Second Edition
Published by Magic Dome Books, 2017
Copyright © M. Atamanov 2015
Cover Art © V. Manyukhin 2015
Translator © Andrew Schmitt 2015
All Rights Reserved
ISBN: 978-80-88231-05-9

TABLE OF CONTENTS:

INTRODUCTION

THE BATTLE was coming to an end. One thousand five hundred dreadnoughts were in siege mode conducting orbital bombardment on the planet below, turning all its space defense structures into dust and preparing landing zones for the space marines. A few hundred lumbering battleships were covering the heavy siege ships, while the faster assault and strategic cruisers, together with the interceptors, happily raced through the star system after the remnants of the enemy armada. All the other allies were out collecting trophies. There was such an abundance of valuable loot this time – it stretched as far as the eye could see. All visible space was carpeted in fragments of broken ships...

I took off my headphones and moved my chair away from the computer desk. I was still so excited from the massive space battle that my hands were shaking. There were thousands of players on each side! I went to take a sip from my beer can. Damn, it's empty already. When had I had the time to down a half liter of beer? I had to tear myself from my chair, stand up and hobble over to the kitchen fridge. There wasn't any more of my favorite local unfiltered beer. The best I could do was a bottle of dark Czech beer at the bottom of the vegetable drawer left there two weeks earlier by a group of old college buddies. It reminded me of my younger days when my friend Pavel used to buy a whole crate of beer that we could never finish. It's not my favorite kind of beer, but it's still a bit better than average. As usual, the opener wasn't where it should have been in the box on the table, so I had no choice but to open the bottle with a fork before taking a foamy swig so cold it hurt my teeth. Praise the Lord!

I walked over to the window. There were some lights hanging from the curtain rod left over from a New Year's party. New Year's was three weeks ago at that point so the decorations should have been down already. All the same, for the hundredth time I was just not feeling up to standing on a stool and climbing up on the window sill. I looked out at the street. Winter had come in all its darkness. A cold wind whistled as it swept its way up the street. It was just past six in the morning, and the cold black sky wasn't even offering a hint of the coming sunrise.

I looked into the cold haze out my window and held back a yawn. I had had to wake up with my alarm clock this morning at 3:30 A.M., then spend a whole hour gathering half-sleeping soldiers for the CTA (Call to Arms!!!) that had been announced yesterday and sneak our whole assault fleet between two stellar regions to the site of the grand battle. The unexpected arrival of our fleet on the battlefield brought chaos to the ranks of our numerically superior enemy. We attacked immediately, even though they outnumbered us twelve to one. We took advantage of the opportunity and got into battle formation, targeting a pre-prepared list of enemy commanders we knew to be talented as we regrouped.

Our plan went off without a hitch. The enemy commanders were sent to medical centers for respawn, which effectively took them out of the game for a while. All they could do was swear pointlessly in chat or try to awkwardly manage their troops through video from allied streamers. They had been deprived of the ability to react in a responsive manner to the quickly changing situation. The enemy armada, lacking adequate command, flew cluelessly in circles through space, which we took appropriate advantage of, radically thinning the herd of our bumbling prey. Moreover, any time the enemy was able to replace a downed fleet commander and get some kind of resistance together, they would already be outnumbered three to one, and in a situation like that there was no way my well-trained high-class soldiers could lose. After that, there were some long firefights and chases, in other words, tons of fun before the bloody battle ended in our unconditional victory.

Shivering from the cold in my apartment, I turned the knob on the radiator slightly and went back to my computer. The enemy station had already been taken over by our alliance. Huge transport ships were hauling in everything our alliance's military and industry would need for our new home. Our boys had already finished looting the wreckage of the enemy ships and were preparing to overtake the reserve combat ships from the intermediary station all on their own.

An atmosphere of unrestrained joy and celebration reigned in game chats. Dozens of unread private messages and chat invitations flashed on my screen. I immediately turned them all down because I was too tired and not in the mood to explain myself to anyone. I was just skimming the first line of the messages, not making a special effort to read them any further. There were people thanking me for a job well done and others wondering how long it would take them to get compensation for lost ships. Allies were congratulating me on the victory and tactfully reminding me about my earlier promise to give them half of the captured territory. Enemies were threatening to get revenge and take back their lost station. Some of them were even sputtering silly threats that they would find my IP-address, find me in real life and break my arms and legs, but there weren't many of them. I even came across enemies who expressed their admiration at the operation in broken Russian or English. Basically, just like usual. I was on the verge of deleting all unread messages without even looking at them, but one message just kept calling my attention. It was from a player I didn't know by the name Space_General123. Much to my surprise, he wrote in perfect Russian:

"Great job! Congratulations! I was listening in on your voice chat and watched the whole battle from the sidelines, start to finish. It was a very precise operation. I especially liked that fake panic you created. Really believable. I'm sure the enemy spies bought it. But enough empty words, let's get down to business. I have an offer that you might find interesting. There's a job that you fit the profile for. A big alliance needs an experienced fleet commander. You'll be paid entirely in real money, no virtual bytes. Let me know if you're interested."

My hand froze on the mouse button as I sat there, not deleting the message. A big military alliance? And also is it a Russian-speaking one or at least one with a lot of Russian-speaking players? I considered it seriously. I was pretty sure I knew all the more-or-less serious alliances in the game. There really were quite a few Russian alliances out there. Well, to be more accurate, mixed Slavic alliances, including the one I was in then. There were three really serious ones, but none of them needed fleet commanders. Though there were rumors that the permanent leader and commander of one of the top alliances was about to get married, or something, and quit computer games completely. But I had talked to him literally yesterday, and he had a ton of big plans, so he didn't really seem like a person playing their favorite online game for the last time.

Plus, this weird guy, what was his name... Space_General123 wrote that he had been listening to our private voice channel. I looked at this mysterious character's information. A complete zero, made just three hours ago. Obviously, it was the alternate character of some other, much more experienced player who didn't want to reveal their identity. Nevertheless, he was listening in on our channel. That means he was either from our alliance or had somehow found out our secret password. In the first case, it would have meant that one of my thoroughly vetted people was working for the competition. In the second, it would have meant that one of our pilots had given top-secret information to a stranger! It's hard to even say what would have been worse. In any case, we'd have to root out the traitor in our ranks, so I sent a message back:

"It's hard to answer right away like this. It might be something I'd be interested in. It all depends on the conditions."

Almost immediately, he sent me a voice chat invitation. I put on my headphones and got ready to listen carefully. I had an ear for voices. Ever since I was a child, I had been able to discern minute changes in a person's intonation and uncover tricks or bald-faced lies. Plus, I knew a lot of my team by voice and would have been able to pick them out, even if they were purposely disguising themselves. All the same, this guy's voice was new to me.

"Hi! I'm glad you agreed to hear me out." Judging by his voice, he was already quite a bit older than 40, but definitely not old yet. "Does it bother you if I speak informally? You're a young guy, it just doesn't seem natural to put on airs for you. You can call me Georgiy Innokentievich."

I did my best to call him by his full name but, in my sleep deprived and slightly drunken state, my tongue wasn't in any condition to pronounce such a tooth-shattering combination of sounds on the first go. My admirer wasn't offended though and even chuckled back at my awkwardness:

"I don't know what my parents were thinking when they gave me that name. Not many people can say it right all the time. My international partners don't even try to pronounce it. To make it easier, they just call me Mr. G. I. You can do the same. Or call me

George, or even Gordy, but that might be a bit too familiar."

"Alright, Georgiy, what do you want from me?" I asked, deliberately not identifying myself by name and also choosing a name option for him that he had not suggested. I also opted to speak informally.

"As I already told you, there's a job to be had, with good pay too. So good that you won't have to work anywhere else, or do anything but your favorite activity. In fact, that would even be a necessary condition of this arrangement. Nothing can be allowed to distract you from carrying out your mission..."

I couldn't hold it in anymore and laughed into the microphone. How naive this guy was! Did he really think you could hire a good fleet commander for the game under these conditions? I've obviously been taken for some kind of complete gaming addict who can sit for days on end in front of a monitor washing down delivery pizza with cola.

"That's impossible," I answered, laughing back. "I have a contract already with this alliance, and it's plenty good for me."

"You contract was completed as soon as you'd finished the mission at hand and taken the base," said my new acquaintance, revealing a surprising level of familiarity with my agreements with alliance leaders. "Now, your soldiers can spend some time fattening up in a new place and saving their money. There isn't supposed to be an active war for at least six months, so the alliance has no need for a fleet commander. And what kind of contract did they give you? Two hundred bucks a month for beer and cigs? Laughable! I'm talking about actually good money."

That's where he really got my interest. I don't know how he'd found out what I was getting paid or the specifics of my contract. Obviously, my employer had been indiscrete. But I really had suggested these exact conditions a few months earlier, and at the time they had seemed like a good deal: two hundred dollars a month, and for that, I'd agreed to train fighters every evening after work and on weekends and make them into a flight team that could win a war against a coalition of Eastern European alliances. For some reason, after Georgiy's speech, the conditions I had once negotiated for no longer seemed like such a good deal.

"What city do you live in?" wondered my mysterious acquaintance for some reason. For a reason I don't even understand, I answered honestly that I lived in Moscow.

"In Moscow!? That's impossible! I'm from Moscow too!" Mr. G.I. cried out in joy, as I suddenly picked up on his theretofore unnoticed native Muscovite accent. "Well, listen up then. Seeing how you're not gonna sleep anyway, let's meet up in an hour somewhere at a restaurant and discuss all of this one-on-one. Is anything open in the capital at this hour? Do you want to go to *The Wishbone* bar? It's by the Sokolniki metro station. Do you know where that is?"

"Do I know where it is? I live right next door!" I even got a bit offended at his lack of trust in my knowledge of my native city. "The only thing is that we need to reserve a table in advance. You can't just show up!"

"At seven A.M., in this blizzard? It's probably totally empty." "Well, I'll reserve a table under my name in any case. Sound good? It's a deal. We'll meet at exactly seven at *The Wishbone!*"

The call cut off. I looked at the clock. It was six twenty in the morning. The mirror on the wall told me I was unshaven, disheveled, wrinkled, and swollen after a sleepless night of beer drinking. My potential employer seemed like a very mysterious person, so I wanted to create a favorable impression. I had to go to the bathroom, looking around my bachelor pad on my way for some more-or-less clean socks and an iron that I knew was hiding somewhere.

At exactly seven, I walked into *The Wishbone*. A pretty hostess took me from the entrance to the coat room, took my coat and pointed to the far corner of a totally empty, early-morning room where a hefty man in an expensive-looking suit was sitting solemnly at the only occupied table. He was younger than he had come across over the phone. Not fifty, but no more than thirty or thirty-five. Next to Mr. G. I., there were two men standing at attention who looked a lot alike, as if they were twin brothers. They were his bodyguards, and they were wearing identical gray suits. Both guards were keeping careful watch over how close I came to Georgiy. As soon as I got within fifteen feet of their employer's table, they both simultaneously reached with their right hands for the holsters hanging from their belts. Holy shit! They weren't even trying to hide the fact that they had guns on them! I was a bit taken aback by the guards' wildly inhospitable behavior, and so I stopped sharply in place.

Georgiy said something very quietly, though both bodyguards heard their employer and pulled their hands back from their weapons. After that, my strange acquaintance said something else, but this time much louder so I could hear it. He asked his guards to leave us alone so we could have a confidential conversation. I took the seat I was offered and stretched out my hand to shake his: "Ruslan!"

Mr. G. I. froze for a few seconds as if he did not know whether to greet me, but then his expression faded into a smile and he answered me with a handshake, "Georgiy! Well, nice to meet you!"

My acquaintance's palm was quite soft to the touch and somehow feminine, as if he had never been subjected to either physical labor or exercise. And so what? It's not like that was impossible. Maybe he was the son of some Moscow politician. He had been living in complete luxury since childhood. He'd never had to worry about money or getting into an elite private school and meeting all the "right" people. Then to celebrate his graduation from University, his parents bought him a job as deputy director at a huge company, and Georgiy had never had to work his way up the career ladder from the very bottom.

As I looked over Mr. G. I. surreptitiously, they brought our food: grilled trout, a huge plate of shrimp with hot sauce, and a charcuterie plate. And alcohol too, of course: there was vodka in a rounded carafe and some kind of wine. I emphatically refused the vodka. Mixing that with the beer I'd just drank would make for a killer cocktail, and getting drunk in front of a potential employer wouldn't be smart. My new acquaintance didn't argue and poured me a glass of light white wine. We toasted to our meeting, and I couldn't hold back any more. I had to ask:

"So, what alliance are we talking about here, Georgiy? It's weird, because I basically know all the big alliances in the game and I can't for the life of me remember any fleet commanders leaving recently..."

"Ruslan, who told you we were talking about that game in particular?" Georgiy inquired, interrupting my awkward attempt at guessing.

His question threw me off. "Then what game are we talking about, if we aren't talking about the one we met in when we talked this morning?" I asked with a smile, thinking he'd been trying to make a joke. But he was dead serious.

"The game I'm talking about is called *Perimeter Defense*. It's a big game with a hundred thousand players.

"*Perimeter Defense*? I've never heard of it..." Seeing my confusion, Georgiy poured us both some more booze and made a toast, given that it had become clear that our conversation would be going on for a while. I noticed that my acquaintance wasn't chasing his alcohol with the food on the table.

"Where do I start?" he began. "You probably realize that rich and famous people also want to get away from hum-drum, everyday life by playing computer games. But add to this that those who have grown accustomed to considering themselves members of the elite are not at all happy with the fact that some players have a less than professional attitude, the so-called 'casuals,' who start to ruin the atmosphere of the game. Plus, games that are out there for normal people don't satisfy such sophisticated gamers at all, neither in graphics nor in plot. Are you following me?"

Who does Georgiy take me for? Does he think I'm a total loser who cannot understand even the simplest words? Why spoon-feed me everything like a baby? Nevertheless, I held firm and didn't let my annoyance show, just nodding quickly up and down. Georgiy continued at a leisurely pace:

"One day the inevitable happened. A few rich people got together, talked it over and decided they would make a totally different game only for an elite private club. It wasn't very hard to make it happen. Most companies that make computer games eked out and still eke out a fairly meager existence and will go ravenous at the sight of a big contract. The made men I just described – you can even call them oligarchs – had everything they needed to bring their dream to life: an ocean of money, excellent designers and artists, the best programmers, and script writers. The clients were finicky and demanded maximum realism and the feeling that you were truly there. Nothing was too small for them, even the most minor details in the game world were reworked dozens and even hundreds of times. They demanded realistic and totally unique voice acting for every character, custom appearances for different species, changing weather, and an elaborate economy. It was a very ambitious project. But, one day, development ended and the game began."

My new acquaintance poured another glass of vodka and wine and offered me a drink. And once again, he didn't chase it, despite the fact that there was more than enough food on the table. Georgiy coughed. It looked like his gulp of hard alcohol had gone down the wrong pipe. Breathing out with difficulty, he continued:

"There are rumors that, in reality, there are a whole bunch of games out there only 'for a select few.' Maybe that's true, but I won't lie because I don't have that information. I personally can confirm the existence of only one such game. It's not likely that you would have heard about it. But just accept it as fact that there is a game that no one ever writes about in computer magazines, isn't advertised on television, and isn't even findable by Internet search. Nevertheless, it is a very high-quality game. Its graphics are practically indistinguishable from reality. You feel so much like you're in the game that you end up just living in that virtual world. Getting in is no easy proposition, you have to have recommendations from other members of the private club..."

Here Georgiy paused, because a waitress had come up to our table to take the dirty dishes. Taking advantage of the pause, we had another drink and he continued, though he had started slightly slurring his words:

"So that's what I'm saying... There's this game, it's called *Perimeter Defense*... But I've already said that... The game is about space and starships. Like the very far future of humanity. There's a huge, practically limitless cosmos, and a character wouldn't even be able to fly to the edge of this virtual world if they had their whole life to do it. And, in it, there is a big and fairly strong Human Empire, which occupies just under one hundred star systems and two or three hundred inhabitable planets. What's more, you can visit every planet with your character, and all these planets are different. You'll never find two that are identical. The designers really put a lot of effort into it. Other than the Empire, there are a few hundred small states with all different forms of government... Some of them are Empire vassals, some are allies, and some are avowed enemies. Close to the borders of the Empire there are mostly Human states, but the further you go into space, the more variety you'll find in terms of species... So, I didn't tell you yet, but there's a whole bunch of alien races, I won't even tell you how many exactly right away... And, actually, I don't think there even are any players who know how many races there are all together... Yeah, and what difference would it make anyway?"

Georgiy poured me another glass of wine despite my protests. I was already feeling like I'd had one too many. I was in a really strange state. I felt like I'd be drunk soon, but I didn't understand how or why. Obviously, being this tired and not having slept was having an effect, because such little wine couldn't have put me in such a state on its own. Nevertheless my acquaintance proved to be stubborn, so I had to pick up the glass and drink it down. After that, he picked up a pickled mushroom on his fork and waved it around, continuing:

"All these races have really confusing relationships among themselves. It's a hell of a mess trying to navigate their friendships, military alliances and irreconcilable hatreds. But none of that matters. What *does* matter is that there are these other, *totally* bizarre species that are one hundred percent different from those ones. I don't even know how to describe the difference between these 'monster' aliens and the 'friendly' aliens. The only thing I can say is that they're one hundred percent different. Very strong. Very dangerous. Very aggressive in nature. There isn't much known about them yet, except that they look different from one to the next, but all of them are deadly dangerous. It isn't even known if there's only one species or a few different ones. We're not sure if they're working together or if they're solitary. But these freaks are attacking our galaxy from different sides, conquering territory as they go. And that's exactly what players are supposed to do: stop the invasion. And those, essentially, are all the rules of the game. What do you say?"

Georgiy took a look at me, clearly waiting for my commentary on his story. To be honest, I hadn't understood a thing, though of course the thought of being able to take a look at this "game for the chosen," even from the corner of my eye, was very tempting. I nodded, and Georgiy poured us both another glass. I mechanically picked up the wine glass and wondered aloud:

"So, what's my role in all this?" Speaking proved harder than I thought. I was also slurring my words at this point.

"You? Didn't I tell you? Really? Strange... Well, listen up then. You'll be leading one of the Human fleets – like, you'll be playing for me. Actually, it's me who's the commander. It's my character, but I'm sure you'll play better than me. You're supposed to defend Perimeter Sector Eight. It's not the hardest sector, but also not the easiest. You'll have a small squadron of ships, as well as some resources and finances. There aren't many attacks on your defensive sector now, but they're growing more frequent. You just need to hold out."

"I don't understand. What interest do you have in this if I'll be playing for you?" I asked in surprise.

"It's hard to say... I'll be honest: It turned out I had no potential as a strategist, and so far I haven't put up impressive results in defense either. But, all the same, I cannot shame myself before the other players. There are very influential people who play this game, and I want them to think I'm a capable fleet commander and a talented leader. It's useful for my career – which is why I'm prepared to pay you well to play for me for a while. Let's say... six months to start. But just keep in mind that it isn't going to be entertainment for you, but real work. You'll have to put all your energy into completing your mission. There are two main rules. The first is that you cannot, under any circumstances, tell anyone that you're playing in my place. The second rule is that you cannot break character, tell other players about real-life news, or tell anyone about your life outside the game. That really bothers people. They came into this virtual world to escape reality after all. If you ever break either of these rules – it's game over, the character is banned and, basically, we'll both be in a lot of shit. I hope you understand that."

"I see, I see..." I responded, finally wondering about how much I'd be getting paid.

Georgiy named an amount. It was about four times more than I was making at my current full-time job. Nevertheless, I immediately sensed a restless waver in his voice and figured that I could be asking for quite a bit more.

And, actually, he turned out to be quite generous in this regard. I was able to negotiate three times better conditions compared to Mr. G. I.'s original offer. I could barely keep myself from screaming in delight for the whole restaurant to hear. It was unbelievable! For that kind of money, I'd have been willing to spend day and night in the game! Of course, I would have to quit my job to devote more time to this mysterious game. But what kind of a job was that anyway? Part-time database programmer... what a joke.

"So, technically, I'll be playing someone else's character? Am I going to be sent the password and screen name?"

"No, nothing like that," chuckled my new acquaintance happily. "I doubt that your computer at home will be able to deal with the graphics and, well, I'd prefer to avoid any potential 'crashes' due to connection problems. So, you'll play from my place. It's a sin to spoil one's impression of an excellent game due to an insufficient level of immersion, which is why I've ordered the finest equipment. I already have a virtual reality helmet. I got the suit too. The virtual reality capsule I ordered is held up at customs for now, but, if they deliver it, your work station will basically be outfitted with all the best equipment."

Virtual reality capsule? It seemed scientific progress had left me in the dust. Unfortunately, I was not able to clarify that point, as the waitress came by again to switch out the dishes and bring us more plates of different delicacies. To be honest, food wasn't agreeing with me at all at that point, and it was even just starting to ask to be let back out. Was it from overeating or had I just drunk too much alcohol? And that after a morning beer?

Georgiy's monotone voice came to me as if through a thick fog. He kept droning on about the game's strict rules and how I could never reveal that I was taking his place. I looked in his direction from under my eyebrows, getting ready to say that I already had it all figured out. But the words were sticking in my throat. For some reason, it began to appear as if Georgiy was not wearing an expensive dark suit from a couturier, but some weird, almost military, dark blue tunic with gold epaulets. I shook my head to banish the illusion. The strange vision passed. Georgiy went back to normal. I put on a dumb smile. What a sight, though!

"Are you listening to me?" Finally, Mr. G.I. had successfully gotten through to my drunken consciousness. "We still have to sign an official contract. We can't do it without a contract, because this is serious money. What are you doing, sleeping? Hello, don't sleep! Concentrate!"

I nodded, but the big stupid grin wouldn't leave my face. All that money! I'll have to get a driver's license and buy a car first thing... After that, I'll have to swap out my rented one-bedroom apartment for something more fitting... Or maybe just buy my own apartment right away? Is it going to be enough money for an apartment? The thoughts were slogging through my head with huge difficulty, which is why I was not able to calculate how much I was supposed to be getting for six months at this job. It was six months that Georgiy said, right? Or was it not six?

The smiling waitress came by again, but this time her tray had a stapled packet of carefully typed-up papers. I noticed that the waitress wasn't wearing the strictly mandated restaurant uniform, but it didn't really register. For some reason, she was wearing a strange, very revealing, semitransparent outfit made of wide pink ribbons that wrapped around her waist, arms and legs with bizarre bobs hanging down. After that, my attention trained in on the papers she'd brought. What is that, my contract? But when would the waitress have had time to print it out? And is printing out papers even a waitress's job? Or had the contract been prepared in advance and she was just bringing it out?

"In duplicate, as legally required. Acquaint yourself with it and sign on the last pages," explained Georgiy, his voice cutting through the haze. For some reason, he was wearing the dark blue military uniform again.

I earnestly tried to read the whole contract, but it turned out to be a pointless exercise. The lines were jumping around before my very eyes and, what was more, something was off with the letters in them somehow. Except for the word "contract" in capital letters on the first page, I couldn't read a thing. One of Georgiy's bodyguards came up to the table, but this time he wasn't a person but some kind of gray, bipedal lizard wearing bone armor. One thing hadn't changed though: he was still wearing a gun on his belt, but this time it wasn't a pistol but some kind of device that looked like a hair dryer.

"My Prince, we must hurry. Time is running short," uttered the lizard in an alarmed state.

"I know!" answered Georgiy sharply in his uniform. "But do you see how smashed he is? We were supposed to bring him in an unresponsive state, but now he's completely asleep! Miya, don't let him fall asleep!"

The girl wearing the pink ribbons skirted around the table, came right up close to me and sat on my knee. Without warning, she took a peck on my lips, and I tasted her floral, dark purple lipstick.

"Hey, hey, that's quite enough!" The one who they called "Prince" dragged his right hand, weighed down by many rings, across the table and turned the contract laying before me to the last page. Miya foisted an obviously quite expensive pen on me. It even looked like a real *Parker* with a golden nib. She jabbed with her finger where I was supposed to sign. Georgiy started to hurry me:

"Sign it now! It's time for you to get to work!"
With my limp hand, I mechanically squiggled out my signature on the long line. Then, I produced another signature on the second copy of this incomprehensible contract they shoved in front of me. And after that my consciousness left me at last, and I fell face-first into my unfinished plate of trout and salad scraps.

Waking Up

"AHHHHH!" I never thought that the sight of my own hand would be so shocking.

I don't even know what it was exactly that scared me more: my nails being painted dark blue and green; the black-green ring on my pointer finger; the gold chain on my wrist, which was thin with a modestly-sized medallion that looked like two bodies merged in an embrace; or my hand itself, which was plump with short fingers that looked as if they were missing the last joint. What left me feeling afraid was probably all of it put together. The biggest thing was that the hand at the end of my arm wasn't mine! The dream vanished as if by magic, I sat up on the bed and looked around.

The place was unfamiliar to me. It was a rectangular space of average dimensions without windows or doors. The walls were made of stone tiles that were rough to the touch and slightly warm as if there were heating pipes behind them. I didn't see any lights but, nevertheless, the dim illumination allowed me to make out the outline of objects. The only piece of furniture was my bed. It was huge, as if made for three or four people. There was a burgundy carpet on the floor that gave a slight spring when you stepped on it...

Wait a second! I caught myself having an unexpected thought. How did I know that the walls were rough to the touch and warm, and that the carpet gave a slight spring when you walked on it? After all, I had just woken up and hadn't even gotten out of bed! In agitation at my discovery, I pressed my hand to the wall and quickly reassured myself that the wall really was warm and rough, as if it were made of porous stone. How did I know that? Maybe I had touched it while asleep. That was probably it. I stood up on the floor. The carpet really did give a slight spring as I'd thought. Maybe, I'd gotten up some time during the night and had found out that way? I took a walk along the wall. There was no door or even anything that hinted at a door. And, what was more, there was obviously not enough lighting in the room.

"Light!" I commanded, and the whole edge of the ceiling lit up brightly.

How did I know how to turn the lights on? I couldn't figure out the answer to that question. Maybe somewhere in the depths of my consciousness, I even knew how to get out of this locked room. For some reason, I began doubting that there really was an exit. And if it did exist, where would that exit be taking me? Was I ready for what I'd find outside? It was only at this point that I noticed I had been sleeping in the nude. There wasn't any clothing in the room at all, just those same plain walls and a big bed. And what if someone is watching me right now? The thought both stumped and scared me at the same time. I sat back down on the bed and covered my shame with a blanket. It was, by the way, a nice blanket, thick and warm, and inside the duvet cover I felt a soft, pleasant-to-the-touch comforter.

I kept sitting for a while, collecting my thoughts and trying to figure out how I'd gotten there. I couldn't concentrate because I was really thirsty. My throat got dry, and my heavy, clumsy tongue felt bristly and like it belonged to someone else. All my guesses and suppositions about how I'd gotten there turned out one less likely than the next. The only thing I could remember for sure is that I had "overindulged" the day before at the restaurant, then started feeling really bad. Did that even happen yesterday? With difficulty, as if through fog, I got through all the obstacles, gradually putting the pieces of yesterday's events back together. I went to *The Wishbone*, next to my house. That I remembered distinctly, so from there I could start figuring out what had come next. I was drinking with some guy I barely knew, named Georgiy. He hired me. I was supposed to play for him in some game. That's right. That's it, exactly. But then when I tried to remember what happened after that, my thoughts started getting muddled.

So, could I already be in the game? If I am wearing a virtual reality helmet, then it wouldn't matter what direction I turn my head, all I'd be able to see is screen. I lifted my hands and felt my head. I couldn't feel any helmet there, though that didn't really mean anything. It was possible I was controlling the game with my thoughts, and thinking about moving wasn't moving my actual body but my character's. But how could I test whether I was in a virtual world? I looked around again at the empty room. Even in the best rendered computer images you can see the pixels! It was a good idea, so I looked closely at the strange ring on my finger and tried to find imperfections. Either the resolution of the virtual screen was very high or the ring was real, but in any case, no matter how hard I tried, I was not able to make out the individual points that it would have been made of, if it were a computer image.

My thirst continued to grow. I stood up again and, after wrapping myself in the blanket, I set out to take a look at the walls of my... what was this place to me anyway? It was too comfortable to be a prison, but too empty to be normal living quarters. When I walked up to the next section of wall, a space noiselessly opened in it. A piece of stone just came out of the wall and slid to the side, exposing a semicircular archway leading into another room, which turned out to be a bathroom. It came in very handy, as it were – as did the entrance to the shower I found next to it. On the ledge in the shower, there was a plethora of containers I couldn't read strewn about, but that wasn't what stopped me at all. There was a mirror on the wall, and I looked into it.

"Ahhhhh!" A scream of despair and fear ripped its way from my chest again.

It wasn't me in the mirror! Looking back at me, from the mirror, was... what's his name... Georgiy Innokentievich! It was his face to be sure, swollen after drinking, looking back at me with cloudy eyes from a rectangular frame. That's his dark hair, his nose and his eyes! How the hell...? I stepped back and practically fell down, obviously the fault of the previous day's activities. Along with all that, I had to constantly focus my vision. There were these dark spots constantly moving to obscure my view, and that bothered me a lot.

Think! Think now! The possibility that I was already somehow playing, and that was why I saw someone else's face in the mirror was seeming more and more likely. It was the face of a character created by a different player. Obviously, I would have to play for him now. But what do I even know about my character? I took another look in the mirror. A dark-haired, middle-aged man. Pretty bloated and with a noticeable gut. If he did play any sports, you'd never have guessed it from his figure. That was probably pretty far from something Georgiy did often. Folds of fat dangled loosely from my manboobs and flapped on my belly. Why the hell would you make such an egregiously repugnant character? By the way, what is his name?

As if answering my question, an information box appeared before my eyes:

Georg royl Inoky ton Mesfelle, Crown Prince of the Empire
Age: 47

That put my bare butt right on the uncovered floor. So, now I was sure I was in the game. What more proof did I need?! And now it was my job to play this "Crown Prince" called Georg who, in his 47 years, has left his body in such a state that you couldn't even look at it without wanting to cry!

I wanted to get some more information about my character, like his characteristics, you know, like, strength, agility, charisma... Though... how could you even think about charisma if just looking at this guy had made me react with complete disgust?! But, try as I might, I couldn't figure out how to get to any screen to see my characteristics. Maybe they didn't have that in this game. The only thing I could find out about Georg royl Inoky came from something like a popup:

Race: Human
Gender: Male
Class: Aristocrat, Mystic
Achievements: None
Fame: +4
Standing: - 27

What's the deal with his standing? Why the hell would it be negative? I got embarrassed for myself somehow. I walked up to the mirror again, calmer this time, and looked at my new face. My eyes were expressionless, off-white with very bright irises that contrasted sharply with my dark hair. They had a reddish tinge, either from being tired or drunk. There were also dark bags under them. A straight nose. Slightly baggy cheeks. A bit unshaven. Teeth... In this department, Georg had actually made me happy. He had a full set, and they were ideally even and white. My real teeth had a chip on the upper right incisor (for some reason, idiot that I am, I once opened a beer bottle with my teeth) and I was missing two teeth on the left side. I was afraid of dentists and disregarded cavities when I was in my last few years of school. So, at least in that one regard, my virtual character was better than the real me.

My neck was solid, but not very long. My body... Well, it was so doughy that you couldn't even properly call it a body. I was reminded of a cruel nickname my friends and I used to call a fat classmate in school: "wide load." Now, I was the "wide load." I had obviously weak arms, and there was an ungainly tattoo on my left forearm in the shape of some kind of cartoon character that was driving me nuts. It was either a badly drawn donkey with bulged out eyes and butterfly wings, or some kind of insect with four appendages and either hooves or claws. I had medium-length legs that were fat and strong. Also, my toenails were painted alternately dark blue and green. Between the legs... Well, at least the Crown Prince didn't have any problems in that regard. I even let loose a whistle and felt a pang of jealousy.

I was getting thirstier, so I took a risk and tried the water straight out of the tap. The local water wasn't too pleasant. It had some metallic undertones, but in any case it sated my thirst. After that, I took a shower (by the way, it was really classy with a big selection of functions and panels), dried off with paper towels and went back to the bedroom because there wasn't anything else to do in the bathroom. While I was out of the room, the bed had disappeared on its own up into a slot in the wall, leaving the room completely empty. I was standing in the middle of the room and looking attentively at the walls, but I couldn't find any doors other than the two to the toilet and shower I'd found earlier. But this can't be?! Funny, I'm stuck in my own bedroom!

"Building map!" I said loudly and clearly, not knowing how to get out of this ridiculous situation and trying the first thing that came to mind.

It worked! A detailed schematic of the floor with hallways, closed rooms, some kind of elevators and a "you are here" marker in one of the rooms appeared before me. But what caught my eye wasn't the semitransparent map that had appeared before my eyes but the writing below it:

Third (residential) deck of the heavy assault cruiser, Marta the Harlot

I didn't even know what to be more surprised by. Was it the fact that I was on an assault cruiser? Or the fact that I asked for a map and it just appeared at my command? Or was it that some moron named a military ship something so strange and unfitting? In any case, I decided to leave all these questions for later. What was important was getting out of my bedroom. Without effort, I expanded the image and found that there were three exits in my room. One to the bathroom, the second was a very narrow door for staff, behind the corner panel. (The plan showed there being a ventilation shaft and power cables there.) The third exit was right in the middle of the wall and went into the big hall shown on the map as the "Guest Room." I walked in the direction of the wall shown on the map, and the wall panel moved noiselessly up into the ceiling. I had finally found the exit!

"Ahhhhh!" I jumped back and covered my nakedness with my hands. "Please forgive me!"

There was a fat old lady sprawled out on a pink sofa in the big hall wearing a long bathrobe and golden hair curlers. There was a thick layer of greasy cream on the aged woman's face. The woman slowly turned her head toward me and bellowed out in an extremely annoyed tone:

"Georg, I'm being serious. That's quite enough! If you're going to scare me and scream like you're being cut every time you take crystals, I'm going to divorce you once and for all. Do you understand?"

There were a few things in her speech that caught my attention right away. The first and most important: that fat cow was my wife. It was extremely hard to believe, because she wasn't to my taste at all. Nevertheless, after looking at her again while averting my gaze, I read the information in the popup window:

Marta royl Valesy ton Mesfelle-Kyle, Princess of the Star Kingdom of Fastel, ruler of the planet Fastel-XI
Age: 38
Race: Human
Gender: Female
Relation to you: Your legal wife
Class: Aristocrat
Achievements: None
Fame: +2
Standing: - 9
Presumed personal opinion of you: -57 (hate)
Kingdom of Fastel's opinion of you: -11 (dislike)

She really was my wife! And, for some reason, she hated me! What a twist!

The second thing I paid attention to was that she had said "divorce you once and for all." What was that supposed to mean? Was it that we already basically were divorced but it wasn't "once and for all" yet? That struck me as strange; however, I was not able to find any more information about why our relationship was strained.

The third thing was also important. It would seem that this wasn't the first time I had reacted this way in front of my wife. Why? Could it be that I had already been in a similar situation? Or maybe this character has already been played by some people other than Mr. G. I. himself?

And finally, the fourth thing. My wife had made a passing reference to crystals. What was that all about? I wasn't even too surprised when a hint about that very question appeared before my eyes:

*Crystalloquasimetal-cis-isomer valiarimic acid (slang: **crystals**). A synthetic narcotic substance with a pronounced hallucinogenic effect. Noted for the extended effect of its narcotic state (from 48 to 86 hours), which presents a non-negligible risk of death to the user due to dehydration. Addiction to **crystals** begins from the first use.*

*Consuming **crystals** became fashionable during the universal popularization of the "drang-musik" musical movement between 658 and 712 and was widely consumed by composers and artists. Later, consumption of **crystals** became popular among scientists and the upper aristocracy as well. At present, the manufacturing and distribution of **crystals** is strictly forbidden by the laws of the Empire* *and can be punished by death, as can consumption of* **crystals** *by individuals who are not on the special list of Mystics, reaffirmed yearly by the Emperor.*

Effects of taking **crystals***: may cause detachment from distracting factors, with concentration of cognitive activity for solving day-to-day problems, often in an extremely nonstandard way. This kind of cognitive activity has produced results: from optimal algorithms for complex systems, to captivating scripts, brilliant financial solutions for firms, winning strategies at various logic games, and much, much more. There have even been recorded occurrences when the individual taking* **crystals** *had a very weak understanding of a subject, yet was able to make a scientific breakthrough in it.*

Side effects: very strong narcotic dependency; the need to redose on crystals every 5-8 days, with a slightly higher dose required each time; serious weakening of the body's immune system; reduction of overall muscle mass; and a high probability of developing chronic diseases of the gastrointestinal tract and urogenital system. Notable reduction in sexual activity in individuals of both genders to the point of complete refusal of sexual contact.

Well, I'll be damned! I couldn't believe what I'd read. I have to play a fat, impotent drug addict! Thanks, Georgiy, you did me a solid. If I'd have known this from the start, I'd have told you right where to stick your "good deal!" And no bodyguards would have been able to stop me from giving you a smack right to the jaw!

"What are you looking at? Is your brain still switched off after the drugs? What are you doing walking naked around the berth, swinging your useless family jewels around? Don't embarrass yourself, go get dressed. Your officers could come in with a report any minute!" My fat wife pointed at a crack in the wall. That must have been where the clothes closet was.

Not giving an answer to her hurtful words, I set off for the closet and started getting dressed, trying not to pay attention to the shameless way Marta was looking at me. By the way, was it her that this ship was named after? I'd have to look up where the name of this cruiser came from and how my wife behaved herself, when I got the chance.

The clothes were bizarre. The underwear were form-fitting and very thin. The unitard was like a jacket and pants sewn together with self-correcting rubber bands, fitting it exactly to the shape of your body. I finally figured it all out and put the clothes on. It wasn't too fast, but there were also no particular problems. I especially liked the boots. They were high, practically to the knee, but soft, and you couldn't feel them on your feet at all. The situation immediately became easier to handle with clothes on. I had barely gotten dressed, when the trill of the doorbell rang out and a gray-haired old man came into the room in a severe, silvery-gray uniform. He bowed deeply and declared in an official tone:

"My Prince, officers from the ship are awaiting you in the entrance hall. Shall I let them in?"

I looked at the old man. A popup told me that the person standing before me was my 135-year-old, loyal personal secretary and butler, by the name Bryle:

Presumed personal opinion of you: +37 (loyal)

"Remind me, Bryle. What am I to discuss with these officers?" I asked my servant.

If he was surprised, he was doing a good job of hiding it. Bryle bowed again and told me that I myself had asked them to bring a detailed report on all skirmishes with the aliens and, also, that I was preparing to share my new defense strategy for Perimeter Sector Eight with my subjects. No more, no less! I laboriously swallowed the lump that appeared in my throat.

"Tell them..." I began, looking for a reason to get rid of these officers who had appeared at such an inopportune moment, but I suddenly changed my mind and said, "No, never mind. I'll tell them everything myself."

Bryle nodded gently at me and placed his hand on an illuminated circle, which opened the entrance door. Trying not to lose my resolve, I went out into the hall. There were six people there in military uniforms and one "nonperson," a ten-foot-tall insect that looked like a praying mantis with six appendages of various lengths. The upper pair of "arms" were hypertrophically huge, with spikes that gleamed menacingly on its chitin armor, and looked scary even when folded up. The middle pair of appendages were thin and maneuverable, the so-called "humanlike arms." And the lower pair looked something more like what you'd call "legs" with backward knees. The first thing to jump out about the insect's face was its eyes. They were enormous, each one was the size of a soccer ball. I could see myself, the hallway, and the frozen soldiers reflected hundreds of times in miniature form in its compound eyes.

I quickly looked around at everyone, but there was only information on two of them: the squat, almost square man in a heavily armored suit and the ten-foot-high praying mantis.

Mwaur Zen-Bey, captain of the Imperial Space Marines
  Race: Human
  Gender: Male
  Class: Military
  Achievements: Has combat medals for participation in interspecies conflicts
  Fame: +2
  Standing: + 2
  Presumed personal opinion of you: -3 (indifferent)
  Empire Military faction opinion of you: -10 (dislike)

There was very little information about the praying mantis:

Triasss Zess, assistant to the ambassador of the Iseyek State to the Empire
  Race: Alpha Iseyek
  Gender: Neutral, third clutch
  Class: Diplomat
  Achievements: None
  Fame: +1
  Standing: + 2
  Presumed personal opinion of you: Unknown

Iseyek race opinion of you: 0 (indifferent)

I wondered what made these two characters different from the other four. Why could I find out more about them, but not the others? Were they real players, while the others were NPCs? That was probably it.

When I appeared, the people froze at attention, as did the extraterrestrial diplomat, pressing his arms to his torso, obviously copying the pose the people were making. I asked which one of them had prepared the materials I requested. The six military men exchanged confused glances. Either they were all counting on someone else to do it, or they all had just equally forgotten about my order. It looked strange. What were they doing coming to a scheduled meeting with the Prince and not even taking the time to prepare? The ambassador saved the situation. Triasss Zess stepped forward and, in a very clean-accented human voice, told me that he had prepared a whole collection of materials on all times people had encountered the mysterious race and added materials to that about encounters the Iseyek race had had with these aliens as well.

Instantly recognizing the opportunity that had presented itself to sit and study the materials one by one while simultaneously finding out more about the overall game world, I dismissed the six military men:

"My good men, I will have to first carefully study the materials brought by the honorable Triasss Zess in order to make any necessary corrections to our defense plans and take all information into account. Please forgive me. It seems I called this meeting prematurely. I'll need some more time..."

I lost track of what I was saying a bit when my gaze accidentally fell on the wide, oval porthole behind the soldiers. Behind the thick glass there were some long metal arms like cranes or claws on the backdrop of the inky blackness of space. It was then that I realized that the ship I was on, *Marta the Harlot,* was not a typical oceangoing ship but a real-life star cruiser.

"... Could you please leave me alone with the honorable ambassador?" I asked, finally having collected my thoughts and turning quickly away from the window.

It seemed that the soldiers weren't too happy with the fact that I wanted to conduct a discussion alone with the Iseyek; however, none of them chose to express their dissatisfaction out loud. I pulled back to the side, letting the ambassador into the hall. It seemed that I had done something wrong, as the praying mantis froze for a few seconds before coming through the door.

"I am grateful to you for the honor you have given me in allowing me to enter your personal chambers, my dear Prince Georg," said the praying mantis as he slightly lowered his head and came through the door. There was a beep in my head as if I'd just received an email. Some lines passed quickly in front of my eyes:

Standing change. Your relationship with Triasss Zess has improved.
Presumed personal opinion of you: +10 (warm)

Standing change. Your relationship with the Iseyek race has improved.

Alpha Iseyek race opinion of you: +2 (indifferent)
   Beta Iseyek race opinion of you: +1 (indifferent)
   Gamma Iseyek race opinion of you: +1 (indifferent)

Thankfully, that cow, Marta, wasn't in the room anymore. Bryle produced a remote control and nimbly pressed a combination of buttons. Immediately, the couch retracted into a gap in the wall, and two armchairs and a big, oval table came out in its place. Then, a ten-by-ten flat screen descended from the ceiling. I asked my butler to bring me a glass of some kind of juice as well as something for my guest. The praying mantis and the old servant shot me equally flabbergasted looks. At that moment, the old man's eyes looked a lot like the shifting compound eyes of the huge insect standing next to him. But Bryle nodded in silence and left the room, and I got another set of messages:

Standing change. Your relationship with Triasss Zess has improved.
   Presumed personal opinion of you: +20 (trusting)

Standing change. Your relationship with the Iseyek race has improved.
   Alpha Iseyek race opinion of you: +4 (indifferent)

Why were they all so surprised at what I was doing? What was wrong with these praying mantises?

My question was answered almost immediately. An indistinct shadow rose up off the flat wall, quickly acquiring the appearance of a huge bipedal lizard. At first, I nearly shouted, but almost instantly I recognized the figure from my drunken dream. This was one of Mr. G. I.'s bodyguard lizards from the restaurant. Obviously, they must have been Prince Georg royl Inoky's bodyguards. In other words, now they were my bodyguards. The information that came up on the lizard told me that he was pretty kick-ass:

> **Popori de Cacha, Bodyguard Division commander**
> **Race: Chameleon**
> **Gender: Male (at present)**
> **Class: Military**
> **Achievements: Has earned athletic awards in marksmanship and no-rules fighting, two-time winner of the famous Gug-V survival tournament**
> **Fame: +7**
> **Standing: + 6**
> **Presumed personal opinion of you: -2 (indifferent)**
> **Chameleon race opinion of you: +1 (indifferent)**

"My Prince," explained the reptilian chameleon, keeping one eye on me, but not taking the other off the gigantic praying mantis. "Soldiers of the Iseyek race are extremely fast and deadly, and, insofar as the ambassador has undergone military training, there can be no doubt that he presents a risk. My division and I will simply not be capable of defending you as long as you are so close to Ambassador Triasss."

"I appreciate your concern, Popori de Cacha, but try to understand me. Our common foe is getting closer every day. No race will be able to make a stand alone. My defense strategy requires us to work actively together with several species, including the various Iseyek groups. Without trust, this is impossible. How can I trust the Iseyek state in the future, if I cannot trust their official ambassador now? What's more, I would even request that you and your soldiers take your leave of this room during the negotiations, so we can demonstrate our openness and level of trust to the honorable Mr. Ambassador. At the same time, I would like you to check the whole cruiser for all potential crystal hiding spots and destroy everything you find, no exceptions."

Both of the chameleon's eyes turned to me at once. It obviously meant that he had been very taken aback, to the point that he even took his eye off the ambassador he had yet to stop being suspicious of.

"Excuse me. Could you repeat that, my Prince? I must have misheard you..."

"Yes, Popori de Cacha, you understood everything correctly. There is very little time remaining, and I cannot allow myself to lose any more to a drugged-up haze. For that reason, you must find and destroy all crystals you find on the ship. And, thereafter, everything and everyone coming on this cruiser must be monitored to prevent even one gram of that junk ending up here. Any attempt to bring it on the ship must be uncovered and intercepted with no mercy. Any person or nonperson who tries to offer me crystals is to be considered an avowed enemy and must be terminated immediately, regardless of their status. That is an order, now carry it out!"

Popori de Cacha let out a quiet, faltering whistle, and immediately three more lizards appeared in what was not even a very big room. What was more, one of my bodyguards turned out to have been on the ceiling, right above my head. The division commander whistled again and all four bodyguards exited the room in an unhurried and dignified manner.

When the door shut behind them, the ambassador, Triasss Zess, stood motionless for some time, looking around the room with his huge compound eyes. It seemed to me that the praying mantis didn't believe that all the guards had really left. Triasss Zess took a sip of a bubbly green drink from a long transparent straw on the side table. He savored the drink, wriggling his wet mandibles, then carefully placed the unusual vessel back on the table and... In the space of a second, the ten-foot-high praying mantis had already made it over to me, somehow having gone over the table that had been between us. In an instant, my neck was being pressed between the blades of the "unique" scissors, curved at the joint, which had once been his upper right appendage.

"How long I've waited for this moment!" whispered Triasss Zess directly into my ear, with a sinister tone. "You people are as blind and naive as you were on the first day you made contact with our civilization. How little you know about my race. How simple it was to trick you! As long as you're born an Alpha Iseyek, all the Empire's much-touted special services consider you harmless and will even let you in to meet a member of an Imperial dynasty... You see, I trace my lineage from the family of Igir-Gugorito, the hatchlings of whom were destroyed on the orders of, as it were, the Orange House of the Empire. The Sival-II Hive Massacre happened just 170 years ago, and you humans have already forgotten about it. But the Iseyek nation has not forgotten! How joyful it makes me to take my revenge on a member of the Orange House!"

I felt the praying mantis's spiny, razor sharp appendage slowly tighten around my neck. The chitin spines pressed into my throat, piercing flesh. It was very painful. I took a breath, but didn't feel even a drop of fear. It was more like a detached interest. Will I see a "You have died" message? "Game over?" Will I have to make a new character? Or will I come back at a respawn point? The screen got darker and darker – and that was the first time I died in the game.

"So, what'd you think?" came a vaguely familiar voice from out of the absolute, pitch-black silence.

It took me a few moments to recognize the speaker's voice. It was Mr. G. I., that son of a bitch! I took in a lungful of air, getting ready to launch into an uncensored tirade directed at the liar and cheat who had tricked me into a game I had never played before. But still I said nothing, as it struck me that I had died in the game but not respawned yet! There wasn't a new character creation menu, nor was there a "continue from previous save" option. What was that about?

"Don't you have anything to say? How was your

first day? Have you spoken with the staff officers yet? Were you able to come up with something worthwhile with them in your one day?" My acquaintance was pelting me with questions, making it impossible to concentrate.

"I haven't had the chance to talk to them as much as I would have liked. I got killed by that praying mantis almost right away," I admitted in shame.

My new employer started to seem confused. Georgiy even asked me to repeat myself:

"What praying mantis? Are you talking about the messenger from the Iseyek embassy? How did he even get close to you? The cruiser is full of guards. Go into any hallway. You can't even spit without hitting a guard. Plus, there are four invisible chameleons that won't let anyone dangerous get anywhere near you under any circumstances."

I had to explain in detail that I had dismissed the officers myself, let the assistant ambassador into my room and ordered the bodyguards to leave. Judging by his reaction, Georgiy had not foreseen this cascade of thoughtless actions on my part. He said nothing for a long time. It even seemed that he was consulting with someone.

"Here's the deal," rang out the familiar voice once again after I had already managed to lose interest. "So, they killed you. Don't worry about it. You'll wake up soon enough in the medical center; the doctor will tell you something about how they were 'barely able to get you out.' It'll be a good lesson for you in the future. There's just one thing I can't figure out. Why would a messenger from the Alpha Iseyeks attack a relative of the Emperor?"

"He said something about broken eggs and revenge on the Orange House. But to be honest, I didn't really understand what he was going on about."

"So, that's how..." my acquaintance remarked in surprise, even becoming noticeably scared. "So the praying mantis really did have a reason, even if it is quite an old story. On first contact with his race, we humans acted with too heavy a hand. Some pioneers found a nice planet for building a distant Human outpost, but there was already intelligent life on it. Our scouts reported that the praying mantis race inhabiting Sival-II was extremely technologically backwards and also too aggressive for negotiation to be feasible. Those people mistakenly decided that no one would ever find out about these events taking place on a faraway planet... Admiral Bayagor royl Stashek ton Mesfelle was acting on incomplete information and underestimated the military and economic power of the Swarm and their allies. Fifty years of interstellar war followed that fateful error. Now both sides have learned to respect one another's territory and interests, and there is peace with the Iseyek. Some unsubdued fanatics do remain among the Gamma Iseyeks, though. These insects, resentful of our race, think that the Orange House, to which Admiral Bayagor royl Stashek belonged, has not paid the full blood price for that long-ago aggression."

There was a plethora of unasked questions spinning around in my head, but Georgiy suddenly informed me that our conversation would be ending, as I would soon be respawning. Immediately after his words, I saw a glaring white light, and the vile scent of ammonia filled my nostrils as I woke up.

AFTERDEATH

"THANK THE Creators, you're alive, my Prince!" Hunched over me was a man with a swarthy face, a big Roman nose, and huge, dark hazel eyes. He was wearing a white, plastic smock and a round, white cap that covered his hair.

Nicosid Brandt, your personal doctor
Age: 128
Race: Human
Gender: Male
Class: Medic
Achievements: Numerous awards for scientific works in the fields of psychiatry and rehabilitative medicine (full list available on next tab). His mastery in his field and loyalty to the Empire have been affirmed repeatedly. Approved to work with members of the upper aristocracy.
Fame: +5
Standing: + 19
Presumed personal opinion of you: +35 (loyal)

I took a sharp smelling flask from in front of my face and let out a sneeze. The doctor's face reflected a mix of tenderness and a certain concern.

"Have I been lying around here long?" I wondered, without greeting the doctor or giving a word of thanks.

"Not very, my Prince. Forty minutes have passed since you were brought to my office. I intentionally did not wake you up earlier, as I needed to examine the wounds on your throat to make sure that they did not present a risk."

After the doctor's words, I felt my neck and there really was some kind of moist bandage. The doctor, as if reading my thoughts, extended me a rectangular mirror. I noticed a wide, white, elastic bandage. Under it, there was some gauze soaked with some kind of yellow ointment.

"Nothing serious, my Prince, just grazes and scratches. They'll disappear without a trace in two or three days. The Iseyek that attacked you merely squeezed your carotid artery until you passed out."

"What happened to him, by the way?"

"Triasss Zess did not resist. In fact, he opened the blocked doors to the cabin and called for medical aid. Your security force tried to kill him on the spot, but Princess Marta's guard intervened. The praying mantis is now sitting in the prison chamber awaiting the judge's ruling. Your spouse has locked herself in her personal chambers with her interstellar legal counsel."

"Should it not be me who decides the fate of the criminal? He attacked me after all."

"My Prince, if what took place had been an attack on a member of one of the Great Houses inside the

Empire, your claim would be indisputable. However, the incident took place on a military starship belonging to the Kingdom of Fastel. Marta royl Valesy is the noblest representative of the Kingdom of Fastel on board this cruiser, which means that, legally, only she may rule on this case. Insofar as I understand, she is presently consulting with a panel of experienced lawyers to choose Triasss Zess's method of execution. They need to assure the Empire remains satisfied, while also keeping the Swarm from being overly offended."

The way this situation had turned out did not suit me one bit. To my mind, if the praying mantis had wanted to kill me, nothing would have been able to stop him from doing just that. But he only knocked me out, then called for first aid and turned himself in. His actions didn't resemble those of a murderer. And so I decided:

"Nicosid, I need to have a meeting with the arrested Iseyek messenger immediately. He is in possession of information of critical importance to the Empire. I must familiarize myself with it."

"Not possible, my Prince," came the doctor, staggering back in fear. "The suspect is extremely dangerous! Especially now that he has absolutely nothing to lose!"

"Popori de Cacha!" I exclaimed, calling for my bodyguard.

I didn't see the chameleon; however, I had no doubt that he was in the room somewhere. And in fact the contours of the enormous lizard did begin to show on the backdrop of a big, abstract picture on the wall. In just a few seconds, the six-and-a-half-foot chameleon was standing in front of me, waiting for my orders. Before beginning to speak with the leader of the guards, I noted the fact that his loyalty to me had made a noticeable drop:

Presumed personal opinion of you: -7 (disapproving)

Obviously, my poorly-thought-out actions that had ended in my ridiculously foreseeable and preventable death had earned my bodyguard's well-deserved annoyance. I tried to correct the vexing misunderstanding:

"Popori de Cacha, you were right about the Iseyek messenger. I admit my mistake. In the future, I will try to listen to your wise advice. And, as a matter of fact, I am presently in need of the verdict of an experienced bodyguard. Can I speak with Triasss Zess without putting my life in excessive danger?"

"The safest method is to communicate via videophone, without coming into close contact with the arrestee," reasoned the chameleon.

"Holy hell, that does make sense," I agreed. "But I'm specifically wondering about a personal conversation with the praying mantis. We may end up discussing very confidential matters, so I would not like our secret conversation to take place over the ship's communication system. This way, we can be sure foreign spies aren't listening in on our conversation. Just tell me your expert conclusion. Could you and your soldiers provide for my safety if I were to go into the praying mantis's chamber, or not? Having a conversation with the arrestee is very important to me, but I'll do whatever you conclude is best."

It looked like my question had put Popori de Cacha into a contemplative state. The chameleon's eyes stopped twitching in all directions, and a cloudy white film descended over them. It was a curious sight. It was the first time I'd seen a chameleon deep in thought. This intensive thought process continued for twenty seconds, after which his eyes opened and Popori de Cacha answered:

"My Prince, I officially guarantee your complete safety during your meeting with the arrestee in the name of the Ravaash race, known to humankind as the Chameleons. However, I will need to enter first, look over the space carefully and prepare the praying mantis for questioning. I'll only need two minutes."

"Excellent, take me there!"

The door to the hallway slid silently aside, revealing a short corridor packed with well-armed humans. I only needed one look to figure out that there were members of two different groups of soldiers present. There were a great deal more of the well-armored guys in light gray uniforms, armed primarily with light firearms. I looked closely at the emblem on one of their shoulders. A message appeared obligingly before my eyes telling me who was in front of me:

Space corporal of the Second Heavy Fleet of the Star Kingdom of Fastel

Mhm. I immediately figured out that the gray soldiers belonged to my beloved wife. Then, can I assume that the ones wearing gold uniforms are mine? I turned to the nearest lumbering hulk of a man.

Sergeant of the Space Fleet of the Orange House of the Empire

It seems I was not mistaken. But there weren't many golden soldiers – no more than 15. They were equipped with either an archaic rifle almost as long as a person is tall, or some baffling, obviously heavy gizmo that looked like a twisted fire poker. Some of them were even armed with nothing but blades. It looked somewhat strange and led me to think that I was seeing the remnants of an army that had been crushed, hurriedly gathered into one group made of different types of soldiers and hastily equipped with whatever weaponry was at hand. The sight of it left me visibly upset; however, I tried to maintain my stony expression despite having a whole bunch of questions running around in my head.

I took a harder look at the "golden" soldiers and determined that the sergeant I had looked at earlier was the highest ranked soldier among them. All the other soldiers were just privates. I turned to the sergeant and he froze at attention.

"Your name, sergeant?" I wondered.

"Tavar Prest, my Prince. Senior gunner from the frigate *Pyro-27* in Your Highness's fleet. One of three survivors from that frigate, after the recent battle."

I started to realize that I was not wrong: they really were the surviving members of the crew of my own personal fleet, which looked to have been completely destroyed. What happened? Why are my people in such a sorry state? I didn't have nearly enough information about the events that preceded my entering the game. Nevertheless, I couldn't show my subjects how confused and ignorant I was. Trying to make my voice powerful and confident, I issued an order:

"Sergeant, organize the survivors into an escort and have them accompany me to the prison chambers. I need to speak with the praying mantis that attacked me."

The sergeant obviously appreciated the high level of responsibility placed on him with this mission to guard such an important person, and quickly and skillfully ordered the "golden soldiers" into a three-part formation. We weren't able to get very far before we were blocked by an officer in a gray uniform. Based on his patches, he was the captain of my spouse's personal guard.

"Prince Georg, I have been ordered to provide for your safety and not allow further incidents similar to that with the Swarm messenger. For that reason, I must request that you either return to the infirmary or go, guarded by my soldiers, to the residential zone. Your wife, Princess Marta, will be very dissatisfied if you leave your designated area on the ship of your own volition."

Behind the insolent officer, other figures in gray were already lining up. It looked as if they were preparing to stop me by force, if necessary. I raised an eyebrow in dissatisfaction, trying to look as pompous and haughty as possible, and declared:

"Captain, can it be that a prince of the Orange House of the Empire is being held captive on the ship of an Imperial ally, the Kingdom of Fastel?"

The officer shook his head "no" in silence.

"Then allow me to pass and do not interfere in my business! Popori de Cacha, there is no need to kill him! This man is simply doing his duty. He is no enemy to us."

I only said the last part because the captain was hesitating about whether to get out of my way. I thought that mentioning the leader of my invisible bodyguards would be enough to push this slightly impudent dog of war in the right direction. But what happened, though, was even better. Behind the horse-stubborn officer appeared a chameleon holding a sharp, curved blade to his throat.

"Yes, my Prince. Disrespect to members of the House of the Emperor is supposed to be punished, but if you insist..."

Popori de Cacha slowly pulled his weapon away from the officer's neck and backed away while giving a very convincing imitation of a human bow. The captain hurried to make way. His people also stepped aside, many of them smiling nervously as they did. When my retinue had reached the end of the hallway and entered the elevator on its way to another deck, my bodyguard wondered:

"My Prince, allow me to ask a question that's been torturing me. How were you able to detect me? How did I reveal my position? I need to understand this in order to correct this shortcoming in the future."

I chuckled back happily:

"Popori de Cacha, you were flawless as always. You did nothing to give away your location. I simply assumed that my very capable bodyguard would be trying to keep the situation under control and would be as close as possible to the person who dared block my path. As you see, I was not wrong."

Standing change. Your relationship with Popori de Cacha has improved.
Presumed personal opinion of you: +10 (warm)

The system message that popped up was unexpected, but very welcome. It seems I was able to get through to my bodyguard and make a step forward in my standing, which had been ruined by my predecessor.

All four chameleons appeared at the doors of the prison chamber. Three of them got the hallway leading to the elevator secured, while the commander asked me to wait as we had agreed. Popori de Cacha entered a code into the keypad in the wall with his long, flexible fingers. Then, he unlocked the door and went into the prison chamber. Popori de Cacha finished his inspection of the room in even less than two minutes.

"My Prince, the prisoner has been subdued and does not present a threat to Your Highness," announced my bodyguard about a minute after entering.

I slid open the metal door and went inside. The praying mantis was lying down by the far wall. His upper appendages were folded up and handcuffed together, so his scary, sharp weapons would remain out of play. The long, spiny legs of the enormous insect were stretched limply out along his body. I don't know exactly who did what to him, but it seemed to me that the praying mantis's legs were broken or paralyzed. And his middle pair of appendages... was simply gone! Where the messenger's "small arms" had been just minutes before, now there was nothing but jagged wounds showing through a yellowish slime. I looked around somewhat dumbfounded and noticed that Popori de Cacha had ripped out the praying mantis's thin arms and was holding them in his hands! The chameleon followed my gaze and took it on himself to answer:

"Alpha Iseyeks have no problem speaking without the middle pair of appendages. I did it for your safety, my Prince: the middle arms were not bound, so I preferred not to take any risks. In any case, the murderer who attacked you is going to be executed, so it doesn't really make a difference."

I hadn't explicitly approved such a harsh method of preparing the prisoner for questioning, but the disabled praying mantis spoke out unexpectedly in agreement with his tormentor:

"Your bodyguard is right, Prince Georg. The small upper arms of my race are in no way connected with the speech function. As such, I will be able to provide you all the information I was supposed to have communicated to you initially: The Swarm first encountered the aliens less than two standard years ago, but have since grown quite afraid of their power – so afraid that evacuation of all egg clutches has begun in all peripheral Swarm star systems. And what would have earlier sounded totally unthinkable is that the eggs are not even being brought to the capital..."

"It's *that* bad?" Though I couldn't understand why that situation should be surprising, as the praying mantis had emphasized it, I decided to support him.

"Yes, Prince Georg. The Swarm came to the conclusion that the Iseyek race is not in proper shape to prevent the capture and destruction of our capital planet, Dekeye, by the alien fleet. Given that, bringing the eggs to the capital would be a mistake that could put the Iseyek race on the verge of extinction. Because of this, the construction of gigantic transport starships made for holding billions of eggs has begun in all Swarm star systems. All these ships will be outfitted not only with standard warp drives, but also with other drives that are more powerful, if unstable. The Swarm thought that, if sending starships to the farthest reaches of known space couldn't save us, it was better to risk sending ships filled with our descendants to a random point in the Universe than to allow those freaks to completely wipe out our species. Now the only issue is the time factor. Although all Swarm resources are currently devoted to their construction, building such huge starships will still take several standard years. Nevertheless, the aliens are coming too fast and no one can guarantee that we'll have enough time. Our analysts have calculated that, given the present situation, the Swarm will not have enough time to launch the transport ships with our descendants. There are many reasons for this. The threat was detected too late and, due to insufficient information, a mistaken decision was made to construct such gigantic ships, but there isn't enough time or resources left to change that significantly. So, the Iseyek race has sent ambassadors to the Empire to seek aid from the Human race. The Swarm is prepared to offer a lot to humanity to get the Imperial Fleet to defend our territory and buy us more time. As soon as the starships are finished and the eggs are sent to a safe place, the Swarm will turn all our many shipyards over to producing military ships, in order to give the aliens a fight and buy more time."

I heard the praying mantis out, furrowing my brow and immersing myself in thought. How powerful must the alien fleet be if the large, developed, interstellar Iseyek civilization is already planning to turn tail? In parallel, I was thinking about something else entirely. There was also another matter that I couldn't help thinking about. For example, it really hurt me when the praying mantis pressed my neck between its spines. But the creature I was interrogating, with his arms ripped out, couldn't seem to care less about the fact that he was missing appendages. Two arms had been ripped all the way out, and nothing, no emotion. I had no doubt that the creature before me was being controlled by a live player. Triasss Zess had an information popup, and he behaved too unpredictably to be an NPC. Why didn't he feel pain? And how was he controlling his extra appendages anyway? Or are there totally different laws about playing alien races? I tried to banish these out-of-place thoughts and concentrate on the plot of the game.

"How long can your fleet hold back the aliens?" I wondered to Triasss Zess.

In response, the messenger could only squint his huge eyes, which was obviously supposed to indicate grief or sorrow.

"Prince Georg, the sad truth is that the Iseyek race no longer has a star fleet capable of offering any kind of resistance against an alien invasion. The Deeho reconnaissance squadron was completely destroyed while traveling in the direction of the nearest cluster captured by the aliens, Aysar. The Ayho fleet, which did a pretty good job of holding back Imperial attacks for many years, was destroyed entirely in the first battle. The only ships spared were not from the main classes. The Virho fleet took heavy losses and retreated to the capital, Dekeya. The Yuho reserve fleet is not fully equipped or manned and is in the Sival system, but it's really more of a response group than a full-on fleet. The Yayho border fleet is focused on its only mission: not letting any ships enter Swarm territory, so the fact that we don't have adequate defense capabilities will not escape our borders. The hardest fact in all this is that there are no more reserves to wait for, because all Swarm shipyards have been completely given over to building transports, not military ships."

"Then why I have suddenly been entrusted with such critically important, top secret information on the deplorable state of Swarm defenses?" I really did not understand why such inappropriate trust would be placed in me, a member of the Orange House, which the Iseyeks themselves had no lost love for.

The ambassador's assistant silently shifted his mandibles, then said, slightly taken aback:

"Who else would it make sense for the Iseyeks to go to than the Crown Prince and official representative of the Empire responsible for guarding Sector Eight, where a large portion of Swarm territory is located? What's more, you, Prince Georg royl Inoky, have already fought against the alien ships yourself, so you have a better idea than other people in the Empire of how freakishly strong a whole fleet of them can be. Well, it was also of no small importance that the strongest stellar flotilla in this region is under your command, making you the most valuable Imperial representative for my race."

In regards to his last point, I could have disagreed with the praying mantis in that I had already figured that a large portion of the military ships out the porthole were from the Kingdom of Fastel's fleet, more subordinate to my plump wife than to myself. However, I did not emphasize that subtle distinction. Trying to take it the other way, I put on the most confident and majestic face I could.

"Very well, Triasss Zess. As the official representative of the Empire in Perimeter Sector Eight, I am prepared to approve military aid to the Iseyek race. Humanity shall aid the Swarm in the fight against the aliens; however, the Swarm must also participate in the defense of Sector Eight, and not only in Swarm territory but in neighboring territory as well."

The praying mantis began turning his huge eyes, oscillating between expressing delight and apprehension. The ambassador's assistant spoke, carefully enunciating each word:

"May I request that you prepare a clear, bulleted list of what aid the Empire is expecting from the Swarm? I would also like to request that you convey that information to my homeland, in that I will apparently not be able to do so, in view of my impending execution."

"First, I will need all the information you have on

all military engagements between the Iseyek race and the aliens: information on noted concentrations of alien ships, and any other information that has been collected. Second, I'll need official permission to move my fleet through Swarm territory as well as comprehensive information and technical support for my fleet. Third, I need the Swarm's military ships. I would not lay claim to the Virho fleet defending your capital, however the Yuho reserve fleet and the remnants of the defeated Ayho fleet must submit to my authority unconditionally. Given these conditions, the Empire will defend Swarm territory with maximum ferocity, as if it were our own."

The praying mantis made a surprising expression. He turned his head on its side and looked at me meaningfully, as if not believing what he'd heard. I thought I'd overplayed my hand with my demands. However, it turned out the reason was something else entirely.

"Does the Prince not require the Swarm's land-based armies? He would be refusing the best Alpha Iseyek assault troops in this sector of the Universe, as well as the famous Gamma Iseyek space commandos. Does the Prince suppose that this war can be won in space alone without recapturing the planets taken by the aliens?"

It seemed that I had once again blurted out something stupid, so I had to correct myself by improvising on the fly:

"My friend, I presumed that the great Swarm warriors would only fight at maximum effectiveness under the command of a talented general of their own race, who knows their strong and weak points. I wanted to charge you with the mission of finding such a great commander. Popori de Cacha, set him free! I completely trust Triasss Zess and am prepared to release him."

I was afraid that my overly careful bodyguard would disobey my order; however, the chameleon opted not to put that part of his nature on display in the presence of a stranger. The six-and-a-half-foot-high lizard appeared next to the prisoner, carrying the keys to his handcuffs. The only thing the chameleon allowed himself was to give me a slight, cautious warning:

"My Prince, Princess Marta will be extremely dissatisfied with this decision. Knowing your wife's character, you should expect a severe reaction from her to such flagrant disregard for the rights of the Kingdom of Fastel to a fair trial. Should we not, in order to avoid excesses, relocate to one of Your Highness's ships?"

"Have there been issues with my release, Georg royl Inoky?" asked the captive, perking his ears.

"Yes, there have been certain complications. My spouse thinks that she may act independently and has other ideas about your fate, Triasss Zess. But I will try to smooth our family issues over. Popori de Cacha, open the handcuffs!"

The handcuffs fell off the praying mantis's enormous folded appendages. The huge insect stood up to his full ten feet, but stopped when he clocked his head on the ceiling. Both huge, compound eyes froze. I saw my own reflection in them hundreds of times over.

Standing change. Your relationship with Triasss Zess has improved.
Presumed personal opinion of you: +30 (trusting)

Standing change. Your relationship with the Iseyek race has improved.
Alpha Iseyek race opinion of you: +6 (indifferent)
Beta Iseyek race opinion of you: +2 (indifferent)
Gamma Iseyek race opinion of you: +2 (indifferent)

Right after that, another message came:

Standing change. Your relationship with Popori de Cacha has improved.
Presumed personal opinion of you: +12 (warm)

It seemed a bit strange that my constantly cautious bodyguard approved of the release of a dangerous prisoner, but the chameleon thought it was the right decision. At the same time, I was perplexed by a slightly related question. How do they do it? How do they show change in relationship to another player? Maybe I can do it too. I had already grown accustomed to dismissing the popup messages blocking my vision, so when one came up without me even looking at it, I froze for a moment and brought the window back, allowing it to temporarily obstruct my view.

__Chance of expressing your reaction (unread__

message # 3254)

    Change in personal opinion of Triasss Zess (choose an option: -5,-1, 0,+1,+5)

        Change in faction opinion of Triasss Zess (choose an option: -1,0,+1, must be approved by the Head of the Orange House)

        Change in Human race opinion of Triasss Zess (choose an option: -1,0,+1, must be approved by the Emperor)

    Change in faction opinion of Iseyek race (inactive)

    Change in Human race opinion of Iseyek race (inactive)

I skimmed the list of similar, dismissed messages containing more than three thousand skipped actions. Geez! Only the last three messages in the huge list were from me. The rest were describing events that I knew nothing about. It looked like my predecessor had been quite negligent in his duties and had simply been ignoring this function. Some messages that I saw were from a long time ago, but still had yet to be closed, even though the reaction time limit had long since passed. A message about some argument with my wife, dated last year, caught my eye:

Chance of expressing your reaction (unread message # 2751, expired).

    Change in personal opinion of Marta royl Valesy ton Mesfelle-Kyle (choose an option: -15, -10, -5, 0)

    Change in faction opinion of Marta royl

> *Valesy ton Mesfelle-Kyle (choose an option: -3, -1, 0, must be approved by the Head of the Orange House)*
> *Change in faction opinion of the Kingdom of Fastel (inactive)*
> *Change in Empire opinion of the Kingdom of Fastel (inactive)*

I did not want to dig through the Prince's dirty laundry, so I permanently deleted all the messages except the very last one. I did react to that one, increasing my opinion of the praying mantis by +5 and choosing the option to inform him about my decision. Triasss Zess bowed in reply, just like a person.

"My Prince, I would still recommend that you flee *Marta the Harlot* immediately and go to one of the ships of your personal squadron," said the bodyguard commander, reminding me.

"The shuttle dock is very near us. It's on this deck," offered Sergeant Tavar Prest, and I ordered him to lead the division there.

We passed through the cruiser's hallways without any resistance from the soldiers in gray uniforms observing us. We came out into a big hall with two identical, sleek shuttles. The sergeant walked up to the closest shuttle and knocked on the panel with his fist. With a hiss of escaping air, a part of the shuttle's chassis rose up, making room for the gangway to come out. Tavar Prest looked over the people and nonpeople swarming around and said perplexedly:

"The shuttle has a capacity of 11, but it looks like we've got more..."

"What's the problem? We'll take both shuttles," I said, asking the soldiers in golden uniforms if one of them could pilot the other ship.

A few hands rose immediately, and I pointed randomly at a pudgy, but very agile technician. Inside the shuttle, the praying mantis had to fold himself in half to be able to fit into the hallway, but somehow the enormous insect was able to ram himself into the shuttle, and just a minute later, both shuttles had left the dock.

It took considerable effort to hold back a cry of joy and amazement when a fabulously realistic map of space opened before my eyes. The game developers had done a first-rate job: both the bright orange sun and the multitude of statuesque ships looked surprisingly elaborate and well-rendered. Honestly, I had absolutely no idea how the mash-up of metallic objects and debris worked, but the others sitting in the shuttle obviously understood the map.

"Over there is where we sorted through the alien debris," remarked a young man in a pair of orange overalls, picking something out of the chaos.

"Well, because, back yesterday, they drove in a big transport ship and unloaded a whole space workshop from the Kingdom of Fastel. The whole rest of the day we spent cutting up debris and collecting everything of value," repeated the sturdy fellow with engineer's patches.

Tavar Prest's question bellowed out of the cockpit:

"My Prince, where shall I dock?"

With horror I realized that everyone else's conversations had gone silent, and they were all looking at me, expecting an answer. And I didn't really know what I was supposed to say! Popori de Cacha saved the situation, though. Seeing that I was in no rush to answer, the chameleon decided for me:

"Pilot, hold course to the Prince's yacht. The remaining ships in the squadron were damaged in the battle and cannot provide the proper level of security and comfort. Also, the yacht, *Queen of Sin*, is where the main fleet headquarters are located."

"I see. I'll set a course for *Queen of Sin*," confirmed the sergeant.

The world began sharply turning around me. The nearby sun disappeared below my feet somewhere. The stars and ships reshifted around us. I had basically never had a problem with sea sickness, but at that moment I was having a hard time holding back the contents of my stomach. The lack of reliable visual landmarks and the too weak, barely perceptible artificial gravity had put my sense organs into a state of stupor. I even had to close my eyes to not look at all the craziness on the other side of the glass.

About a minute later, there followed a smooth jolt, and I opened my eyes. The shuttle was on the snow-white deck of a long, cigar-shaped ship. The robotic arms turned the shuttle around and pulled it into an open gate. I breathed in with relief. The flight was finally over! I even managed not to make a fool of myself in front of my subjects. I was one of the first out the door. As soon as the little pressure gage by the door changed color to green, I was off the shuttle. Then I stopped, skimming the information on the stately officer welcoming me:

Oorast Pohl, captain of Queen of Sin

Age: 38
Race: Human
Gender: Male
Class: Military
Achievements: Two-time winner of the Imperial Space Racing Championship in the Frigate Class. His mastery in his field and loyalty to the Empire have been affirmed repeatedly. Approved to work with members of the upper aristocracy.
Fame: +3
Standing: + 15
Presumed personal opinion of you: +55 (trusting)

The captain stopped five steps from me and took a low bow.

"I'm glad to welcome you on board your yacht, Prince."

"I'm glad to see you as well, Oorast, but now is not the time for pomp and circumstance. Marta will soon find out that I've taken a captive out from under her nose. So, give an order to all our ships: be prepared for departure at a moment's notice."

Despite the irregularity of the order (or perhaps it was the other way around, because orders like this from the eccentric Georg were not a rarity at all), the captain was not surprised in the least and merely asked me to clarify one thing:

"Where will we be going, my Prince? We can jump to three warp-zones from here: either to Fastel, to the recharging station at Himora, or to the Forepost-12 zone, toward the Iseyek border."

"Well, definitely not to Fastel," I smirked nervously. "Let's go to Himora."

"Prince Georg royl Inoky ton Mesfelle," said the praying mantis, addressing me. "Would it be permissible for me to take my leave and set off toward the Swarm to complete my assigned mission? Any ship in your fleet would be suitable. As soon as I can get to secure communication devices, Iseyek ships will be sent to any point in Sector Eight that you ask. I am also prepared to hand over all information on the aliens I have right now."

With these words, Triasss Zess pulled out his neck, finding a row of spiracle cracks in his thin, gray-green skin, one of which contained a round metal ball. Keeping a careful eye on the praying mantis's actions, Popori de Cacha reached jerkily for his weapon, but the assistant to the ambassador made no sudden movements and asked:

"Due to my temporary lack of small arms, I myself cannot reach the drive. Could one of you do it? It's just a normal memory crystal. It presents no threat to the Prince."

Nevertheless, the vigilant chameleon looked the ball over carefully, even scanning it with a shining plate before taking it in his sticky hands.

"My Prince, I can spare a frigate for the honorable Ambassador, *Pyro-14*," offered Oorast Pohl, looking at something on a handheld screen. "It has full energy drives, so the frigate will be able to bring him home and quickly return to the main fleet."

I consented to this choice and parted ways with the huge praying mantis, who doubled himself up again to fit into the Human shuttle. After that, I ordered them to send a second shuttle back to *Marta the Harlot* to pick up my remaining people: the doctor, butler, and maybe some others who were still there. Then I followed the captain, left the airlock and, trying not to be too surprised at what I'd seen, went up on a high-speed, gilded elevator, before arriving at the officer's deck of my own luxury yacht.

As I had already figured out from the captain's words, it was here, on an unarmed, civilian starship, that Prince Georg kept the headquarters of his fleet. The only reason I could figure for what could generously be called a strange decision was that the facilities on the yacht were much more comfortable. I secretly admired the idiocy of that decision and, also, the fact that no one in the Empire had told the Prince how surprised they were at his choice of flagship for a military fleet. Two royally armed guards in gilded armor suits preemptively opened the doors before me, and I passed through into a huge control hall.

"Get me a detailed report on losses sustained and what remains in service and what condition it's in!" I proclaimed loudly, having barely come into the hall.

The nearest officer, a girl, sprung up from the seat at her desk and practically ran to hand me a flat, almost weightless tablet computer, then froze next to me at attention. I looked in some wonder at my quick subject after reading the information that popped up:

Nicole Savoia, lieutenant of the Star Fleet of the Orange House of the Empire
   Age: 22
   Race: Human
   Gender: Female

Class: Military
Achievements: Top of her class at the Academy
in officer tactics
Fame: 0
Standing: + 1
Presumed personal opinion of you: +4 (neutral)

On top of this, the lieutenant was even nice just to look at. She was young, with dark hair and prim and proper facial features. The fact that she wasn't wearing makeup served to highlight her natural beauty. Under my overly analytical stare, Nicole got embarrassed and even blushed slightly. I sniggered bitterly to myself – they say you've got nothing to be afraid of, little girl... Your Prince Georg is a hopeless impotent... Not wanting to further embarrass my subject, I looked away, immersing myself in the rows of the table.

Prior to the fast-paced battle three days earlier with enemy ships, identified as standard *Recluse*-class alien destroyer scouts, the Sector Eight Fleet had two heavy assault cruisers, five light cruisers (including two cloaked cruisers), 11 destroyers, and sixty frigates. After the only 11-minute-long battle, all that remained were two light cruisers (one badly damaged), four destroyers, and 11 frigates.

"Play back the recording of the last battle! Pay attention, everyone!" I demanded, locking my eyes on the hologram that appeared in the center of the hall.

The battle began with a hussar charge by twenty high-speed frigates at one lone target. The alien ship threw open its gates, and a stream of drones started coming out. Jesus, what noobs! Instead of reducing the number of enemy combat drones, the small ships of my fleet were trying to get through the enemy's energy shield. After that, a heavy ship came, and it just got better from there. By that point though, there were barely any ships from the initial frigate wave left. It looked really rough. The alien ship would let loose one cannon volley, and one frigate from my fleet would go down. After the alien ship had taken down the small fries, it concentrated on the big cruiser. It was destroyed after five or six hits from the terrifying cannon. The second heavy cruiser that had also come to the battle didn't survive much longer. If it hadn't been for the Kingdom of Fastel fleet coming to finally take the enemy ship down, the defeat would have been even more terrible. The recording of the battle ended. I ripped myself from the screen and, after looking around unhurriedly at my silent subjects, depressed after being made to watch their defeat, I said calmly:

"Even though that battle was reported to the rest of the Empire as a victory, let's face facts. That was nothing short of them bending us over and having their way with us. And now I want every one of you to tell me why we got our butts handed to us, and what conclusions we can take from that painful lesson. Nicole, you start."

She straightened up even more and said loudly and clearly, looking past me somewhere ahead of her:

"I have no idea, Your Highness! It's beyond my level of competency!"

I slowly walked around my unmoving subject before stopping directly in front of her and repeating, softer this time:

"First thing, at ease, lieutenant. Second, when speaking with someone, make eye contact. It's hard to have a conversation with your ear or the back of your head. Well, and third: although you are a junior staff officer, if you really have no idea about the reason for the battle going the way it did, you aren't in the right line of work. So, Nicole, let me have it. Don't be shy − tell me your conclusions."

She blushed even harder, stumbling a bit, then spoke out loudly, eyes on me:

"My Prince, when the battle was beginning, an unconscionable lack of coordination was allowed to take hold on our side. Our second most important gun, the heavy cruiser *Gentleman of the Night*, only appeared on the battlefield after our first heavy cruiser, *Flamboyant*, had already essentially been taken out of commission. Thus, at no point did the alien ship have to fight against our two main ships at once."

"Excellent observation, lieutenant. You've proven that it's not for nothing that you work at my headquarters. In an hour, I want you to make me a detailed report on the timing of our ships' arrivals to battle position and a conclusion about why this inconformity in action between our two main ships occurred. So, who wants to talk next?"

After a few seconds of silence, a massive, chubby man with space corporal badges stepped forward.

"My Prince, allow me to speak. What I have to say may come across as direct and rude, but if panic hadn't taken hold, leading to six ships leaving the battle immediately in the second phase, the outcome would have been better."

"What was the reason for the panic?" I wondered, turning toward the corporal.

"The main reason was the heavy losses sustained in the first phase of the battle. Our fleet lost a third of its ships in four minutes," he said quietly, his eyes pointed down. "The second reason was your Highness's orders. They were not always appropriate to the situation at hand in the battle, and were nowhere near the caliber required to create the ideal conditions for maintaining discipline."

Everyone gasped at the space corporal's insolence. It looked like the staff officers gathered there were expecting me to rain down wrath. But, instead, I stated loudly and clearly:

"Popori de Cacha, there's no need to kill this person! It took a lot of bravery to say what he said, and he said exactly the words I was hoping to hear."

As I had assumed, the commander of my bodyguards appeared directly behind the space corporal. The chameleon pulled his blade away and stepped aside, returning to invisibility as he went. God damn is that effective! The staff officers, already walking a tightrope in the Prince's presence before, started breathing in turn. When I spoke, everyone paid an inordinate amount of attention.

"Getting offended by the truth would be a dumb move on my part. Yes, ladies and gentlemen, I too have never before come face to face with an enemy so fierce, so I lost heart, like many of you. However, I have already taken this new information into account and come to my own conclusions, and I promise everyone present that it will never happen again. Now I want the same from each of you. It is very important to me that you understand that this hard lesson was not in vain. I await your comments, advice and observations on the battle. You can relax. There will not be any punitive measures from me today."

At first they were shy, but the officers gradually gathered more courage and started speaking out. The last to speak was the head of the staff officers, the gray-haired Admiral Kiro Sabuto, who said:

"My Prince, the error was due to our initial underestimation of the enemy. We should have joined up with the Kingdom of Fastel's fleet initially, before attacking the alien ship. We didn't want to share the victor's laurels and we paid dearly for that."

"That is partially true, my friend. But I promise everyone present that our fleet would have been capable of taking out the extraterrestrials' ship if it hadn't been for our numerous errors. Our frigates were just screwing around. Instead of destroying the many drones to reduce the amount of damage the enemy could do, they tried to do a job they weren't made for and, for some reason, shot at the main target. The light cruisers didn't go down from just one hit. No one was stopping them from fleeing the battle. There were about twenty seconds between shots from the enemy ship. So why then were our cruisers dropping like flies?! It's plain to see that it was due to weak preparation of our captains and commanders. They clearly haven't learned to react quickly to changing combat conditions. The heavy cruisers took a long time to be destroyed. Their energy shields held out for a few strikes. Note that some frigates and destroyers tried to support the cruisers' shields. If these "healers" had not remained occupied until that moment and those that remained would not have died under attack from enemy drones, we would have been able to save the cruisers. Now, pay attention to what happens at 3:43. Don't tell me no one noticed something off?"

The hologram operator rolled the section of the battle clip a few times, as I ordered. The officers present remained silent. Finally, Nicole shyly postulated:

"It didn't shoot?"

"That's right! The alien ship didn't shoot, despite the fact that it had had enough time to recharge its cannon. Analyze all recordings and find me the reason why the enemy was not able to shoot. If we can figure that out, we'll have the key to defeating the aliens..."

Standing change. Your relationship with the Empire Military Faction has improved.

Present Empire Military faction opinion of you: -7 (mistrusting)

The message arrived unexpectedly and threw me off a bit. I stumbled through the middle of the phrase. I wonder who here did that? It was impossible to figure out. There were too many players around me. But, in any case, it was pleasant news: my speech had been judged worthy by those present.

"My Prince, what are our further instructions?" inquired Admiral Sabuto.

I noticed that the officers were listening avidly, and trying to speak confidently and clearly.

"You all realize that we need repair and reinforcements. The Kingdom of Fastel's fleet helped us in that battle, but it will soon be going back home, and we will not be going with them. We are going to the Himora station, where we'll be sending our ships in for repair, undergoing several training sessions and expecting reinforcements."

"Will more ships be joining our fleet soon?" asked the admiral, not hiding his joy at the good news.

"They absolutely will, admiral. The frigate *Pyro-14* has just departed with the mission of bringing us reinforcements. And I am preparing first thing to deal with the specific problem of reinforcing our battered fleet. So, give our whole fleet the order to prepare for departure. In exactly 10 minutes, we'll be leaving through the warp jump to Himora."

FAMILY AFFAIRS

I WAS STANDING next to Captain Oorast Pohl when we made the warp jump, so I was lucky enough to observe the fantastic event as it unfolded before my very eyes. The cosmos rolled itself up into an endless tunnel as all nearby stars grew dim and began shifting around the sky.

"The flight to Himora will be eight hours and forty minutes, my Prince," explained the captain in a nonplussed tone, not paying any attention to the light show taking place on the screen. "Where would you like to dine?"

"Oh, come on," I said, trying very hard to make my voice sound bored enough, even though it wasn't very easy given the level of sensory overload.

"In the large dining hall with the other senior officers, or in the small one?" asked the yacht captain, clarifying my choice while making some notes on the screen.

"In the small one. It would be even better if I could take it in my office. I'll eat alone," I said, somewhat afraid at the perspective of eating strange food and having to follow etiquette rules I didn't know with whoever happened to be there.

I took a small risk, given that I wasn't sure that there was a "my office" on the yacht. But there were no questions or clarifications, so I figured that I would be able to eat lunch in my office. Now I just needed to figure out where "my office" was. It occurred to me that I could ask someone to take me there, but that might lead my servant to the logical question of why the Prince suddenly doesn't know how to get around his own ship. So, instead, I called up the map.

Deck four of Queen of Sin

The area I was looking for turned out to be on deck two. In fact, Prince Georg's huge apartments occupied practically the whole second deck of the 1,000-foot yacht. After picking the right cabin, which was marked "Office," I first tried my best to memorize the order of turns and staircases, but then I found the "create route" function in the properties of the map, and it worked just like GPS in a car. This brought up a "distance to destination" box and a brightly colored marker to show me what direction to go in.

I felt like a cyborg as I walked through unfamiliar hallways with absolutely no fear of getting lost. No, this is cheating. It isn't even fun to play this way! Would the story of Theseus be of any interest to us now if he could have just pulled up a navigation system and walked out of the Labyrinth? The hero shows up. He's been training since childhood to become a strong, agile master of hand-to-hand combat. And he kills the ill-fated, stupid and clumsy beast created by the geneticists of Olympus. Where's the heroism?

Of course, with my build, I wasn't exactly in the same league as the muscular and athletic Theseus. The body bothered me. My eyes were a different distance from the floor, my fingers were too short and awkward, and I wasn't used to having such a big gut. Once, I even got stuck in a door frame, and hurt myself quite badly. And there was the wheeze, too. I couldn't even make it 10 feet at a clip without having to take a breather. I wonder if physical exercise in a virtual gym would help my virtual body? I'd like to understand how a character's body is defined in the program code, and how and what numbers are stored. I had a pretty good idea how databases worked. Maybe I'd be able to fix it...

It was with these fairly strange and distant thoughts that I walked through the halls of the huge space yacht, only making note of the attention-grabbing luxury. Any metallic detail that struck my eye was gilded (or maybe even solid gold, who can tell?). The sheer number of pieces of art on display was enough to make your eyes light up. There was so much gem encrusting in the interior that you couldn't even stop to admire it for feeling so strongly that you didn't belong there. The ship looked so over-saturated with luxury that you immediately felt it was fake. It could only be possible in a virtual world where it was possible to draw any number of diamonds and emeralds without paying for them. Basically, as a customer and a player, I was dissatisfied with the result and wouldn't have given higher than a three out of five to the programmers and artists that made the decorations for the prince's yacht in the game.

Once I arrived at the office, my already familiar butler was setting the table. Even in his advanced years, Bryle worked nimbly and carefully. I even marveled at how precise he was in placing the dishes on the table. Then my eye was caught by the second set of silverware, which the old man placed on a napkin to the right of the first set for some reason. And the second seat at the table also made me uneasy. I thought I had been clear that I wanted to dine alone.

"Crown Princess Lika wanted to accompany you over lunch," said Bryle, explaining the unexpected preparation.

I held my tongue, though I really wanted to ask "and who is she?" It seemed like that question was a step too far, even for such an unflappable and loyal servant, assuming that Prince Georg really was well acquainted with this lady. And I didn't even say out loud how dissatisfied I was with the fact that some Crown Princess thought she could overrule my orders on my personal yacht. But I couldn't say for sure. Maybe she really did have that right? After all, I hadn't had the chance to study the rank tables around here yet, and didn't really have an understanding of my place in Imperial Royalty. It was completely possible that this Lika person was above me in status and thus *could* overrule my commands. The only thing was that this Crown Princess being there turned a normal lunch into a new test that could end in me looking like a jackass. After all, I had no idea how table manners worked here, and all the dishes on the table were really weird and unfamiliar.

Maybe I should refuse lunch and blame it on my bad health...

I can't say what conclusions I may have reached though, because just then the doors swung open, and a long-legged little girl flew into the room. She looked to be about ten years old with dark short shorts and a light-gold, sleeveless blouse. Her long hair was an unusual shade of bright green, and I immediately began gawking inadvertently. As I stared, I noticed that nestled in among her green locks was a thin gold band in the shape of a crown.

"Hi, dad!" said the young Crown Princess carelessly, as she confidently took a seat in the second chair.

I rushed my way through the character notes, already having a pretty good idea of what I'd see:

Likanna royl Georg ton Mesfelle-Kyle, Crown Princess of the Empire
    Age: 11
    Race: Human
    Gender: Female
    Relation to you: Your legal daughter
    Class: Aristocrat
    Achievements: None
    Fame: +1
    Reputation: +3
    Presumed personal opinion of you: +99 (completely trusting)

"Hi, Lika. What are you doing here? Aren't you supposed to be in class?" The reply just came out on its own. I was just utterly convinced that an eleven-year-old Princess probably should be studying a bunch of different kinds of sciences and skills, starting with dances and music and ending with genealogy and etiquette.

"Of course I'm *supposed* to be," retorted my daughter, agreeing mildly as she nimbly manipulated what looked like a big pair of tweezers to bring a plate of unfamiliar, oblong, dark blue-purple fruits towards herself from the common dish. "I just heard on the news that you and mom fought back an alien invasion, so I decided to fly up and take a look. I was worried."

For some reason, Lika ignored the other fruits, intentionally picking only the dark blue-purple fruits that looked like little weirdly colored apricots. I wonder if they're the tastiest? Before my daughter had a chance to empty the dish, I also picked up a pair of the tweezers and grabbed one, tossing it in my mouth. Yum. So it really is an apricot, even though it's not the color I'm used to. Lika snorted back happily:

"I've always told the table etiquette teacher it'd be easier to eat right from the grabber without putting it on a stupid plate first."

I chuckled too, happy to myself that my mistake, which had been due to my unfamiliarity with table manners, was taken as a joke by my daughter. Nevertheless, it was a good idea to be more careful and only eat the same exact way my daughter was doing.

"Don't spoil your appetite on fruit. Save some room for the main courses," I suggested to Lika, but all she did was carelessly brush it aside. "Well, I ate not too long ago when I got to the battlefield. There wasn't even anything alien to see there on the backdrop of broken pieces of Imperial and Kingdom of Fastel ships. So I figured right away that actually it was just you and mom fighting with each other."

"And I bet you'll say it was mom that almost bit right through my neck too," I said, pointing at my bandage.

Lika started guffawing, and I joined her. Then my daughter unexpectedly started complaining:

"Dad, Joan royl Reyekh is teasing me again. She tells everyone that I don't have an ear for music. And it's all because I'm gonna be playing in the school orchestra instead of her."

"That's not called teasing. What she's doing is called gossip," I said thoughtfully, correcting Likanna. "And what am I supposed to do about Joan royl Reyekh now then? Bomb her home planet to dust or just break that unbearable little snot's arm?"

At first, Lika froze in fear with her food half way from the plate to her mouth, but then she began giggling again:

"It's always fun with you, dad. Of course, it would be nice to punish that pain-in-the-butt and bomb the Purple Palace to the ground, but I'm afraid the leader of the Purple House, Duke Takuro royl Andor wouldn't allow it. To put it lightly, he has no love lost for our Orange House. And I won't be able to break Joan royl Reyekh's arm either. She's a crown princess too, unfortunately, so laying a hand on her would be illegal."

I smiled at my overly serious daughter and took the risk of starting my meal in earnest, as my stomach was groaning in hunger. I only took food that

I could tell how to consume in polite company: a thin, pureed soup (there was only one spoon among the tableware, so there was no way I could make a mistake with that), pieces of dark bread, cheese balls, and a light wine.

Lika saw my appetite and enounced thoughtfully:

"You know what? I think I'm gonna join you. I haven't had anything but fruit since yesterday."

That turned out to be really helpful and I was finally able to watch how you're supposed to consume all these tartlets, round thin sausages, and jelly balls. Some time passed in silence, but then my daughter broke it:

"Dad, my summer break's starting soon, so I'm not gonna go back to school. Sound good? I'll just spend some time with mom on Fastel-XI."

"Alright, but we aren't on our way to Fastel right now. We're going to Himora. The fleet needs to be repaired."

"If you say so," agreed the Crown Princess, somewhat reluctantly. "If we're going to Himora, then Himora it is. I mean, it is literally the most boring place in the Universe, but it's only five hours from Uncle Roben's flying palace on Tesse. Can you tell my teachers that I'm with you then? They won't give *you* any crap for me playing hooky. Dad, can you pay a couple bills for me? On my way here, there weren't any adults with me, so I told everyone that the Orange House was paying."

"Of course I'll pay. It's not a question," I agreed. Not one second later, I heard a sound as if I'd gotten an email.

I opened the window that popped up:

Total payment due: 3076.89 credits. Pay (yes/no)?

I could also go into detail and see every item on the bill. I probably wouldn't do that with any other character as not to pry into their private life, but with my daughter I would play the father. I opened the list, and my eyes darted across the lines.

"So, what is this? 'Alcoholic cocktail: 2.3 credits?' Who sold it to you?" I asked indignantly, while shooting my underage daughter a severe look.

"That was at the cargo terminal station Unguay-3. I got stuck there for half a day. There weren't any space flights in or out of that one-horse shithole. I was thirsty, but the bar didn't have anything for kids. And, dad, there aren't any restrictions on selling alcohol to kids in the Unguay system, so I didn't break any laws."

The picture I was imagining was an eleven-year-old girl hitchhiking with no money wandering into places that weren't exactly made with kids in mind. In the real world, that situation would scare me. Either there weren't problems with criminals in the virtual game, or Lika had just been lucky.

"And how did you get out of there, then?" I wondered, not able to hide the worry in my voice.

"Duh, dad. I jumped an ore-carrier that was unloading at Unguay-3. I demanded to meet with the captain and ordered him to immediately bring me to the Vorta beacon near where the battle happened. I promised that the Orange House would pay any expenses. You should have seen the captain apologizing for the mess. His team absolutely scoured the halls! It didn't look like it had ever been cleaned until I came on board. What was even funnier was how they tried to hide an illegal immigrant prostitute on their tiny little ship, then tried to pass her off as staff. She had to pretend to be their washerwoman, cleaning dirty underwear. It was just too rich!"

I had no words. When I was eleven, I not only didn't understand what the word "prostitute" meant, I had never heard it before. And this underage space Princess travels in the company of a prostitute and a bunch of sullen stevedores and thinks it's fun! But Lika had no understanding of why I was so upset.

"You can get mad if you want, dad! But what could possibly happen to a Crown Princess on Imperial territory?! Not even the baddest crook in the Galaxy would dare lay a finger on the heir to the Imperial throne, because the punishment for it is unavoidable and final. Plus, everyone in the Galaxy knows that Princesses never travel alone. Who cares if there's no bodyguards visible? That means nothing. Your chameleons aren't visible, but they're probably with us here right now."

"But you didn't have any guards with you!" I insisted.

"That's right. But who knew?" Lika sneered.

I just shook my head and paid my daughter's bills. What's more, I even had to pay double for the ore freight from the *Avaricious Miner* to compensate the crew for their trouble. I'm sure some nerves were fried by having an impudent young girl with a title on board. After that, we continued our meal over an uninhibited, very friendly conversation. Mostly Lika spoke, enthusiastically telling me about her private school for the upper aristocracy in the Throne World. I responded with nods and "yeah, yeahs," while thinking about something else entirely.

I never had kids in the real world. I had had girlfriends, and even two or three long-term relationships with regular sex. But I never saw the necessity of deepening an existing relationship, or taking one as far as marriage. Nevertheless, I discovered in despair at that moment that I had always wanted a daughter deep down. I would do all it took so she would turn out like Likanna: careless, happy, with a boundless trust of the world around her and utterly convinced that her parents are capable of anything.

Of course, it was entirely possible that Likanna was actually being played by some rich retiree looking to have a second childhood, or maybe even some fat, bald guy sitting at his monitor as he scratches his sweaty balls and wipes his greasy fingers on the keyboard. But for some reason, I got the impression that Lika wasn't just playing a child, she really was a child. It came so naturally to her that no actor could possibly have been behind such an authentic eleven-year-old girl.

After lunch, Lika stood up from the table and said anxiously:

"I think I ate too much. I'm gonna go down to the gym and swim for an hour in the pool. Look at me, I even had a wrinkle show up on my skin. I guess I'll never fill out." She tried her best to find and show me the wrinkle, but it was no use.

When Lika had left, I finally had the opportunity

to really study the game world for the first time since I started playing. In my less than a whole day, I had already accumulated hundreds of questions: What are the Empire and Great Houses? What are the relationships between the two like? What are the roles of the mystics and the aristocracy? What kinds of ships are there? How fast do they go? What star systems are in Perimeter Sector Eight, and what countries are in it? What moves are possible between the beacons in the zone I'm responsible for, etc. and so on.

I spent five hours sitting in front of the huge screen in my office until my eyes were fried and my head refused to take in any new information. After a light dinner with my daughter, I spent another hour studying the characteristics of the military ships and went off to find the gym.

My whole body was aching. Every muscle fiber was shouting to my brain as if to say "I'm here, and I'm not happy with the violence you're inflicting on me!" I wondered if the Prince had made it down to pump iron even once in his nearly half century of carefree life. As if! The fitness instructor at least tried to pretend there was nothing wrong with me, but the sympathy was written on his face a bit too clearly. "Don't worry about it," I said to reassure myself. I have another half year left to turn this amorphous lump of fat into something that resembles a man's body.

In the shower, where I went to clean off the

abundant sweat that was pouring off my body, there was a surprise waiting for me. It turned out that the space yacht had three nice-looking girls on staff whose job description included sponge-bathing Prince Georg's body and being responsible for his hygiene in general. Initially, I wanted to protest, but eventually I gave in to their skilled, capable hands. I was massaged, lathered and rinsed, shaved, and sprayed down with a number of lotions and colognes, before having my hair done and finally getting my finger- and toenails repainted. I tried to refuse the polish, but it was obvious they didn't understand what I was asking for, instead thinking I was just sick of the color. For that reason, my nails got painted orange and pink. It was horrifying, of course, but I didn't argue, because changing Prince Georg's habits too quickly would risk me being unmasked.

A warning signal rang out over the intercom. "Ten minutes to warp tunnel exit." I hurried to fleet headquarters, trying not to look too bow-legged after how sore I'd made myself. As soon as I noticed that Prince Georg had his own personal seat in the headquarters in front of the big screen, I hurried to take it. The staff officers were obviously surprised at my showing up, but no one said a word. Though it was already too late, I considered the fact that such a commonplace occurrence as coming out of warp hardly merited the personal presence of a Crown Prince, but I wasn't going to leave my post at that point. As it turned out, I had not miscalculated.

"Sound the combat alert!" The siren wailed. It's not like my ship could've just come out in regular space. That'd be too easy.

Reports and comments from the staff officers rained down one after the other. I hardly had enough time to read through them all.

"The ship isn't answering standard identification system requests!"

"Distance to target: one hundred miles. It appears to be a *Flamberg* heavy cruiser."

"Confirmed. It's a *Flamberg*."

"Search the ship database for that make."

"There is a 97% chance that it is the *Payoff*, the flagship of the pirate squadron, the Brotherhood of the Stars. They have a base one star system over."

"The *Payoff* has firepower that exceeds that of any of our flotilla's ships."

"Immediate retreat is recommended!" proclaimed Admiral Sabuto on the basis of the data he was given.

"As you were!!!" I shouted, hurrying to interfere. "All I see is one antiquated heavy cruiser. We've got a whole sixteen ships to go against him!"

"If I may, my Prince, we have fifteen ships, and not one of them is a cruiser," interrupted the admiral.

"Remind me after the battle to have a serious talk with the captain of the delayed cruiser. But there's no time for that now. Even without our late and damaged ships, we've got double that cruiser's firepower. Let's tear him to shreds! All frigates and destroyers on the attack! All power to forward shields!"

A swarm of tiny dots ripped themselves out of place and, quickly gaining speed, made a beeline straight for the enemy. One of the frigates bloomed with the fire of an explosion.

"Curve in on it and change trajectory. Don't let the cruiser's cannons get a clear shot! Do not reduce speed, slow it down and don't let it warp out! If it uses drones, shoot them down the second you see them!"

"We've got it!" came Officer Nicole, providing commentary on the message about the enemy's warp drive being blocked.

"Great! Focus on the cruiser. Let's put some pressure on its shields!"

"There's a message from the enemy ship. They're surrendering!" The communications officer was bewildered and couldn't even believe our luck.

"Cease fire. Send boarding teams, plug up the propulsion drives and deactivate the cannons," said Admiral Kiro Sabuto, now demonstrating the very picture of calm, as if he hadn't recommended turning tail five minutes earlier.

"Congratulations on the victory, admiral," I confirmed, also trying to move past what was undoubtedly not the most heroic moment in the commander's biography. "It looks like our fleet has a new flagship!"

The people in the hall applauded as the enthusiastic screams of our fleet's captains could be heard over the speakers.

Standing change. Empire Military faction opinion of you has improved.

Present Empire Military faction opinion of you: -4 (indifferent)

Messages flashed up about personal relationship improvements with Prince Georg directly from a few players. Among these, I noticed I had received one from the admiral, Lieutenant Nicole Savoia, and even the grumbling space corporal.

"My Prince, incoming call from Princess Marta royl Valesy ton Mesfelle-Kyle," said the communications officer.

Happiness was blowing in like the wind. The crew of the yacht turned out to be surprisingly well informed about my none-too-simple relationship with my spouse.

"Put her through," I demanded, donning my headphones so my underlings wouldn't have to look down every time I came around after what they'd hear.

I didn't really hear anything new in Marta's five-minute-long, wrathful rant. After the stream of curses and accusations went dry, the plump cow announced that she would be cutting off my income from the Kingdom of Fastel. It seemed to me that she was expecting an immediate apology or for me to debase myself even further begging for forgiveness, but I kept silent, which clearly caught her by surprise. Marta continued a minute longer just to make sure, then started another tantrum with a renewed ire:

"Don't expect any more help from the Kingdom of Fastel! Instead of more ships from my fleet, all you'll get from me are official divorce papers from my lawyers! And how could you trade me in for that dirty whore Miya! If it weren't for Lika being on board, I would gladly leave your yacht in ashes! I don't even want to look at you!"

The call cut off, but I sat there another minute without taking off my headphones as I worked through all the mud that had been slung at me. When I finally did stand up and take a look around, I discovered that none of the officers were working. Instead, they were all silently staring at me. Apparently my facial expression was enough for everyone to figure out that it hadn't been an especially pleasant conversation.

"My Prince, think nothing of it. The only thing these highborn bitches are good for is making trouble," said the same space corporal, as straightforward as ever. Perhaps more than necessary.

"Thank you," I answered. Then I observed to him, "Today, I skimmed through your personal records, Patrick toyl Sven. Allow me to give you some advice, space corporal. Your tongue is your enemy. It is the only reason why at fifty-six years old, you're still the lowest ranked staff officer. You could already be a major based on your merits in battle. But today I need just such an honest man at my side. I invite you today to the small dining hall and warn you in advance that I will be getting drunk as a skunk. All the other ladies and gentlemen here, I value and love you, but you are not invited. I don't want you to see your Prince like that."

"We have completely captured the pirate cruiser! The enemy crew has been placed under arrest!" reported one of the officers in a deliberately vigorous tone, obviously trying to improve my mood. "What are your orders for the captives?"

I didn't have time to answer before another message popped up:

"*Algol Hulk*, a light cruiser in our fleet has come out of warp." Fifteen minutes was all he needed then...

"Admiral, get me a profile on the captain of that ship," I demanded, turning sharply on my heels to face Kiro Sabuto.

The admiral squinted and looked aside:

"You know my feelings about him, your Highness. Captain Crasav ton Lavaelle is the grandnephew of Count Amelius royl Mast ton Lavaelle from the Green House. His high birth is the only merit that led to him becoming captain of a star cruiser. He's too independent and shows it in every way. The only reason he survived the encounter with the alien ship is because he fled the battle. This is all in my reports, your Highness. I have already made formal complaints about Crasav ton Lavaelle for disobeying direct orders and even recommended he be relieved from his post as captain of *Algol Hulk*. However, you ignored both of my reports..."

"I need to speak with him this instant," I demanded. A few seconds later, a handsome young dark-haired face came on screen with a magnificent, curled mustache like a hussar.

"My Prince, you have my full attention," came the captain without even a hint of guilt or repentance.

"I ordered all ships in the fleet to warp to Himora at the same time. Explain the reason for your fifteen-minute delay."

"Uhhhh. I never got the order from the communications officer. I wasn't told," Crasav ton Lavaelle lied flagrantly, not fooling me.

"*Algol Hulk* communications officer!" I demanded. A frightened, twenty-year-old girl with space corporal patches appeared on screen. "Was the order to quickly move the fleet received and transmitted in good time to the captain?"

"I can assure you it was, my Prince," said the girl clearly. "The order was received and transmitted in good time. However, the captain was in the dining hall when he received it and replied that he would be finishing his breakfast first."

"That is untrue! She's lying! She never cared for me!" screeched the captain, and I demanded to be transferred to his first assistant.

The gloomy, middle-aged soldier in a golden uniform was watching some recordings and answered:

"The space corporal is right. According to the log, the order to prepare for relocation was received at eleven forty-three, and was transmitted to the captain eight seconds thereafter."

"Admiral," I addressed Kiro Sabuto, standing next to me. "Consider your reports reviewed and approved. The captain of *Algol Hulk* is to be removed from his position on the cruiser and placed under arrest. As soon as we arrive at the Himora station, cut him right the hell loose with nothing but a bag of personal belongings. Let him cry to his crown-wearing grandfather."

"But Himora is in the middle of nowhere. Passenger liners only go there once a month."

"It's nothing. He's a grown man. He'll figure it out. My daughter traversed half the galaxy on her own, and she's an eleven-year-old girl. What's more, an ore carrier, *Avaricious Miner*, should be at Himora. Let him fly off to his grandfather on it. It's been cleaned and organized especially for him. They even have a prostitute on staff!"

Internal Problems

"**O**W... MY HEAD is splitting..."

"My Prince, yesterday you allowed yourself an inadvisable amount of alcohol," explained Dr. Nicosid Brandt, as he massaged the active points of my head while rubbing some eucalyptus-scented ointment into my temples.

"Inadvisable, but not unintentional," I said, disagreeing with my doctor. "I wanted to forget after the row with Marta... Ow! That's where it hurts the most. Ooh. Yep, that made it better."

"The after-effects of alcohol consumption should pass within half an hour of taking the medicine. But the overworked muscles will ache at least another five days. There are a number of micro-tears and a great deal of lactic acid. Perhaps you'd like a painkiller after all?"

"No, don't worry about that. Everything is how it's supposed to be."

I refused further treatment and left the hospital wing of the yacht, trying to come to grips with an important matter that had been bothering me since I first woke up. My first conscious thought this morning wasn't regret at the strong hangover, but actually confusion. Exactly that: confusion! Basically, I presumed, I was even totally sure, that after a full work-day in the game, I'd fall asleep and wake up in the real world. How could it work any other way? I put in a whole day, and I did a good job too. I even died once! But when I woke up again, I was still in the game! How the hell? When are they going to let me finish my shift and leave the game?

But, on the other hand, I felt completely rested and was getting ready to spend the whole day learn-learn-learning, just as a certain bald revolutionary politician had once instructed. Nevertheless, I was interrupted just before I could start.

"Incoming call from an encrypted channel in Swarm territory," remarked the communications officer. "Should I put them through?"

I answered in the affirmative, and an Alpha Iseyek appeared on screen. It clearly wasn't Triasss Zess. This new one was a darker color and had all its appendages.

"Good health to you, Princcce Geor-g roul Ee-noki. I are Admiral Kheraisss Vej. Are control Swarm flit. Is two of. Flit Yuho and flit Ayho. Swarm order me go serve flit Eight Sector. I am wait command, my Princcce."

"Nice to meet you, Admiral Kheraisss Vej. How many ships do you have at your command?"

The praying mantis turned his head on its side. As I already knew, this pose meant that he was perplexed and had no idea what was going on. The admiral must have had trouble understanding something in my question. I decided to put it more simply:

"In your fleet: how many ships and what classes? Will there be backup? And when can you come to join my fleet?"

The praying mantis became visibly happy and answered:

"With me, flit Yuho. *Legash* type ship: one. *Umoyge* type ship: four. *Vassar* type ship, rocket: two, laser: nine. *Safa* type ship: five. *Tria*: one, but full load. Flit Ayho is come one day you. Three *Legash* type ship, all improved. Four *Vassar* rocket. After, I comes to Princcce for order. Backup Swarm to give broke *Uukresh*. No place Swarm fix dockyard. Ship with propulsion, but much broken."

I even had to call up a hint to have any idea what the Admiral was saying. *Legash*, what's a *Legash*... But the ship database wasn't giving me anything. I had to answer the praying mantis without having all the information:

"Admiral, all those ships must be quickly relocated to the Tesse system. That's where the closest dockyards capable of repairing your ships are. When can you be in Tesse?"

The praying mantis grated his mandibles and said:

"Four days, all ship, but no *Uukresh*. For *Uukresh* need tug and escort. That ship is too break and vulnerable for trip without convoy. Risk is no can. To move only when tug and guard to come."

"Great, I'll wait for your other ships at the meeting point, and find a tug and other ships to accompany your valuable *Uukresh*."

The Admiral bowed exactly like a person, then signed off. I set straight off for my fleet headquarters.

"Ladies and gentlemen, hello. Who among you has an understanding of Iseyek ship classifications and Swarm terminology? I want to know what a *Legash* is."

The staff officers began looking from one to another hesitantly. Then Lieutenant Nicole, just like a school girl in class, raised her hand and offered an answer:

"My Prince, my apologies. It sounded like you were saying "Legatsh." It's an antiquated Iseyek heavy cruiser for circular combat. It's not like the heavy assault cruisers people have with reinforced shields and most cannons in the front hemisphere. It has an equally distributed shield and has 360-degree shooting capability. In Imperial classification they are called Swarm *Vandal* heavy cruisers. They have proven not very effective in modern combat due to the practical impossibility of firing with all cannons and are considered outdated."

"Thank you, Nicole. Maybe you can answer another question for me while you're at it. What's an 'improved *Legash*?'

The girl shook her head in embarrassment. Admiral Kiro Sabuto answered in her place:

"My Prince, there have been rumors that the Iseyeks created a replacement for their antiquated circular combat cruisers, taking into account their experience of half a century of war with us. Our intelligence has noted several modified cruisers in Swarm territory.

The Admiral quickly tapped his fingers on the

touch screen and sent a few pictures to my display. Silhouettes and photos with tables: *Vandal-2* heavy cruiser, *Vandal-3* heavy cruiser, and *Vandal-4* heavy cruiser.

"Unfortunately, we have very little data," admitted the admiral. "Experts note only a basic reinforced shield and an array of changes in the cruiser's appearance. Its combat characteristics are unknown."

"Then, we'll find out for ourselves. In four days, we'll see four of these Iseyek cruisers with our own eyes!"

I was expecting a flurry of happiness from the officers, but for some reason their reaction was strangely spooked. The reason my team was acting that way was revealed when one of my tacticians cautiously asked:

"My Prince, will we be fighting with or against the Swarm ships?"

"With," I said, calming everyone down. "What's more, these ships will be joining our fleet. It's the Swarm's contribution to the defense of Perimeter Sector Eight."

Then a thunder of overjoyed shouts started in earnest. Everyone came to life and began smiling. I walked up to Nicole and addressed her:

"Lieutenant, given that you have a better idea than most about praying mantis ship names, illuminate me all at once. What are 'umoyge,' 'vassar,' 'safa,' 'tria' and 'uukresh?'"

After a second of strained thought, the girl's face changed to uninhibited joy:

"*Umoyge* is a Swarm light cruiser specialized in electronic warfare. *Vassar* isn't the name of one model of ship, it's a type of ship. They're support ships. Something between our light cruisers and destroyers. There are all kinds of different *Vassars*. There are rocket *Vassars*, anti-rocket *Vassars*, electronic warfare *Vassars*, shield support *Vassars*, cloaked *Vassars*, anti-frigate *Vassars*, and lots more. As for *Safas*, they're little ships. Frigates, in our classification. And as for the last two names, I don't know," she said, beginning to blush.

"Then this question is for everyone. The Iseyeks are sending us a fully loaded *Tria* and a 'very broken *Uukresh*.' Who can help their Prince figure out what to prepare for?"

All staff went silent and looked at the floor. I had to lend some spirit of liveliness to the lazy swamp that had taken hold around my table:

"No, ladies and gentlemen, that's not how it goes. You understand that I am capable of finding the answer myself. But then I'll start wondering why the hell I have twenty assistants at my fleet headquarters, if none of them can find the answer to a pretty easy question! I'm giving you until six this evening to find the answer: what we should be preparing for, and what docks we are going to need for the *Tria* and the *Uukresh*. Whoever answers first will get an acknowledgment in their personal file and a valuable prize from the very hand of an Imperial Crown Prince. If anyone doesn't give me the answer, that person will have to redo their qualifications and retake the exams in all Space Combat Academy disciplines, starting with Physical Education and ending with the combat characteristics of all ships from the Empire and all nearby races!"

I was already half way out the door when I stopped and turned sharply because of something I remembered.

"Lieutenant Nicole, yesterday I received your detailed report on the timeline of the battle at the Vorta beacon. Unfortunately, I have not yet had the time to familiarize myself with your calculations and conclusions, but I promise you I will. In any case, I'm satisfied with the work you've done, and the knowledge you've demonstrated today. Take the rest of the day off. That's an order. Also, what I said about retesting peoples' qualifications does not apply to Admiral Kiro Sabuto. I hope everyone realizes that. I expect all other officers' reports by six tonight. Everyone must do the work on their own without their colleagues' help. Admiral, make sure they do! A big war is coming, and I need the best of the best in my fleet, so you're all going to have to prove why you're here!"

Standing change. Empire Military faction opinion of you has worsened.

Present Empire Military faction opinion of you: -5 (mistrusting)

And almost right away, I got another message:

Standing change. Empire Military faction opinion of you has improved.

Present Empire Military faction opinion of you: -4 (indifferent)

I chuckled to myself. Some officers here aren't

liking the changes and screw tightening the Prince is bringing. Nevertheless, I had my allies in the headquarters so, at the end of the day, I'm back to the status quo. What's next!

"The frigate *Pyro-14* has returned from its mission and has just now docked at the Himora station," came a message from the yacht captain.

"Better late than never! Communications officer, gather all frigate and destroyer captains in the small hall in twenty minutes. Also, have them bring the navigators and senior communications officers from their ships. Our whole fleet is now docked at the Himora station, so I don't see any reason why they shouldn't all be able to come to this important meeting.

There were around seventy people gathered in the small hall. All the staff officers and the crewmembers I'd called from the smaller ships. While the fussy technician set up the electronic display and connected the microphones, I watched with unhidden satisfaction as the staff officers surreptitiously scrambled with their tablets under the tables, searching for more answers, looking over summaries and studying the Iseyek ships.

"So, ladies and gentlemen, let's begin! The topic of today's meeting, as you may have guessed by now is the role of frigates and light ships in modern warfare..."

I was quite rudely interrupted by someone from the crowd:

"What other role do you think they could have? Fighting the enemy's little ships, taking them down and helping the main ships!"

I wanted to tell the man off, but first I read the information about the gray haired officer.

> **Maur Cassei**
> **Age: 96**
> **Race: Human**
> **Gender: Male**
> **Class: Soldier**
> **Achievements: Has combat medals for participation in interspecies conflicts**
> **Fame: +9**
> **Reputation: + 21**
> **Presumed personal opinion of you: -23 (opposed)**
> **Empire Military faction opinion of you: -4 (indifferent)**

"Mother of my wife! This geezer is ninety-six years old, but he is still serving in an active fleet! It can't be easy for the player to get into the role of a character like that believably. You'd need to have a real understanding of what it means to be old. I requested more information about this legendary figure. Seventy-five years in the fleet and all that time the captain has been on light frigates of various makes.

"Our respected elder, who was doing heroic deeds on frigates back when the rest of us were still soiling diapers, is right as always. It's the classic war plan. It's stood the test of time. The little ships fight off the little ships, while the heavy ships deal with others like themselves."

The old man was flattered by my words. He smiled and said something to the person next to him. As I continued, I sharply shifted from good natured and relaxed to a severe tone.

"As we have seen, the classic plan doesn't work at all against the aliens. Our fleet lost fifty-five small-class ships out of seventy-some total! Seventy-seven percent losses! And that was only against one ship. And it wasn't even the most powerful one, just a *Hermit*."

"This is war. Losses are unavoidable. What matters is that our fleet did its job and eliminated the enemy. Losses are secondary!" came the very same old man, interrupting me again.

"Ok then, let's suppose you're right... Bring up the image on screen!" I showed a recording taken from the material Triass Zess had provided. "This was shot one month ago in the Aysar cluster, eight days flight from Himora."

A swarm of unidentifiable spots filled the big screen. There were thousands of them, maybe even tens of thousands. I zoomed in so you could make out individual spots from the seething mess. They were starships, a huge horde of alien combat starships. I pressed pause and pointed my laser pointer at one of the outlines.

"So, right here we see a *Hermit*. Not too long ago, just such a ship almost tore our whole fleet to pieces. As we can see there are hundreds and thousands of them here, and these aren't even close to the largest or most dangerous ships in the alien armada. Here you can see a bigger figure. It's an *Ascetic*-class destroyer. It has double the firepower of the *Hermit*. And over there is a cruiser. The name us humans have given it is the *Sledgehammer*, because one blow from it can take down any make of human cruiser. Now look over here. This one's even bigger. It's easier to see closer to the middle, here. I can't even guess if we've ever come across one of these, but based on its size it's a battleship. And you can make up your own name for that giant in the very middle. It's about one hundred times longer than my yacht."

The audience grew quiet, depressed and even scared at what they'd seen. Before the officers had a chance to collect themselves, I continued in an even tone:

"As you can see, we don't have enough ships to keep losing sixty of ours for each one of theirs. As luck would have it though, tactics for frigates to use against high-firepower ships have been around for a while. That is exactly what we're here to talk about today. We need to study and practice one of these tactics. Given that new knowledge will give our fleet advantages in modern warfare, this material is top secret and not a word of it is to leave this fleet. So, this tactic is called 'long-bombing.' I've drawn up a plan. The enemy ship is in the middle of the board. Below it, are two little spots."

This wasn't the first time I'd had to explain what was a fairly elementary tactic, but the last time I'd done it, I was talking to players of a totally different game.

"The enemy ship is in the middle. But it's very strong. Each cannon shot it gets off is one less frigate on our side, not to mention the lives of all our people on board. The goal is to keep it on the battlefield as long as possible while minimizing losses. To do that, in the initial phase of the battle, we'll need one frigate, let's call it 'receiver number one,' to fly away from the target at maximum speed until it's well beyond the range of the enemy cannons. We'll figure out the range through trial and error. Maybe it's a thousand, maybe fifteen hundred, or maybe even a couple five thousand miles – it doesn't matter. The second frigate, 'receiver number two,' goes in the opposite direction from the target to about the same distance. Only after the 'receivers' are in place and have told the fleet their coordinates, does the main battle phase begin."

I drew a dotted line from one frigate to the other.

"At any point in time, every frigate in the fleet is accelerating, either toward the first 'receiver' or the second one. When you get the warning signal that the enemy ship is targeting a frigate, you warp jump to the receiver at a safe distance. That's when you turn it around. Warp back into the battle at the coordinates of any of our fleet's ships near the enemy, and immediately start accelerating toward the other receiver. The main thing we'll really need from the frigates is to catch our formidable enemy in a warp disruptor as soon as they get on the battlefield to jam the enemy's warp drive so they can't run away. There must be at least one warp disruptor on the enemy at all times, and the frigate that placed it must not jump to either receiver until absolutely sure someone else has placed another."

"But, my Prince, with this plan some of our ships are out of the battle from the start. We're going to lose a good deal of our damage dealing ability," noted one of the captains.

"Yes, that's true. But in the first phase of the battle, what matters is immobilizing the enemy without losing any ships. Actually destroying the enemy is a job for our main guns, when they're out at optimum shooting distance from the target. The frigates' job is to serve themselves up on a platter as a sacrifice. Of course, no one is saying you shouldn't be shooting at the enemy, but shooting is secondary and must only be done after a warp disruptor has been placed."

"And what if the target places a warp disruptor on the frigate?"

"That means we made a mistake, because the frigate didn't make the jump to the candle while the enemy was targeting it. But, if that happens, turn the main propulsion thrusters up to full power and go far enough away that you're out of the enemy warp disruptor's effective range and save the ship. If for some reason that is impossible, then go very quickly toward the enemy and fly in the smallest circular orbit you can. With high angular momentum, there's a chance that the enemy won't hit you. Nevertheless, that rule only applies to enemies with high caliber guns and fixed turrets. That not-too-big *Hermit* will hit you no problem, even if you squeeze a *Pyro* for all its worth and bring it up to near maximum speed."

"I understand the technique, but it requires perfect coordination between our ships," said the gray-haired captain, shaking his head. "One crewmember makes one wrong move on our side and the enemy goes free. And all maneuvers will have to be made at high speed, so this will be quite the extreme challenge..."

"Yes, Maur Cassei, that is true. We need our frigate crews to be in perfect physical condition. That is why only the strongest and toughest can work that job. But space combat does not typically last long. Ten minutes and it's all over. What's more, it's always possible that a frigate with a crew that's already tired could take the role of one of the receivers, while a fresh team takes their place. However, if you aren't confident in your own physical condition, your frigate could be a receiver and help us out that way."

"My Prince, pay my age no mind. My whole life, I've always passed physical tests with flying colors, so even when I'm a hundred years old, I'll still be in good shape."

"I was hoping you'd say that, Maur Cassei. Formation flying is long, hard work. It won't be easy to get used to the new conditions. What's more, we're expecting reinforcements soon, and there will probably be a whole bunch of green novices among them. Those young pilots are going to need an example to look up to of the kind of authoritative patriarch whose footsteps they'll be following in."

"Do not worry, my Prince. I will not let you down!" The old man puffed out his chest, obviously proud at the big assignment he'd been entrusted with.

Standing change. Your relationship with Maur Cassei has improved.

Presumed personal opinion of you: -8 (disapproving)

It looks like I've been able to clean up most of the

negativity toward me. And would you look at that! With time, you can even bring an authoritative veteran over to your side! But the next message made me even happier:

Standing change. Empire Military faction opinion of you has improved.
Present Empire Military faction opinion of you: -2 (indifferent)

Bit by bit, things are getting better!

"Dad, it's so boring here in Himora!" Lika told me over lunch. "It's a teeny little technical recharging station with just three hundred people living on it. There's nothing to do. When are we going to Tesse?"

"Tomorrow night, we're going," I said, reassuring her. "Six of my ships are damaged and need at least some repair so they won't break down on the way. And that pirate cruiser too... It's a valuable trophy, but we need to check it thoroughly to make sure the pirates didn't leave any surprises behind. Our engineers, electricians and mechanics need no less than a day to look over all the *Payoff*'s systems... I really don't like that name. It'd be nice to change it to something more memorable."

"Like that time when they trusted you with naming that cruiser in the capital of the Kingdom of Fastel?" giggled Likanna. "I bet they've never been more caught off guard by a name than they were by *Marta the Harlot*. No one could have been expecting that."

I smiled too. So that's what it was! It's not surprising that after such extravagances, Prince Georg royl Inoky ton Mesfelle wouldn't be on such great footing with his spouse's relatives."

"Lika, do you wanna name the new cruiser?" I offered, and the girl's eyes lit up.

"Yeah, duh! Can I call it whatever I want? Are you sure?"

I gave a kindhearted nod. Lika thought for a few seconds before giving her answer:

"I want to name the cruiser 'Big Fat Joan!' Dad, come on, you promised!"

"Hrrmm... Well that *is* what we call 'making fun of someone.' Your little classmate is definitely not going to like that. But a promise is a promise. Let's go to Tesse tomorrow and change the name."

The incoming call signal rang out unexpectedly. Before I'd had the chance to check, I already had the feeling that something unpleasant had taken place. When I got to the captain of *Queen of Sin*, who had called me, he was seriously alarmed:

"My Prince, we've received an emergency message from *Algol Hulk*, which is in for repair at the Himora station. There's been a double attack on Orange House soldiers. Sergeant Tavar Prest has been killed by unknown individuals. The same sergeant who brought your Highness here from *Marta the Harlot* yesterday. He was transferred onto that ship just last night, and this morning he was nowhere to be found. His corpse was discovered in cold storage during routine inspection. The sergeant was killed by a blow to the back of the head by a heavy object. We also found another corpse in cold storage. That of the female communications officer who spoke out against Captain Crasav ton Lavaelle yesterday. Space Corporal Victoria Min received two puncture wounds to the chest and her extremities have suffered severe frostbite. She is alive, but in critical condition."

I frowned:

"Both attacks were committed against individuals who exhibited their loyalty to the Orange House and to me personally. And, as such, I consider this an attack on my very person. Forbid anyone from leaving *Algol Hulk*! Provide twenty-four-hour security to the injured Victoria Min! Popori de Cacha!"

The chameleon appeared a step from me.

"You heard everything Captain Oorast Pohl said. I need to visit the wounded victim."

"Not possible, my Prince. It is too reckless! Two attacks have been made on Orange House soldiers in a short period of time. The loyalty of the crew after the change of captain is under strong suspicion. Your enemies are probably expecting you to come to the cruiser. They didn't kill the girl after all. They could have."

Of course, I could have stuck to my guns, but I would have been seriously risking spoiling my relationship with my bodyguard. And the chameleon could have been totally right. Everything that happened looked too much like a defiant challenge. And doing that really could have provoked Prince Georg into coming onto the cruiser.

"So then..." I said, in serious thought. "It looks like you're right, Popori de Cacha. It looks too much like a trap. But I don't have the right not to react. So,

I need a map of *Algol Hulk*..."

The other ship's map didn't come up automatically. I had to ask the communications officer for it.

"So look," I said, blowing up the map on the big screen and pointing at the hospital blocks. "The wounded communications officer is here. Let's do this: I'll send my personal doctor and a few Orange House soldiers to the patient to protect her. Take note: there is just one hallway here, so we'll only have to have two guard posts, just for show. Then the doctor, in the presence of the other officers from the cruiser, will tell the captain that Victoria Min is in critical condition, but will be able to identify her attacker as soon as she wakes up from the sleeping pills we've given her."

I zoomed the map in and pointed at the screen:

"Look, there are ventilation shafts and service tunnels leading to the medical wards. I believe that my foes will attempt to make use of one of these paths to keep this dangerous witness quiet. They'll think that there won't be any guards in the sterile wards, because they're all in the hall. So they'll come for sure! How many invisible chameleons are we going to need to be able to guarantee the enemy is killed or, even better, in custody?"

Popori de Cacha trained both of his agile eyes on me and answered:

"We'll need only one, my Prince. And that invisible guard for the wounded girl will be me."

* * *

It was six P.M. I took a seat in my office in front of the screen and began reading incoming messages. The first staff officer to complete the assignment, no matter how strange it seemed, was Space Corporal Patrick toyl Sven. Yesterday he made an alright drinking buddy, despite the fact that he "went under" pretty fast, even though there was plenty to eat. Today he revealed his other talents:

The Tria is a large Alpha Iseyek landing craft. It is capable of transporting up to four hundred thousand landing soldiers in a state of deep hibernation. The ship is not armed and is quite vulnerable in space combat. It requires around three hours of preparation time before beginning a landing operation (perhaps to wake the soldiers up and explain their combat assignment). Presents a huge threat for planets with weak anti-space defense systems, in that an Iseyek landing party coming from a Tria is capable of capturing a landing zone in less than an hour, which will be able to support a full-fledged invasion.

The Uukresh is a new model of Swarm mother ship, corresponding to a carrier in Imperial classification. It is a huge spaceship, capable of transporting up to eighty frigates of various makes and models. It is distinguished by the massive capacity of its energy shields, which allow it to spend a long period of time under dense fire from an enemy fleet without taking substantial damage. Its only noted weaponry is anti-rocket systems.

Alright then, it's a mobile, well-defended base for eighty small ships. That's quite a valuable thing, even if it is in a "badly broken" state without any frigates inside. It occurs to me now that it probably costs a pretty penny to repair such a vehicle. But what to do with the *Tria*, I still had no idea. Four hundred thousand sleeping praying mantis landing soldiers. Do I even have enough space in my heart for that much joy?

The other officers' reports confirmed Patrick's, so my doubts subsided. I was getting one "aircraft carrier" and an ark with a landing party. By the way, not all the officers were able to finish the assignment. Four staff officers still had yet to fish an answer from the stream of information. I opened their personal records and skimmed through them. It's just as well. They're candidates for elimination anyway. In any employee base, there must always be some natural selection, just like in nature. The strong survive and the weak die out, otherwise you get stagnation, disease, and death.

That said, there was one girl in that group of four losers, and she was miraculously good looking! I spent a while staring at the picture in her personal record. I wonder how someone who looks so much like a model scraped her way into a job as a space fleet officer? It was a lot easier to imagine her in a totally different, much worldlier profession. She's beautiful, no question. I closed her personal record and let out a sigh of disappointment. Yep, the Crown Prince kept plenty of beautiful women around. But, Georg royl Inoky, you screwed me with your crystal habit...

New message. It was a bill from Himora management for repairing and charging the drives of all ships in the fleet. Almost three hundred thousand credits, but what could I do? It served as a reminder that it was high time for me to get my financial affairs in order. I opened my own information page and read through the items in the income and expense columns. The Prince's main income source was taxes from the population of the planet Tialla. It looked to be something like the personal demesne of a medieval noble. Tialla was giving me around seventy thousand credits every day. The second income source, comparable in size, I had cut off yesterday with my own two hands when I cursed out my wife. The planet Fastel-XI, right up to yesterday, had been sending fifty thousand credits a day to me through my spouse, their leader.

The expenses column was a bit more crowded. The main expense, as strange as it was, wasn't even fleet upkeep, but buying various luxury items for my personal yacht, *Queen of Sin*. The second biggest item on the list was a series of expensive gifts and huge money transfers to someone named Miya. Miya, Miya, Miya... Who could she have been if Prince Georg had spent more than a million credits on her in the last month alone? I remembered that Marta had mentioned that name in her wrathful speech...

Unfortunately, there was no popup message to answer this question, though it was very important to me. It turned out that there was someone named Miya, who was very close to the Prince and knew him very well. This mysterious female would be fully capable of recognizing that I was a stranger in the body of the man she knew so well.

Well, and finally fleet upkeep. I didn't understand

why Prince Georg had to carry the burden of funding a fleet on his own, but it looked like that was the case. The Prince's personal army and star fleet were a part of the Orange House forces. My other aristocratic relatives from the "orange" family also supported their own militaries, though I had no way of finding out what the exact sizes of these forces were.

The remaining expenses were mere trifles in comparison with the three I already mentioned. In addition to this, I had discovered a fairly large number of small, unpaid bills. It looked like the Prince paid no attention to these trifles. I paid them all at once to finally rid myself of burdens from the last player. I wasn't sure how, but it seemed like something that could bite me in the ass later. When all was said and done, it didn't amount to much. About half a million, a fact which left me breathing easier.

So, Georg had one hundred twenty million credits left in his account. After the split with Marta, the income had fallen to two million credits a month. After I put a stop to these payments to this unknown Miya and reduced purchases and luxury spending all the way to zero, I saw that my income was on the level of around half a million a month. I had a surplus! I breathed a sigh of relief.

PURGING THE RANKS

I WALKED into the medical department with my right arm hanging motionless in a sling tossed around my neck. The nurse on duty jumped out of her chair startled, either ready to give me CPR on the spot or faint herself. In any case, I reassured her:

"Don't worry, I just pulled a muscle in the gym."

"It was my fault, I wasn't paying enough attention," added my hulking fitness instructor, hovering timidly behind me.

"I already told you: you're not at fault here. I overestimated my own strength."

The nurse gave her huge eyelashes another series of quick flutters and explained that Dr. Nicosid Brandt was tied up with another patient right then, but she would be calling another doctor for the Prince right away. I was not able to solve the ethical problem of how proper it was to pull a doctor away from a patient to get my own precious hide treated before the doors to one of the hospital rooms flung open and officers with Orange House star fleet patches began coming out into the main hall. I immediately recognized the graying Maur Cassei among them. He was leading the members of his crew, who were walking arm-in-arm. Upon seeing Prince Georg royl Inoky, the whole company stopped sharply. The elderly veteran pushed his crewmembers aside and took a step forward.

"My Prince, as you see... it would seem that I overestimated my own abilities. My heart seized up during a turn. I had to stop training immediately... It would seem that the time has finally come for me to give up my flight helmet to the Space Fleet Museum. Half a century ago, they were already asking for it as an exhibit... I wanted so badly to die in battle, not on a hospital bed like this... My Prince, I would like to apply for retirement."

"Nicosid Brandt, do you have any comments?" I demanded of the Doctor.

"A heart attack... Today the frigate pilots spent a whole six hours with just a few short breaks zipping around, being subjected to up to eight G's to practice some new approaches. There have been a lot of visits to the infirmary today in general, but this is the most serious case by far. I recommended that the pilot avoid heavy loads for the next two weeks. And, in the future, he shouldn't keep running himself ragged. He's not a kid anymore..."

"Got it. Maur Cassei, your application for retirement has been denied. Here is your fleet commander's order: *Pyro-1* will play first receiver for the next two weeks for any training exercises or military actions that we may take part in. Two weeks from now, you must undergo another medical examination and, if the doctor has nothing new to say, all restrictions will be removed, and you can go back to *Pyro-1* having whatever role your vast experience deems most fit. In order to avoid gossip and chit-chat, we will announce to the whole fleet that you pulled your arm during some sharp turns at high speed."

Standing change. Your relationship with Maur Cassei has improved.
Presumed personal opinion of you: +7 (warm)

Only my personal relationship changed that time, no factions involved, but I was still very satisfied with the result. The old man, despite his sharp tongue, was a distinguished veteran and enjoyed considerable authority among the pilots. His presence alone could be good for the fleet, even just sitting on a couch in the hall of a luxurious yacht. Meanwhile, Maur Cassei, clearly feeling timid, which was uncharacteristic for the fearless pilot, spoke up:

"My Prince, allow me to speak on a personal matter."

So he could surprise me after all. "A personal matter?" He can't have been thinking of marrying at his age, right? But it turned out to be something else entirely.

"My Prince, the Orange House Space Military Academy is holding its graduation in ten days. My great-grandson, Alessandro Cassei, will be among those graduating, top of his class, by the way. And I request that your Highness send a request for young frigate pilots to join our fleet. Of course, there are all kinds of job offers coming in to someone about to graduate, be they from influential aristocrats, corporations or any number of individual planets. But with your influence and abilities, my Prince, the Academy leadership will certainly not refuse a request for pilots."

Well, well, the old man is talking sense! I didn't have a very good idea of how these vacancy filling requests worked for regular staff, much less combat pilots, but it sounded very interesting. I promised Maur Cassei to submit the request and got another personal relationship change message:

Standing change. Your relationship with Maur Cassei has improved.

Presumed personal opinion of you: +22 (trusting)

It was really that easy to bring the veteran over to my side! Well then, I hope that with time the other officers will also reevaluate the skeptical attitude they've formed about Prince Georg. When the group of officers had left the infirmary, the doctor took a look at my arm. As he injected some painkillers and other medications, Nicosid Brandt wondered to me:

"My Prince, would you mind explaining why you did this? Why hurt your crystal-weakened body with heavy exercise? If you could just tell me as your personal doctor, it would make it a lot easier for me to understand and prepare for possible complications in advance."

"And? You just answered your own question. I have decided to totally stop using crystals, and now I'm trying to get a bit more in shape."

The doctor spent a long time looking at me in silence, then spoke out in reproach:

"My Prince, it seems you do not understand that there is no turning back. Crystals are not a normal drug. With normal drugs, the chemical traces can be removed from the body, and the psychological dependency fades with time. Crystals imprint themselves in your consciousness, your memory, your way of thinking. Mystics can't just decide one day to stop doing crystals if they want to keep living."

"No, doctor, you're the one who doesn't understand. I declare to you as a mystic that there is a way out, and I am preparing to take it. Are there any crystals on the yacht?"

"Yes, of course. Both you and Miya are in the Official Imperial Registry of Mystics, which is why I keep a few doses of crystals here especially for you two in a safe in the medical center."

"Destroy them immediately! That is an order! Popori de Cacha... Ah, shit! He's not in the building. Whoever is here in his place now, make sure it happens. And I repeat once again: any person who tries to offer me crystals is a sworn enemy, regardless of that person's status or position in society, and thus must be terminated without delay!"

The doctor, dumbfounded, opened the armored door with his keys and watched in silence as the chameleon fairly carelessly swept a pile of transparent boxes with some shiny balls inside from the safe and stuffed them into a dark plastic bag. Then my bodyguard opened a door, which turned out to lead to a garbage incinerator and tossed the bags of crystals down it.

"Done, my Prince," reported the chameleon before camouflaging himself again.

"Doctor, what is the status of the girl who was found wounded today on *Algol Hulk*?" I wondered aloud, just to change the topic.

The old doctor turned to me and said with sorrow:

"You haven't heard, my Prince? She died before I even got to the cruiser. She had severe puncture wounds, and her extremities were frozen solid. But I did everything the commander of your bodyguards asked of me. I laid her body out flat on the bed, put an oxygen mask on her face, and covered her torso with a blanket. Then it was declared in the cockpit that the wounded girl had seen a criminal and was prepared to identify them, but that she should not be disturbed before tomorrow morning due to her weak state... My Prince, just so you know, normally as a doctor I am a neutral party and must not interfere in conflicts or play into one side's hand, but I am also a living man and want to see those responsible for the death of this young girl punished."

"Thank you, Nicosid Brandt, and I will try to bring those responsible for her death to the appropriate punishment. As for my quitting crystals, you're one of the Universe's best-qualified doctors in rehabilitative medicine, and I'll more than likely need your help but, in essence, you understand my decision. I'm going cold turkey!"

"So, how's the game going?" The call came at night after I had just finished chasing away a restless,

incoherent dream.

"Georgiy!" I said, instantly recognizing his voice and filling with joy. "Where have you been? I've already worked two whole days in-game. When am I gonna be able to go back to real life?"

"Hold up, we signed a contract! It said in black and white that you'd be playing for me for half a year, and only after that can you go back home. Think of it as a business trip!"

"A half year with no breaks?!" I let out, afraid and shocked at the just-revealed prospect of spending six months trapped in a computer game. "I did not see that in the contract! Plus, I just can't do that. I have a job, friends, and a cat at home to feed."

"Come on, don't lie. You don't have a cat at home. The only thing you were keeping in that rented apartment was a bunch of empty beer bottles. How can you even drink that shlock?!"

"Why did you go into my apartment? And how did you find out where I live?"

Georgiy chuckled happily but, in that moment, his laughter brought me nothing but spite.

"You wouldn't believe it if I told you. And don't you worry about the apartment. Your landlord and I came to an agreement. I told him you were working a half-year internship in another country, and that one of my acquaintances would be living in your apartment for a time."

"Miya?" I blurted out under the spell of a surprising insight.

Mr. G.I. kept silent for some time, but ended up confirming my suspicion.

"I don't know how you guessed, but you're right.

Yes, it's Miya. Don't try looking for information about her in the game. It won't do any good. I was careful to delete all records of her. Her account has been suspended for six months, and she has disappeared from the game world. You could even say that she was banned by the game administrators. So, it looks like you'll need to look for another Truth Seeker to take her place. Because Miya is mine and mine alone!"

Beep-beep-beep-beep!

The incoming call signal woke me up in the deep of the night, interrupting an important conversation. Or maybe I was asleep the whole time and the conversation with Mr. G.I. was just a dream?

After a moment of looking around for the beeping device, I jerked it up to my ear and accepted the call.

"My Prince, the criminal has been neutralized. You were right. He came in through the ventilation shaft."

"Please tell me he's alive! I need to speak with this beast!"

"Yes, my Prince. He's alive. All I've done is bound and gagged him. I am preparing him for interrogation now. Then he will be brought to *Queen of Sin* under the protection of your soldiers."

"Just don't overdo it with the preparation! Peoples' arms aren't directly connected with their ability to speak either, but he won't talk for long without them."

"I understand, my Prince," said the chameleon, signing off.

I suddenly lost the desire to sleep entirely. I called for the night nurse and asked for a pick-me-up. I was brought a high-walled wine glass with a dark, bubbly liquid. So sour! But it really did clear my mind and restore my energy. While the chameleon dealt with the captive, I took a seat at the screen and set about experimenting with game options I had yet to try.

A bunch of minor organizational issues had piled up, and I didn't really understand how to take care of them. For example, I needed to tell my daughter's teachers that Lika was fine but wouldn't be coming back until after break. On a purely technical level, how could I do that? Or did I need to warn the leader of the Tesse star system, my brother Roben royl Inoky ton Mesfelle, according to the storyline, that I was going to be coming to visit soon with my whole fleet? How could I even? It couldn't be that I needed the fleet communications officer to do that, could it? There was no easier way? Not everyone in the game had officers at their beck and call, but somehow they all got along. I poked my nose into all kinds of information panels and couldn't find my own brother's contact information anywhere, so I decided I would need a personal assistant as soon as possible.

I first thought that my old servant, Bryle, could handle this work, but then realized I was wrong. Bryle was more of a household butler. He could make sure the cooks, cleaners, and other servants were doing their jobs, but his age was advanced. What I needed was a vivacious personal assistant who could organize meetings, make a daily schedule and carry out any other orders I might give. It can't be that in such a well-developed game there was no button for hiring a personal assistant, right? I refuse to accept that!

I took a seat at the information panel and found what I was looking for before long. It was set up in-game as a staff recruitment website. You could set criteria, and the system would search for the right employee (or maybe it just made them up, who knows?). So then, I need a personal assistant. Requirements? Education? Age? I think I'd prefer someone who at least looks like a person (though the list of species available was substantial), with experience in the field and a college education. They should also know at least three nonhuman languages and be no older than thirty-five. Even if I applied the "authorized to work with members of upper aristocratic families" filter, the list of job-seekers that came up took up no less than one hundred pages.

I needed to thin the herd somehow. What else could I even ask for? Alright, let's find an assistant that does sports as a hobby (another list popped up, and I ticked, practically at random, "mountain climbing," "diving," and "single combat"). The list of potential applicants shortened up noticeably. I tried just putting in some extreme requirements for experiment's sake, like "no less than twelve children," or "truth seeker," but in both cases the resulting list was empty. I pondered for a second. Did that mean that the system wasn't generating new characters? Were they really choosing from available NPC's in the game? Or had I just entered some contradictory requirements? So I kept experimenting with the settings, you could even say I was just messing around, but it ended in me finding (or creating) HER.

The girl of my dreams. First, she had snow-white hair (plus it was natural, as I had clearly asked for in my search requirements) and an exceptionally well-developed intellect (I moved that slider to max). She was also an expert shot with a laser sporting pistol and a queen of the mountaintops. She had a degree in law and knew the languages of the Iseyeks, the Ravaash and some other brutes I'd never heard of. She was twenty-seven, honest to a fault and had work experience and excellent recommendations. Beyond all that, she had a surprisingly beautiful figure and the face of a model. A dream come true!

The fact that someone with all these talents was for some reason not authorized to work with upper aristocracy was of course surprising, but did nothing to stop me. Another thing was that her salary requirement wasn't as inflated as that of other beautiful girls with significantly more modest features. It wasn't that a high price would have stopped me. With the Prince's resources at my disposal, I'd have been able to buy Miss Universe, but her yearly salary was still surprisingly low. Just six thousand credits for someone with such an advanced degree. My new assistant was called Bionica Klein, and she could start in four days. What the hell, let's do it!

"He has been prepared for interrogation and presents no risk," said Popori de Cacha, stepping to the side.

A beat-up, dark-haired man of about forty with a huge bruise on his cheek bone was sitting on a chair. His arms were tied behind his back, and his legs were tied to the metal legs of the chair. The patches on his jumper told me that he was the senior electrical technician from *Algol Hulk*.

"Tell me your story," I proposed to the criminal. "I'll

decide the severity of your punishment relative to the truthfulness of your words."

And with that the technician opened up. It looked like he'd gotten caught up with some Green House spies three years earlier, and since then he'd been given the assignment to keep an eye on Orange House ship movements. He'd left spy bugs at stations and on ships, and informed on the location of Orange House aristocrats and their contacts. Around half a year earlier, he had been promoted, which brought him to *Algol Hulk*, where he continued working for the Green House. Almost the second he arrived, the captain called him and said that he was aware of his activities. Captain Crasav ton Lavaelle was himself the coordinator of the Green House spy network, and many of the crewmembers from that cruiser had either been blackmailed into spying or were even career spies working undercover for the Green House. On top of that, there were more spies on the other ships.

"Tell me their names!" I demanded, and the technician told me eleven last names. I couldn't believe it. The second assistant to the captain and the chief communications officer from *Algol Hulk*, the captain of *Pyro-8*, the first assistant to the captain of *Pyro-14*, and a few security officers and technicians from the crew of *Queen of Sin*...

"Arrest everyone on this list without exception!" I ordered the commander of the yacht's "golden" guard.

The gloomy muscular goon in charge of the nearly one-hundred-strong detachment of elite warriors furrowed his brow in dissatisfaction:

"My Prince, the only evidence you have is one

technician's word. There are many respected officers on that list. I'm afraid a number of them will not like it. The blow back from this will be serious. It's entirely possible that the arrestee lied to save himself. Would it not be better to check with a Truth Seeker? It would take Miya only an instant to check if all this finger-pointing has any truth to it and determine if these people are guilty."

At first, I couldn't believe my eyes and ears. The security commander of my personal yacht dared question my orders? But still, I didn't stomp my feet or demand submission. It couldn't be that the Prince and the head of security had that kind of relationship, right? Maybe the Prince really did follow his subject's sage advice? What was more, this Miya just kept coming up... You couldn't spit on this ship without hitting some trace of Georg royl Inoky ton Mesfelle's strange companion. I was learning bit by bit just how important her role had been in the Crown Prince's world.

"Miya will not be available for some time. She has gone on an important mission. So we'll have to get by without a Truth Seeker. And I may be no Miya, but I'm a mystic as well. There are some things I can do. Commence apprehending the suspects! Place each of them in a separate chamber, isolated from the others. I will be talking to each of the arrestees myself."

By morning the fleet was abuzz like a battered bee hive. The number of arrested was rising at a frightening pace. While interrogating every traitor, I found it helpful to tell them that the Truth Seeker was listening in on our conversation. Every time I did this, the arrestee immediately stopped being stubborn and gave up all their associates. I even began to fear that this process would never end and that I would have to place the whole fleet under arrest. But the total number of conspirators never rose higher than thirty-six. I was told all known names.

Two captains, four first assistants, many other officers... The list of traitors turned out to have been extensive. None of them were players, just NPC's, which wasn't very surprising. What real player would want to play such a vile and humiliating role for so many years? But even without living players, the problem looked very serious. What could we do with the traitors? Some of them were guiltier than others. Their levels of repentance and preparedness to aid the further investigation also varied. I wasn't ready for a trial yet, but I also couldn't draw the process out. I was informed that the crews of some of my ships were on the edge of revolt after the previous night's arrests and the subsequent lack of information that followed. I took another look at each detainee's record and discovered that they were all members of the Imperial Military Faction, so I decided on a change of plans.

"Oorast Pohl, gather the fleet officers in the large hall in one hour, and arrange for the meeting to be broadcast live to all ships! What's got these people upset is a lack of information, so we'll do this as out-in-the-open as possible."

An hour later, I went into the hall. The large size of the room notwithstanding, it wasn't able to fit everyone who wanted to attend. There were soldiers standing in the hallways and along the walls, as well as sitting on the stairs. When I arrived, silence took hold. All faces turned to me.

"Dear officers! I've gathered you all here today for an exceptionally important reason. I've known for quite some time that there were a number of Green House agents among the upper officers on *Algol Hulk*. I knew about it but didn't think it was very important. In any case, the Green House is part of the Empire, just like our Orange House, or any other Great House. Maybe we aren't all friends, but still we are not enemies. The situation changed drastically when our fleet encountered the aliens and joined the war. Many of you probably noticed that *Algol Hulk* refused to obey orders and fled the battle. Thereafter, upon fleet warp, *Algol Hulk* yet again ignored a direct order and arrived much later than the rest of our ships. It was the only reason the cruiser did not take part in the battle with the pirates, though we were counting on them. That was the last drop. The cup of my patience has spilled over and the captain of *Algol Hulk*, Crasav ton Lavaelle, has been removed from ship command and dishonorably discharged from our fleet's ranks due to cowardice and repeatedly disobeying orders from the fleet commander."

The hall began to come alive. It looked as if many of them really didn't know the story and naturally wanted to discuss it with their neighbors.

"Captain Crasav ton Lavaelle's dismissal had an unforeseen consequence. It revealed the long-festering ulcer of treason. The Green House spies, who had multiplied to unforeseen numbers in our fleet, have been deprived of their coordinator and have begun to act on fear and take risks, carrying out orders received earlier or acting in their understanding of their role. They've harmed us before in various ways, trying to lower the effectiveness of the fleet and, ideally, even destroy it. But now they've begun flat out killing Orange House soldiers and officers!"

The audience whirred in indignation. Many shouts could be heard calling for the traitors to be punished harshly. I raised my hand, calling for quiet.

"As you understand, the audacity of the Green House spies has crossed all conceivable boundaries. This is why the traitors have all been arrested and interrogated. This infection of treason was able to overrun the ships of our fleet. All told, thirty-six members of our crew were caught up in the enemy spy ring. So none of you worry that Orange House soldiers might be detaining innocent people; I'll be sure to let you hear the arrestees' confessions yourselves. And thus we come to the most important thing. Why I've brought you all here. As fleet commander and Crown Prince of the Empire, I possess the full legal authority needed to convict the traitors myself. However, I noted that all the accused are Imperial soldiers. I value soldiers as a class very highly, and I admit that there may exist particular aspects of the military justice system that I may not be aware of. For this reason, in order to avoid making any mistakes, I consider it fair that all of you gathered here today judge the traitors in full accordance with the law as Imperial soldiers."

Standing change. Empire Military faction opinion of you has improved.

Present Empire Military faction opinion of you: 0 (indifferent)

Great news! I got some responsibility off my shoulders and let the Military know that I respect their traditions. I was finally able to crawl out of negative standing.

Kiro Sabuto took the floor and let out an incomprehensible phrase:

"34-11, what do you think here?"

"I do not agree, admiral. 37-12A! This aspect also should be considered," objected Captain Oorast Pohl.

"With all due respect to you, no!" came a destroyer captain, standing up from his seat. "The murder in no way took place during combat, which is why I think a totally different article of the Star Fleet Charter applies here..."

"Wait up, guys," interjected another captain, having decided to express his point of view. "After the last battle, our commander did not give our fleet leave and did not allow the crews to exit their ships to Himora. So, as before, article 34-11 is still in effect here, but subparagraph C!"

It seemed that the trial would be more drawn out than I expected, so I asked them to provide me the final decision of the military court in no less than fifteen hours. I then headed to my bedroom to sleep off the endless, crazy night.

I was awoken by the beep of an incoming message from the communications officer. My officers were generally not supposed to disturb me while sleeping unless it was for events that really were very important. If I had been woken up, it must have meant that something extraordinary had happened. I read through the short message, not coming to its meaning right away:

The Head of the Blue House, Duke Malvik royl Stefan ton Miro, has resigned.

So, why did they wake me up? What does this have to do with me? I'm not from the Blue House! But just then, Lika ran into the room, her hair wet after swimming in the pool. Without a pause, she jumped up onto my bed and shouted excitedly,

"Dad, have you heard? That two-hundred-year-old fart finally admitted that it's time to give someone else a turn on the Blue House throne! For my whole life, all I can remember Duke Malvik doing is getting sick, getting better, then getting sick again."

In my two days in the game, I had managed to more or less familiarize myself with the most notable members of Imperial aristocracy, so I was able to confirm confidently:

"Likanna, I am older than you, and my memories of the Duke are no more varied."

We both let out a chuckle, then Lika uttered a phrase that I didn't know how to react to:

"Admit it, Dad. You made this happen, didn't you? Remember how you told me that with the help of a very strong Truth Seeker, it would be possible to make this happen, and many times you declared that Miya was one of the strongest Truth Seekers in the Universe. Plus, I heard that you sent your girlfriend out on an important mission. So it all came together!"

I answered in the negative, which left her clearly

upset. Lika got sad, hugged me around the knees and thoughtfully remarked:

"These decrepit old aristocrats do like to take their time to make way for the next generation. This is the first time in my memory that the line of succession has moved from a dead stop. Ughh, too bad it wasn't someone from the Orange House who resigned..."

As Lika kept silent in thought, I quickly called up a hint and looked over the rules about the lines of succession to the Great Houses. I had already called that information up before, but it was on my first day in the game, and I barely remembered because I had more important things to deal with at the time. All I figured then was that the Imperial throne presented no threat to me, given that my position in the line of succession to the Imperial Throne was somewhere in the high fifties, and the first hundred in the "living line" hadn't moved for twenty years at least. I had to disenchant my daughter of her dream:

"Lika, just think about it, though Duke Malvik has lived two hundred and eight years, he has only moved up to third in line to the Emperor's throne. So, Lika, there's no way the throne will shine its light on us for at least another two hundred years..."

"*You're* not moving beyond number forty-eight, no, but I've got somewhere to go still from one hundred eleven... You're right though, you know. There's really no difference... But it is totally possible for me to become Queen of Fastel in like a hundred years and, as for you, there's not just the *Imperial* crown to think about, there's the Orange House crown too. Your brother and sister are just a tiny little bit older than you. It must hurt, doesn't it?"

I smiled and let out a sigh.

"Lika, it hurt when I was still a little kid, but I got used to it. Roben is four years older than me, and my twin sister, Violetta, was smart enough to be born first. But they're before me in the line of succession, so there's nothing to be done... Alright, seeing how you finally woke me up, let's have breakfast."

While Bryle set the table, I got myself in order and inquired with the admiral if the soldiers had been able to reach a verdict.

"All thirty-six of the Green House spies have been sentenced to death!" announced Admiral Kiro Sabuto. "The sentences will be carried out today at seven P.M., at the moment our fleet starts off for the Tesse system."

Seems harsh, but... I thought I might limit the punishment to some of the crustiest old saboteurs. The ones who had brought the most harm to the Orange House. But executing them all en masse? The admiral then continued:

"In accordance with ancient norms, your Highness, as representative of the Imperial family, has the right to exercise his will and pardon one of those sentenced."

"Dad, can I pardon someone and exercise my will too?" begged Lika from behind me. "I'm a representative of the Imperial family too."

"You can," I said, bringing the list of criminals and their personal records up on the screen on the wall.

"Let that one go," Lika blurted out before she'd even had time to look at all the pictures. "He's got a cute face."

I weighed the difficult choice for a long time. There

were thirty five NPC's whose further existence in the game now exclusively depended on my whims! And I could only pardon one of them according to the law. If they were real people, I probably wouldn't have been able to make this choice. But there I sat at the dining-room table continuing to look over personal records, even though Lika had given me a suggestion. Finally, the hard choice was made. It would be the senior gunner from *Algol Hulk*. He was a jolly fellow. All the women loved him. At his young age, he was already a father of five from three different women, and they were all counting on him for support. He was forced to accept an offer from a Green House spy one month ago because he needed a little extra money to feed his kids.

I told the admiral my decision and my daughter's. Kiro Sabuto also reminded me that there were almost four hundred pirates from the *Payoff* awaiting their fates. He recommended also allowing their cases to be heard by the military court, but I refused.

"The *Payoff*, from the Brotherhood of the Stars, gave up practically without resistance. For this reason, I intend to release the rank-and-file right here at Himora. The station owners have been complaining of a severe labor shortage. They have several station development projects currently on hold due to a lack of manpower. Let it be a condition of their release that they sign a five-year contract with Himora. And then, who knows, maybe some of the former pirates will decide to settle down here. But as for the captain and his assistants as well as the other senior officers, I intend to keep them locked up in my ship for now. Who knows? Perhaps I'll be able to find out the coordinates of their beacon."

I was already familiar with the story of the beacon in the Hnelle system. The Hnelle system, which had taken almost twenty years for our scouts to reach, turned out to be very convenient from a logistics standpoint. You could reach four star systems directly from its warp jump, which had previously been quite remote in the transportation network: Himora, Tesse, Forepost-11 and Tialla (the last one was my system, by the way). A warp beacon was built in the Hnelle system, which quickly spawned a space station and it snowballed from there. And when earth-type planets capable of supporting a full-fledged colony were discovered by scouts several years later and a bit deeper in space, the flow of shipping through Hnelle grew by hundreds of times, and with it the population of the station grew as well. And the station itself just kept growing. They set up shipyards for building ships of various classes, factories, laboratories, and space plantations. The inhabitants of the Hnelle system formed their own government independent of the Empire and called it the Brotherhood of the Stars. Then something happened that no one in the Empire expected. There was a military coup in Hnelle, and the new government turned the beacon off...

A situation arose in which a series of Orange House star systems became cut off from the unified transportation network. It soon became apparent that the Brotherhood of the Stars had not turned the outpost all the way off and was using the situation to their advantage to organize pirate raids on the neighboring Orange House systems. The Brotherhood of the Stars' ships would turn up unexpectedly in

Himora or Tialla, plunder and hijack passing peaceful ships or bombard the station, demanding a payoff. When an Orange House fleet would show up, the pirates would just warp immediately to the Hnelle beacon, which would light up for one second, then turn off to cover their tracks and avoid retribution. Sending a whole fleet of combat ships on the twenty-year flight to the Hnelle system and leaving our own defenses weakened for such a long period was, of course, something that no one wanted to do. The Empire had more important things to do than deal with the presumptuous pirates, so combat ships had to always stay in those areas for defense. Adding to that, combat ships weren't made for such long flights. Only scout ships were built for the purpose of being able to travel autonomously through space for many years or even decades.

And now, for the first time in many years, the Orange House had captured a Brotherhood of the Stars cruiser, and the captain and navigator were on board. It was a trophy that had value in itself. I was already informed that this century-and-a-half-old model of heavy cruiser had huge modernization potential. After being fully upgraded and refitted with weapons, it could become a true pearl of the fleet. But what made this cruiser especially valuable was that it was potentially able to jump to the Hnelle system, which was otherwise unreachable. And I was going to figure out exactly how it did that.

* * *

More than three hundred former *Payoff* crewmembers accepted amnesty in return for signing a five-year contract with Himora. I received full approval from the station leadership. Fresh blood and working hands were in high demand on the remote space station. Even the fact that it was a contingent made up of people who were recently working as pirates didn't seem to really bother the inhabitants. The locals were prepared to accept even more infamous villains, because they had experience in retraining new settlers and keeping them in line with harsh methods.

There were around twenty people left in the prison chambers of the former pirate cruiser. The captain, the officers and a few others who had chosen not to accept forced labor at Himora. The Orange House team guarding the *Payoff* guaranteed we could get the ship to Tesse, where we would be able to fill the crew out. At exactly seven P.M. general time, my fleet, composed of one heavy and two light cruisers, four destroyers and ten frigates, left through the warp tunnel to Tesse. As the ship was entering warp, I received the following game message:

Standing change. The Green House's opinion of you has worsened.

Present Green House faction opinion of you: -11 (mistrusting)

Standing change. The Green House's opinion of the Orange House has worsened.

Present Green House faction opinion of Orange House: -4 (indifferent)

Captain Oorast Pohl, who was standing not far from me, screwed up his face and commented on the worsening relationship between the Great Houses:

"We can't have captured all the Green House spies. The news about the agents' execution must have been sent immediately."

The captain, seeing the lack of understanding on my face, explained:

"The prisoners sentenced to death were on the *Payoff* in isolation chambers."

The warp drive turning on was always accompanied by a colossal blast of energy. Also, for a few microseconds the temperature would go up to five thousand degrees. A momentary, painless death.

BROTHER DEAR

I WAS FAIRLY well prepared for the meeting with Georg's brother. I had studied all the background information on Crown Prince Roben royl Inoky ton Mesfelle, and so I wasn't at even a slight risk of being uncovered. Other close relatives might get a bit suspicious, but not Roben. He lived the playboy lifestyle. For the past quarter century he had concerned himself exclusively with gladiator fights, blowing any and all remittances he got from our father as well as all the income from the rich planet Tesse-III on the best fighters in the whole galaxy. It was Roben who had been behind the Galaxy's largest money transfers in recent years, and his gladiator team, the "Tesse Assassins," had been the unchallenged Imperial champion for the last four years in a row. He played that kind of character. A deep-pocketed playboy. The player himself probably had a similar nature, as a more responsible person wouldn't be interested in acting that way.

Being the sovereign leader of the planet Tesse-III, with its six-million-strong population and developed industrial capacity, Roben was fabulously wealthy. Even he didn't know the exact size of his demesne, as he had fully entrusted all financial issues and the administration of the star system to authorized representatives. My older brother wanted nothing to do with politics. He would only show his face in the Throne World at obligatory events or at the finale of huge gladiator tournaments. The Tesse star fleet was an object of well-deserved pride for Roben and was made up of two battleships and more than forty cruisers of various types. Formally, the Tesse fleet was part of the Orange House forces but, in fact, after a conflict with the head of the Orange House, Duke Paolo royl Anjer ton Mesfelle, it had spent the last few years in Tesse, keeping guard.

Roben received me and Lika in his flying palace. It should be said that the photos I saw hadn't given me the full picture on my brother's dimensions. I wasn't thin myself, quite the opposite in fact. But, compared to my immeasurable older brother, I looked like a matchstick.

Roben royl Inoky ton Mesfelle, Crown Prince of the Empire, ruler of the planet Tesse-III
   Age: 52
   Race: Human
   Gender: Male
   Relation to you: Your brother
   Class: Aristocrat
   Achievements: None
   Fame: +5
   Reputation: - 4
   Presumed personal relationship: +55 (loyal)

"Georg!" exclaimed my brother, his layers of fat billowing in a way that not even loose clothing could cover up. He hurled his 450-pound bulk in my direction.

"Roben!" I responded, opening my arms for a hug and running out to meet him.

Bammm! Just as Newton's First Law would've predicted, I was sent flying a few yards back. I couldn't recover from the imbalance and ended up falling on my back.

"Look at you, brother dear! You're losing weight!" cracked my older brother in good spirits, grabbing my hand to help me up.

"Uncle Roben!" Lika yelped out joyfully, as she jumped up to hang off his shoulders.

"Lika! My dear niece! You've finally come to visit!" exclaimed Roben, as he picked her up. Compared to his huge figure, Likanna seemed like a little bug. "And, just like I promised last time, I built a castle especially for your arrival. It's just two hundred fifty miles from the capital. It has eight towers and about a hundred rooms. We filled it with all the toys we could find on Tesse. There's a quiet bay next to the castle, and it already has a mooring where your personal yacht is waiting for you. When you grow up, my niece, you'll be able to take boys you like out on the ocean."

The girl's joyful shout popped my ears.

"She just loves you," I told my brother, as he basked in satisfaction at the effect his gift had had on his little guest.

"All kids love me," chuckled the huge Roben, carefully putting the child back down as he pointed at a group of youngsters playing on the lawn. They were a group of normal, carefree boys and girls having fun: flying a kite, throwing a ball... Not all of them were playing though. For some reason, my eye was caught by an eight-year-old girl with dark blond hair in a short frock. There was something not right about her. I didn't figure out right away what it was exactly about *that* kid that made her stand out, but then I noticed. Most of the kids were running around the flower beds barefoot, but she was still wearing her boots. So what? She didn't take her shoes off, OK... But then I figured out what was really putting me on alert. The girl was just pretending to frolic in the grass chasing after butterflies. Her facial expression was staying inappropriately serious the whole time, as a matter of fact. Then the girl... no, no. Yep, she turned toward me. Really weird. I read the information about her character.

Millena Mayer
Age: 8
Race: Human
Gender: Female
Class: Mystic
Achievements: None
Fame: 0
Reputation: 0
Presumed personal opinion of you: Unknown

She was a mystic at such a young age??? I wondered if the Emperor had included this dark-blond girl in the list of people allowed to take narcotic crystals just for her abilities. We walked slowly along the little alley that wound fantastically among the bushes and bright blue flowers. Little herds of kids were running all around, and Lika joined them, but the strange girl was walking in parallel with our path, staying close by the whole time. The conversation wasn't about anything important, and at some point I inquired about the health of my brother's wife and young son just to be polite.

"Verena was preparing to meet you, but since this morning she hasn't been feeling too well..." started Roben, but I immediately guessed that he was lying due to his change in tone and carefully thought-out words.

He also figured out that I knew. My older brother took a deep sigh and admitted:

"Who am I trying to lie to here?! In fact, you know quite well what Verena thinks about your choice of women."

Somehow, I knew right away that my older brother was not talking about Princess Marta just then.

"It is because I know what your wife thinks that I did not bring Miya with me this time." I didn't know why she had such a strong dislike for Miya, but I wasn't going to upset a young, nursing mother.

"Well, you must agree that Miya was acting quite strangely that one time. Then the complications with her pregnancy coincided with that, as it were... It was just Verena spooking herself up."

"I'll repeat again. Miya isn't here, and she wouldn't make a move without my permission. And I have never harbored any ill will for you, much less for your wife or son. You can even call your own Truth Seeker and check my words," I said, before turning and pointing at the approaching girl who was clearly listening in on our conversation.

Apparently I had guessed correctly about this kid's abilities, as the sovereign of the planet stopped sharply and also turned to Millena Mayer. She was standing five steps from us waiting for my brother's word, but the Crown Prince was hesitating. I understood his doubts. Checking someone's words like that was considered grossly indecent.

"Don't worry, Roben. It's OK. She can check. I'd do anything to get rid of this unspoken suspicion that has been poisoning my life as well as that of your wife."

The fat man waved his hand, and the girl with a thin braid walked up closer. I had read about Truth Seekers when I was looking for information on the mysterious Miya. So, I stretched out my hand with my palm facing up and proclaimed clearly:

"Neither I nor my companion Miya are party to the complications that arose during the birth of my nephew."

She put her palm on top of mine, and it felt like being electrocuted. I felt the full spectrum of emotions from the little Truth Seeker, the strongest of which was fear.

"She's devastatingly afraid of me!" I remarked with a fair amount of surprise.

"She's never had the chance to check a mystic before. And your personal Truth Seeker has quite a singular reputation. That kind of thing can scare a kid. Well, Millena? What do you see?"

"This person's conscience is totally clear, my Lord. He is withholding nothing. Your brother is speaking the truth. He's never thought anything but nice thoughts towards you and your family. And he is not aware of anyone else, including the Truth Seeker by the name of Miya, having wanted to bring harm to your family either."

"I already knew that. I didn't have to check," said Roben, feeling somewhat embarrassed. "My apologies, brother dear, it was quite foolish of course."

Standing change. Roben royl Inoky's opinion of you has improved.
Presumed personal opinion of you: +70 (trusting)

I answered in kind so we could put that ugly episode behind us once and for all.

* * *

"Believe me, I understand your problems, Georg, but I can't give you any ships."

My brother and I were in a green pavilion on the edge of a precipice. The flying palace slowly drifted above a dark blue sea, taking us in the direction of my daughter's new castle. Next to us on the table was a whole load of platters filled with any and all kinds of food you could imagine. A barrel of ancient wine was towering over us from the center of the table. Apparently, Roben wasn't planning on going anywhere until the whole eight-gallon barrel was dry.

"W-why not?" I pleaded, my tongue letting me down slightly. Nevertheless, my conscious remained clear, and I didn't lose the thread of the conversation.

"Because I promised. To my Duke. He's your Duke as well, by the way. And I'm still paying more taxes to the Orange House treasury than anyone else. I also want to be sure that Tesse won't be left unguarded. Geeze, the cursing and foot stomping Paolo can do... Just to think, he even insulted me!"

"It cannot be!"

"It is, brother! Duke Paolo royl Anjer insulted me with the vilest of words. And then I made him a promise that the fleet of Tesse would be staying here. And I am a man of my word, so I cannot give you any ships from my fleet."

"And what about ships not from the Tesse fleet? The shipyards in this planet's orbital belt are so big that any size ship could fit. Is there anything in stock that was built recently?"

My brother waved it off:

"There are no production facilities here. We've got repair docks, transfer bases, and the biggest storage facilities in the whole of Sector Eight. This is where the main path from the center of the Empire to the Orange House is, after all. Huge transport starships unload on Tesse all the time. There are docks, but it's been a long time since anything bigger than a frigate's been built at them."

"In that case, I am prepared to purchase all the frigates you've got!" I declared.

The fat man clapped his palms together and, as if from underground, a small man in old-fashioned livery appeared next to the table.

"I need a list of every finished combat ship built at the shipyards."

Not even a minute later, a flat screen appeared,

hovering in midair right above the dining table. I studied the none-too-rich offerings. Eight *Pyros* and four of the more modern *Warhawk* frigates. The *Pyros* had a two-hundred-thousand-credit price tag, and the *Warhawks* were three hundred fifty thousand.

"I'll buy all these frigates!" I declared.

"My Prince, may I remind you that these *Warhawks* are already contracted to the Kingdom of Fastel?" asked Prince Roben's assistant.

"Screw it! We'll build more and pay whatever penalties needed for failure to meet delivery date. Georg needs them more."

I transferred the money as fast as I could and in contemplation I said:

"It's a bit better, but my forces are still pretty weak. Are you sure you can't give up one cruiser?"

The servant, having already turned off the screen before leaving, stopped and said with a bow:

"Your Highnesses, forgive me for interfering in your conversation, but three heavy assault cruisers are nearly finished being built at the military shipyards of the Second Citadel. Literally two days ago, they sent us an offer to sell because there had been a disagreement on price with the initial customer."

"Do you have more complete information? What kinds of cruisers?" I scrambled, given that the topic was very, very relevant.

I had already thought up a few tactics for fighting alien ships on my own, but to actually pull any of them off, my fleet would need heavy-class ships. If I couldn't get heavy cruisers, I could forget about battles and victories, and my mission in the game would end in failure.

Perimeter Defense Book One — hold on.

The servant opened the monitor back up and displayed a full report. Three *Katana* heavy assault cruisers. They were built after an order from an Orange House trading company without a down payment. The plan was to flip them. During construction, there were changes in the state of affairs on the heavy metals market, and the cost of building the ships went up, so the buyer changed his mind. They are more than 95% completed, and they could be finished twenty days after receipt of payment." They were cutting-edge cruisers: a powerful force in the right hands. However, the price tag stung a bit. The shipyards were offering either the individual cruisers for eighty million credits each or all three wholesale for two hundred ten million.

"What do you say?" wondered Roben, lazily slurping wine from his high-walled glass. I had no choice but to admit that I didn't have the funds.

"Stop crying poor, brother dear. You've got Tialla, which brings you almost no benefit. When was the last time you even visited that little planetoid? Five years ago? Or was it ten? Think for yourself: why do you need that settlement on the outskirts of the universe? You have no son to be your heir, and your daughter, the Crown Princess, is already provided for. Are you keeping it around for the pittance of an income it provides? How about I buy it off you for an OK price? The amount I'll pay you in one lump sum you wouldn't even get from Tialla in ten years! I have a son, and he'll need a holding to keep his title."

It was a tempting offer, but I still refused. Roben started proposing other ways of getting the money:

"Your yacht is full of chachkes, and you've still got

the right of inheritance to think about. There are many who would pay you to give up your right to the throne, both of the Orange House and the Empire. So, think about it, brother dear. After that trouble you stirred up with the Green House, don't even hope they'll forgive you. I'm sure they've gathered all the muck there is on you and will be taking it to the Throne World soon. I'd put up my best gladiator against a red flier that any day now you should expect to get your ass chewed out by the Emperor."

My older brother's ideas were very convincing. His words were also adding to a strange but strong sense that hadn't left me since my first day in the game: I needed to beef up my fleet post haste! The only question was whose money to do it on. Where could I get the money? I wasn't going to give up my right to power, I had no idea what *Queen of Sin* was even approximately worth and also I still needed it. I wondered aloud about the price of Tialla.

"Two hundred fifty million," offered Roben. His eyes and voice offered no hint that he had been drinking. "It's a bit more than its real value, so don't pass on it. It's a pretty good deal."

"Two hundred fifty million, and you'll repair and modernize all of my ships in your shipyards for free, including the three *Katanas* I'm planning to pay for now, and the ships of my fleet that have yet to come to Tesse. It's just that, tomorrow, the rest of the fleet is supposed to come, and the *Uukresh* has a broken propulsion drive, so it'll need seven days to be dragged here by tug."

"Alright, but I'll only repair and upgrade all your ships one time, not whenever you need it," clarified

Roben, and I agreed.

"Let's shake on it!" agreed my brother, and just a half hour later we had washed up and officially signed the contract.

By evening, Roben, having drunk a fair bit, unexpectedly admitted:

"You know, little brother, about Tialla... I didn't tell you, but very soon, in a few months at most, they're going to put up a new warp beacon in the Parn system. Scout ships have already brought all necessary equipment there. Basically, all that's left is assembly. In two months, a short path between Sector Eight and Sector Seven will finally be open, connecting two huge regions directly without having to go through the Empire. Just imagine, little brother, what kind of ship traffic is going to be going through there. Every station on its path will be showered with gold! So then, the short way will go through Forepost-31, the Closed Laboratories, Tialla and Unguay. But I didn't trick you at all. I bought Tialla from you for what was a fair price at the time. But, in a few years, it will be three times more expensive at least."

I just smiled and kept quiet, thinking to myself, "Well, brother dear, I didn't tell you everything either. You're in for quite the surprise when the *Uukresh* comes in for repair."

* * *

"Well, hi! For some reason you hung up abruptly last time..." came Mr. G.I.'s familiar voice from inside my dream. I'd just barely had enough time to crash down into bed and fall asleep after spending the whole day

at the banquet with Roben.

"There was a reason. I'll have you know that there were three dozen Green House spies in your fleet!"

"Oh, yeah, I'm sure..." Georgiy said, dismissing it with a wave of his hand. "Crasav ton Lavaelle was working at such a flurried pace to get his agents in among my officers that it would've been hard not to notice. But until recently they've been behaving themselves, so there was no particular reason to upset that hornet's nest."

"I have dismissed Crasav ton Lavaelle for cowardice and disobeying orders. He was discharged at Himora. And right after that was when the attacks on people loyal to me began. Two have been killed so far. I had to act harshly. Thirty-six Green House agents were exposed and brought to trial. The military court quickly sentenced them all to death."

"What a mess..." gasped Georgiy, obviously shocked at the news. "You should be expecting some nastiness from the Green House now. At least you figured out that you had to let the grandson of Count Amelius royl Mast ton Lavaelle go. The Count is the second most important member of the Green House after all, so executing Crasav ton Lavaelle would be equivalent to a declaration of war on the Green House... But maybe it's for the best that you purged the fleet's ranks of traitors. What else is new?"

"I met Roben. We spent the whole day drinking together. By the way, what's the story there with the pregnancy complications? They tried to really bring the hammer down!"

"Oh, that... Pay it no mind. It just turned out that way. They thought Miya wanted to kill Roben's heir."

"Did she really though, or not? It's just important for me to know, so I can understand how I should act with Roben's family," I clarified, framing my question. Mr. G.I. gave an unexpectedly honest answer.

"Miya was acting on my orders. She was just able to stop in time and cover her tracks before they unexpectedly started suspecting us. You see... the temptation was too strong. Roben has a huge fortune and didn't have children. If anything were to have happened to him, the treasures of Tesse would have been split up among his closest relatives, his brother and sister. No, don't think anything untoward. I never arranged for an attempt on my own brother. And, in essence, that wasn't necessary. Roben drinks and eats a great deal, which is ruining his health right before our eyes. I know from reliable sources that Roben's personal doctors are sounding the alarm and begging the Crown Prince to give some thought to his health. They say that, if he doesn't do something soon, he'll suffer unavoidable, terrible consequences, like a stroke ten years down the line. I was prepared to wait. But suddenly Roben married someone from a vassal family, a lower noblewoman, and she conceived him an heir. The first pregnancy had a bunch of complications. On several occasions, the doctors said it was a miracle they saved the fetus. All an experienced mystic would need to do is give a little nudge in the right direction and the unexpected obstacle standing between myself and the treasures of Tesse would have once again ceased to exist... Would you not have tried?"

"I don't know. But I can tell you something good: their suspicions have been completely allayed. His Truth Seeker confirmed our shared innocence."

"Roben got a Truth Seeker? And he sicked her on you? Now that's something!"

"It was my idea. I was having a hard time getting through to him. Your brother had suspicion in his mind in regards to you and Miya. I needed to prove your innocence."

"Yes, that was a good idea. It looks like we've found a way to worm our way out of any meeting with a Truth Seeker, even the Dark Mother herself. Interesting perspectives are coming to light..."

"Don't even think about it!" I cut in, putting my foot down to keep from having to continue covering for the Prince's sins.

Then I told him about selling Tialla, expecting a strongly negative reaction. But Mr. G.I. considered the decision justified, if for a different reason than me:

"My brother is right. You'll be called to the Throne World soon to give a report. I myself already knew that quite well, which is why I thought to get someone else to play for me. But I was hoping you'd have enough time to distinguish yourself. Now though, to be honest, I don't even know what to expect from that meeting. There isn't much in the way of positive results, and these ill-wishers are always digging into the negative. And if the Emperor isn't very impressed with your and my actions, he very well could decide to impose a punishment. Having your holdings revoked is one form of punishment that can be imposed on an aristocrat. So now it's good that we don't have that hanging over our heads."

* * *

"Have you totally lost your mind, little brother? Bringing a whole insect fleet to my system! And a big landing ship to boot!" roared an annoyed Roben through my headphones, forcing me to wince from a headache flare-up.

"Roben, calm down. I warned you yesterday that I had more ships coming. What's more, you even signed a written contract promising to pay for their repair and modernization."

"Yes, I remember. But you just left out the little fact of who would be inside them! I don't even know if our docks will be able to repair them."

"They can, I looked into it. Many of their ship systems are compatible with human ones and can be swapped out and modernized as well. So, I'm counting on a repair and an upgrade."

"Little brother, I always do what I promise and pay my debts. It's no problem, let them come to the orbital docks and swap out whatever they want. But I swear to you: if any of these ships tries getting any closer to Tesse-III than that, it will be destroyed," proclaimed my older brother, hanging up.

I cackled to myself mischievously. The Crown Prince and sovereign of Tesse would not have been so annoyed if his fleet hadn't unabashedly slept through the "invasion." I bet my brother's commanders are going to get quite the thrashing! Just to think, it took the first Tesse fleet scout frigates twenty minutes to reach the Swarm ships. In twenty minutes, three dozen Iseyek ships could have had their run of this foreign system! An attacker would have been able to destroy the warp beacon with time to spare, for example, or make mincemeat of all the docks and storage facilities. Of course, this time the Iseyeks were coming in peace and not showing even the slightest sign of aggression, but the fact remains...

For me personally, the wake-up today was also unforgettable. The combat alert siren put *Queen of Sin's* whole crew on its feet, and the situation on the other ships was the same. I ran into the headquarters, buttoning my uniform up mid-stride. I took my seat at the combat console, arriving even before some of the officers. And by the way, the mood in the headquarters was near panic. The monitors convulsed on, someone caught the cable with their foot, tipping over the device-laden desk. The second tactician screamed in hysteria as he added enemy markers to the tactical map:

"Distance to target: nineteen thousand miles. It's a group of ships! Eight cruisers, four of them heavy! Up to twenty support ships showing! One target is very large, tentatively a landing ship..."

It was the words "landing ship" that finally brought me to my senses and got my brain working.

"Turn off the alarms! Those are our ships! Get me Admiral Kheraisss Vej on the line!"

One minute later, the enormous Alpha Iseyek greeted me with a slight bow from the big screen:

"My Princcce, I to carry out you order and bring two fleet to Tesse system."

"Excellent, admiral. Stay at the pre-warp point for now, do not approach the beacon. First I need to give your ships the codes to the Friend or Foe ID System and add your ships to the Imperial Fleet Database so the automatic defense systems on Tesse identify you correctly."

An hour later, the admiral's shuttle docked on *Queen of Sin* and a pair of praying mantises climbed out of the lowered hatch. The admiral was accompanied by Triasss Zess, and I immediately recognized my old acquaintance by his missing limbs.

Triasss Zess, Ambassador of the Iseyek State to the Empire
Fame: +3
Standing: + 5
Presumed personal opinion of you: +30 (trusting)

"Would you look at that. The crippled praying mantis is making a career for himself after all! As far as I remember, he was just an ambassador's assistant a few days before, and his fame and standing were somewhat more modest. By the way, Triasss Zess's coloring had changed as well. His chitin armor had become brighter. I didn't understand the pants-color-based differentiation system, but obviously these changes had some significance in the life of the intelligent insect.

"My Prince, I have carried out your orders," explained the diplomat. "General Savasss Yakh is on the *Tria*-class ship with us. And though he is a Gamma Iseyek with genetically unfixed mutational signs of brilliance, it was he that the Swarm considered the most appropriate candidate to command the assault and landing divisions. He has a great deal of experience from the war with the subterranean Arite race, the storming of several planetoids and space stations from different races, and he well and truly has a wealth of knowledge in strategy and tactics for terrestrial operations. Without any exaggeration, I can say that Savasss Yakh is a brilliant commander. He has the kind of greatness that only hatches from a Swarm clutch every hundred years. There are four hundred thousand soldiers on the ship with him and, my Prince, in the appendages of such a great strategist, that is a terrifying force. Beyond that, I have been authorized by the Swarm to tell you, Prince Georg royl Inoky, that if you should ever lack soldiers to carry out any mission whatsoever, the Swarm shall provide you with boots on the ground up to five billion strong."

I needed a few seconds to digest what I'd just heard. I couldn't wrap my head around the number, so I asked the ambassador to repeat what he'd just said. Triasss Zess obediently repeated, adding:

"We are very low on resources; everything is dedicated to building the transport ships. Due to the lack of food supplies, we will have to put whole villages in hibernation if they aren't directly taking part in the construction of the starships. The ground combat forces have actually been put into a state of suspended animation. The Swarm wanted me to tell you that you can have up to five billion soldiers and technicians as soon as you like."

Five billion praying mantis assault troops! My imagination just froze up, refusing to think up any combat operation that could possibly require that many soldiers. And where would I get the funds to transport five billion creatures? That's the population of a whole planet!

* * *

The huge Tesse Orbital Repair Complex was abuzz with work. Crane operators were grabbing the Iseyek cruisers with their magnetic claws, turning the hulking bodies of the huge starships in their several-yard-long mobile arms and putting them in place at the repair docks. The repair complex was reminiscent of a gigantic bunch of grapes with different-sized fruits, from the modest frigates to the huge heavy cruisers. Through the semi-circular observation porthole in the manager's office, I watched the docking procedure in the company of the two admirals and the leading technical expert of the station.

"Replace and modify all computer equipment on the ships," said the expert, noting the client's wishes on his tablet. "Install Empire-standard communication systems and signal coders on the Iseyek ships. Apply anti-radar coating to all frigates, modernize propulsion systems and energy shields on all ships. Anything else?"

"Yes, modify the *Warhawks'* artillery modules, replace the combat drones on all *Legashes* with Imperial models and, well, frankly a lot of other things," I added, sending my list to the technician's computer.

He began skimming through the file rather quickly, but suddenly got tripped up on a line:

"Prince Georg, is this right? You would like to remove the warp disruptors and energy shield recharge generators from the heavy ships?"

"That's right. I need ships with that exact setup."

I'd already grown tired of arguing about this. I'd already proven my idea, first to Admiral Kiro Sabuto, then to Admiral Kheraisss Vej and the cruiser captains. The military men's inertia was simply impenetrable. "Every combat ship must have a warp disruptor to keep the enemy on the battle field," "a ship will not survive a battle if it cannot recharge its own energy shield," and other such fossilized dogma. And even if I was more or less able to explain why heavy class ships don't need warp disruptors – keeping enemy ships immobile is a job for the frigates and small ships after all, then the shield recharging was much more of a sticking point. The idea of recharging the shield, not of one's own cruiser, but of an allied ship was met with hostility. The fear of being on a ship under fire and being helpless, without being able to "heal" your energy shield proved so strong that I had to even pressure my subjects and lean on my authority as Crown Prince of the Empire to push the difficult decision through.

The idea of "spider tanking," when players heal other group members instead of just themselves, has been firmly established in online games for some time. As a rule, one player cannot heal all the damage done to them and, if they try to heal only themselves, they will inevitably bring about their own death. But if everyone in a group or fleet immediately heals the ship that was attacked, its chance of survival rises sharply. As weird as it was, the Iseyeks accepted the idea more readily than the humans. It seemed that the idea of collective action was closer to the intelligent insects than it was to the individualist humans.

"The repair and modifications to the ships comes to forty-two million credits," explained the expert, sending me an itemized list of all planned work. "The ships presently at dock will be finished within six days, and the three *Katanas* will be ready one week from the day they arrive here in Tesse."

I signed the sheet and sent it on to Roben. An alert chime rang out, telling me that my older brother had paid the bill. Great, in six days I'll finally have the basis for what will become a menacing fleet!

"Now, let's fly to the *Tria*. I want to finally meet the great strategist and see the Alpha Iseyek warrior host with my own eyes."

"My Princcce, me probably to with you?" wondered Admiral Kheraisss Vej with a light half-bow. "No one on *Tria* speak people."

Yes, the language problem was really quite poignant. None of my people could understand the insects' language, and only two of the Iseyeks could understand human speech. But Triasss Zess has already left for home with the tug and three support ships to ferry the *Uukresh*. And using Admiral Kheraisss Vej as nothing more than a translator didn't feel quite right. Ugh, when would my translator-slash-assistant finally arrive...?

I was in no rush to answer the admiral. An emergency call came in from the headquarters of *Queen of Sin*. It was code red – something very important must have happened.

"Your Highness," explained the communications officer, his voice wavering in worry. "A request from the Emperor's Communications Service has come in. Crown Prince Georg royl Inoky ton Mesfelle, you are to report to the Throne World at once."

The officer didn't even have time to hang up before a call came in from Roben.

"I already know. Anyway, the Green House did it. Hold tight for now, brother dear!"

THE PATH TO THE EMPIRE

T
HE FACT THAT I had been called to make a report before the Emperor, much less "at once," required me to abandon all my affairs and fly as hurriedly as possible to the Throne World. I even suspected that special employees of various services would evaluate the minute-by-minute timeline: how fast did I get ready and under way? How fast did I fly? Did I forget to announce any unjustified delays under way, thus showing disrespect to the Emperor?

"Oorast Pohl, arrange for the fastest possible route to the Throne World, we will go at maximum speed."

"Yes, my Prince," he said. *Queen of Sin* was just then undocking from the station and accelerating to the next warp beacon.

I set off for my office. For whatever reason, even though there were many different kinds of cabins for work and relaxation on the luxury yacht, I preferred the very office where I had once dined with my daughter for the first time. It was the place where I could do my best thinking. The furnishings didn't annoy me with excessive luxury and did not distract me from my work. I left Likanna on Tesse, which didn't worry me at all. It would take more than a week for my daughter to play herself out in her own real castle, where she had all imaginable kinds of entertainment at her service, and Uncle Roben could provide for her safety in his own star system.

On my way into the office, I was unexpectedly stopped by Popori de Cacha coming out of invisibility.

"My Prince, your secretary has arrived on the yacht and is awaiting you in your office. But my subordinates need some more time to make sure it's safe."

The image of the chameleons preparing Triasss Zess for interrogation flashed before my eyes involuntarily. I even shivered, though I understood that my bodyguards did not suffer from excessive bloodthirstiness and would not be crippling her without reason.

"My Prince, you may enter," announced Popori de Cacha one minute later, before disappearing again.

I took a step into the open door and sharply stopped. There was no doubt about it, what I saw shocked me to the core. There was a big box right next to the door with its top taken off, lying right next to it on the floor. Inside the box, covered with packing peanuts, lay a totally naked girl. She had had to press her knees to her stomach and tuck in her head to fit in such an uncomfortable package. Next to the box on the floor lay a few sets of clothes, carefully folded into plastic packets and two pairs of shoes, one of them sneakers and the other high heels. The girl was conscious, and her bright blue eyes were darting around, following what was happening in the room, though she did not try to budge or climb out of the package.

A chameleon appeared from nowhere and handed me a packet of papers and bent down over the box. He unceremoniously turned the girl's head a bit to the side, brushing a lock of yellow hair from her temple before entering some information into his electronic bracelet, constantly checking it against the single visible digit or letter. With difficulty, I tore myself from contemplating the box with living contents and took a look at the brochure I had been given.

"Android Servant. Model № 034-6781. User's Manual," I read at the top of the first page.

So that was it... That was why the expected salary was so modest! It seems I had ordered not a living assistant, but a robot servant... I walked around the box and noticed a label on one side, "Bionica Klein, android. Immediate delivery. Bill of lading: 71566-AAB Tesse."

"Have you finished checking?" I wondered to the chameleons.

"We're almost finished, my Prince," declared Popori de Cacha. "In essence, everything's in order, the base command unit is sealed, all restrictions are in place. No foreign objects have been detected in the box or the android's body cavities. But two irregularities are bothering me. First of all, the date on the security seal on her processor unit does not match up with her release date. That means this model has been sent out for repairs and some adjustments have been made to the operating system. Second, this model's firmware is very out of date. It's been more than twenty-five years since a new patch or update was installed. I must find an explanation for these irregularities before I can make a conclusion on whether this secretary can be used safely."

"Maybe we could just ask her... or it, or how should I call it?" I wondered, going far off track as I didn't know how to properly identify the gender of a robot in conversation.

"Perhaps, but we cannot consider the android's answers fully credible, in that we cannot check them," objected the chameleon. "But asking can't hurt."

I walked up closer and met eyes with the girl lying in the box. She looked at me attentively as if waiting for something.

"Can you speak?" I asked.

"Yes, of course. I can speak," came the android's lifelessly mechanical voice, expressing no emotion whatsoever.

Apparently, disapproval or disenchantment was being expressed on my face, because Bionica then rushed to answer:

"Reading expression. Master upset. He was expecting something else. My appearance can be set on a sliding scale. My ability to learn new information and abilities is virtually limitless. My level of humanness can be set."

"Normal voice, not like a mechanical puppet!" I demanded. "And your speech must be coherent, without broken phrases. Set humanness to maximum!"

"Does this voice for a secretary and translator please the Crown Prince?" asked the girl with a pleasant, young, utterly vivacious voice.

"Fully. Do you know who I am?" I asked, catching

on the girl/android's last phrase.

"With a chance of over... That is, my apologies, I recognized you Prince Georg royl Inoky ton Mesfelle, which is why I am at such a loss for words."

"Explain," I commanded, not having understood her answer.

"It is very nice that a member of Imperial upper aristocracy had an interest in my talents. But, at the same time, the choice saddens me. It is completely obvious that from now on, my value has risen sharply in the eyes of your Highness's foes. My intelligence and the wisdom I've acquired over twenty-five years speak to the fact that, even if I am left to lie in this box, either way after the end of this contract, there is a nearly one hundred percent chance that I will be purchased by other aristocrats with the goal of finding and extracting all information I have on Prince Georg royl Inoky. Clearly, your Highness will not allow that, and such information will surely be destroyed together with its carrier. I may not be a human but, like all people, I love and value life. So, my perspectives here have upset me."

Huh, damn... With my stupid choice, I had sentenced this android to death. Even though she wasn't a living being, I still felt a bit beside myself with guilt.

"You may stand up out of the package."

Bionica immediately took advantage of the permission, stood up and adopted the classic "bashful pose." One arm was covering her breasts, while the palm of her other hand covered her crotch. As I was her owner, I felt it appropriate to walk a circle around her, looking shamelessly over the android girl who was getting embarrassed just like a human would. What a body. And her skin was very natural. There was no way of telling that the thing in front of me was not a living person.

"Answer my bodyguard's questions," I demanded.

Bionica, not seeing the chameleon, turned her face toward me and proceeded to tell her story.

"I was sent to the service center for repair on warranty just three months after I was first purchased. My owner's son took advantage of his absence and threw a party with his friends. Though they didn't have super-administrator rights, they decided to take advantage of my model's expanded range of functions all the same."

"Explain," I asked, not having fully arrived at what she was driving at, though I could have guessed.

"If I were a living person, it would have been classified as gang rape. I tried to the best of my ability to obstruct the unauthorized access, but androids are not allowed to harm people, though people themselves have no such restriction... The external appearance of the model was damaged, and the warranty was used to get the necessary repair. The client was given a similar model instead of me, and my self-teaching programming unit was modified to erase the negative experience. The second answer is to the question about missed patches. My third owner thought that it was accumulated life experience that allowed androids to perfect themselves and become more human. He thought it wasn't necessary to change what was already working fine and that changing out the unique, naturally formed character with something average and manufacturer-recommended would only ruin me. So, he turned off automatic updating of installed programs, and all my subsequent owners simply paid the matter no mind."

I waited for a reaction from Popori de Cacha, but the chameleon remained invisible. So, I made the decision on my own and addressed the android girl, who stood petrified as a statue:

"In order to explain all questions you might have right away – yes, it was me who ordered you. And as you've probably figured out, I made a mistake. But today I was struggling with a severe deficit of translators from the Iseyek language, so I need a specialist in that, and it is of no importance whether that is a living person or an android. And I also need a personal secretary. So, get dressed and get to work."

As the ship came out of warp, I was instantly met by two system messages:

Global fame increase. Current value +5

Global standing decrease. Current value -28

I did not understand the reason for these changes. Either the Green House had unfurled various insinuations about me in the Throne World, or my choice of a second-hand android as a personal servant had been made known to the noble public and put me in a negative light. It wasn't really important. Much more important was the fact that I had had my first drug withdrawal symptoms. My fingers were clenching involuntarily, my leg muscles were shaking, and tears were rolling down my face. I never took drugs my whole life, so I had no idea what was happening to me and became quite scared.

I immediately called for Nicosid Brandt, who quickly made a diagnosis and gave me an IV with some solution somewhere between glucose and vitamin complex. It helped, but my heart continued to beat in fear for no less than an hour.

"My Prince, I warned you," scolded my elderly doctor. "No one has yet been able to overcome crystal addiction."

"That means I'll be the first," I insisted in continuing stubbornness, reaffirming my decision as hard and final.

I spent the next two hours just torturing myself at the gym to build up my atrophied muscles. Even the fitness instructor looked scared; he could only watch as the high-born prince fought through pain, sweat and tears to complete cycle after cycle of exercises. My exercising hadn't had any effect on my figure yet, but I was still feeling something. My first day of exercising, I spent an hour in the gym and was just dying. But now, after two hours, I still had the strength to take a shower and head to the pool.

By the way, it was in the pool that an incident occurred that nearly lead to my being unmasked. I was running to jump into the water when two of my chameleon bodyguards appeared in front of me and grabbed me in what was not the most careful of ways. I fell to the floor with them, rolled and skinned my knee.

"My Prince, that was not very smart!" The alarmed

Popori de Cacha hurried to the place I'd fallen to help me get up. "That's the deep end, and you don't know how to swim!"

I almost answered that I can swim very well, but I bit my tongue just in the nick of time. How lucky I was to have been stopped by my bodyguards! It would have been a sight to see if the truly unable-to-swim Prince Georg royl Inoky suddenly started swimming confidently, be it a crawl or a breast stroke...

"Sorry, Popori de Cacha, I was dreaming way too big. But your worrying was for naught. Take a look at my body," I offered, extending a layer of skin with my fingers. "Can a person really drown with so much extra fat?"

The chameleon's eyes both darted to the part of my body I was pointing at, then to the open wound on my knee that had a fair amount of blood dribbling from it.

"My subordinates did not have enough time to account for the buoyancy of the human body," said Popori de Cacha, turning toward the three bodyguards who had blocked my way to the water. "So, my Prince, they acted on their life experience, which said that, if a Ravaash individual falls into the water, they will inevitably drown and die. That is why the bodyguards considered the threat to your life critical and acted in kind. If the front pair of guards had not been able stop you at the edge, all four of us would have jumped into the water to help our master reach the edge and get out alive, even if it cost us our lives."

Tired, I sat on a bench to allow the pool employees who had run up to me to disinfect my knee and attach a wide bandage. I opened the relations menu and saw a message about a possible decision:

> ***Chance of expressing your reaction***
> ***Change in personal opinion of Popori de Cacha (choose an option: +15, +10, +5, 0)***
>> ***Change in faction opinion of Popori de Cacha (choose an option: +2, +1, 0, must be approved by the Head of the Orange House)***
>> ***Change in racial opinion of Popori de Cacha (choose an option: +1, 0, must be approved by the Emperor)***
>> ***Change in faction opinion of Chameleon race (inactive)***
>> ***Change in human race opinion of Chameleon race (inactive)***

I chose the maximum possible personal improvement with the head of my bodyguards, stood up from the bench, and took a critical look at my quickly swelling knee before announcing:

"Apparently, swimming has been canceled for the day. Popori de Cacha, bring me to the changing room."

It wasn't that I really needed the help. I was fully able to walk, but I just wanted to have a talk with the chameleon. He and his subjects were always invisibly present around me, keeping many threats at bay, but I knew so little about who they were.

"I am grateful to you and your coworkers, Popori de Cacha, and in general I am very satisfied with the job you do. If there is anything you need for work or just for life in general, now is the time to let me know."

Without thinking for even a second, the chameleon answered:

"My Prince, what worries me the most is the fate of two soldiers of my group who you took for some important mission. Their transmitters are not responding, and I don't even know what to think."

All I needed was a few seconds to figure out that the two big armed lizards in the *Wishbone* cafe where those very same armored chameleons.

"Popori de Cacha, I have sent your soldiers to guard Miya, a person very dear to me. Miya sensed a threat and told me that, for her security, she would need to go into hiding for some time to keep away from the eyes of the many watchers. I myself do not know how my Truth Seeker got off *Queen of Sin* nor where she is hiding now. All I can say is that Miya and your soldiers are alive and well but can only return to the others in around half a year."

The chameleon, standing at the changing room door, opened it before me and announced with a bow:

"My Prince, thank you for the trust you've placed in me. You can be sure that my soldiers will not steer you wrong."

Standing change. Popori de Cacha's opinion of you has improved.
Presumed personal opinion of you: +17 (warm)

As the second half of the day began, I was taking a seat in front of my work again. The material Triasss Zess provided turned out to be truly priceless.

Recordings of more than two hundred local skirmishes with the aliens and eighteen exhaustively analyzed battles with a timeline of all events and the characteristics of all ships that took part. I studied the recordings, finding interesting moments for myself.

... the alien *Ascetic* destroyer has truly miraculous firepower for such a little ship, but it is quite unwieldy and accelerates slowly.

...in battle against the Iseyeks in the Aysar cluster, there were three times that the *Sledgehammer* cruiser was not able to shoot after reloading. Each of them was when it was being attacked by the *Umoyge* light cruisers. That means its defenses against electronic warfare are pretty middling.

...the *Hermit* destroyers can release twenty combat drones. The damage each of them can do is comparable to that of a *Pyro* frigate.

...the alien fleet did not attack the beacon in the Umwi system, which made it possible for the beacon crew to take advantage of the emergency shuttle and make it into warp. Manpower is key. At the very end of the video, you can see the little alien ship has a landing party that captures the beacon.

There was very little photographic evidence on the aliens themselves. And the specimens we did have were of a very low quality. That wasn't very surprising – it was hard to imagine that the corpses would be well preserved after a hit from a proton torpedo or the explosion of a ship's reactor. Nevertheless, the bodies of at least three different species of alien had made their way to the scientists for study. Also, these species were so strikingly different that many researchers suggested that there were actually three independent alien armies, not just one.

I looked carefully at the reconstructions of the external appearance of the aliens, and I also wasn't able find anything in common between them. Something filled with hydrogen and methane, levitating with thin tentacles dangling down like threads; a glob of slime without typical sense organs; an incomprehensible bush-creature with a large number of branches. The last species of alien described was protein-based, though its set of amino acids was unfamiliar and had nothing in common with the creatures humanity knew of. The two first were not protein-based life forms at all.

I was tired from the many hours of studying pictures and numbers, and I was also downright starving, so I went off in the direction of the small dining hall. On my way, my attention was caught by a light coming from a branching corridor, and I turned to see what was going on. Bionica Klein was standing by the wall in the hallway, holding her boots and the package of her clothes. Her eyes were closed. I called her name, and the android immediately opened her eyes and gradually woke up.

"Good evening, master," she said, greeting me.

"Why are you standing here and not going to your room?" I wondered.

"Captain Oorast Pohl said that androids and robots don't get their own rooms. Because I'm not a crewmember, I wasn't assigned a room, which is why I'm having a bit of trouble here. I don't know where I can put my things and wait out the night. I also don't know where to recharge yet."

"Recharge? Are you hungry? Or what's the deal there, how do you recharge?"

The long-legged blonde smiled and told me:

"My Prince is repeating the very same questions that each of my previous masters has asked me. It's all laid out in detail in the instruction manual, but for some reason people don't like reading instructions. My model has enough energy reserves to work around-the-clock for six days, then I need a recharge. You can power an android either via the power grid or food. What is recommended is a combination of both recharging methods."

"Bionica, do you not need to rest?" I asked in surprise.

"My program has human behavior imitation built-in. Each day, the model may go into inactive mode for a few hours. But, by and large, that is not at all necessary given enough energy. Current charge level is eleven percent, enough for twenty hours of uninterrupted work."

"In other words, you wouldn't mind having some time to freshen up?" I insinuated, immediately filling with enthusiasm. "Bionica, are you trained in table etiquette?"

"Yes, master. I am aware of all subtleties of table manners in all kinds of social circles. I am programmed to behave properly and do not allow myself even the slightest infractions."

"Great! Then you're coming to dine with me!"

The reason for my amiability wasn't just that I cared about the good-looking robot (that was part of it though). It was just that, in one day, *Queen of Sin* would be arriving on the Throne World, and beyond a conversation with the Emperor, I had talking with nobles in store as well. I had already received an official invitation to dine with the head of the Orange House, Duke Paolo royl Anjer. I had also been invited by my sister, Crown Princess Violetta royl Inoky ton Mesfelle-Damir, to her palace in the Throne World. It should be said that I was even more afraid of these meetings than making a report before the Emperor. The Emperor I could just tell a sob story about the fleet I was entrusted with, but not getting confused at a table in the highest society in the Empire would be much more complicated.

The old man, Bryle, quickly organized the chefs and, as I requested, set the table with the great variety of dishes that I could expect to see on the nobles' tables. I sat at the head of the table, and pointed at the chair next to me for Bionica to sit.

"So, let's begin. Consider this a test. You have to demonstrate how to use the tableware and the correct way of consuming all these delicacies. It is important to me that you try as many different dishes as possible, if even just a little."

The girl smiled her pleasant smile and set about filling her battery, as I tried to study and memorize her actions.

"Can androids drink wine?" I asked Bionica, and she broke into a joyful laughter.

"Of course we can. My Prince, I'm not trying to shame you but, all the same, read the instructions at your leisure, and many of your questions will be answered. The brain of an android is fully computerized and is in no way connected with the stomach. Let me answer your next question right away, which all my masters have asked right after asking if I can drink alcohol. No, I cannot get drunk. An android's body sees no use in ethanol, except as a high-energy fuel."

"I wasn't really thinking of getting you drunk," I said bending the truth, in that I had already given some thought to the possibility. "Red? White? Green?"

"I prefer dry whites," she said, taking a high-walled glass from my hand and looking at me through the transparent drink with a smile.

I still couldn't believe that the person before me was a robot and not a worldly lioness. Based on her behavior, voice, appearance and gestures, Bionica was impossible to tell from a living person.

"Then tell me: what questions do your masters normally ask? So I don't repeat them. Well, and answer them all too."

"Does it matter that some of them will deal with topics that are not to be discussed at the dinner table in polite society?" the blonde giggled coquettishly.

I gave my approval, and Bionica gave her fingers a flex:

"The most popular question is 'can an android get pregnant?' The answer is no. Reproductive functions have not been provided for in the body of an android.

The second most popular question is 'how is an android different from a cyborg?' Cyborgs are living creatures with computer parts implanted or part of their organs changed out for robotic prostheses. Despite these change-outs, cyborgs remain living beings. This contrasts with androids, who are in essence robots from the get-go and are in some way or another similar to humans. It should be said that scientific progress is making these differences less and less significant all the time. The share of mechanical components in cybernetic organisms is increasing gradually, while at the same time androids are being implanted with various systems from living organisms, for example the digestive and excretory systems. It is not impossible that the line between cyborgs and androids will become blurrier or fade away altogether.

The third most popular question is 'how important is cleanliness to androids? Do we wash ourselves,' excuse my directness, 'do we wash our private parts after going to the bathroom or having sexual intercourse?' I cannot speak for all android models, as I do not know, but model № 034-6781 androids, like myself, maintain sterile cleanliness. And something that especially worried my masters, who would always ask squeamishly: there are no biological traces of my previous masters inside me, of course not."

"Alright, that's enough of that. Let's change the topic." I really was a bit taken aback by how direct my android servant had been, and by how inappropriate the topic had been for the dinner table. "Now I am interested in the limitations of your programming. That an android is not able to kill or harm a human I already figured out. But imagine this situation: we're in battle, I order the fleet to attack. You, as my translator, must translate my order to the Iseyek ships under my command. Would you give them the order, given you know that by doing so you'll kill a certain number of fully intelligent enemies, maybe even people?"

"Of course. Due to programmed-in limitations,

androids are not able to hurt or kill an intelligent creature. But we are not supposed to stop one intelligent creature from killing other intelligent creatures. It's not like you can really stop that from happening anyway."

It should be noted that the android girl was making a very positive impression on me. She was quickly figuring out how to be a secretary and sending me everything I really needed to see. She absorbed new information easily, and quickly found her bearings in any situation. She also helped me a lot as a teaching aid, demonstrating proper table manners. There was a whole sea of subtlety there, but Bionica was able to tell me the purpose of every little fork and file in the tableware and demonstrate their proper use in action. From time to time, I even forgot that before me was not a living person, but a robot. After the end of dinner, I gave Bionica permission to be in any residential room on the second floor assigned to Prince Georg and also marked one of the sleeping cabins on the yacht map as her own.

Queen of Sin followed the chain of warp beacons through Sector Eight without any delays, and entered the central regions of the Empire also known as the Core. By the end of the next day, Captain Oorast Pohl warned me:

"My Prince, we've entered the last warp tunnel. In seven hours we'll arrive at the Throne World."

THE THRONE WORLD

THE ARRIVAL of my yacht to the Imperial capital was accompanied by a large number of call notifications. The signal lights flashed all at once, indicating missed calls, and the color-code of most messages was either orange or red.

"My Prince, there's an urgent call from the head of the Orange House, Duke Paolo royl Anjer ton Mesfelle. It's a code red!"

"An urgent call from the Imperial Secretariat, code red!"

"Three missed calls from Crown Princess Violetta royl Inoky ton Mesfelle-Damir, code has changed from orange to red!"

The communications officer was somewhat shocked by the overload of information crashing down on him.

"Let's talk to the Duke first," I decided and, just a second later, the old man was yelling through the speakers to the whole hall:

"Where have you been hiding, Georg?! The meeting with the Emperor is in an hour and fifteen minutes, and no one knows where you are! Come to the Silver

Palace at once! I'll try to delay the start a bit so you can make it..."

"Captain, what's the matter?" I bellowed harshly to Oorast Pohl, though he had also been thrown for a loop.

"Your Highness, I swear on my honor: we got here at maximum possible speed, and we came out of warp at the smallest possible distance from the recharging station, so close that it was dangerous even. There must have been a mistake... I'll review all the data now and figure it out."

"Alright, our mission is to reach the Silver Palace from orbit in an hour and fifteen minutes," I announced to my frozen crew. "I welcome your suggestions, dear officers."

The hall grew silent, no one made a sound. After that, Space Corporal Patrick toyl Sven stepped forward and suggested:

"My Prince, typically, a safe descent takes three hours. But in combat landing conditions, the standard target time for reaching the surface of a planet is twenty minutes. So, what we could do is take the shuttle and enter the atmosphere hard and fast, as close to the edge of shield failure as possible. I can drive. I've already had to do this once in the battle of Algol, so we'll have no problem muscling our way in. Just one piece of advice: don't put on your ceremonial attire now. During entry into the lower layers of the atmosphere, it vibrates so hard that even interceptor pilots in training get shaken up."

Other than the pilot and me, only the chameleons and four guards were able to cram themselves into the shuttle. Old Bryle gave me my ceremonial uniform, packed in cellophane, and wished me luck. The shuttle accelerated directly toward the wall, and only at the last second did the doors open before us, letting us out into a rounded corridor. The airlock opened with a hiss, and the shuttle took a sharp dive into the blackness of space, falling out on its side. I tried my hardest to suppress the nausea. Yep, I'd already forgotten that flying on a shuttle can be a nasty experience. In the Tesse star system, I had used the yacht's shuttle a few times, but we were flying carefully, and I even liked the feeling of flying through space. Now, those impressions seemed long gone...

"Who of you knows where the Silver Palace is?" came the pilot's voice from the cabin.

The soldiers, buckled into their seats, exchanged nervous glances.

"What? No one? Well, alright then, I guess we'll figure it out after we land. I hope we're at least in the right hemisphere."

I felt a sharp jolt, then I got pushed back into my seat. The shuttle fell downward while gaining speed at the same time. At first, there was nothing especially scary about it, but then I noticed that the tips of our flying machine's wings were on fire.

"Is that supposed to happen?" I asked the pilot, receiving an answer in the negative.

At some point, it started to vibrate. First it was barely noticeable, but then it sharply increased in intensity until it felt like our shuttle had fallen into a cement mixer. The flames on the wing tips started burning with more and more intensity. Also, a strange, frightening glow began wrapping around our ship. Bolts of electricity ripped themselves from the chassis, and the air was crackling. But the graphical tricks weren't having a very strong effect on me anymore. I was feeling really sick. What reassured me was the fact that I wasn't the only one feeling bad. Even the chameleons were nauseated. The pilot asked me something, but it took a while to register:

"My Prince, explain to the anti-space defense services of the Throne World why we are taking such a dangerous trajectory, otherwise they're going to shoot us down now."

"Put them through to me," I groaned, gathering my strength. I then confidently and even haughtily explained who I was and why I was in a hurry to the Silver Palace.

"You've been heard, Crown Prince Georg. Order your pilot to lower speed and take the recommended course and bearings. Escort ships will approach you now and accompany you to the Silver Palace."

The shuttle's flight evened out, and the flashing stopped. Everyone around breathed a sigh of apparent relief. I also started gradually coming back to reality and got right up to change into my ceremonial uniform. Our shuttle, accompanied by eight streamlined atmospheric/near-space class fighters, soon came to a big island covered in green, surrounded by the ocean, and made a landing on the pad in front of the silver-hued palace. I was already preparing to disembark when I was stopped by a pilot:

"My Prince, incoming call from Captain Oorast Pohl!"

"Your Highness," said the Captain, his voice wavering in agitation. "As I thought, there was a scheduling error. *Queen of Sin* has set a new record for travel between Tesse and the Throne World: fifty-two hours and seventeen minutes! We beat the previous record by almost two hours. Here's the official record from the Ministry of Interstellar Transportation!"

"Excellent, captain. Well, time to make someone squirm then!" with a combative attitude, I left the shuttle onto the landing pad in front of the palace.

There were people waiting for me there already. A young man in an Orange House uniform rushed in my direction, gesticulating wildly. I took a look at his information.

Marat ton Mesfelle, Sector Seven Fleet Commander
 Age: 33
 Race: Human
 Gender: Male
 Relation to you: Your second cousin
 Class: Aristocrat/Military
 Achievements: None
 Fame: +2
 Standing: + 4
 Presumed opinion of you: +4 (indifferent)

"Where have you been, Georg?! Everyone's already in there. They're only waiting for you. The Green House is already in quite a decisive mood. There's no sense in giving them another excuse for chicanery."

"Who's there from our side?" I wondered on my way. We really had already given up all pretense to aristocratic dignity and were running at full-steam to the hall, given that arriving late to a meeting with the

Emperor was considered extremely bad form and could have serious consequences.

"The Duke, your sister, and myself," answered Marat. "Roben was also called, but he refused to come. As for me, I just happened to be in the Throne World. The Duke found me here and called on me for support."

We walked down the corridor between two lines of soldiers, who were frozen at attention in shining ceremonial suits of armor, into the reception hall back at a normal pace, regaining our breath. Marat stopped, and before me opened the enormous fifteen-foot-high gilded doors. I went through into the luxurious hall, which was all decked-out in pink.

"You barely made it, Prince Georg. One more minute and I would have had to consider you late," declared the tall, gray man harshly. He was standing near a wall next to a set of strange bronze plate armor, clearly made for a creature with a greater number of arms than a human. I bowed deeply to the old man, reading his information at the same time. No, of course, I knew who it was before me, but I just wanted to see the characteristics of a real top player:

August Royl Toll ton Akad, Emperor
Age: 338 years
Race: Human
Gender: Male
Relation to you: Your great uncle
Class: Aristocrat
Achievements: (see Attachment)
Fame: +99
Standing: +234

Presumed opinion of you: Unknown

His age, fame and standing were of course impressive, but nothing more. I was expecting something more... I don't even know what... Some unique characteristics or something. Well, or just some more grandiose phrases in his character description. And also the old man's appearance wasn't anything to write home about. He looked like a dried morel with long, gray hair in which you could just barely make out a thin gold band. The Emperor was dressed in a gold-embroidered black velvet suit, which spoke to the meeting's official nature.

"I would really like to come face to face with the person who scheduled this meeting for me," I pronounced loudly.

"I set the time," piped up a chubby man named Rahim ton Lavaelle, whose popup confirmed that he was the Emperor's senior secretary. "What would you like to know, Prince Georg?"

I immediately figured that his last name, Lavaelle, meant that he was related to the Green House. Everything became clear at once. Oh, well then. I wasn't going to lower myself to the point of telling that tub of lard that his actions had almost forced me into a bad light before the Emperor himself. With people like that, the best defense is a good offense.

"Answer me honestly, Mr. Senior Secretary: was it due to incompetence or malice that you demanded that I arrive on the Throne World from Tesse a whole hour faster than the officially confirmed starship speed record? Only the fact that my yacht, *Queen of Sin*, really is an excellent ship that my captain piloted at maximum speed, coupled with the fact that we descended from orbit according to space marine combat standards instead of civilian ones, posing a serious risk to our lives, allowed me to arrive to this event on time. By the way, in my rush here to have this meeting with the Emperor, I set a new speed record, beating the previous one by two whole hours. The record has been confirmed by the Ministry of Interstellar Transportation," I added, bringing up the red certificate with signatures and stamps from officials on the screen.

"Is that so...? Well, that changes things entirely," said the Emperor, approaching the screen and carefully studying the pretty certificate. "Rahim, I would also like to have an answer to the question posed by the Prince. Why did you find it necessary to subject my grandnephew to such an unjustifiable risk to his life? It would have been entirely possible for us to meet and discuss all these issues a bit later without him having had to race."

The secretary grew noticeably embarrassed and was definitely upset that his crafty plan to set me up had been foiled. But I was sure that such an experienced court figure would probably have some escape plans ready. And that was exactly what happened. Rahim ton Lavaelle jabbed his fat fingers into the screen of the handheld computer, then asserted with a tone that did none-too-good a job of imitating regret:

"My Emperor, it would appear that my subordinates have made a vexing blunder. In preparing the urgent order for Prince Georg late at night, they were in such a rush that they did not notice that the next day had already begun. Look at the time the order was sent, it was just a few seconds after midnight. So actually, Prince Georg royl Inoky should have been given a whole day more time. But it's good that he was able to get here in the more compressed timeframe."

He wormed his way out of it, the pest! For some reason, the Emperor took his servant's word that the mistake was just a coincidence and paid no more attention to the minor episode. He asked Rahim to call the other attendees in from their separate chambers for the meeting. The secretary took a weighty silver bell from the table and gave it a few shakes. A clean, crystal sound rang out, serving as a signal. Several doors opened, and all kinds of different people began entering the room. Three were in orange garb – the ancient Duke Paolo royl Anjer; leading him by the hand was my sister, the Crown Princess Violetta; and also Marat, who I'd seen earlier.

There was one more person in green than in orange. The first to come out, the head of the Green House, Duke Kevin royl Olefir ton Lavaelle, was quite a lively geezer for all his two hundred ten years. Count Amelius royl Mast ton Lavaelle came next. He was the great uncle of Captain Crasav, who I'd banished from my fleet. Then came the two inseparable twins, Rigo and Keno, who were as alike as two peas in a pod. By the way, they were both my first cousins on my mother's side. The Green House delegation was filled out by a tall, pretty girl with chestnut hair. I didn't recognize her, so I quickly read the popup:

Katerina ton Mesfelle, speaker of the Green

House
   Age: 28
   Race: Human
   Gender: Female
   Relation to you: Your second cousin
   Class: Aristocrat
   Achievements: Master of Rhetoric
   Fame: +2
   Standing: +7
   Presumed opinion of you: Unknown

Other than the members of the two Great Houses, also in the hall there were: Space Marshal Abram Kovel, from the Imperial Star Fleet, and an elderly woman in dark, long clothing, whose face was obscured by a hood that was down over her eyes.

I read about the space marshal – he was a worthy soldier, a good strategist and had participated in a great deal of military conflicts. Abram Kovel was a supporter of the concept of the decisive battle: trying to pin down the enemy with the huge, unified Imperial Fleet and, all at once, crush them. I was aware that the space marshal had tried several times to change the law on reassignment of Great House forces, so that they would be subordinate directly to the Imperial Joint Staff, but each time he met with very strong resistance from the aristocracy.

But I was much more interested in the old lady. The Dark Mother was the strongest Truth Seeker in the Universe, after all. Nevertheless, I wasn't able to get any additional information about her. Don't tell me such a high role is played by an NPC?! On the other hand... That's probably how it should be in a balanced game. You can't give a real player such great opportunities as the most powerful Truth Seeker in the game would have. Just imagine the potential consequences.

The attendees took their seats around the table – the orange ones to the right, and the green ones to the left. The others took the seats closest to the Emperor.

"So, let's begin," my second cousin stood up and announced the criminal charges she'd memorized in a well formulated tone. "The Green House accuses Crown Prince Georg royl Inoky ton Mesfelle, present here today, of negligence in his duties as the Sector Eight Fleet Commander. The fleet completely lost its combat strength in a fight with just one small alien ship. At present, all that remains of the fleet are two light cruisers, one of which doesn't even have an experienced captain, as well as a few dozen support ships."

My accuser paused, giving the Emperor the chance to take a note on the screen of the computer lying before him. Finally, August royl Toll raised his head and with a motion of his palm, indicated that she could continue.

"Second, with his exceptionally incompetent command, Crown Prince Georg has spooked off our historically staunch allies in Sector Eight, the Kingdom of Fastel. The Kingdom of Fastel's fleet has separated from ours and has refused to participate in further joint operations with the Orange House fleet. Beyond that, the commander neglected his direct duties and allowed Iseyek military ships to make an incursion into Imperial territory unpunished."

"That really is quite serious," proclaimed the

Emperor, taking another set of notes.

Katerina ton Mesfelle waited once again until the Emperor had finished writing, and continued:

"Our third accusation: the Crown Prince was unjustly harsh in suppressing the dissatisfaction of his fleet's captains and officers, which was brought about by his own incompetent leadership. Cruiser Captain Crasav ton Lavaelle was sent back to the Empire in a humiliating way on a dirty freight ship, while the thirty-four other fleet officers were executed. And at last, our fourth and final accusation: the fleet commander has blemished his standing with links to suspicious characters, the attempted assassination of his own brother Roben's heir, and finally with his choice of an old android as a girlfriend and sex toy, which has become the focus of gossip everywhere outside alien territory. And with that the Green House rests."

When my second cousin had finally taken her seat, the Emperor sat in silence for a bit, then declared, addressing me:

"These accusations are truly very serious, Georg. Do you have anything to say in your defense?"

I stood up and, looking at Katerina, said mockingly:

"I have yet to hear one word of truth come from my second cousin's mouth. Because of that, I've actually been left a bit confused – I can't seriously be expected to refute such artless lies, can I? Either my second cousin wasn't paying attention in her rhetoric courses, or the Green House has no real accusations against me."

"Come now, Georg, go a bit easier. There's no need for insults," interjected the Emperor, obviously dissatisfied. "What have you got on this case? Any facts to back up your assertions?"

"Of course," I smiled. "So, point by point. In regards to what my second cousin said about the strength of the Sector Eight Fleet: 'two light cruisers, and a couple of little ships,' is that right?"

Katerina nodded slowly, staring at me with an expressionless gaze.

"So, here are the facts: At present, the Sector Eight Fleet has fourteen cruisers, of which eight are heavy class..."

"That's a flagrant lie!" exploded the head of the Green House, no longer able to hold himself back and jumping up from his seat.

I turned to the old woman and, with a slight bow, asked her to come closer:

"I ask the Truth Seeker to check my words. At present, my fleet is composed of one *Flamberg* heavy assault cruiser, three of the newest model *Katana* heavy assault cruisers, four *Legash* heavy cruisers, and six light electronic warfare cruisers."

"He speaks the pure truth, Emperor," said the old lady in a trembling voice.

"Thus, I consider the first accusation against me a flagrant lie," I snorted, as I bowed mockingly to the head of the Green House. "The Sector Eight Fleet is stronger now than it's ever been. What were the other accusations? That the Empire supposedly has been left without allies in Sector Eight, and that Iseyek ships had made an incursion there? Let's define our terms here, so I'm clear which of these mutually exclusive accusations I am to answer to – what is it? Are we without allies or have the Iseyek come? In actuality, it is the Iseyek who have become our allies and given us their ships at no expense, as well as allowed the Imperial fleet passage through Swarm territory for the first time in a century."

The "jury" buzzed. It seemed they were not aware of these details. I made a serious face and added:

"Yes, I really did have to face a difficult choice – three Kingdom of Fastel cruisers that would never become part of our fleet and would continue to act of their own accord, or nine Iseyek cruisers under full Imperial control. I chose the second option and made some of the most loyal allies you're liable to find. Yes, my choice did upset my wife, Princess Marta, but it's plain to see that a complete break in the alliance has not been made. The Kingdom of Fastel is still as loyal to the Empire as ever and is still guarding its part of Sector Eight. So, the Empire hasn't lost a thing, and instead has acquired new allies and their fleet. And if anyone remains in doubt, I'll say one word: '*Uukresh.*'"

The jury members exchanged uncomprehending glances, but the space marshal had heard the name before:

"*Uukresh* is the name of the insect mother ship. It's their strongest ship. What are they doing, giving us one?"

"They've already given us one. As we speak, that huge carrier is on its way to the Tesse system for repair under the guard of my ships. That giant will become the pearl of the Sector Eight Fleet."

"Why don't we get that information checked, just to be sure," suggested Katerina. "It sounds so good it hurts. Too good to be the truth."

I gave my hand to the Truth Seeker again, and the

old lady said:

"That is also the truth, my Emperor. The huge Swarm ship now belongs to Prince Georg."

The attendees began making a din. It was very positive news. The head of the Orange House gave me a gesture of approval, saying I'd done a good job! I then continued:

"So, I suppose that the falsity of the second accusation has also been proven. Let's move on to the third. Regarding Crasav ton Lavaelle... What do we really know about the captain? Dark Mother, stay close, please. I'll need your help again soon. So, I'll say this as frankly as possible: I still don't know if Crasav ton Lavaelle is truly capable of commanding a cruiser!"

"What drivel is this? My grandson was captain of *Algol Hulk* for a long time!" exclaimed the Duke, deeply offended in his finer feelings.

I reached for the hand of the Truth Seeker and started speaking, choosing my words carefully:

"In all my time having command over *Algol Hulk*, it was almost never Captain Crasav ton Lavaelle commanding the ship, but his first assistant. And of what the captain himself did: he was written up twice by Admiral Kiro Sabuto for ignoring orders. The admiral advised me to fire Crasav ton Lavaelle twice due to his being unsuited to command the cruiser, but for a long time I refused – he is a member of the respected Lavaelle family after all, the great-grandson of the Duke, and all that. But then, Crasav ton Lavaelle displayed cowardice in battle with the alien ship and fled, taking his cruiser out of the battle. Then, after receiving a direct, explicit order from the fleet commander to make the warp jump to Himora, he instead decided to sit down for a meal. This resulted in Crasav ton Lavaelle also not taking part in the battle with the pirates in the Himora system. That was the drop that caused the cup of my patience to run over. I couldn't stop myself, so I discharged Crasav ton Lavaelle. Why do I need a coward as a captain? He's afraid to fight, he disobeys orders, and all he does do is try to enlist my officers in his spy ring, turning them against the Empire and the Orange House! Of course, according to all military laws, he should have been sentenced the same as the other traitors, but he's still a member of the honorable Lavaelle family after all..."

"Dark Mother, what is your verdict? Is the Prince speaking the truth?" wondered August.

"Yes, my Emperor. All the Prince's words are truthful, with the exception of 'honorable Lavaelle family.' In reality, he harbors a slight disrespect for that family."

Some poorly restrained giggles could be heard, and Duke Paolo royl Anjer completely lost his composure, beginning to whinny like a mare. I even noticed a smile flash quickly across the Emperor's face. I could have ended there in regards to the third accusation, but I preferred not to quit while I was ahead:

"I suggest we speak a bit more on Crasav ton Lavaelle and his agents in my fleet. As I've already stated, I still am not sure that captain is capable of commanding a cruiser. But I am sure of something else: he lied flagrantly to his commander, and he ascribed his sins and faults to his crewmembers to shelter himself. Also, in his latest bout of deceit, he didn't even pay the captain of the ship that brought him to the Empire – he promised to pay, but still he fled without having done so!"

Here the Duke was forced to blush for his great-grandson, who everyone in the room had begun shooting reproachful glances. The Duke muttered something about how he'd be paying all of Crasav ton Lavaelle's debts personally that very day. I made a harsh face, stretched out my palm to the Dark Mother, and said:

"The spies and saboteurs implanted in my crew by Crasav ton Lavaelle went completely off tether after the captain's disappearance and proceeded to murder those loyal to me. Ladies and gentlemen, I think you'll agree that such behavior violates all possible bounds of proper conduct, even for spies embedded in an openly hostile state. The spies were uncovered in a surgical operation, but I did not think it my right to decide their fates, so I allowed the military court to handle it. The criminals were executed in full accordance with article 34-11, subparagraph C of the Star Fleet Charter."

The Dark Mother reaffirmed my words. The others present remained silent, somewhat shocked at what they'd heard. I went on to the last accusation.

"So, about my standing. This 'shadowy figure,' if I'm understanding Katerina correctly, is the Truth Seeker Miya. Or am I wrong, and the Green House had someone else in mind?"

"No, cousin," said Katerina, clearly mocking me. "You've understood perfectly. The whole Empire gossips about the details of the longstanding excessive intimacy between the Crown Prince of the

Empire and the Truth Seeker of such questionable standing."

"If that's true, then they know more than I do!" I chuckled. "To begin, dear cousin, read the details on the pharmacological effects of crystalloquasimetal-cis-isomer valiarimic acid, which Miya and I have taken, as mystics. I think, after that, a lot of the fantastic stories about myself and Miya will seem quite silly. The facts are as follows: Miya is one of the strongest Truth Seekers in existence. I myself do not know the limits of her abilities. Not long ago, she sensed a danger and went into hiding. It's possible that she foresaw this very conversation about her and preferred not to bother high society with her presence, and instead disappeared temporarily. Where Miya is now, I do not know. To be more precise, I have some guesses, but I am not prepared to share them, as she is very dear to me, and I don't want her being bothered. I was merely told through an intermediary that it was pointless to seek out Miya and that she would be coming back on her own in half a year."

"Half a year?" asked the Dark Mother, to confirm. "It's very curious that such a powerful Truth Seeker could be frightened off. Unless..." the old lady did not finish her thought, instead turning to the Emperor and quietly saying: "We'll discuss this issue later one-on-one after the meeting."

"Yes, I consider this matter settled. But what about that accusation about Roben's child?"

"The accusation was false. Georg and Miya's innocence was proven by another Truth Seeker. I have already been informed," said the Dark Mother.

Everyone remained in silence for some time, so I

had to continue myself:

"So then, the only accusation against me that remains is the android I purchased?" I sniggered happily, adding:

"Is it not surprising to you that my purchasing a simple secretary and translator is being judged at such a high level? The Emperor, two Dukes, a Count, a Crown Princess, a space marshal, two fleet commanders... It's scary to think what could have happened had I acquired a cleaning robot or a robot dance instructor, instead of a translator. Would it have been necessary to convene the large council of all Imperial allies?"

"Yeah, it is a bit absurd," agreed the space marshal. "My Emperor, if that is all, then I suppose I'll be on my way. I have a great deal of matters to attend to more important than investigating the purchase of servant robots..."

Keno ton Lavaelle shot up from his seat and shouted:

"Georg did not buy a simple android, but a model for sexual gratification! What's more, it's not a new one but an old one, used many times over, stinking and vile!"

I suspect that my cousin's nerves gave out seeing all the accusations against me melt away. But making this personal was a bad choice on his part. He of all people should have known not to do that. I also stood up and angrily said:

"Look who's talking about stink! That android is much cleaner than you! Even from here I can smell the piss on your clothes!"

That was, of course, a blow below the belt. All close

relatives knew that Keno had suffered from bedwetting as a child and that he was treated and operated on for a long time (this information was even included in his character notes, which is how I had come to know it). There were rumors that even now, if strongly upset, this forty-year-old man would involuntarily urinate in his pants. I, of course, had acted nastily by touching on such a delicate topic, however he started it.

"That is untrue!" shouted Keno.

"Dark Mother!" I demanded, stretching out my hand.

Everyone in the hall froze. If the Truth Seeker confirms these words... it would be the end of Keno ton Lavaelle's standing. Just imagine if this medical information, such a delicate topic for him, were to be officially confirmed. However, that time the old lady was in no hurry and turned to the Emperor.

"Keno ton Lavaelle, leave the hall and get your nasty clothes in order," said August, obviously having decided that that was the best way to avoid a quarrel and, if I really happened to be right, give Keno the chance to avoid bad publicity.

My cousin's cheeks were aglow from shame and anger; however, he stood up quietly and left. And I, it seemed, had made a mortal enemy for life.

"Let me explain my actions in any case, but without unnecessary emotions," I said calmly. "Half the ships in my fleet are Iseyek, and none of my people understand their language. I needed a translator very badly, and whether that was a human or a robot was of secondary importance. Now I'm even glad that I chose an android. As far as I know from the information in the guides, the Beta Iseyeks have strong psionic powers. I really would not like it to be possible for the insects to read the thoughts of a living translator like an open book."

"And your own thoughts, Georg?" wondered my sister, Violetta. "When Miya was with you, you were protected. But now?"

"Yes, you must find another Truth Seeker," said the Emperor, who then suddenly wondered. "And, by the way, *can* a strong psionic read an android's thoughts?"

The Dark Mother shrugged her shoulders.

"A weak one cannot, but a strong one... I do not know. To be honest, I have never tried."

"Alright, would anyone mind if we checked?" I asked in surprise, pointing at the head of the Green House. "I hope that Duke Kevin royl Olefir will not refuse us in this modest experiment?"

A few seconds of dead silence followed, after which there came a predictable, but highly negative reaction from all members of the Green House. I was accused of going insane, as well as being a boor and a gadfly; they even threatened to make me regret my impudence... But it was too late to stop me. I went around the table, walked right up to the Duke and placed my palm down on it.

"Honorable Duke Kevin Royl Olefir! If you would like to prove that you are not an android, I would ask you to take your bejeweled dagger, the symbol of your ancient power and nobility, and prick your palm with it. If it bleeds, I swear to you that neither I nor anyone else from the Orange House will hold any grievances against you whatsoever. I pray that you take your blade and do it."

Everyone around froze in anticipation of the Duke's reaction to such a flagrant provocation. Kevin royl Olefir took out his blade decisively, gave it a wave... and lowered his arm.

"You yourself know that I cannot do that..." said the old man fatalistically.

A system message appeared unexpectedly. Everyone present flinched in unison:

The Head of the Green House, Duke Kevin royl Olefir ton Lavaelle, has resigned.

The old man had long ago been led away by the guard, but the Emperor remained sitting with his head low and his hands covering his face. No one dared leave the room.

"How could he? How could he?!" repeated August royl Toll ton Akad again and again.

My sister Violetta moved her chair closer to mine and asked quietly:

"Have you known long?"

"No, I figured it out here at the meeting. I've been spending a lot of time in the last few days talking with my android, and I started noticing all kinds of minor tics that even robots have. For example, if a person turns their head one hundred times, every time it will be a bit different. An android does it the exact same way every one of the hundred times, down to the little details – as long as you don't specially ask it to mix it up a bit. The Duke was sniffling the same way every time, in imitation of a light cold. On the fifth or seventh time I was already pretty sure, but by the tenth time, I had no doubt. He was also massaging his sore hand with enviable regularity. If I hadn't been purposely monitoring an androids behavior before that, I never would have guessed."

"Georg, why did you sell your holding?" wondered my sister.

It made no sense to lie, so I admitted honestly:

"Where was I supposed to get money for all my ships? The three *Katanas* will become the core of my fleet, but their price tag is nowhere near cheap... All I could afford right off the bat was the down payment and, as it were, I'll be paying the remainder with the sale of Tialla."

"But didn't the Orange House help you buy ships?" suddenly wondered the Emperor, as I unexpectedly discovered that my private conversation with my sister was being heard by everyone in the room.

The head of the Orange House became very embarrassed at the question and quickly assured the Emperor that the Orange House would help Prince Georg and give him the money to purchase the three ships under construction.

"No need!" the Emperor suddenly declared decisively. "I will pay for the construction of the three *Katanas* for Crown Prince Georg from my personal funds. I am very satisfied with your work, Prince, and let this be my contribution to strengthening the defense of Sector Eight. My only wish – well, you might even call it an order – is that after the contract with the android is up, or as soon the necessity for it fades, the robot must be destroyed. It may have information in its memory bank that is too valuable to fall into the hands of a stranger. You do understand that, right Georg?"

I nodded in silence. The Emperor then, clearly satisfied with my pliability, wondered:

"Perhaps you have some other questions or wishes of me?"

I contemplated it for a second and said:

"Just one thing. I officially request to be removed from the list of Mystics!"

Everyone in the room gasped at once. Nevertheless, I continued, trying to speak firmly and decisively:

"My mission is to defend Sector Eight from any and all threats. And I cannot allow myself to lie around in a drugged-up dream for several days in a row, then spend another chunk of time waking back up. Yes, I am aware of the general opinion that it is impossible to recover from crystal addiction. But it was as a Mystic that I examined this path and realized that there still is a way out. Yes, it will be very difficult, but I will manage! I want you all to know that I have destroyed all doses of crystals on my ships and given an unambiguous order to my guards to immediately kill any person who tries to foist that drug on me."

"Crown Prince, give me your hand!" demanded the Dark Mother.

The old woman held my palm for an unexpectedly long time. For the first time, I even overheard some muffled echoes of her emotions, then she said delightedly:

"Prince, your faith that you will succeed is simply unsurpassable! I am even inclined to believe that this faith may overcome the unavoidable. A certain chance exists, though it will not be easy."

"Good, the request is approved!" proclaimed the Emperor.

Class change
New Class: Aristocrat

Global fame increase. Current value +6

Global standing increase. Current value -25

"It's good to be the Emperor," he said, as another player's numbers changed with great ease. The meeting was over, and everyone began leaving the hall. I wanted to speak with Violetta, but my sister was delayed by a conversation with the Green House Duke. So I went out into the hallway alone.

The two pea-pod brothers were waiting for me there. Keno was blocking my path:

"What, Georg, you think you've won? Not likely!"

Both of my relatives simultaneously rifled through the inner pockets of their clothes before producing two transparent boxes containing glowing spheres:

"How long has it been since you took crystals? You think you'll be able to refuse?"

I didn't have time to answer or react in any way to the provocation. A criss-cross flashing of blades came out of nowhere, leaving both Green House aristocrats collapsed on the stone floor, sliced down the middle by the frightening blows. Popori de Cacha carefully placed his bloodied blade before me and laid down on the floor, not trying to hide and accepting his fate.

The startled, but numerous guards spent another

second staring at the chameleon who had just murdered two members of Imperial upper aristocracy and then threw themselves on him from all sides. My consternation also passed, and I unexpectedly threw myself forward, covering the chameleon with my body:

"Stop! He was following my orders!"

I was shoved fairly unceremoniously on the floor, my arms were pushed behind my back, and I heard the clink of the handcuffs.

Atonement in Battle

M Y CELL WAS not very big. Just six-by-ten feet. Windows had not been provided for, and all the "conveniences" were right in front of me. The one special feature of this space was that it was completely isolated from the outside world – I could not send or receive game messages or call up guides or information; a large proportion of the game's functions were not working. I was only allowed to install a data reader to get the information from the Iseyek drive and a computer with no connection to the outside world for interpreting the information. So I spent two days in front of a screen, watching battle recordings and studying the aliens' errors.

I worked myself to the point of exhaustion, spending the minimum possible time on sleeping and eating. I had no choice if I didn't want to go insane or be overwhelmed by the innumerable questions swarming around in my head. Two players had been killed right before my eyes by a third player! Is that even possible?! Then what about when Mr. G.I. said that death was "nothing to be afraid of, you'll come back in the medical center." As far as I understood, neither Rigo nor Keno had respawned and both were finally and irrevocably dead in the game. This is a game, right?

I was mentally returned to my first day on the job. The arguments I had considered sufficient to call this world virtual – the popup messages, the ship maps and everything else – really could have just been the result of highly developed technology. Built-in identifiers in important individuals, a unified system of relations between governments, factions and the like that all races could understand. After all, it's a real hassle to meet someone you don't know – figuring out who this person is, and how you should interact with them, etc. But now, one look at the popup and it becomes clear immediately if someone is friend or foe.

I was called for interrogation four times while detained. I never met with the same investigators twice, and the Truth Seeker that accompanied them was also different each time. But it always went the same way: it was suggested that I admit that my bodyguard acted alone, because of some incomprehensible hatred he'd formed for the Green House. I was assured that, if I agreed to that version of the tragic events, I would be immediately declared totally innocent and released then and there. But in that case, Popori de Cacha would get the death penalty.

That deal wasn't good enough for me, and every time I gave the investigators the same example: Two idiots see a power transformer and read a warning sign: "Do not enter, you will die!!!" Furthermore, they understand well what an electric current is, and how dangerous it could be. Nevertheless, they neglect the rule, break open the transformer door and go inside; then, predictably, they die. Who is at fault in that situation? Is it the construction workers who installed the transformer? Or the scientists who discovered electric current? No – it is those two idiots who climbed inside a transformer, despite the obvious warning.

The investigators would admit that the two situations were obviously similar, then ask some questions of little merit and return me to the cell. I even formed the impression that all these interrogations were just a smokescreen and the real negotiations about my fate were being carried out on a different level altogether. I also had no doubt that I was being observed round-the-clock, and that fact would soon receive a clear confirmation.

My muscles began writhing. For some time, I consoled myself with the hope that it was just a spasm due to the cool air in the cell, but I would soon be forced to admit that it was another drug withdrawal episode. I didn't even have time to become very afraid before the doors opened and the prison doctor entered, implements at the ready. In truth, he was quite ham-handed and bruised up the whole crease of my elbow and wrist in his search of my deep veins before he was finally able to get the needle in, but his treatment didn't help right away. And it also confirmed that unseen observers were keeping a watch over me.

At the end of the second day of detainment, the doors to the chamber opened, letting an unexpected visitor in. It was Duke Paolo royl Anjer, head of the

Orange House. I moved over on the bed, offering my visitor a seat, but he did not accept. He took a disgusted look around my cell, pausing on the monitor on the wall. On it, as it were, the space battle was being played back at a very slowed-down speed.

"You can't seriously still find that interesting?" exclaimed the old Duke in surprise, pointing at the screen.

"Of course. It's the destruction of the Virho fleet in the Aysar cluster. It's the final phase of the battle. The battle has already been lost, individual Iseyek ships have survived and are trying to escape, but the chances aren't good. In the distance, the *Uukresh* is being brutalized. The carrier's powerful shields are down, practically all the mother ship's frigates have been destroyed, and the enemy is finishing up by taking down the utterly defeated giant. And here, look, the fleet commander, Admiral Ogesss Toosk, is abandoning his last remaining forces to rescue the *Uukresh*. There are four battleships, one of which he is on himself. Why? The admiral cannot understand that attack is hopeless and that all the battleships will be destroyed. He is fully capable of saving the four, very valuable battleships, but is openly sacrificing them in an attempt to save the *Uukresh*. You must agree, it is strange! The combat value of a carrier is about the same as four or five battleships, but it is undamaged and has a full set of frigates. What we see here is the burning skeleton of a mother ship, not representing even half of its value, and the Iseyeks have nowhere to fix it – all their docks are busy with other work. Take a look here, the enemy has totally refocused its attention on the recently-arrived battleships, and the *Uukresh* leaves the battle, saving itself at the very last moment. In a few minutes, the battleships will be destroyed one after the next, the Virho fleet – the main Swarm strike force – practically ceases to exist. Put yourself in the Iseyek admiral's place. What could be so valuable on the *Uukresh* that the admiral would sacrifice his best ships and even his own life? Your thoughts, Duke?"

The head of the Orange House thoughtfully stroked his aquiline nose:

"Except perhaps his own son and heir... But the Iseyek are insects. They basically don't have direct blood relationships."

"Yes, you are correct, Duke. They have communal egg clutches and three genders. They do not know their own children. So, the idea about the heir is no good. But what exactly was on the carrier, I do not know... However, Duke, you did not come here to listen to my theories. Has something changed in my situation?"

"Yes, you could say that. A half hour ago, I was with the Emperor. The moment, to be honest, wasn't the most appropriate... but it's all relative. Everyone really was not interested in talking about you, the whole court was going nuts – there has been an alien incursion in Sector Fourteen. Our enemy has captured a poorly defended warp beacon and cut off three distant allied kingdoms from the unified transport network. The Red House is planning a counter attack with the united forces of Sectors Fourteen and Thirteen. The Imperial space marshal has already supported the idea and promised support. As we speak, the military men are sitting in their seats having a meeting. The Emperor is also with them. When I snuck up there with your papers, August signed them without even looking, as long as it got me out of the way so he could go back to more important matters. But, nevertheless, the Emperor did say one thing about you: "At least that one does something useful, unlike most other princes. Release him, let him atone for his guilt in battle."

"So is my fleet to fly to Sector Fourteen and participate in the attack?" I clarified.

"No, that didn't come up. And also how would you even do that? It is forbidden for Great House military ships to enter the Imperial Core, and there is no other way of getting from Sector Eight to Sector Fourteen without going through it. And even if the Emperor gives his approval to your fleet's passage, the Red House will perceive Orange House ships appearing in their territory as aggression and a declaration of war. It is simply recommended that you get out of the Core as quickly as possible, return to your fleet and go about your business. In regards to August's words about 'atoning in battle,' do not take them literally. But if a situation should arise where you can do something notable in the Emperor's eyes, don't miss the chance. For example, try to solve the problem with the Brotherhood of the Stars. The Orange House is still blamed for the loss of these territories. It would be nice if we could extract the code to the pirate warp beacon from the captain you've detained. I don't know how, and I don't want to, but get that information out of him. Then we'll be able to call a general assembly and descend upon the pirates for a visit with all of the Orange House's forces!"

"Has my bodyguard also been released?" I clarified just in case, as Paolo royl Anjer and I were already walking down the prison hallway to the exit. The Duke answered in the affirmative:

"As I've said, the Emperor signed everything without paying special attention. They should be releasing the chameleon soon, and I told them to send him to my ship. So, pick up your servant and return as quickly as possible with him to your yacht and get out to Sector Eight. Once you're there, no one will be able to reach you. And I would strongly recommend that you not return to the Core systems without a particularly good reason. When the Green House finds out about this, they'll certainly file an appeal of your release, and you could be arrested again. It could be significantly more complicated to get you out a second time."

I thanked the Duke for his help and wanted to clarify all the details of my release, but the old man unexpectedly put his finger to his lips, saying that it wasn't a good idea to discuss this as there may be people listening in. But near the airlock doors, the head of the Orange House unexpectedly stopped and said, fairly deliberately, clearly and loudly, obviously wanting his words to be heard by all the microphones installed nearby:

"At the meeting with the Emperor, I promised to help you with the ships. And even though my help was not needed at that time, I have not forgotten my promise. My steward recently purchased new ships for defending the Orange House Capital: ten frigates and five destroyers. Right now it's all still packed up on a transport ship here on the Throne World.

Though there is no crew yet for the military ships, I think you'll find people. Crown Prince Georg, take all these military ships as aid from the Orange House, and keep the transport for yourself too. And maybe it's not cruisers this time, but this gift will also be of use to you."

The tricky devil! I didn't even know whether to be happy at the gift or indignant. The three heavy cruiser *Katanas* cost two hundred ten million credits. I deposited the thirty percent down payment from my money, and the head of the Orange House had promised to pay the rest in the presence of the Emperor. Though the Emperor personally covered the deficit that time, the Duke's promise, which he claims he "has not forgotten," amounted to one hundred fifty million credits – nowhere near the three and a half million or four in the best case, which is what the frigates I was being offered were worth. It seemed like quite the uneven exchange.

Nevertheless, I chose not to show my outrage or argue and thanked the head of the Orange House with a bow. The metal doors opened before us, and I saw Popori de Cacha. To put it lightly, the chameleon had seen better days. There were a multitude of burn marks on his soft skin, a scar from a collar or choker that had cut deep into his neck, and bruises and abrasions on his whole body. My bodyguard had obviously been tortured in an attempt to beat the desired confession out of him. The picture shocked the Duke, who was standing at my side.

"They had no right to treat an authorized representative of the Crown Prince like that! I will not let this go unpunished and will be filing a complaint."

"You have to file a complaint, Duke. But my bodyguard and I will try to be as far from here as possible at the time of its review."

I walked up to Popori de Cacha and hugged him. The chameleon noticeably flinched; apparently my touch was quite painful to his wounded body. Nevertheless, Popori de Cacha raised his head, trained both eyes on me and said, touched:

"My Prince! I never lost faith that you wouldn't abandon me!"

"You think I could have left you in the hands of these torturers?! And where would I find another bodyguard like you? So skillful, so loyal! Plus, you put up with all of my antics and whims!"

Standing change. Popori de Cacha's opinion of you has improved.
Presumed personal opinion of you: +47 (friendly)

Standing change. Chameleon race opinion of you has improved.
Chameleon race opinion of you: +3 (indifferent)

I replied by raising my opinion of him and hurried behind Duke Paolo royl Anjer, who was leaving without me. The Orange House leader's plane brought us in the blink of an eye to our space shuttle, which was already ready for liftoff from the planet surface. Someone was waiting for us next to the shuttle: an important-looking lizard in a bright red armored suit was standing surrounded by six bodyguards. When our ship set down, the whole group set off to meet us.

I looked quickly at the information to figure out what to expect from this meeting.

Pandedede de Rua, plenipotentiary ambassador to the Empire
  Race: Chameleon
  Gender: Genderless at present
  Class: Diplomat
  Achievements: None
  Fame: +4
  Standing: + 0
  Presumed personal opinion of you: +5 (warm)
  Chameleon race opinion of you: +3 (warm)

The ambassador was clearly seeking out a meeting with me, as he was waiting right next to my shuttle. But when he saw the head of the Orange House, he begged his forgiveness and approached the more senior figure in the court hierarchy. I have no idea what they talked about through an interpreter over there. A few times, their discussion began in raised tones, but then a system message popped up about a one-point improvement in Chameleon opinion of the Orange House, and the Duke answered in kind. Five minutes later, they were shaking hands, and the ambassador finally came to me.

"Crown Prince Georg royl Inoky, I am very glad to express my gratitude to you from the whole Ravaash nation, which you people, for some reason, insist on calling chameleons." Obviously that was some kind of joke, given that the ambassador went silent, waiting for my reaction.

Only after I smiled did the ambassador continue:

"The joy and sorrow of my nation is the rocky, lifeless terrain that covers almost the whole surface of the planet Sss. It is quite poorly suited for raising crops. Only in a few, not-very-large valleys on Sss is it possible to survive or grow food. They are surrounded on all sides by hundreds and even thousands of miles of nothing but radioactive rock faces. These severe conditions are a serious limit to the population of my species. There really aren't many chameleons – around forty thousand in total, a tenth of which are soldiers. And though our soldiers are strong and capable, the Ravaash nation understands that the first conflict we have with a strong spacefaring nation would quickly become our nation's last."

Here I fully supported the ambassador's opinion. When the Swarm carries out an operation, it has a huge star fleet and billions of soldiers for land-based battles, and the Empire is also capable of fielding an army and fleet no smaller. Without even wanting to, with neighbors like that, you start to gain an appreciation for peace.

"The joy of my race was that the cliffs and crevices of Sss were rich in heavy and rare metals, which are so very necessary for building starships. Because of this, we were able to offer something to people on first contact, and in return we got technology, vehicles, fertilizer, grain and even domesticated animals. All the same, we are not small, unintelligent tadpoles. We studied the history of human expansion in space as carefully as possible, and we figured out that such an impulsive race could decide one day that they no longer want to pay for resources when they can simply be taken by force."

"That is dead on!" I laughed back unhappily, also having studied the list of species made extinct by humanity in the process of its expansion through space.

"Yes, Prince Georg, no offense intended to you as a human, but humanity has gone to war with forty-eight species out of the fifty-two they've come across in space, and has made eighteen of them completely extinct. That's a scary statistic to my mind. So, the Ravaash nation has spent long decades putting as much effort as possible into not giving humanity a cause to consider us an enemy. At first, that was not difficult; people didn't take us seriously and sold – and sometimes even just gave us – quite valuable technologies. Perhaps, your species underestimated the abilities of our scientists, I do not know. All the same, after the Ravaash were able to figure out warp technologies and copy the star frigate specimens we did have, human opinion of us changed sharply. The epoch of repression began: for forty long years they stopped selling us weapons and new technologies, and people also de facto stopped buying rare metals from us. Our attempts to trade on our own were harshly intercepted by the Orange House. When you, Prince Georg, came to us on Sss with your companion Miya, the Ravaash nation perceived that visit as a sign of warming relations with the Orange House. It was the first time a member of Imperial upper aristocracy visited our homeworld. We greeted you with special honors and six of the best soldiers of our nation became your bodyguards. At that time, it seemed to be the right decision for us... And suddenly the murder of two relatives of the Emperor happened, and the murderer turned out to be a chameleon!"

The ambassador theatrically clutched at the left side of his chest with his upper appendages, symbolizing a heart flutter, which I involuntarily laughed at – chameleons don't have such an internal organ, I had read that in the encyclopedia.

"For two days the fate of my race hung by a thread, and only by your stubbornness and tireless effort were the accusations against Popori de Cacha cleared. The head of the Orange House has just promised me that the Orange House military fleet would soon be leaving the Sss star system. The Ravaash nation is extremely grateful to you, Prince Georg royl Inoky, and asks you to accept another six bodyguards of my race, just as expertly trained as the first six. I also ask you to include two Ravaash frigates in your fleet, which were such a thorn in the side of the Empire when they were first built. The crews of both starships are trained in human language, as are all members of my race that leave Sss."

I thanked the ambassador for the soldiers and ships he'd given me. Though I still thought to myself that the chameleon ships could become a burden to me. Two illegal copies, and probably not the highest quality at that, of Imperial frigates that were already antiquated a half century ago... Not the strongest ships in the fleet, to put it lightly. While, at the same time, losing either of the frigates would lead to the death of a quite noticeable proportion of all living soldiers of that extremely low-population species. I quickly calculated, using the Earth of the twentieth century as a model, that losing one frigate would be equivalent for the chameleons to the earthlings losing four million soldiers. Just one frigate, but the relative losses would be larger than those of Poland, France, the USA, the UK, Romania, Yugoslavia, Italy and Hungary put together over the whole course of World War II! So, I guess I'd have to keep the chameleon ships safe...

"My Prince, how glad I am to see you once again on board my shuttle!" cried Patrick toyl Sven, greeting me. "For two days all the news channels were only talking about you and the chameleon, slandering you with all their might. You probably can't wait to get off this hell-hole, right?"

"That is correct," I agreed, taking a seat in the chair and buckling right in. "Visiting the Throne World has left me with quite negative emotions and memories. I was expecting to be able to look over all the beautiful palaces unhurriedly, make appearances at fancy dinners with the upper nobility, and hold a bunch of negotiations... But instead of that, I spent the whole time either rushing, washing myself clean of false accusations, or sitting in a prison cell. Let's get off this inhospitable planet as quickly as possible!"

The shuttle lifted itself up off the surface gradually and evenly, after which it carefully began rising up through the atmosphere. I risked repeating the earlier bout of sea-sickness, but this flight passed exceptionally smoothly, so I didn't even need the paper sacks.

My arrival to *Queen of Sin* was met with enthusiastic screams. Members of my team greeted and congratulated me in every hallway. The staff officers were all standing at attention and giving military salutes as I walked by.

"Shall we return to Tesse?" offered Captain Oorast Pohl, as soon as the ovations had slightly quieted down.

"Yes, but on the way we will stop in the Nessi system. It is on our way, after all. The Orange House Space Military Academy is having its graduation ceremony there, and it would be nice to be able to take a look. Beyond that, a transport with ships and two chameleon frigates will be flying with us."

"I suppose you mean the two frigates that have been cutting circles around our yacht for the last three hours," chuckled Admiral Kiro Sabuto. "Those two museum pieces? I'm familiar with the story."

I asked him to tell it, as I was very interested in hearing the Orange House version. With great displeasure, the admiral began:

"The chameleons' system was discovered relatively recently, just eighty years ago. A scout ship reached the star system after a few years flight and immediately noted a small planet that was as radioactive as a nuclear reactor with its protective housing removed. A huge deposit of actinides and platinoids were detected there, whole mountains of tantalum strata and other rarities, so a warp beacon would have been placed in any case. In addition, a native civilization was discovered with a fairly high, if pre-space level of development."

Popori de Cacha was standing behind me. Due to the damage to his skin, he had temporarily lost the ability to camouflage himself. He added his comments to the admiral's story:

"Actually, our nation had already begun its first flights into orbit. The first artificial satellites had already been launched by the time the huge starship came to the Sss system."

The admiral nodded, not about to argue over such a minor point. He continued:

"After the story with the Iseyeks, which ended badly, people behaved as properly as possible with this newly discovered race. We installed a warp beacon and began trading with the chameleons, exchanging various vehicles and products for valuable ore. Almost immediately, our traders noticed that the chameleons wouldn't buy the same type of technology more than once; they would buy just one specimen, figure it out and then rivet up their own the exact same. We tried explaining to them that that isn't how it's done – you need to pay for patents, for licenses, for technology at the end of the day, but we could not find common ground on this issue. Apparently, in the culture and manner of thinking of the chameleons, there simply wasn't such a concept as a patent or invention..."

That time, Popori de Cacha nodded, in imitation of the admiral. No comments from his side followed, so Kiro Sabuto continued:

"For some time, we turned a blind eye to their theft of technology or at most tried to fine them, but the chameleons didn't pay even one fine for violating patents, so it still did no good. But one day they began reproducing technology on a very high level. At the station by the warp beacon, the chameleons collected two copies of *Tusk* frigates, one of which they got practically at cost. Of course, *Tusk* frigates are very antiquated, but in any case they are military starships, capable of navigating the warp beacon system to reach any part of the known Universe! There's a ton of technologies, patents, and active exclusive licenses from various corporations that the chameleons made theirs for free just like that! A trial was held that reached the verdict that the Chameleon race should pay a hefty fine for damages. All Chameleon accounts were frozen until the debts were paid, Orange House trade with them stopped, and attempts by the chameleons to trade ore in circumvention of the Orange House were intercepted. The ships were confiscated together with their cargo, no questions asked. And here we are now with the situation fossilized. The interest and penalties over these years have run up so high that we could practically take the whole planet but, as before, the Chameleons do not recognize the debt's existence on principle."

Popori de Cacha shuddered and, looking at the admiral with both eyes, asked:

"For what do the greedy human corporations want to force the Ravaash nation to pay? For the fact that our mechanics were smart and understood how this or that mechanism worked? Or for the fact that our scientists made the right choice and learned something? That is, would a stupid race have been able to make use of it without paying? Then those are bad, incorrect laws, as they promote stupidity. They contradict common sense."

How nice it was to finally return home! I spread my arms and crashed down back-first on the soft bed in the second, small bedroom. I usually preferred the large bedroom, but today I decided to mix it up and visit the usually unused cabins on the huge yacht. I took a look around. It turns out this room is pretty swanky too! Rosewood furniture, some stone flowers or corals, a picture of God-knows-what on the wall, and a statue of a girl, which, on the opposite end of the spectrum, was quite unambiguous and erotic.

"My Prince, will you allow me to enter?" The old doctor, Nicosid Brandt shyly peeked in through the doors, not wanting to spoil my rest after exercise in the pool.

"Come in, of course! Unscheduled medical examination, is it?" I laughed.

"You could say so, my Prince. I have spent several days in contemplation and experiments, creating a rehabilitation plan to get you off crystals for good. And I wanted to familiarize your Highness with my conclusions."

The wizened doctor sat down carefully on the edge of the bed and showed me a screen with a bunch of graphs. Not standing up, I asked the doctor:

"Could you tell me what it says, in brief? It's just that I spent the last two days staring at a screen and I'm not in the mood to take in any complex information right now."

"If you want it in brief, chemical traces of crystals remain in the body for a very long time, around three years. The blood vessels, the liver and the brain must all be cleansed. I have developed an intensive purge program: physical exercise, vitamin mixes, pills. In order to avoid having to use a needle regularly, I recommend that you inject these nanobots, which will cut the attacks off at the beginning by injecting the chemicals you need into the blood. Two capsules two millimeters long in each shoulder, and you can forget about withdrawal for half a year before having to change them out again."

"Sounds good!" I filled with joy. "When can you make these capsules?"

"My Prince, they are ready now. I just wanted to get your permission and warn you about the side effects. There's one important thing: if a person has these capsules implanted in their body, taking crystals will lead to two mutually exclusive processes beginning in the body, which can end in a fatal conclusion."

"That is serious..." I agreed. "But my decision is firm, so let's do it. Implant your nanobot capsules!"

The doctor opened a plain case and laid his implements out on a tray. He rolled up my sleeves above the elbow and got a blue, flat flashlight and shined it from my hand to my shoulder.

"You've got deep veins, your Highness, it's always a challenge to find them. Oof, they really beat up your arm, it's all bruised... Wait up, what's that?"

The doctor picked up a pair of glasses with customizable spinning lenses and spent a long time looking over my needle-wracked arm.

"My Prince, three microcapsules have been implanted in your right arm. They weren't there before..."

"It was that doctor in the prison hospital," I said, instantly figuring it out. "I thought he was just inexperienced, given how long he dug around in there, but it turns out he was implanting spying devices while treating me! Remove them immediately!"

Nicosid Brandt put on a mask, injected me with painkillers and reached for the scalpel. In a few minutes, on the tray before me, there were three tiny metal balls rolling around, each half the size of a matchstick.

"Done, my Prince. But capsules like that can still present a threat even outside the body."

"Popori de Cacha, crush all three capsules in a vice and throw the remains in the trash incinerator!"

When the doctor and leader of the team of chameleons had left the room, I poured myself a splash of hard liquor from a bottle I found behind the bar and lost myself in thought. Who needed to attach a leash to me in the form of unnoticeable implanted capsules? The Emperor? That was hardly believable. Such a powerful figure wouldn't have to act in secret. But then who? Whose toes have I stepped on, or who have I frightened with my independent behavior?

An alert signal interrupted my thinking. The communications officer said:

"Incoming video call from the Kingdom of Fastel, Princess Marta royl Valesy. Will you accept?"

I thoughtfully swished the snifter of strong brandy in my hand. I had absolutely no desire to talk to Marta now and hear another stream of abuse and accusations.

"Tell my wife that I'm busy. Say that I'm on a mission from the head of the Orange House to meet Princess Astra royl Kant ton Veyerde. If Marta really needs me, she can call back in a half hour."

I finished the very fine drink and placed the empty snifter back on the table. The malignant smile wouldn't leave my face. I would have paid a million credits just to see my former wife's face. She was probably looking up information on the character I told her I was meeting, reading carefully and looking at the portrait of a young, doll-faced girl. Then she'd read it again and look in the mirror... Let her compare two princesses and consider how irresistible she really is in my eyes for me to have to bear her scolding and threats every five minutes.

I had found the pretty face of the unmarried princess by complete coincidence while looking over the stellar transportation map and studying the states that control this or that corner in the warp beacon network. The Kingdom of Veyerde was not in Sector Eight but was a vassal of the Orange House, so let Marta think up a reason for my interest in the young Princess on her own.

In exactly half an hour, Marta sent another videochat invitation, but that time I accepted it.

"Georg, what is it, are you drunk? Or have you lost the last remnant of your brain?" as usual, my scandal-loving ex-wife opened with a shrieking, hysterical tone.

"It's actually the other way around, Marta. For the first time in so many years of drunkenness, I've finally sobered up. I take my affairs and fate seriously now, after receiving full approval from the Emperor for any, even less popular steps I've made..."

"How can you allow yourself to behave this way with me?" interjected Marta. "You've already been deprived of Tialla, and now it depends on me alone whether you'll walk this world with your hand outstretched or not."

"You think so?" I laughed. "Then let me make you

really sad, Marta. I no longer have a need for your financial backing. And without the ships of your fleet, I will also manage just fine. So you can keep your blackmail to yourself. The times have changed. You just haven't figured it out yet."

"The Kingdom of Veyerde?" asked Marta, and I understood that I had predicted her behavior quite accurately. "It isn't as rich as mine. And that girl Astra is already engaged, too."

"I don't know what you're talking about and I don't want to. But by the way, the Kingdom of Veyerde is a vassal of the Orange House and will do whatever Duke Paolo royl Anjer orders. So, please, send the divorce papers as soon as possible. There's no hope left. Stop dragging your feet."

"Well, now things have changed! I'll never do it now! You'll come back on your knees begging for me to sign!" Marta revealed her inconsistency at its finest. First she blackmailed me with divorce, and when I suddenly turned out not to be opposed, she sharply changed her point of view.

"Well, whatever. If that's all, I'm hanging up..."

"No, wait!" Marta hurried to scream out this sentence so as not to lose the chance. "You've changed a lot, Georg; I don't recognize you anymore. Tell me honestly, what's happened?"

"Marta, after all your streams of curses, threats, blackmail and unfriendly actions, give me just one reason why I should be honest with you. Give me just one reason why I should be with you at all!"

She answered with silence, and I, with clean conscience, hung up.

* * *

"I haven't been able to reach you for two days now. Miya and I were starting to get worried something had happened. What can you tell me? Did you have to make a report before the Emperor?" Mr. G.I. appeared in my dream quite tactlessly, interrupting a cheerful vision of summer, the beach, grilling, and friends.

"It's not surprising you couldn't reach me. I spent two days in a prison cell in the Throne World in full isolation."

"Come now, it can't have gone that bad with the report on the condition of the fleet?!" I picked up on clearly panicked notes in his voice.

"The report couldn't have gone better. All Green House accusations have been cleared up, and you got full approval from the Emperor. August royl Toll even personally gave me a hundred fifty million credits for buying new ships for the fleet. But then, after the meeting, it got worse – Popori de Cacha killed Keno and Rigo Lavaelle."

"Yes, I know them. Those twin brothers always infuriated me with their chicanery, so it serves them right. But who is Popori de Cacha?" wondered Georgiy.

I took a deep sigh, struck by how weak the Prince's knowledge of his own servants was.

"That is your personal chameleon bodyguard. You should be ashamed not to know!"

"What, I have to memorize the names of all my servants now?! I asked the chameleons not to show up so they wouldn't annoy me all the time. How'd it end then?"

"Well, to put it very briefly, in the end you were

released with a stern wag of the finger and a demand to occupy yourself with fleet matters and not get involved in politics. The only thing is that the Green House has included you in the list of criminal elements subject to termination if present in their territory."

Mr. G.I. started laughing:

"Not a huge loss. I didn't have any plans to mess around in Sectors Four or Five anyway."

I did not join him in rejoicing and demanded strictly:

"So now, explain to me how it happened that two players died, though you claimed that death was nothing to be afraid of."

Georgiy objected after a short pause:

"I didn't tell you that death is never something to be afraid of. It's just that if there is a chance of survival, the player will always survive and be patched up in the medical center. If not, that's all, game over, create a new character and load up the game afresh. So, protect my body, it's in our shared interest!"

I was awoken by the smell of coffee. Not having opened my eyes yet, I was already imagining a mug of the aromatic, hot beverage on the table next to my bed. I opened my eyes and began beaming an idiotic smile. My dream had come true!

"Good morning, master!" Bionica, in her best dress, was placing a sugar bowl and a dish of crispy sweet rolls on the table.

"And good morning to you. Hot coffee in bed was a great idea!"

The robot straightened up and said:

"The ground and roasted nuts of the firo tree from planet Anbach-VI are called coffee. I will learn it. That word wasn't in any of the dictionaries downloaded to my memory. Coffee." Bionica repeated the word again, clearly trying to memorize the new term.

After trying the coffee, I could barely hide my disappointment. It wasn't coffee. The smell was the same, but the taste was closer to hot dry-fruit compote. Nevertheless, I thanked the android for the gesture. Bionica smiled:

"I thought about it for a long time. I wasn't prepared to make a choice. On one hand, masters usually have a positive reaction to breakfast in bed. They like being greeted in the morning and brought a light breakfast. No one was doing this for your Highness, and I could take that role on myself. On the other hand, people don't like when someone comes into their personal space without asking, and the bedroom is generally considered one of those 'personal spaces.' I couldn't decide how to act, but then I considered it important to tell your Highness two pieces of news. First, over the last few days I have completely memorized all terms from the star fleet dictionaries and found their translations to the languages of the Iseyek and chameleons. Now I'm completely ready to work as an interpreter for the fleet commander. Second, an unknown employer has paid in advance for the year-long contract that comes into force after my service to your Highness has finished."

I instantly remembered the Emperor's unambiguous order and grew sad.

"Bionica, your new contract doesn't have a very good chance of coming into effect. There's some news that's important to you as well..."

The android listened as I told her the news about the Emperor's order and, for her part, she maintained her imperturbable exterior.

"Don't be upset, master. I figured out right away that my contract with the Crown Prince would be ending in exactly this way. Do not worry, I'll carry out my duties right up until the very last second of the contract."

"Look at you, a walking hunk of metal... I asked you to turn up your humanity setting to maximum! It can't be that hard to make a sad face, can it? I'm getting the impression that saving your life is more important to me than it is to you! The Emperor ordered it 'on completion of contract,' but didn't give any limits to the length of the contract. Can I extend your employment contract by a few years right now?"

"Of course you can. The maximum possible initial employment period for an android is twenty five years. It can be extended thereafter an unlimited number of times."

"So then, why is this an issue? I gave you the right to take care of day-to-day matters in my name. Extend your own contract by twenty-five years."

Bionica smiled in gratitude, then spoiled the whole impression given by her pretty, human smile when she declared in a lifeless, totally mechanical voice:

"My Prince, due to programmed-in restrictions, I am required to inform my master about important changes in the conditions. The price of my year-long contract next year is one hundred seventy thousand credits, and I do not have the right to charge your Highness any less."

A not-safe-for-work reply ripped itself from my lips. Someone really, really wants to buy Bionica after her service with Prince Georg. One hundred seventy thousand credits! That's just unthinkably expensive for a contract with an android. That means the client isn't so much interested in the android itself, as much as the information in its memory banks.

"I accept. Pay the twenty-five-year contract at that price before they get it up any higher. Bionica, you are now the richest android translator in the Universe!"

Bionica became clearly embarrassed:

"The majority of the money goes to the company that manufactured me. I will personally only get eleven percent. And that's good. A few years back it was just four percent, barely enough for clothes. My Prince, the contract has been paid. Four million eighty thousand credits have been transferred from your account. Remaining account balance: two million credits. And I simply don't' have the words to describe my feelings! No human has ever done anything like that for an android. My thankfulness to you is simply running over. I'll put all my effort forward so your Highness will not regret this decision!"

THE BROTHERHOOD OF
THE STARS

"**T**HERE IT IS, the Orange House Space Military Academy!" the shuttle approached the huge, many-mile-long, ring-shaped space station, and Patrick toyl Sven quite carelessly veered the shuttle to the right so as to fit between two tall spires.

"No need to hurry, we have plenty of time before the ceremony begins!" After the landing on the Throne World, I was already dealing with flight much better but still didn't like sharp maneuvers.

The shuttle slid into the outstretched robotic arm and stopped at the airlock, marked with lights, which allowed a magnetic arm to pick us up and pull our ship into the station. The headmaster of the Space Military Academy met me right as I got off. The old, important-looking, mustached man had come out personally to meet his important guest.

"Crown Prince Georg royl Inoky ton Mesfelle, it fills me with joy to have the honor of welcoming such a highly placed guest to our academic institution. The graduates are already gathering in the large hall. As I understood from your message, you'd like to give them a speech?"

"That's right. Today, your fledglings will leave the nest and choose from among many employers' offers that which is most to their taste. At the end of your official part, immediately before the right of choosing, I'd like to give a little speech."

"Prince Georg, in that case, you'll have to wait almost an hour and a half..." said the headmaster, somewhat upset.

"No matter, I'll wait in the stands. Do you think I could get the personal records of the most capable graduates to familiarize myself with?"

The headmaster grew embarrassed. Clearly that wasn't something they were supposed to do, but still he gave his permission. I went up into the box for important guests and looked over the perfect rectangles of lined-up graduates. Two thousand young people, who today will become full-fledged pilots, navigators, tacticians... Teachers and leaders of the Academy said various things on their many years of difficult work, about their pride for the new class, about the big world opening up before the graduates, and all the while I waited patiently, looking through personal records, selectively noting the candidates with the best perspectives. Finally, the Academy headmaster announced that a member of the Orange House of the Empire, Crown Prince Georg royl Inoky ton Mesfelle, would be saying a few words.

I noted to myself that a few of the graduates, having grown bored over the hour-and-a-half-long ceremony suddenly jumped back to life. Obviously, they don't see members of Imperial upper aristocracy very often. It might have even been their first time. I stood and saw myself on the big screen – a dark-blue, severe uniform with green epaulets, a proud profile and a strong gaze. A true fleet commander!

"Graduates, I have looked over the job offers and vacancies sent by potential employers on the occasion of your graduation. It should be said that I am quite disenchanted. What most of them need are good-looking boys for transporting decrepit old ladies on their trips through the galaxy; pretty, uninhibited girls for rich millionaires; and guards for corporation transports. If any of you has sought out such a fate for yourself, you can go; I don't need such graduates. My words are intended only for those of you who remember why the Imperial Combat Fleet exists in the first place!"

No one stirred or left the fastidiously-arranged rows. I waited a few seconds and continued:

"Just a few days ago, a diplomat of an allied race complained to me that humanity cuts its path through the Universe like a bushwhacker, relying on strength and destroying the weak. And yes, we really have gone to war with forty-eight races and completely wiped out eighteen of them. All of them were our enemies, and eliminating them cleared the path for the more capable and strong in the future. But now, for the first time in millennia, our race has come across those who are stronger than us and want to cross us out of the future! I'm talking about the aliens.

Don't believe the reports of victory. Yes, the Red

House recently was able to take down a couple of enemy destroyers in Sector Fourteen, but they lost more than seventy combat ships in doing so. All the news channels reported the battle as a victory, but left out the fact that the emergency evacuation of residents of remote systems has begun. The Orange House battle at the Vorta beacon was also reported as a victory, as were other skirmishes with the aliens. But every one of those times they hushed up the fact of how high a price humanity paid for these victories. At present, we lose around thirty to fifty military ships to destroy just one alien ship. That's the truth they aren't telling you. And just seven days' flight from here, there's an alien fleet of tens of thousands of starships ready to invade, and that's also the truth! There has never been such a real threat of total annihilation hanging over our race, and that is the pure, horrifying truth!

One could justly note that, as they say, if we destroy the warp beacons, the enemy starships would take years or even decades to arrive at our planets. Yes, that's true. But by doing that, we aren't changing our fate, but just drawing out the inevitable. Sooner or later, the enemy will still reach the Orange House Capital, the Nessi system, the Throne World and, ultimately, all star systems under human control. No, we need to fight now, delay our enemy's arrival while studying them and finding their weak points. The skeleton of a fleet is coming together right now. It uses new techniques and nonstandard battle tactics, specially developed to be used against alien ships. That fleet is being formed with the goal not of simply dying a hero's death in encounters with the aliens but of winning. I am the commander of that fleet! I need young, talented captains and officers with open-minded outlooks, who are able to learn new things and quickly take on the spirit of the victor. Ships will be found for them: cruisers and destroyers and frigates. Everything necessary to survival we will teach. Enemies for testing your abilities will also be found. Now it is up to you to decide if you are truly capable of becoming part of a newly forming force, or if you'd rather take a more relaxed position."

"My Prince, we've received six official complaints about your behavior in Nessi from various Orange House corporations," said the communications officer. "For the first time in many years, the corporations were not able to fill all their vacancies with Academy graduates."

"Don't react to them," I said, brushing it aside. "War is coming, and we hired crews for all our ships. That's what matters. We have no choice but to turn our backs on their grumbling."

The fleet was training intensively for the second day. The frigates were perfecting their group combat techniques. Five heavy cruisers were learning to spider tank and experimentally figuring out how long you could survive in such a cluster. I was preparing to interrogate the detained captain of the pirate ship and was a bit nervous.

The investigator who began the work with the detainee had already told me that they had discovered a brain block installed in the Brotherhood of the Stars captain; any attempt to give him drugs or truth serums, as well as any strong physical pain, would cause the pirate captain to die before giving up the valuable information. The only way to get the information from him would be with his consent to work together.

So, we had to act carefully. I had especially insisted that the pirate captain be blindfolded during my landing on the yacht. There was absolutely no reason to demonstrate my fleet's composition to an enemy that was still near the station. I was trying to play off that actually, hoping they'd still think we had a weak fleet.

"My Prince, he is ready for interrogation," said Popori de Cacha, letting me into the prison cell on the yacht where he had been placed two days earlier.

The middle-aged pirate captain, Velesh ton Rayf, was sitting on a chair with his arms bound behind his back. His legs were left free, clearly the chameleons didn't consider this prisoner too dangerous.

"Oh, finally it's the master of these knaves! I'd grown sick of waiting!" came the pirate, greeting me derisively.

"I was hoping that I wouldn't have to solve this issue personally. But now that there is no other way, I'll be brief, as I find it unpleasant to be in the same room with a criminal." I was trying to demonstrate haughtiness and contempt with all my might. "I need the coordinates of the Hnelle warp beacon. I'm prepared to take them, whether it be the nice way or the not-nice way. In the first case, you'll get a million credits, a new identity and be released to the four winds, alive and unharmed. In the second, I'll wait for the Truth Seeker, and she will try to get the information out of you regardless of the psionic block. The chance of finding the truth is quite high, but you will die. Have I explained myself clearly?"

"Clear as day," agreed Velesh. "But why do you want the beacon coordinates? The station there is very well protected, and there is a defense fleet as well. What if I lead your fleet there and you can't capture the station? I'd become a traitor in the eyes of my friends and still wouldn't get any reward."

"Alright, you'll get the money transfer as soon as my ships arrive to Hnelle, regardless of how this plays out. If my fleet wins, you'll get another million. And now tell me: what should I be expecting there?"

The captain kept quiet for a while, then answered nevertheless:

"You've got a way with negotiations, Prince Georg. I'll tell you, even if it is to my detriment. In the Hnelle system there is the defense fleet – two cruisers, one of which heavy, and three destroyers. With your fleet, you'll have to sweat to take them down."

I pretended to mull it over for a long time. Then I said decisively:

"I have no choice. After the debacle at the Vorta beacon, I need to rehabilitate myself in the Emperor's eyes, so I am prepared to risk it. Plus, your captured cruiser has become part of my fleet, so we have enough forces to win, even if it won't be easy. How can I get the beacon coordinates?"

"Prince, near the captain's console to the right there is a metal box with a lid. You need to lift up the plastic cover from the keyboard, press 1 and 6, then wait for an answer. In reply, there will be a brief period when the beacon will be turned on. Before doing that, you need to be in starting position, ready for a jump. And as soon as the beacon is activated, don't blink, jump right away."

I walked out of the room with the prisoners and went into the next one over. The little girl with blue eyes was sitting on the floor, drawing flowers and butterflies with colored pencils on a sheet of paper.

"Millena, did you hear our conversation?"

"Yes, of course. He was lying. There aren't two cruisers in the Brotherhood of the Stars fleet, there are four. And they're all heavy. Signal 16 is the code for 'My ship has been captured but can be recovered. Prepare for an engagement.'"

"Thank you. You can go back to Roben now. The shuttle will take you to my brother's flying palace. As soon as Roben comes to, thank him from me."

Roben had grown angry with me and had been drinking heavily for three days already. I was not expecting that the *Uukresh*'s arrival would cause such a stormy reaction from my older brother.

"Six hundred twenty million! You've gone bonkers, little brother! You have no conscience!" Those were the very words that the sovereign of Tesse had used upon receiving the bill presented to him for payment.

He paid the bill but demonstrated his dissatisfaction with his whole appearance. Then he went on a bender, put all his affairs on autopilot and stopped answering calls. I'd had to negotiate with the little Truth Seeker on my own. The child did not object and immediately agreed to help in the conversation with the pirate captain.

* * *

"Prepare for warp in three minutes!" Admiral Kiro Sabuto announced to the whole fleet.

The ships were already picking up speed and drifting toward the far-off, barely visible star. My palms started to sweat from trembling, and I tried to dry them on my pants in a way that no one would notice. It was noticed, though, by the derisive gaze of the android. Yes, Bionica was in the headquarters today too, sitting in the seat next to me. Not all officers responded positively to the robot's being stationed in the fleet's holiest of holies. I heard dissatisfied whispers, but no one expressed themselves out loud.

I turned on the microphone:

"One minute! Be prepared to receive the signal!" I reminded all the captains to set the jump to pre-warp twelve hundred miles away from the beacon. The last thing we needed was more surprises, like mine fields.

Bionica, sitting next to me, chirped out a long tirade of squeaks and creaks, repeating my words to the Iseyeks. One after the next, the ships confirmed that they were ready to receive the coordinates.

"Ten seconds. Nine. Eight. Seven."

Tensions mounted.

"We've got a signal! New beacon!" cried three or four officers at once, scanning the cosmos.

"All ships warp to the coordinates!" I yelled at full-throat.

"Een-teesaka-teero-leesss!" shrieked the android next to me.

A tunnel opened, and space darkened as usual. It

worked!

"Four hours to warp tunnel exit!" said Captain Clay ton Avelle, former first assistant to Oorast Pohl.

Oorast Pohl had accepted my offer to become captain of *Joan the Fatty*. The former pirate heavy cruiser had become the most terrifying unit in my fleet after modernization, and I was planning to transfer my headquarters there as soon as possible. Doing that quickly, before the beginning of the operation, had upset the bureaucratic inertia. While they were registering the new name for the ship in the Orange House register, they got its friend-foe codes. While they were filing for the captain's transfer, and hiring officers and assistants, the time for combat operations to begin had already come.

"Now let's just hope that the rest of our ships were able to come after us. I wouldn't like to race up to a fleet of enemies on nothing but an unarmed yacht," grumbled Admiral Sabuto.

"Dad, when are we gonna fight the pirates?" rang out Lika's voice from behind me.

I turned around very slowly.

"Likanna, how did you get on the ship?"

My daughter lowered her eyes to the floor.

"The young Crown Princess arrived fifteen minutes ago on a shuttle," said one of the officers.

"So, everyone knew, but no one had enough smarts to guess that an eleven-year-old girl has absolutely no business on a ship on its way to a battle?" I asked sternly, looking all around.

The officers and even the admiral looked away guiltily. My daughter hurried to interfere, going on the offensive:

"Dad, how could you? I haven't seen you for eight days! You came back to Tesse and didn't even take a peek at me in the castle, but I really wanted to see you! Obviously, I missed you, so I flew to see you myself. Your people actually didn't want to let me in to the dock, but who can stop a Crown Princess?! I ordered it, and they let me through."

"Alright, Lika, for the next three and a half hours, I'm all yours. But after that, you're gonna spend the next half hour sitting in a space suit in a rescue shuttle, and you're not gonna leave without my permission. Got it? If you're a good girl, I'll let you name one of the *Katanas* under construction."

"Two *Katanas*, and you've got a deal. Just promise you won't change the names. *Joan the Fatty* just isn't as offensive as the name I gave you, 'Big Fat Joan.'"

"Alright. Everyone else gathered here, I order to take a three-hour leave."

When my daughter and I had left the headquarters, Lika whispered:

"Dad, have you noticed that all the girls in your headquarters have started wearing make-up? They used to sit, gray and timid, and now they've suddenly decided to take a liking to one of the men. It isn't you, is it?"

"You see it too!" I laughed.

"And who's that cute blonde you've got sitting next to you?" Likanna wouldn't drop it.

"That is an android translator to the language of the praying mantises."

"Well, that's no fun," said my daughter, puffing out her lips. "What am I supposed to gossip about later with my friends? What can I tell them? It was supposed to be like an adventure – fighting the pirates, but now I have to sit the whole battle out in a shuttle."

"Tell them about your palace on Tesse," I offered, but Lika could only sigh sadly.

"On Tesse there... I don't even know how to say it. It's uncomfortable or something. There's an atmosphere of general fear. The main news on the planet is like: 'how's the heir's health, it hasn't gotten worse, has it?' Did you know that Roben's son survived a clinical death four days ago? The doctors just barely saved him, and it's not the first time either... Aunt Verena only lives through her son; she doesn't even want to see anyone else. Uncle Roben is also really worried. Every day he drinks himself to a blackout because he isn't strong enough to bear all that fear..."

I pondered for a second. It wasn't due to the cost of remodeling the *Uukresh* that my brother was so worried – what was six hundred million credits to him? The reason was something else entirely. It's too bad Roben didn't tell me that. And what a good guy I am! Three days I spent on Tesse, and I didn't even take a peek at the local news...

As we left warp, all the staff officers exhaled in concert and a flurry of curse words burst forth. The Truth Seeker had not been wrong. The enemy really did have four cruisers, and all four were heavy assault *Flambergs*. But the little girl had left one thing out: in addition to the heavy cruisers, there were three

Surgeon-class destroyers, specialized in recharging the shields of the heavy ships and ninety (!!!) frigates, half *Pyros* and half *Tusks*.

There was good news too. All our ships had made it out of warp.

"There are multiple targets. Five hundred miles to the enemy," came Nicole Savoia, slightly distracted by the commotion. For some reason, I just noticed that she was, in fact, wearing lipstick.

"Alright, good. Let's get to work." I hurried to take the helm of the fleet so the soldiers could hear their commander's confident voice and get the butterflies out of their stomachs. "You know the drill. *Pyro-1*: first receiver, *Pyro-2*: second receiver. Heavies will form the forward group. Keep an eye on your distance. Destroyers and light cruisers, take position twenty miles behind the heavies, hang out toward the third planet. *Tria*, fly out four hundred miles away from us, also in the direction of the third planet. *Safas* and *Tusks*, hold by the *Tria* for now. Other frigates, hold on, just don't stay in one place, take free orbits around *Queen of Sin*."

Meanwhile, a verbal sparring match was under way on the public channels. Quick-witted soldiers from both sides were facing off in a battle of rhetoric. Yes, I know that soldiers like to get their two cents in before a battle – their nerves are acting up. But I was always a supporter of discipline in the fleet, and now I was hurrying to put an end to this nonsense:

"So, this order applies to all my officers. If you want to gab, go to the encrypted fleet channel. But you don't talk to your food. Weren't you taught that as children?"

The battle began somehow suddenly. A cluster of enemy ships began reducing the distance between us at breakneck speed.

"Anti-support, keep your guards up! Let them get wrapped up in the heavies, but if they come any closer, cut them the hell down! Work together in groups of no less than four or five, concentrating on one target. I don't have any need for damaged ships, so go for the sure shot and don't scare off our booty. Heavies, target the *Surgeon*. I've marked it on the map. Do not fire before my command! On the count of three. One, two, three!"

The far-off destroyer was replaced with the bright fire of an explosion, which instantly faded to black. I gave some new orders, having finally settled into the new atmosphere:

"The next *Surgeon* we see is the primary target. The one after that is the secondary. Shoot only on my command. One, two, three! Anti-support, take those animals down now! Don't let them escape! Great! *Safa-4*, what are you doing? You're supposed to be next to the *Tria*! Brainless spider, where do you think you're going?! Go to hell!!!"

The Iseyek frigate decided to help the pinned-down *Joan the Fatty* for some reason and didn't survive even a few seconds.

I commented on that moment with relish, so much so that Bionica, sitting next to me translating, demonstrated outwardly that androids can also blush.

"We can't hold *Fatty*! Its shields are going down faster than we can recharge them!" rang out Oorast Pohl's calm voice, as if it wasn't his ship he was talking about.

"Understood, hold on! All heavies, fire on the marked cruiser. Its name is *Happy Sloth*. *Pyros*, to the first receiver! We can't let *Sloth* escape alive! Anti-support, don't sleep, cut down those frigates around *Fatty*. *Warhawks-1, 2,* and *3,* get those enemy drones off our light cruisers. Electronic fighters, come the hell on! You've got six ships! Take *Corpse Sword* out of the battle already! *Warhawk-4,* your mission is to take down the last *Surgeon* before it gets away."

"*Fatty* is in the weeds! Shields at twenty percent!" Notes of nervousness had appeared in Oorast Pohl's voice.

"It'll get easier from here on out. *Queen of Sin,* warp to zero to *Fatty*!"

Some of the officers sitting next to me gasped. But I knew what I was doing. The shields on my yacht were strong, almost as strong as a heavy cruiser's. Let the enemy go after this valuable target and give the cruiser a break.

The ship jerked forward into the very thick of the battle.

"A warp disruptor has been placed on us! Two even! Three! And two stasis webs!" said Captain Clay ton Avelle with obvious interest in his voice, as if he was just curious whether his yacht would make it out alive or not.

I felt the ship give a jolt. One of the enemy cruisers unloaded its cannons on *Queen of Sin*. After that, a bright flash lit up the screen, even the light filters suddenly kicking in didn't help, and I was blinded for a couple of seconds.

"*Happy Sloth*'s reactor blew up," commented Nicole.

"Great! Focus all heavies on *Corpse Sword*! *Pyros*, the enemy support ships have been decimated and are fleeing, so all three cruisers take point on the battlefield. None of them can be allowed to escape. *Warhawk-4*, what the hell are you doing sleeping? Why isn't the *Surgeon* under the disruptor and web yet? I'm giving you thirty seconds to catch it! I'll cut off your balls myself if he gets away!"

"Commander, I'm afraid I'm a girl..." came the captain of *Warhawk-4*, correcting me with reproach.

"Oh, yeah? Well, I don't give a crap about your personal issues! You've got twenty-five seconds to catch the *Surgeon*! *Safas* and *Tusks*, prepare to warp to *Warhawk-4*!"

"The *Surgeon* has been captured," reported the captain of *Warhawk-4*.

"That's more like it. See? You *can* do it when you want to! *Safas* and *Tusks*, warp to the *Surgeon*. Maul that cowardly beast!"

"*Corpse Sword* is ready!" reported Oorast Pohl. "*Fatty*'s shields are recharging, already up to thirty-five percent."

"Great! All heavies, focus on *Hunchback's Heir*. Anti-support, move out and wipe up the rest of the frigates. *Warhawks* from one to four, cut speed, exit to near orbit around the cruisers and hold them down."

I relaxed slightly. The battle had clearly moved into the final phase. All that was left was to catch the last few enemies, who were flying off in all directions. And here... a big group of enemy frigates warped simultaneously to my first receiver! How? Where'd they get the jump coordinates?! I was the first to figure out what was happening.

"*Pyro-1*, warp immediately to heavies!!! Get out of there right now!"

"It's too late, my Prince. I have a disruptor and web on me..." There was no fear in Maur Cassei's voice, just a statement of fact.

"All frigates, warp immediately to *Pyro-1*! Hold out for five seconds, old man! Help is on the way!"

"Thank you, my Prince. I can die happy!"

Standing change. Your relationship with Maur Cassei has improved.

Presumed personal opinion of you: +38 (friendly)

A second later, *Pyro-1* was no more. The herd of frigates sent to help arrived in a cloud of debris. I let out a sinister howl and shouted on the public channel:

"You've killed a legend. I'm giving you exactly one minute to surrender. Whoever does not will be eaten alive by Iseyeks!"

A chorus of rattling, chirping insect voices on the channel confirmed to the incredulous that I wasn't joking.

"My Prince, they're surrendering!" said the admiral.

"Cease fire... Hold disruptors on all those who've surrendered. If one of them tries to turn on their warp drive, destroy them on the spot!"

"No emergency rescue capsules have been noted on the battlefield," said one of the tacticians sorrowfully.

I stood up with difficulty and ran my utterly insane gaze over the staff officers. For some reason, they were all standing at attention. With a crisp gait, Admiral Kiro Sabuto approached me and unexpectedly lowered down on one knee.

Standing change. Empire Military faction opinion of you has improved.
Present Empire Military faction opinion of you: +1 (indifferent)

"My Prince, that was an unbelievable thing you did! We came up against a fleet of approximately the same size and lost just two frigates! I still can't believe our luck!"

"I don't smell a whiff of luck here, admiral. From the get-go, we were a bit stronger and more organized, so to me our victory was rightfully earned. Losing *Safa-4* was just totally dumb, but I have no idea how we weren't able to save *Pyro-1*... Call the captain of *Pyro-27*. Put him through to all ships in the fleet. I need to speak with him about his heroic great-grandfather."

Standing change. Empire Military faction opinion of you has improved.
Present Empire Military faction opinion of you: +2 (indifferent)

Two improvements in a row?! Apparently one for the victory, and another for honoring the fallen hero. I didn't speak long, but I was penetrating and sincere. The young Alessandro Cassei, who had graduated just one day earlier, heard me out without hiding his tears. When I suggested renaming his frigate *Pyro-1* in memory of his heroic great-grandfather, the boy only had enough strength to nod in silence. The sheer number of messages about personal opinion improvement overwhelmed my eyes, so I closed them all at once.

"Admiral, report on the results of the battle."

Kiro Sabuto straightened up and reported plainly:

"My Prince, two *Flamberg* heavy assault cruisers have been captured. One of them is in serious need of repair; the second is absolutely undamaged but has lost all its combat drones. A *Surgeon* destroyer has been captured. It's so damaged it's practically scrap. Eighteen frigates have been captured. Eight *Pyros* and ten *Tusks*. Our losses: one frigate, *Safa-4*, and another frigate, *Pyro-1*. The space station is not responding to our messages. Its defense systems have been put at the ready. But all they really have is a number of high-speed turrets and one low-radius rocket system. It shouldn't be any problem for an Iseyek landing party."

"All captured ships are to be transferred to Tesse. Bionica, send Prince Roben royl Inoky a message in my name: I request that he repair and modernize all ships sent. I will be paying. And I need you now, as well as Space Corporal Patrick toyl Sven. We're headed to the *Tria*. I want to see how a praying mantis landing party works with my own eyes."

"My Prince, I had to turn off the obscene vocabulary filter in order to translate some of your orders," said my android translator on our way to the hangar. "I wasn't expecting to hear such words from the mouth of a crown prince."

"Obscene?" asked the space corporal to clarify, and Bionica explained:

"Improper, abusive, or insulting language."

Patrick toyl Sven whinnied like a mare:

"That's right. But at the same time, it was all easy to figure out, even when the odd unknown term came up. Point, primary, secondary... That was the first time I'd heard those words, but I figured out what they meant."

I kept silent, deciding not to comment. Yes, during the battle I had slightly fallen out of the noble prince role, let loose the odd curse word and used a couple of terms from a different game. I'll have to be more careful next time. Though... my behavior didn't confuse anyone. The unusual terms were fully understood, so everything's fine.

Lika was sitting inside the shuttle, looking absurdly huge in the heavy, armored space suit. She was bursting with anger out of the shame of having been made to miss a real space battle.

"Well, you're gonna be one of the first humans in history to go inside a real Swarm landing ship!" I said, reassuring her.

I was accompanied by four gloomy, serious men from my personal guard and God knows how many chameleons. I saw only Popori de Cacha, who was still not making any attempts to camouflage himself, though his partners were probably also invisibly present. The angular and dark *Tria*, four times larger than my yacht, was about a half a mile from *Queen of Sin*, so flying over took less than a minute.

I was greeted by Admiral Kheraisss Vej, who had come to the *Tria* from his *Legash-1* specially to show his fleet commander the Swarm landing ship. The huge, dark-colored praying mantis was walking around today without escort, and, despite how colossal the *Tria* was, I didn't see any crewmembers.

"All automate. Soll-diers in suspended animation sleep. No need more mouth to feed," explained the admiral.

The dock of the landing ship made an impression on me, and not even with its gigantic size, but with its never-ending rows of armored spindle-shaped capsules, ready to be launched. Each landing module was just ten feet in diameter, but counting the reactive drive in the tail section, its length exceeded fifty feet.

"Small landing projectile. Control beam laser from *Tria* or eyes see pil-oht," explained the admiral, who had noticed my interest in his race's technology.

We walked, bouncing at times due to the weak gravity on the insect ship, to a glowing tube of transparent plastic, inside of which was an elevator, a cylinder with a metal lattice floor and ceiling that zipped from floor to floor. When the elevator suddenly jerked downward, my legs even lifted up off the floor. The human guards were also wavering, and Lika I just barely caught when she was up by my head. The praying mantis and Popori de Cacha did not experience such difficulties, as they had been smart enough to grab the handrails on the wall (or they just read the inscription about that on the wall of the elevator, who knows?). Bionica was also more or less holding the handrail, though the android girl was having her own problems with using the elevator: the bottom of her long dress had flown up over her head, exposing a pair of long, fit legs and dark lacy underwear.

"You have good taste. Great underwear!" commented Likanna on my translator's difficult situation.

"I was almost left without a dress..." Bionica grew embarrassed and set about hurriedly fixing her clothes.

The admiral though, clearly in order to distract us from the episode with the excessively fast elevator, decided to talk about the recent battle with the pirates.

"My Princcce, all cap-i-tain Iseyek lose-mind happy from victory. But cap-i-tain me ask one question, but I miss these chance and no know answer. They very interest in know how to be original of Prince phrase that in Swarm language translate soundeded like thisss: 'I fertilize your whole clutch eight time, and every time do that is different, and all wrong?' And also 'you are spider without full set of appendage and without nerve bundle in head to drag you body, stupid like parasite, to home, human insect?'"

"Bionica?" I turned to my translator.

"Yes, my Prince," the blonde innocently batted her eyelashes, clearly not understanding what complaints I could have had.

"For some reason, I don't even remember coming close to using such loaded language," I admitted.

"But that is the most literal translation of some of your phrases and commands. Saying it another way would have been even more bizarre."

"Is that so? Well, ok then," I said, not about to argue.

The elevator took us to a long, darkened hallway. It was a strange place, reminiscent of a mountain gorge. It had endlessly high walls on both sides and a narrow space between them. From far away, a bright bluish light shone through. It was the only source of light. Gravity was barely perceptible. It seemed to me that with my magnetic soles, I would be able to walk on the vertical walls as well, but I didn't decide to check. We went forward toward the light and up an inclined path that ended in the control hall.

"That's what I'm talking about!" Lika wasn't able to hold in her shriek of excitement.

I was also impressed. In fact, the picture that revealed itself frightened me. Everywhere you could see, along all the walls and on the ceiling, there were endless rows of hexagonal cells. Inside each cell were metallic hemispheres arranged in perfect hexagons. A huge number of identical, carefully arranged, perfect hexagons with six hemispheric sides.

"Six plus seven is thirteen, plus eight, that's twenty-one..." my daughter began calculating the number of hemispheres in each cell.

In response to the child, the admiral chirped something back in his language, and Bionica helped out with the translation:

"Ninety-one capsules inside each hexagon. Inside each capsule, there is one sleeping soldier. In each hexagon is one ready division – a commander and his ninety subordinates, trained and accustomed to one another."

"They're all sleeping? That is, in a state of

suspended animation?" I clarified.

At first, the admiral tried to answer me in human language but lost his way, not able to find the term he needed. Seeing this, Bionica took up her role as translator:

"Yes, Prince Georg, the four hundred thousand soldiers on the ship are in a state of suspended animation all the time; otherwise, the *Tria* wouldn't be able to hold enough food, water and air. Only the crew of the starship remains awake, but it is quite small, around forty creatures, primarily Gamma Iseyeks. But they aren't here. They're on the other end of the starship. Here is where the army commander, Savasss Jach, is stationed, as well as the general's servants. As a matter of fact, we're on our way to see him now."

I picked the general out of the group of insects right away. He had a huge, fuzzy body, a head and breast that grew up into a unified whole, rows of spidery black eyes in the front part of the torso, all kinds of whiskers and antennas, articulated appendages, other protuberances, and a long tail that dragged along on the floor behind him for fifteen feet, ending in a sharpened spike. Around the general there were semicircular, glowing panels with a multitude of circular and rectangular screens and at least a thousand buttons that all looked identical. All the screens were on. They lit up, flashed rhythmically, twinkled and changed color, but I couldn't understand a thing.

I rubbed my eyes, tired from the flashing, and the creature in front of the panel chirped out something, not turning to the recent arrivals. Bionica translated:

"The frame rate is too high to be visible to the human eye. But just for their high-born guest, they'll turn the holographic screen down from a frame rate of forty-eight to something you'll be able to see. General Savasss Jach welcomes his boss. He apologizes for missing the very beginning of the battle, but at that time he had yet to be awoken from suspended animation. So, he asks, how many were they?"

"They? Ah, probably he means enemy ships. Tell him there were ninety-seven, four of which heavy. Our side had sixty-nine, five heavy."

The general listened carefully to the android translator and whistled out an answer. Bionica translated.

"General Savasss Jach expresses his admiration of the Orange House Prince's talented command and says that he wants to tell you something very important."

The utterly enormous insect continued his speech. I noticed Popori de Cacha tighten up and even place his palm on his weapon. The soldiers in the heavy orange armor followed his example. It was quite strange. I saw no threat in the awkward, sluggish general and, besides that, the five or six small servant creatures standing at a slight distance were unarmed. The android listened to the long message attentively and translated:

"General Savasss Jach would like to confess something to you, Prince. It is he who has spent more than one hundred and twenty years as the 'elusive head of the Gamma Iseyek fanatics, unwilling to recognize the end of war with the Empire.' The general remembers the clutches burnt with napalm in the

Hive on Sivala-II. He watched with his own numerous eyes as those thirty-six million eggs burned up in flames from the heavens. It was at that moment that he swore to his personal soldiers to destroy the Orange House, which had caused that slaughter, monstrous in its senseless severity. Even when the war between the Empire and the Swarm officially ended, the general's agents rooted out and assassinated members of the Orange House through embedded agents. There are fourteen deaths of your relatives on the general's account. But today General Savasss Jach, who has outlived many enemies and friends over the last one hundred seventy years, has been put in a difficult situation. It wouldn't be hard for him to wake up any of the Iseyek divisions, who were put into suspended animation during the war with the Empire, and then the soldiers wouldn't even have to be told – just seeing a person would be enough reason to kill them. But such an action would threaten the weakened Swarm, practically totally deprived of a star fleet, with a new war. The general does not have the right to forgive an ancient enemy and break an oath; however, he confesses that the conflict is untimely at the moment. So, the general suggests signing a temporary cease-fire between the Gamma Iseyeks and the Orange House for eighty-three years, one month and two weeks."

"Why that amount of time specifically?" I asked, surprised.

"Dad, what are you talking about? Even I know that!" Likanna became surprised. "That's how long it takes for their home planet to rotate around their sun!"

"Huh, I guess I forgot," I admitted candidly. "But what the heck? I, as a representative of the Orange House, accept the cease-fire offer."

Standing change. Iseyek race opinion of you has improved.
Alpha Iseyek race opinion of you: +7 (warm)
Beta Iseyek race opinion of you: +3 (indifferent)
Gamma Iseyek race opinion of you: +4 (indifferent)

I actually had no idea if I had the right to make such a serious agreement; however, I didn't see any other way out. The tops of the capsules had already started opening in the nearest hexagon, and ninety, strange-looking praying mantises and change began forming even rows on the platform five steps from me. It became clear immediately how the normal Alpha Iseyeks, like Triasss Zess or Admiral Kheraisss Vej, were different from these specially-bred soldiers. The soldiers were a bit taller and twice as wide. Their vulnerable eyes were sunken into their skulls and covered in chitin nodes. And they had wide and thick-spined shields on their upper appendages that were reminiscent of mattresses. An assault soldier could simply cover itself from fire behind these impenetrable shields.

"Good division, new genetic line VI-896-A. Assault soldiers in the sixth generation. All necessary genes have been added and enhanced. Raised relatively recently, twenty years ago," Bionica said, translating the general's words. "Reinforced front appendages, highly durable, extremely fast reaction time, genetic modification for intellect, and trainability included. They are expert marksmen with any firearm, are skilled in explosives and electronics, and are capable of detecting power cables inside a two-foot-thick wall. Able to live and work in a vacuum for one minute, twenty-six seconds."

"Impressive," I agreed. "But it can't be that just one division is enough to capture a space station, right?"

"Princcce," answered the admiral, "no one is quessstioning your ability as flee-eet commander. If general Savasss Jach wake up just one little egg of soldiersss, that meansss it's all we'll need."

The division chosen by the general flew suddenly from their places and darted off into the distance along the inclined wall. Savasss Jach himself was conjuring something up on his console, pressing buttons and moving sliders with his numerous appendages. And suddenly, in the air before me, a rectangular screen began to flicker on. Some parts of a picture began forming – some details and plans. The details became more numerous. They spun and overlapped between themselves, forming something whole, though it was not yet clear what it was. Bionica translated the general's crackling:

"Reconnaissance drones from the *Tria* are orbiting the space station, scanning it and sending back a picture in pieces. The computer is making a model of the station, noting the installed weaponry and blind spots. Eight thousand inhabitants, but almost all self-identify as peaceful civilians. There are no more than two hundred defenders. Easier than expected. The enemy is preparing to defend the residential areas and not the section of the station with the warp beacon. We could pass from the direction of this station module. It covers the range of the automatic turrets. Further is the airlock, the shuttle dock, and down this hallway one group is holding the warp beacon, and the others are cutting the hallway off in the direction of the hub so as not to let attackers enter. It's always bad when something looks too good..."

"Why bad?" I asked through the interpreter.

The answer shocked me:

"Some loss percentage is simply necessary. The soldiers need to eat."

"The assault soldiers... What!? Eat their own dead???" I exclaimed in surprise.

"Not only their own. Any dead. But enemies aren't always edible, and killing them isn't always part of the mission. Now, Prince, you've set the mission to not kill the inhabitants of the station, get to the station module and turn on the warp beacon. So there won't be any needless bloodshed, only armed defenders, but there won't be much food. So we'll need to sacrifice some of our own. This is a very ancient Swarm soldier tradition: the survivors eat their fallen and also wounded. It's easier to raise a new soldier from an egg than it is to heal one that has been so badly wounded. This is how a soldier becomes equal to his group-mates. Every soldier knows about it and is happy that he can bring benefit to his comrades, even if he dies or is wounded. By the way, the model of the station is done."

Walls, hallways, and a whole labyrinth of rooms were depicted in a maze of green lines on the hologram. The orange dots marked defense systems and places where defenders were concentrated. A bright blue spot inside a long spire was the warp beacon, which was still off.

"I'm still a bit uncomfortable with us needing to lose our own," I confessed. "General, what if I just decide to provide your soldiers with enough food after the assault? And now we can cover the attack groups from the turrets and rockets, to protect landing troops with one of the fleet's frigates."

"Have it your way, Prince Georg," translated Bionica. "The assault divisions are already in the projectiles and ready to start the operation. As soon as your ship covers the turrets, my soldiers will begin the assault."

I asked for a microphone set to the fleet frequency, and the general's servant instantly handed me a metallic tube, while another was handed to Bionica.

"Check, check. Fleet commander speaking. I need two or three frigates, a couple destroyers, preferably *Warhawks* and *Vassars*. Come in a straight line between the *Tria* and the station, as close to the station as possible. Cover the turrets to make a path for the attack groups."

Answers came in immediately:

"*Warhawk-1* has accepted. *Warhawk-4* has accepted. *Vassar-9* has accepted. *Warhawk-2* has accepted. *Vassar-11* has accepted."

"The ships are in position. The assault has begun."

The green dots on the screen moved toward the station, getting faster and faster. Then the landing modules made a maneuver, using the drifting ships as cover and leaving the firing zone. And now they're at a safe distance. Or are they? A bright dot on the screen meant that one of ten landing capsules had gone down.

"A cloaked enemy frigate!" several voices spoke at once on the channel about the change in the situation. The enemy frigate uncloaked and attacked the landing capsules! A *Ghost* frigate, exiting the station.

"Get that son of a bitch!" It immediately became clear how the enemy fleet had been able to strike the *Pyro-1* so cleanly in the recent battle. I began to thirst for revenge.

"*Warhawk-4*, take point on the enemy! Put a web on him! He won't get away now!"

"Great, girl, you're learning quick!" I commended the captain. "And now, everyone together, kill that bastard!"

"My Prince, the enemy is surrendering on the common channel. They're requesting mercy," said Admiral Kiro Sabuto.

"Here on the *Tria*, I don't have access to the common channel, only to our fleet one. The enemy attacked and killed our landing troops. Is there even a single reason that we should spare his life?"

"The captain of the enemy frigate says that the head of the Brotherhood of the Stars, King Janis the First, is on board the cloaked ship. In exchange for saving the life of Janis the First, he will order his subjects to put down their weapons."

"A pirate King? How interesting. Well, let's see how much the subjects love their ruler. Send a message to the *Ghost*: if the station defenders fire even one shot, their monarch will be learning to breathe in a vacuum."

TRUMP CARD DEAD END

I'M SO TIRED... Five hours of uninterrupted negotiating is enough to leave anyone feeling beaten down. I would gladly put this work on someone else's shoulders, but many of the issues required me to be present: subjugating the Brotherhood of the Stars to the structures of the Orange House, the rights to the Hnelle system, the further fate of the space station, placing a contingent of guards at the warp beacon (what do you know, you need to take the errors of the past into account), etc. I got a lot of help from space lawyer Gleb ton Veyer, who was discovered among the staff of *Queen of Sin*. Without him, I definitely would not have been able to navigate the infinite possible collisions and submerged rocks that make up the sea of Imperial law. At long last, the final version of the agreement was decided on, and I placed my personal seal on the document.

Sovereignty Change
The Hnelle system has been placed under the

jurisdiction of the Orange House
  Crown Princess Likanna royl Georg ton Mesfelle-Kyle shall become sovereign of the Hnelle system

And, with a five second delay, some messages came in about me:

Global fame increase. Current value +7
Global standing increase. Current value -22

The hard business was finished. I picked myself up sleepily, preparing to return to *Queen of Sin*. My bodyguards and the local soldiers, still having yet to change their black-green uniforms out for orange ones, formed a single escort group. Popori de Cacha cantankerously corrected the positioning of a pair of soldiers in the escort, but did not speak out against the presence of the Brotherhood of the Stars soldiers. And I also was already feeling like the locals were my close allies.

My initial plans were to deal with those who took part in the long-ago mutiny and those party to piracy. They broke on reality. The people of the station met the coming of Imperial forces with joy as true liberators. It quickly became clear that the population of the Hnelle station was at least two-thirds captured crewmembers from ships looted by pirates. Some of the captives had spent more than forty years here in the Hnelle system, long ago assimilated, found themselves work on the station, started new families, had children, and were not at all preparing to return to some historical homeland. There turned out to be no pirates or participants in the military coup at the station. Most of the pirates were on their ships during the battle; the others were taking a vacation from interstellar flights on the planet Unatari-VII, which is a huge ocean with a scattering of islands and archipelagos.

It was the Unatari system, the warp beacon of which was reachable from the Hnelle system, that was the base, the so called "capital" system of the Brotherhood of the Stars. It was a planet with a population of eight million, orbital docks for building and repairing ships, and luxurious palaces built for the pirate captains on the shores of the warm sea. I was slightly worried that the pirates would find out about the incursion of Imperial forces into their territory and turn off the warp beacon in the Unatari system, but I was reassured by the fact that it was quite unlikely. Risking treason from their own, not-too-reliable allies, the "council of the four Kings of the Brotherhood of the Stars" made the Unatari warp beacon totally automated and well defended, capable of withstanding multiple days of heavy-ship bombardment.

My interest was, of course, piqued by the personalities of these four space pirate "Kings." One of them, Janis the First, was in a prison cell on *Queen of Sin,* but who are the other three? It quickly became clear that the second of the "Kings" had been commanding *Happy Sloth* during the recent battle and had surely died in the reactor explosion. The third owned *Scalp Collector,* one of the two heavy cruisers brought to me, but in the last battle it was being commanded by his assistant, as the "King" himself was in a crystal-induced sleep in his palace on Unatari-VII. The fourth "King," it turns out, I already knew. He was the former captain of the *Payoff*, Velesh ton Rayf, or Velesh the First, as he called himself. I remembered how I had promised him a million credits and full freedom for his assistance. So what now? It was just a million. Money comes with time. But releasing that bloodthirsty pirate unpunished... I pondered the difficult choice for some time: either release this flagrant criminal or break the Prince's word before Admiral Kiro Sabuto, who was accompanying me, asks about it. From the admiral's point of view, there was no choice. A nobleman's word was considered inviolable, and breaking it threatened the most severe consequences, up to the point of losing one's title...

I experienced true elation when I saw the local star maps, which confirmed even my boldest suppositions. The Hnelle system could potentially be an extremely important transportation hub. It had five connections to other warp beacons. Quite a rare thing! From here you could reach Himora, Tesse, Forepost-11, Tialla and Unatari. It was precisely as a transportation hub that I should plan the development of the station here. It would need more docks, new space links for recharging ships, freight terminals, cavernous hangars, new residential areas... But everything I described required huge amounts of money to pour in and two to three years to build. The average estimate for how long it would take for all this to pay for itself, according to the optimistic estimates of local economists, was around fifteen years.

The station's coffers were empty. The station had

never harbored huge amounts of funds, and also King Janis the First had transferred everything to the last cent to his personal account right after the unsuccessful battle. And though some of the local inhabitants were burning with enthusiasm to beat banking information out of the criminal "King," the rest advised us not to put too much hope into that option – this "King's" brain also had a psionic block in it. Both groups looked at me with pleading eyes, as if they were looking at the only one who really was capable of paying for the development of their station. And I did seriously get hung up on that.

I was supposed to spend the money on developing the station now from my own in-no-way bottomless funds while all the "goodies" from spending the money would only come after my contract, and would be left for Mr. G. I. It was my consciousness of such blatant injustice that became one of the reasons why I placed the Hnelle system under my daughter, Likanna. Maybe she was being played by a kid I didn't know, but that kid was doing a masterful job of playing the role of an eleven-year-old Princess. Also, I had another potential scenario in mind: that everything happening here wasn't a game at all, no matter how much Mr. G. I. tried to convince me it was. The world around me was just too realistic, the characters reacted in a way that was too lifelike. And if that was so, then let Crown Princess Likanna receive a nice holding before she comes of age, one that she won't have to be ashamed of before the best suitors in the universe.

One hundred seven million credits... That's two cutting-edge, heavy assault cruisers for my fleet. Or thirty light cruisers. Or three hundred destroyers. Parting with the money left me in tears but, all the same, I made the payment. The people around me were exultant, and I heard joyful shouts in support of the Orange House and me personally. I tried to hold the proper smile on my face but inside cats were scratching. The fleet had grown, and upkeep had also become more expensive, but instead of more income, I kept accumulating new expenses...

Though, the hope remained that I could fully cover all my losses in the other Brotherhood of the Stars systems. Above all else, I was interested in the capital of the pirate region, Unatari-VII, with its luxurious palaces, many of which were built with dirty money from the sale of stolen goods or drug trafficking, up to the point of trafficking the strictly forbidden crystals. Basically, all the industry on the planet was piracy-based – entertainment complexes on tropical islands with servants captured in slave raids, banks that launder money of questionable origin, and firms for selling stolen goods. The profits of the criminal business on Unatari-VII numbered in the billions, and I was hoping to put an end to that by confiscating the assets of the criminal Kings and their circles.

It also wasn't a good idea to forget about the two recently discovered systems, access to which had been found by scout ships during the Brotherhood of the Stars period. In the Tivalle star system, there were vast ice asteroid fields, rich in tritium and other rare isotopes. Also, the Brotherhood of the Stars had already begun mining them and smuggling them into Sector Eight through shell companies. Thinking about ice mining, I was immediately reminded of my sister,

Crown Princess Violetta royl Inoky ton Mesfelle-Damir. Our father gave Violetta the Damir system, famed for the endless ice rings around its planets. It was there that the largest space ice processing facilities in the Empire were located. Tritium, helium-3, lithium-8, nitrogen-12... Thermonuclear reactors in the whole known Universe needed these rare isotopes in huge quantities, and a large share of the reactor fuel was mined, as it were, at my sister's facilities. It wasn't for nothing that Violetta had acquired the nickname "the Ice Princess." I supposed that my sister would doubtlessly be interested in the Tivalle system and would be willing to spend quite a bit to drown out potential competition before it even got off the ground. It isn't right to divide up the pelt of a bear that hasn't been killed yet, but I had already decided for myself that I wouldn't be selling my concession for ice mining in the Tivalle system for less than eight hundred million credits.

And, finally, the Sigur system. The warp beacon there was only activated eleven years ago. There was extremely little known about the system, though there probably was some reason for building a warp beacon there. It was as if the Sigur star system didn't exist – there was a warp beacon, but I was not able to find any information about it in the system. No one was able to explain me the reason for such secrecy. Well, alright, we'll figure it out when we get there, as they say.

"All ships at the ready in ten minutes!" The time had come to take all these hypothetical pirate riches in my own hands. "Fleet, begin acceleration toward the Unatari system. Captains, set the pre-warp settings to two thousand miles from beacon. We have reason to believe that the beacon has defense systems installed, and I think we can all agree those are best avoided. Our target is the seventh planet and its orbital docks. Serious resistance is not expected, but all the same, everyone should stay on their guard. General Savasss Jach, we'll need a terrestrial operation: capture a few small islands, and strategic locations – cliffs and thick forest, non-defensive structures. So, wake your soldiers up as soon as possible..."

"Unknown ships in system!" the officer's scream interrupted my speech.

"Sound the combat alert!"

Everyone began scurrying around. The officers took their seats hurriedly. After that, messages started coming as if from a cornucopia.

"Group of targets, distance: 900 miles. Around eighty ships."

"Big dot! A battleship! I repeat, the enemy has a battleship! And several heavy cruisers!"

"I got the right answer from the friend-foe system!"

"The fleet is identifying itself as Orange House forces. It's the Tesse fleet!"

Everyone grew silent, waiting for my reaction. I shrugged:

"What's to ask? Cancel the combat alert! That's my brother's fleet. Well, to be more accurate, half of his fleet. Just one thing I don't get: what did they come out here for?"

"As a matter of fact, we invited them by turning on the Hnelle beacon," answered the admiral.

Ah, ok. That probably was what happened. My

allies knew that my fleet was on its way to a battle with pirates in the Hnelle system. The turning on of the warp beacon after so many decades meant that I had won. And now the allies were rushing to the already finished battle to divide up the pirate treasure. What a shmuck I am! What was the point of first beating the pirates and declaring the conquered systems mine, only to turn on the warp beacon in this little pirate dead end?!

A video call invitation came in.

"Crown Prince Georg royl Inoky, glad to meet you! I am Admiral Nill ton Amsted, fleet commander for Crown Prince Roben royl Inoky. We came to help you clear out this pirate nest!"

I tried to hide my annoyance and answered the uninvited guest politely:

"Admiral, thank you for the concern, but we've already taken care of the enemies. The pirate fleet has been totally destroyed. Three of the four ringleaders of that criminal underworld have already been either killed or captured."

"But the Unatari system is left. We would gladly participate in its liberation!"

"Admiral, I repeat: there is no need for your participation. My fleet is preparing to warp to Unatari this very moment. You've caught us by surprise, in fact. There are no enemy ships there, so liberating Unatari is not a difficult mission. Your fleet still needs a few hours to recharge for the next warp jump, but my ships are completely ready to go right now. So you can give my thanks to my brother Roben for his concern, but in this case it was unnecessary."

"This has nothing to do with your brother... Crown

Prince Roben was unavailable, so this whole operation of moving the Tesse fleet was entirely my and my captains' idea. My people were starting to stagnate without anything to do. They've spent many years cooped up on Tesse. The military officers thirst for battle. They want to fight with pirates! And though my fleet is much larger than yours, I'm prepared to split the loot and pirate captives down the middle."

So that's what the hell! As I suspected, they really were hurrying to split up loot that I already considered my own. I don't know how it would have ended, but Nicole Savoia's heart-rending half-scream half-yelp interrupted the conversation:

"ALIENS IN SYSTEM!!!"

"Sound the combat alert!" the siren wailed gratingly, and the relaxed officers threw themselves into their seats.

"The alien *Hermit* destroyer is six hundred miles out! And..." Nicole's voice cracked from worry. "And with them is a *Sledgehammer* cruiser!"

Now it's serious. I suppose no alien ship could cause such a panic among my people as a *Sledgehammer*. The powerful starship could take out any ship smaller than a heavy cruiser in just one volley, guaranteed. Yes, and heavy cruisers wouldn't make it much longer – two or three volleys from the *Sledgehammer*'s cannons is all it would take.

I rushed to take my position leading the fleet:

"Soldiers, the time has finally come for your first test! Not quite as many aliens as I would have liked, but at least we'll be able to check if you've been learning anything these last couple days! We'll split up the alien ships and draw them away from each other. *Pyro-1* is first receiver. *Pyro-2* is second. *Safa-1* and *Safa-2*, make two more receivers. *Tria*, go away toward the sun. Both *Tusks*, protect the *Tria*."

"Prince Georg, what should we do?" came the voice of Admiral Nill ton Amsted over the common channel.

Come right on! What's he getting himself into?! He's not ready for an encounter with the aliens and would lose a lot of ships if he entered the battle!

"Nill, I don't want to have to justify to my brother why I lost his ships! So your job is just not to get in the way! If you want to help, use your whole fleet to guard the huge praying mantis landing ship. I've only got one, and I can't afford to lose it. And do not allow your ships to come closer than 300 miles from the skirmish!"

"The enemy has begun maneuvers! The *Hermit* is going on the approach to *Pyro-2*! The *Sledgehammer* is lagging behind, but it is also closing the gap!"

"Good, they're splitting up! *Pyro-2* and *Safa-2*, blast off toward the heavies! Bring the alien support ships out to our big guns! Heavies, form a single group, check your connections! Destroyers and light cruisers, go forty miles out, take cover behind the heavy cruisers. *Pyro-3* and *4*, make a wide arc from different sides of the fleet and make me another second receiver to replace the ships that leave. Other frigates, warp to the first receiver."

"The *Hermit* has locked on *Legash-3*. It's releasing drones!"

"Anti-support, reduce distance to forty miles and

mow those drones down! Remember, there's twenty of them. As soon as you're done, tell me. Heavies, focus on that beast!"

A well-orchestrated volley from the cannons of five cruisers had no effect whatsoever on the enemy ship. Too high a speed, too unpredictable a trajectory. The volley just sailed by.

"This is *Pyro-3*, receiver in position."

"Great, now we're really playing! *Pyros*, the *Sledgehammer* is presently 200 miles behind the *Hermit*. Your mission is to not allow it to come any closer to the battle site! Stasis webs and warp disruptors must be on the cruiser constantly. If there is even a tiny risk, get out to the receiver! Just hold it in place while we deal with the support!"

The conveyor belt began rolling – one after another the little *Pyros* jumped into the battle, took the cruiser and held it before passing the baton to the next frigate. I watched this carousel of ships and became convinced that the enemy would not be able to target the nimble *Pyros*, and so I turned my attention to the second alien ship.

"All twenty drones are down!" came one of the destroyer captains.

"Great! All anti-support, focus on the *Hermit*. Light cruisers, approach to thirty miles from the heavies, get your electronics firing on all cylinders. Release drones. Heavies, do the same. All four *Warhawks*, warp to the *Hermit* at zero, place your webs and take point. Stop that bastard for me, even if it's just for a couple seconds! Destroyers, you approach too. I need stasis webs on it. Lots of webs!"

It was a worrying moment. The heavy cruisers need

the nimble alien ship's speed to be reduced to be able to hit it. For that, the frigates and destroyers had to get close and be in the combat zone. All our hope was placed in the electronic warfare ships, which were supposed to stop the *Hermit* from aiming normally. According to my calculations, the *Hermit* would have up to twenty webs on it in thirty seconds, which meant it would come to a complete stop. The heavy cruisers won't miss an immobile target. But in those thirty seconds, the *Hermit* will be able to get off two shots... That means I'll lose two frigates...

The seconds ticked by, but there were no losses. One after the other, the captains reported that they had placed webs on the *Hermit*. The small enemy destroyer disappeared in the swarm of combat drones. The alien ship's shields began quickly deflating.

"Heavies, at the ready! Shoot from all cannons, fire at will! Anti-support, *Warhawks*, put some pressure on it!"

In a few shots, the enemy shield had fallen to zero, and a few seconds later there followed a bright explosion! "The *Hermit* has been destroyed! We did it!" A roar of joy bellowed out on the channel from a multitude of voices, not nearly all of them human.

"Great! All frigates, warp to the receivers! *Tusks*, join up too. Heavies, go slowly in an organized group toward the *Sledgehammer*, go up to 30 miles out. Electronic warfare, follow twenty-five miles behind the heavies, don't come any closer. Destroyers, don't come, go out to the *Tria*, this is not your battle."

"Dad, are we gonna win soon?" Lika's voice rang out from right above my ear. I turned and jumped up.

Behind Lika, there were two uncanny-looking,

huge, armed praying mantises.

"What's this then?" Despite the untimely nature of the moment, I decided to clarify why these Alpha Iseyek assault soldiers had come on my yacht.

"Uncle Savasss Jach gave them to me when you were on the station."

"Bionica?"

Clearly, my facial expression was very threatening, as the android recoiled as if I was about to hit her.

"My Prince, Likanna asked General Savasss Jach to give her a couple of the biggest and strongest praying mantises to give her something to brag about to her friends," explained the blond android, innocently batting her eyelashes. "The general did not refuse her that little caprice."

"If that's what you call little..." Each praying mantis was more than 10 feet tall.

"Because the general did not consider Crown Princess Likanna of legal age, he did not make her the primary controller, but you. The Princess can talk to them and give them some orders, but they will only obey and serve you, the Crown Prince."

"How will they understand me or Lika?" I asked in surprise.

"They are learning human speech bit by bit. While you were out negotiating, Lika was playing with them for a few hours, and I helped. They already understand some words and commands. These bodyguards' vocabulary is still very limited, but they are very quick learners."

Well, screw it... Quite the gift! I'll need to have a chat with the general after the battle. But for now, both Lika and these insects needed to be kept busy and out of my hair.

"Bionica, order these praying mantises to carefully and promptly take my daughter to the shuttle hangar. Nicole Savoia will show them the way. Make sure Crown Princess Likanna puts on her armored space suit, then carefully sit her down inside an emergency rescue shuttle. And make sure she doesn't crawl back out!"

The offended shrieks and screams from the young Crown Princess slightly bewildered the huge bodyguards. One of them lifted the young Princess in its pair of small arms and pressed her close. Another took a big piece of soft, gray fabric from a plain belt-bag and in literally two seconds had the kicking child swaddled up in a tightly packed cocoon. After that, both insects, carrying the cocoon in several pairs of pincers, followed Nicole Savoia out of the headquarters. The thick door closing behind them sharply cut off my daughter's dissatisfied screams.

I was probably doing something wrong with my daughter, as the officers all looked at me in shock. Ah, yes. I remembered that it was forbidden to touch a Crown Princess even with one finger. Oh well, we'll figure it out after the battle.

"*Joan the Fatty*, get to position!" the voice of Captain Oorast Pohl sounded out at precisely the right moment, reminding those gathered that this wasn't some playground squabble, but a real, heavy battle.

"Release combat drones. Fire cannons!" I commanded.

The enemy's shield condition was displayed on screen. The little pillar jumped up and down a few times, then returned to one hundred percent. Now *that's* shield regeneration!

"Stop! Reload the cannons. Shoot on my command. On the count of three. One. Two. Three!"

The *Sledgehammer's* shield fell to zero, but a few seconds later was restored back up to maximum. I wonder if we did any damage at all? And, if yes, how serious? The admiral anxiously said:

"The enemy is firing on the *Legash-1*. Each volley takes forty percent of the shield; we won't be able to recharge it fast enough!"

"Light cruisers, approach to fifty miles! I need the *Sledgehammer* not be able to get off a shot every time! It has fairly weak sensors; the Iseyeks were able to jam them. Heavies, have you reloaded? On the count of three. One. Two. Three!"

The camera showed a couple shots hitting the cruiser nevertheless. I saw explosions on the *Sledgehammer's* armor. But how serious are these hits for the enemy? And by the way, the alien ship's energy shield was already back up to maximum. Aw, hell!

"Crown Prince Georg, your ships clearly cannot do anything to the alien cruiser. Perhaps you could use our help after all?" Admiral Nill ton Amsted could clearly see what was happening on the battlefield perfectly.

Maybe I really should call my allies in? No, I decided. It's too early.

"Nill, we're in no rush here. The *Sledgehammer* has been successfully pinned down, it's not going anywhere. My goal here is to train soldiers and try out various approaches, as we've had the luck of capturing an alien ship. If your ships are needed, I'll call you in."

"I need a frigate to volunteer for a dangerous mission," I said on the fleet channel.

"*Tusk-1* ready!" the chameleon frigate managed to answer a half second before the others.

That's what you call bad luck. I'd be burying a ship crewed by such a low-population race if my theory was wrong... But I couldn't refuse now without offending my allies.

"*Tusk-1*, listen carefully. Your mission is to check in practice if the *Sledgehammer*'s cannons are able to hit fast-moving targets. Jump to the cruiser, get up to full speed and take a small orbit. Change trajectory and basically just act unpredictably. Also, place a web on the enemy, take point and shoot from your cannons. That is your order!"

"Order heard!"

Silence took over on the channel. Everyone froze, watching to see how the experiment would end. The frigate looked very small in comparison with the cruiser. It began spinning tight circles. Twenty seconds went by, and the *Sledgehammer* made a shot at the *Legash-1*, having ignored the fast-moving target.

"All frigates warp to the enemy! Do the same as the *Tusk-1*! Before the heavies shoot, make a pause in the shooting, and everyone fire with them at the same time! Heavies, get ready. On the count of three. One, two, three!"

This time the result was much more successful – a whole scattering of bright dots bloomed up from the alien ship's armor. And though the enemy's energy shields recharged in a second again, I could visually make out damage to the *Sledgehammer*'s hull, and one of the cannons wasn't shooting anymore.

"Great! Let's do it again."

After a harmonious volley from the alien ship, some ship fragments flew off it. The ship had clearly taken a serious blow.

"Prince, I'm simply delighted!" Clear admiration could be heard in Admiral Nill ton Amsted's voice.

"Yes, Admiral Nill, we've figured out all we wanted. If you'd like to join me for a meal, I invite your battleship and heavy cruisers to dine. But only them. If support ships come, I swear on everything that is holy that I'll order them shot down."

A minute later, the huge battleship, *Master of Tesse,* and five heavy cruisers of various types came to the place where the alien ship was being shot down.

"Shoot on the count of three!" I ordered on the common channel. "One, two, three! Volley!"

Finally! Where the *Sledgehammer* had been, a bright white flower bloomed. The joyful screams were enough to make you deaf! I took off my headphones and turned around. The staff officers were clapping and shouting. Admiral Kiro Sabuto jumped up on the touch-screen table, cleaving the screen in half with his boots and did some bizarre, wild dance while shouting at full-throat:

"No losses! We did it without losses! That's just not something that happens! But we did it!!!"

Standing change. Empire Military faction opinion of you has improved.

**Present Empire Military faction opinion of you:
+3 (indifferent)**

**Standing change. Chameleon race opinion of
you has improved.
Chameleon race opinion of you: +4 (indifferent)**

The sheer number of standing change messages
was blinding. I closed them all without paying much
attention, before my conscience suddenly told me a
bit too late that I had just seen the number +100
somewhere in there. I was curious who had been able
to raise their opinion of me so much, so I flipped
back. Huh, I never would've guessed – it was the girl
officer with a model's looks, who I had almost purged
from my ranks and forced to redo all examinations to
prove her professional abilities. Her name, by the way,
was Valian ton Corsa.

I looked around for the girl among the officers and
caught her beautiful smile. She saw that I was looking
at her and walked up closer:

"Prince Georg, I'm simply indescribably delighted
and don't know how to express my admiration. Would
you be offended if I kissed you in front of everyone?"

Without waiting for my agreement, she took a step
closer and actually kissed me right on the lips. In
addition, the girl's gaze was promising much more,
and she whispered, barely audibly, through the scent
of cherry lipstick:

"Prince, all you have to do is call..."

"It's a good thing Miya isn't around to see this,"
said Nicole strictly, standing nearby.

Bringing up the name of the Truth Seeker had

somewhat sobered Valian up, and she left right away after muttering some apologies. I walked up to my seat behind the console and took the microphone:

"Great work, soldiers! Today we acted harmoniously, as a unified whole, and earned that beautiful victory. But don't relax yet. We've still got the pirate capital, Unatari, to go. It's time to pay that pirate's nest a visit before they figure out what's going on! All ships, prepare to warp in three minutes. Captains, check energy levels for warp jump. Admiral Nill ton Amsted, I thank you for your help in the battle, but we really can deal with this all ourselves."

"I have no doubts, Prince Georg. I still haven't come to my senses from all the admiration with which I observed your fleet's work. We're going back to Tesse just as soon as my ships recharge. Good luck in Unatari."

"Thank you, Admiral. We'll meet again!"

I turned off the common channel and asked the communications officer to create an encrypted channel with the local station. I was interested in the guard group at the warp beacon.

"Sergeant Paul Vell on the line, my Prince!" reported the beacon guard division commander.

"This is my order, Paul Vell. As soon as the Tesse fleet leaves the star system, turn the warp beacon off."

"Uhhh, could you repeat that, my Prince? I don't think I heard you right..."

"You understood perfectly, sergeant. The alien base must be very close, given how fast they got to the warp beacon after it being turned on. When we need a portal back, I'll let you know. But I don't need any strangers showing up in the Hnelle system!"

A Hole in My Pocket

A HOT SUN, which was almost the "correct" color, an endless blue sky with thinly scattered white clouds, a light, pleasant breeze, a calm sea that stretched to the horizon. From the low cliff, a surprisingly beautiful, calming landscape opened up. It was so similar to the surface of earth, that it actually surprised me. All it would have taken for me to finally believe I was on Earth was some soaring seagulls with their unique iodine smell.

We arrived to the former residence of Velesh the First on our third day in the Unatari system, after nearly all hotbeds of resistance on the planet Unatari-VII had already been suppressed by the Alpha Iseyek landing troops and the governors of all large towns had recognized the legitimacy of the new regime. The small tropical island, which had once been selected by the local "King" for his palace, had been carefully checked over by unified divisions of praying mantises, humans and chameleons. But other than two hundred confused, frightened servants, there was no one in the residence. The notably lusty criminal King's personal guard and the large part of his concubines had left on the first day of the invasion, taking one of the four planes and a recreational submarine from the underground base with them. The runaways had taken a multitude of expensive pieces from the criminal King's extensive collection of paintings and sculptures. Also, according to eyewitness accounts, before their flight, the guards had taken a big safe from the wall where Velesh the First kept his valuables.

I wasn't too worried about the stolen valuables. First, as a Crown Prince of the Empire, it wouldn't be proper for me to own things of suspicious origin. Second, I already ordered my new palace decorated with artwork from *Queen of Sin*. I publicly staked my claim on the former residence of Velesh. I chose the twenty-acre island because of its beauty, but since it once belonged to pirates, technically it should have been confiscated. None of the local powers had opposed my demand and on the interactive map, the island was already marked as property of Crown Prince Georg royl Inoky.

As a matter of fact, I had declared my right to another similar paradise island to give to my daughter. First of all, Likanna really had been seriously offended by my rude behavior during the battle with the aliens, and I hadn't been able to reconcile. I was planning on using this gift to apologize to the Crown Princess. Second, I still felt a certain discomfort with the fact that my brother, Roben, had been able to give my daughter a palace, but her own father hadn't.

However, there had been a problem with giving the palace and island to her: a real gate to hell was discovered in the basement of the otherwise excellent palace. It once belonged to the pirate brotherhood's treasurer and contained whole halls filled with sophisticated instruments of torture, while in the dungeons, in a great many cells, there were haggard, maimed prisoners from captured ships. The pirates would stop at nothing to beat banking information from rich passengers and starship captains. There was no way I could give a palace like that to my daughter, even after the whole sinister basement has been cleaned out – too much evil has been done there for too many years for new inhabitants to be able to live there happily.

Thankfully, I was able to fully reconcile with my daughter soon enough without any palaces. I happened to look in at the language class that Lika and Bionica were giving to the two praying mantis bodyguards. After watching what was not quite a lesson, not quite a game for a few minutes, I suggested the pair of huge, sinister looking, ten-foot-high insects be named Phobos and Deimos (Fear and Dread) and that their chitin armor be painted for a more impressive effect.

"Can I really?" asked Lika, her eyes lit up in surprise.

I said yes. Actually, before that, I'd have to have a long conversation with General Savasss Jach about giving two dangerous killer assault soldiers to an underage girl. I had to hear out the fairly long and complex explanation about the system of subordination priority in the Iseyek race, but the important thing I understood: for Phobos and Deimos, the whole system of values had been realigned under two people – my daughter and me. Now, protecting the lives of Crown Prince Georg and Crown Princess Likanna and carrying out their orders had become the most important and only reason for their existence, fully replacing concepts like the "Swarm" and "clutch." There was no circumstance under which either of the bodyguards could even think about allowing aggression or violence to come to me or my daughter. The general pledged that either of these Alpha Iseyeks would give their life without a second thought to stop any possible threat to the individuals they are guarding. Popori de Cacha was present for this conversation and fully reaffirmed the general's words. The chameleons had come across such "overly attached" bodyguards before.

I apologized to the general for my cutting words (yes, I confess, it happened) and mistrust, and wondered about the Alpha Iseyek soldiers' day-to-day needs. I was interested in everything: what they eat, how often and how much, how the other end of the process works, whether they need to sleep and they continue to grow, if they shed their armor... I had a whole ocean of questions, and I received very detailed answers to all of them. Bionica accompanied me and acted as my interpreter, so now the android was also in the loop on the special features of these huge "house pets."

For the last few days, my daughter had been experimenting with the paint sprayer. Phobos and Deimos had changed their colors over one hundred times since my suggestion. Sometimes I helped Lika;

sometimes Bionica also joined our art sessions. And now at breakfast time, to my right was the silent and serious, hot pink Phobos, and to my left was the also statue-stiff Deimos, painted in a folksy, floral pattern. Over her food, Lika was making plans to bring her guards to school, imagining how surprised her classmates would be. From time to time, I would say yes and laugh with my daughter, not wanting to upset her before I had to. General Savasss Jach had warned me – and in this issue I was in full solidarity with him – that it was entirely impossible for her to bring those bodyguards to school, as all it would take is Phobos and Deimos misinterpreting one little joke on Likanna for someone to get killed.

"Good morning, Prince!" the android, holding flippers and a breathing apparatus in her hands and wearing a swimming suit, walked up to the vine-covered alcove where I was having breakfast with Lika.

"Hi, Bionica! Are you joining us?" I pointed at the full bowl of fruit and the plate of pastries.

"I would like to, of course, but all the same I cannot. I need to watch my figure." The robot ran her palm over her ideal thighs in a worried fashion, just like a person. "I'm on my way to the lagoon right now. I want to swim and check the underwater torpedoes we found in the palace. Well, and at the same time, as it was on my way, I brought three bills: from Tesse, for the repair and modernization of two heavy assault cruisers and frigates; from the new management of the Unatari docks, for buying equipment and materials for the remodel; and also a bill for fleet upkeep for the last month. I dealt with the little ones myself, but these ones are the biggest, and they need to be approved by your Highness."

"And how much is it in total?" I wondered, pouring myself a glass of local berry juice, which was bright blue like a copper sulfate solution but unexpectedly tasty.

"Thirty-five million eight hundred thirty-one thousand seven hundred ten credits," calculated the android.

I gagged on my juice.

"How much?!"

The robot repeated the sum and sent me a detailed report. I opened it and read the dry lines of numbers. So, this is right – eighteen million for the repair and modernization of the captured pirate ships. I understood that, and it was a reasonable price. *Hunchback's Heir* was fundamentally damaged, and the *Surgeon*, well, I still don't know how it didn't explode. I was expecting the repair to cost more. Thirteen million credits for modernizing the docks... So, I'll have to figure this out. How did that number get so high? Well, I'll allow it, it's a one-time expense after all. But now, four million thirty thousand every month for fleet maintenance!!! There was just no way I could make room for that.

I looked at it in even more detail. The main expenses were coming in from the ten heavy cruisers. Buying ammunition and drones to replace those that were destroyed, fuel for the reactors, salaries for the officers and team members, battle payouts, provisions, station upkeep... It was all right, unfortunately. The numbers for the other ships were also right. I breathed a heavy sigh. I had to admit to myself that my fleet had grown significantly, and my expenses had grown with it. But what would the future hold? In a month and a half, the *Uukresh* would be in working order. That's another seven or eight million credits every month for upkeep. And if we can restore the docks...

The topic of the docks was one of the most discussed in the last days. We had not saved the orbital docks at Unatari; we hadn't had the chance. The pirates blew up the space docks, warehouses and repair workshops immediately when my fleet had just barely come out of the warp tunnel near the seventh planet. Blowing up the ten megaton thermonuclear mine was either a gesture of despair or an attempt to damage my fleet. It was more likely an attempt to cover the tracks of their criminal activity, as it was at the repair docks and moorings where the large part of the starships captured by the pirates were kept, sometimes in pieces and sometimes with broken identification chips. Many ships had long ago acquired new names and been successfully legalized, making them able to travel freely throughout the Empire.

In any case, a great many of the docks and ships were totally destroyed or irreparably damaged. The shuttle moorings, freight hangars, repair workshops with complex systems of robotic arms... Everything needed to be rebuilt practically from zero. It was all the more surprising that one of the badly damaged docks had in it the two-mile-long carcass of a battleship under construction. Energy shields had been installed on the ship, and they took the brunt of the damage. The combat ship had suffered in the explosion, but the specialists who looked it over confirmed that the *Tyrant* battleship could easily be finished if the docks were restored and the necessary materials and financing were found. The bill Bionica had brought only had the price of restoring the docks and hadn't included the completion of the battleship, but nevertheless the total ended up being quite substantial.

I grit my teeth and paid all three bills, then looked longingly at my remaining nineteen million credits. After all, it wasn't too long ago that I had more than three hundred million. I hadn't added any ships to my fleet since then, but still I had just over a third left... I supposed that the time had come for decisive action to correct this negative financial tendency. But first, I'd have to officially become the ruler of the planet Unatari.

The beautiful silver liner touched down on the landing pad. I looked out the viewing port at the forest-covered island and the huge white skyscrapers like mushrooms growing out of a green rug. Eight low-atmosphere fighter planes, fresh off a mission, accompanied us from the front before passing us off to the airstrip's defense system.

"Astorimma is the biggest city on Unatari-VII. Its population is seven hundred thousand. It is the unofficial capital of Unatari," Bionica commented to Lika on the landscape unfolding before us.

"Just seven hundred thousand? So little?" the girl became surprised, being accustomed to the megalopolises of the Imperial Core.

"Given that just eight million three hundred six thousand people live on the whole planet, that's plenty. One in twelve Unatarians live in Astorimma."

I didn't interfere in their conversation; I was too busy negotiating with the numerous participants in the forthcoming ceremony. As always, a bunch of minor details had to be decided at the last second. A multitude of events had to be synchronized. The audience appeal of the whole grand event depended on it. It was decided that the regime change on Unatari and the coming of Crown Prince Georg royl Inoky ton Mesfelle to the capital would be furnished with great pomposity, so that even the most skeptical inhabitant would have no doubts that this wasn't the occupation of Unatari, but the return of legal governance after forty-five years of pirate chaos.

The liner hung in the air and began slowly setting down on the Astorimma airport landing pad. I took one last look through the viewing port. I saw thousands and thousands of people behind the fence, gathered to take a look at a never-before-seen spectacle. The liner touched down softly, swayed slightly and came to a full stop.

"The Prince will enter with his retinue in two minutes and forty seconds," Bryle's voice rang out in my microscopic earphone.

The old butler accepted my offer to lead the ceremony with a low bow. He thanked me for the trust I had placed in him and promised that everything would go in full accordance with all accepted Imperial traditions. I stood up from my chair and took a pause in the spacious passage. I allowed some servants to fix my hair, put the thin band of a crown on my head and smooth the wrinkles in my uniform.

"You're on in ten seconds!"

Lika, standing next to me, was noticeably nervous. She was wearing a smart, long, light-blue dress and a gold crown in her emerald green hair. Likanna looked quite spectacular, a true Imperial Crown Princess. I winked to my daughter, and she finally smiled.

"It's started!"

Sovereignty Change
The Unatari system has been placed under the jurisdiction of the Orange House

Sovereignty Change
The Tivalle system has been placed under the jurisdiction of the Orange House

Sovereignty Change
The Sigur system has been placed under the jurisdiction of the Orange House

The Brotherhood of the Stars has ceased to exist.

Crown Prince Georg royl Inoky ton Mesfelle shall become the sovereign of the Unatari system

Global fame increase. Current value +8
Global standing increase. Current value -14

The military orchestra thundered out the Imperial anthem. I went down the gangway, smiled and waved welcomingly. At the same time, though, I found myself quite confused. After the destruction of the Brotherhood of the Stars pirates, I had requested three star systems as holdings – Unatari, Sigur and Tivalle. However, only the first request was approved, while the latter two had been declined. Insofar as I understood the existing order, only the head of the Orange House, Duke Paolo royl Anjer ton Mesfelle had the authority to do that. But why would the old man want to limit my rights?

I went down the gangway and stopped at the beginning of a long carpet path. Popori de Cacha, having been officially appointed head of my security service only yesterday, was waving a staff in his hand. At the same time, the nine chameleon bodyguards surrounding me camouflaged themselves, while two chains of soldiers in Orange House ceremonial uniforms stood frozen at attention. On both ends of the carpet, the crews of all my ships were arranged in two even rectangles. There were ten people from each frigate, twenty per destroyer, fifty per light cruiser, and one hundred from each heavy cruiser. Behind them, standing in flawless rows, as if measured with a ruler, were the Alpha Iseyek assault soldiers from the *Tria*. Nine thousand terrifying-looking praying mantises, decorated in orange and stiff as statues. Beautiful and terrifying, devil take me! It was hard to pick out the few black and green divisions in the sea of orange rectangles. They were the local self-defense soldiers participating in the ceremony, already having sworn their loyalty, but having yet to receive new uniforms. Any observer would immediately comprehend the power relationships in the recent conflict and the greatness of the Orange House.

Slowly and ceremoniously, I walked along the rows of my soldiers, approaching the local dignitaries that stepped forward to meet me. Lika was walking next to me with the proud bearing of a natural-born Crown Princess, and she had a slight, appropriate, bored smile on her face. To the right and left of my daughter in the procession, Phobos and Deimos were walking without letting their guard down and with Orange House coat of arms painted on the little shields on their upper appendages. Two steps behind my daughter and I with a proudly puffed out chest, Bryle was walking in his ceremonial uniform. The old man was supported by Bionica, who was in an excellent dress that the android had ordered herself on the occasion of the ceremony. The two admirals and the general walked further, covered closely by Popori de Cacha.

I was greeted by the governors of every city on the planet. They were a big group of civil servants with ingratiating smiles, clearly spooked and not knowing what to expect from the new government. I saw a great many faces staring at me for a few seconds. Clearly, the local city heads had been reading up on the Crown Prince, and it was only proper that his negative standing worry them.

The tall, thin man who came out to meet me turned out to be the viceroy of Astorimma. With a bow, he handed me a symbolic ring of keys to the planet's cities and pledged his full support to the Orange House. The rest of the group followed the first's example and, one by one, pledged their allegiance to me. After that, the time had come for my first speech as ruler of the planet. I went out onto the stage and saw dozens of camera lenses trained on me.

After the prepared introduction about the responsibility placed on my shoulders, the role of the Orange House and the Empire in bringing order to the planet, and other traditional matters, I came to the part I considered the most important:

"People of Unatari! For decades, the very name of your star system would cause anyone in the Empire to immediately think of bloodthirsty pirates, murderers, slavers and drug traffickers. As the new leader of Unatari, I intend to do away with its criminal past as quickly as possible. That is why I am declaring the beginning of a great hunt for pirates and their treasure. Every Unatarian that informs the authorities about uncovered pirate assets, whether real estate, bank accounts, stocks, luxury items or other property, shall receive twenty percent of the value of said assets. Every Unatarian that points us in the direction of a pirate, slaver or drug trafficker on the lam shall receive a cash reward of one thousand credits.

And now for the most fun prize of the great hunt. A day ago, my people intentionally released the three space pirate "Kings" on different islands on Unatari – Velesh the First, Janis the First, and Gaspar the Second. Of course, you are all very familiar with the names of these bloodthirsty bandits and would recognize them if you saw them. Each of the pirate Kings has been given a bank card with a million credits and a one-thousand-credit-per-day spending limit. In addition, any time one of these cards is used, it will be broadcast in the news with a delay of exactly twelve hours. The reward for the head of each of these three Kings is one million credits plus whatever is left on their card. And also, if any of these three Kings is killed by a wanted criminal, that criminal will be given full amnesty regardless of the seriousness of their crimes. And so, let the great hunt begin!"

Global fame increase. Current value +9
Global standing decrease. Current value -16

I furrowed my brow in consternation. Not everyone had taken to my radical approach to ridding the planet of pirate contagion. But what difference does it make to me what strangers think? The important thing is that eight million people who suffered many long years under pirate oppression can stop living in fear of their tormentors and will now learn to see them as nothing more than a valuable trophy.

"Incoming call from the Veyerde system," said my communications officer late in the evening. "Shall I put them through?"

I tore myself from the computer screen that I had spent the last few hours at trying to calculate the optimum composition for a high-mobility fleet and straightened out my tired back. Veyerde? Uh, a tiny Kingdom in Sector Seven. What could they possibly want from me? I didn't really know anyone from the Kingdom of Veyerde, and it wasn't like their territory was in my Sector. Should I refuse the call? However, natural curiosity and the desire to take a little break from my work overpowered me all the same. I ordered them to be put through. An imposing man in a red robe appeared on the screen. His gray beard and silver hair spoke to his many years.

Kant royl Pikar ton Veyerde, ruler of the Star Kingdom of Veyerde
    Age: 88
    Race: Human
    Gender: Male
    Class: Aristocrat
    Achievements: (see Attachment)
    Fame: +4
    Standing: + 11
    Presumed personal opinion of you: Unknown
    Kingdom of Veyerde's opinion of you: +1 (indifferent)

Oh my God! It turned out that who wanted to talk to me was the monarch of the little kingdom himself! I wonder what he wants from me? I just didn't know what to think. Could the aliens have invaded? But how could I come to his aid? A direct connection between our Sectors hasn't been discovered yet, and my fleet wouldn't be allowed to pass through the Imperial Core. However, the topic of conversation turned out to be something else entirely. After greeting me, the King suddenly declared:

"Crown Prince Georg royl Inoky ton Mesfelle, news has reached me that you have taken an interest in my daughter, Princess Astra."

There it is! But how could he have found out about my conversation with Marta?! Naturally, I asked that question to the King. And he, it seemed to me, sighed sorrowfully:

"Over the last few days, my government's counterintelligence service has caught some five or seven spies from the Kingdom of Fastel and, with various levels of pushiness, they were all interested in my youngest daughter Astra's plans. It was from these captives that I discovered, to my great surprise, that in the Kingdom of Fastel it is considered practically inevitable that Astra's betrothal to Baron Henrik ton Lavaelle will be broken, as your Highness has taken an interest in my youngest daughter. So that is why I, as a loving and caring father, wanted to speak directly with you and get the whole story first hand."

I tried to reassure the King as much as I could. I told him that I hadn't really wanted to complicate his daughter's life; I had just brought her up in a conversation with my wife as an example of a beautiful Princess. Kant royl Pikar became clearly upset.

"Too bad... It's just that I, like many others, was watching the broadcast of your enthronement ceremony on Unatari-VII and immediately noticed that the seats that, according to protocol, should be for your wife and favorite were empty. Rumors have been flying for a long time about your not-overly-simple relationship with Princess Marta, but it was only confirmed today. So, I decided that the information from the Kingdom of Fastel might have had some basis in fact. Because, if the Crown Prince didn't even take his wife to such an important triumphal procession, that must mean that Marta really has made a serious fall from grace."

I hadn't looked at the parade through that lens, I admit. It seems that the aristocrats had looked on the ceremony as a demonstration of the fact that Marta had fallen from favor and had been sent packing back to her little Kingdom. It seemed to them that it wasn't Marta that had gotten mad at me, but I that had sent the disagreeable Princess into exile. I wonder how Marta herself had perceived it? She had probably gotten even madder. The King continued:

"Princess Astra really is my crown jewel and, as you noted correctly, is an exceptionally beautiful girl. That is why I began forming conclusions and supposed that your Highness really could have taken an interest in her, because my Astra deserves better than Baron Henrik, who's only possession is platinoid mining rights on one remote, uninhabitable planet."

I remained silent, not wanting to slander Baron Henrik, who I'd never even heard of. The Lavaelles represented the Green House, with which my relationship had publicly grown more complex, and I didn't want to aggravate that divide any further. The King clearly understood that and decided not to push the difficult topic further, instead suggesting:

"Ok, Crown Prince Georg. In general terms, I understand the situation and will not distract you further from important matters. All I ask is that you have a talk with my daughter Astra. It's just that all this fuss and uncertainty around my girl has left her very spooked and nervous, and she would like to hear that there's nothing to worry about first hand."

"And why not? I am prepared to apologize to your daughter if I caused her any discomfort. Is she there with you?"

"Oh, no. It's already late night here. She went to sleep a while ago. Princess Astra will get in touch with you as soon as she's available."

King Kant bid me farewell and signed off. I continued staring longingly at the tables of calculations and discovered that my recent conversation had totally knocked me out of working condition. Out the window it was late evening, almost night, but I had no desire whatsoever to sleep yet. I poured myself some juice and went out on to the veranda with cup in hand to get a breath of fresh air. With a starry sky overhead, everything was blooming and a pleasant smell was wafting over me. Below, under the cliff, an angry sea roared.

Bionica came out onto my veranda along a path inlaid with multifaceted stone tiles. The android girl was holding flippers and a breathing apparatus again, but this time she had two of everything.

"Where are you going off to for the night?" I asked in surprise.

"I saw that you swim well, Prince Georg. So I decided to suggest that your Highness and I take a night swim together in the lagoon," said the blonde, pointing at the diving masks in her hands.

"Well, the sea is pretty rough right now." The sound of the waves breaking on the rocks really did give me a certain scare, but Bionica waved it off:

"The lagoon is surrounded by cliffs and is only connected to the sea by an underwater tunnel, so the water there is always calm. Also, my Prince, after all the strain today, you clearly need to blow off some steam."

I began looking for a reason to say no, but then suddenly made up my mind. And why not, actually? I had never had the chance to go scuba diving, but Bionica assured me that it wasn't hard at all and was totally safe. The main difference between the equipment here and what I'd seen on Earth was the fact that the oxygen for the diver to breathe wasn't stored in bulky canisters, but was filtered directly from the water by a device that worked like fish gills. One filter pack could last for five hours, which was more than enough for our purposes. I followed the girl up the stone stairway, which was hewn into the cliff. On the way, I asked my personal secretary about the results of the great hunt.

"Better than we could have expected!" Bionica smirked happily. "By the end of the first day, over three hundred individuals suspected of piracy and drug trafficking had been arrested, now the local criminal police are working them over. Around two hundred palaces and villas built on dirty money have been brought to light. The employees of all banks on the planet have been just racing for the last few hours to check all their clients' accounts. They've frozen criminal assets worth almost a billion and a half credits. Well, and of the three "Kings," Gaspar the Second has already been killed. The head of his own personal guard took him out, thus earning amnesty."

I mentally applauded myself − a billion and a half had already been found. Half would go to the planet's budget, twenty percent has been promised to the lucky hunters, ten percent goes to Orange House taxes, and another twenty percent goes to me as ruler of Unatari. As soon as all necessary checks have been completed in a few days and all formalities have been observed, I'll be transferred three hundred million credits. Not bad, not bad at all... And then, there'll be auctions to sell the confiscated islands, palaces and other pirate property. I suspect that that will also end in a decent addition to my coffers.

With these pleasant thoughts, I unexpectedly reached a wooden bridge that brought me up to the very brim of the exceedingly black water. Bionica stopped next to me and started preparing the equipment on the spot. She opened and inserted new catalytic filters into the wide, flat box that attaches to the diver's back, turned some valves and checked the data readers' output. The fact that I wasn't wearing swim trunks suddenly dawned on me. I was wearing underwear, but they weren't exactly made for swimming.

"My Prince, there's no one around. You can't seriously be embarrassed to be seen by a robot, can you?" Bionica asked in surprise, when I told her about my predicament.

Yes, it really was stupid. I still couldn't get used to treating my android secretary as a genderless object. I decisively threw down my clothes, put on the mask and attached the filtration box to my back. Bionica helped me tighten the straps, put flippers on my feet and showed me how to use the valves.

"It's only 25 feet deep here, so it's a good place for a beginner to learn. Let's swim toward the underwater tunnel. There's whole bushes of luminescent seaweed there. It's really beautiful!"

After these words, the girl put on her mask and fell into the black water back-first. I followed after her.

Huh, the water isn't cold at all! The only thing was that I couldn't see my companion under water, despite her neon yellow swimsuit. Fortunately, Bionica quickly turned on a bright flashlight, and I was finally able to get my bearings.

We swam along the very bottom, which was covered in a layer of minute, colorful shells. I quickly learned the ropes, and soon I was practically leaving the experienced Bionica behind. Finally, the girl turned and pointed with her hand somewhere up ahead. She said something through the mask, but I didn't understand a word. Then she simply turned her flashlight off so I could see for myself – the bottom in front of us was covered in illuminated blue and red spots. We swam up closer and Bionica uncurled a vine from one of the bright submarine plants, demonstrating their illuminated, slightly pulsating vein lines.

After allowing me a sufficiently long time to stare at this miracle, my companion pointed somewhere in the distance and swam off in that direction. I couldn't do anything but follow after her. It got darker and darker, and I almost lost sight of her, but she was smart enough to turn the flashlight back on. We were next to a vertical cliff at a depth of 15 feet. Bionica flashed the flashlight left and right on the wall and waved her hand, trying to get my attention. A wide crevice went through the cliff, and it was there that the girl was headed, fearlessly squeezing herself between the seaweed covered stones.

After a bit of wavering, I followed after her. I had to swim forward and up. The space grew smaller. For some time I kept trying to swim, but soon I had no choice but to just stand up, as the depth was now less than 5 feet. My head was above water, and I saw that Bionica had already removed her mask.

"Welcome to the most authentic pirate cave around!" Bionica said to me.

She shined her flashlight in all directions, and the walls answered back with thousands of tiny glints. The cave entrance was lost somewhere in the darkness. The air was fresh, clearly having seeped in through cracks in the rocks. I even felt a light cross-breeze.

"My Prince, come here!" said Bionica, calling me from the darkness.

I followed her voice, went around a turn in the corridor and stopped. It was a small cave, the sole entrance to which we had just gone through. There was no water here. Under my feet, I heard the crunch of sand mixed with little shells. Bionica shone her flashlight on something big and dark. At first, I didn't understand what it was, until I got closer. It was a treasure chest with bronze plate sides. Oh yeah, we've found the pirate's treasure!

The girl moved her light aside, and I looked at the folding table from the other side of the cave. On it, there was a dish of fresh fruit, a little cake with candles and a bottle of wine with a pair of glasses.

"I found this cave yesterday morning, and it has a treasure chest in it," Bionica said, answering my unasked question. "I didn't tell you right away, as not to distract your Highness from the preparations for the ceremony. But it also gave me the opportunity to set up a little surprise to celebrate your success. Phobos and Deimos helped me bring the table and two chairs here. Praying mantises can stay underwater for up to half an hour, so it was no problem for them."

I walked up to the treasure chest. It was massive, well-built and had a huge lock hanging from it. Next to it on the sand, there was a key-ring with what looked like either keys or lock picks.

"Have you opened it yet?" I wondered.

"Yes, of course," she answered, deftly opening the lock and throwing back the lid.

Inside the chest there was gold and silver jewelry, goblets, and chains. Basically, your typical pirate treasure, like you see in picture books.

"Have you calculated the value of the treasure yet?" I wondered.

"Um, around half a million, more or less," answered my secretary, fairly carelessly.

It was this wanton estimation from the normally scrupulously accurate Bionica that was the last straw that finally cleared away my doubts.

"Eleven percent of the total for your four million eighty thousand credit contract comes to slightly less than half a million. Or did you also put the money you had saved up before coming to work for me in there?"

The girl lowered her eyes in embarrassment, and her toes squirmed in the sand.

"No, I basically had no money left when you hired me. But how did you guess, my Prince?"

I pointed at the treasure chest.

"It's too theatrical. Of course, I can understand why the pirates in the ancient world did it, but why would a modern pirate store funds in the form of valuable objects like this? It's inconvenient, hard to sell, and it leaves a trail when bought or sold. And also, in such a damp cave, bronze should tarnish fast, so right away it was clear that this chest had been brought in, if not today, then yesterday at the earliest. Not to speak of the fact that it's hard to imagine Velesh the First looking all around and making off into the night with such a huge chest on his humpback."

Bionica laughed and said seriously:

"Androids don't need much personal money, so I'll be returning what you spent on my advance, whether you want it or not. You've done a lot for me, Prince, and I really am endlessly grateful to you. Ok, let's forget about the chest. It was a clumsy attempt. But are you going to say no to a late dinner in the company of your robot?"

"I will not," I smiled. "Yes, and your plan with the chest was quite fun and unusual. I liked it a lot. Thank you!"

The girl adeptly opened the bottle and very evenly, as if from a burette in a laboratory, poured a thick dark wine into both glasses.

"To the new ruler of Unatari!" my secretary toasted.

"And to his wonderful assistant!" I added.

We clinked glasses loudly and took a drink. The wine was sweet and quite strong, with a distinct note of those berries used to make blue juice on Unatari. While the girl poured us a second round, I turned to the table to try the fruits. When I turned back to my companion, I froze. Bionica had removed her swimsuit and was standing before me naked with two wine glasses in her hands. She was a blindingly beautiful blonde with a flawless body and skin, which was impossible to tell from the genuine article.

"My Prince, perhaps I'm doing the single most reckless thing I've ever done in my life, but I can't go on like this. If I cannot express my feelings to you with treasure, let me do it another way. Or order me to lower my humanness level..."

Bionica went silent mid-sentence, looking downward in my direction. I already knew exactly what she was looking at. And what of it? Doctor Nicosid Brandt had assured me that this would happen one day in the process of curing my crystal addiction. There was no way I could tell the android girl I didn't like her now...

I took one of the glasses from Bionica's hand, drank the wine in one gulp and took a decisive step toward the robot.

BLACK CLOUDS GATHER

THE NEXT MORNING, it was planned that I would visit the orbital docks or, to be more accurate, what was left of them. But the storm that descended on the island spoiled all my plans. With such strong wind the shuttle pilot refused to take off into the atmosphere, explaining his decision with the fact that it was a space shuttle after all and wasn't rigid enough to be an adequate low-atmosphere plane. I probably could have ordered him to do it, and he would have obeyed, but it occurred to me that this wasn't the right time to be throwing my weight around.

That was why I spent the morning sitting in a glass-walled room in my new palace, drinking a hot cup of the local coffee-analogue, half-watching the news and observing the chaos going on outside. Trees were being ripped from the soil. It looked as if real waves were running across the tall grass and bushes. Taut strings of rain lashed against the glass. Lightning painted the dark sky shades of pink and orange. An incoming call signal distracted me from the display of nature's rage.

"My Prince, incoming call from the Tivalle system," said my communications officer.

I accepted the call and brought up the picture on the big screen.

"Your Highness, this is Lieutenant Ramon ton Klest speaking, commander of the guard team for the warp beacon and ice harvesting plant in the Tivalle system. We have received the following strange message from the Orange House Capital: **'Viscount Sivir ton Mesfelle shall become the holder of the Tivalle system. *Confirm? (yes/no)*'**"

"What nonsense is this? Say no immediately! Lieutenant, I give you my permission, and even order you to accompany your 'no' with vulgar commentary! Tell them that the Tivalle system belongs to Crown Prince Georg royl Inoky, and any usurpers can go sit on a... Well, you can write the rest. Use your imagination. If more such messages come in, ignore them!"

"Will do, my Prince!"

The lieutenant signed off, and I seriously weighed the issue. What is this incomprehensible fuss going on behind my back? After I was unexpectedly and utterly groundlessly refused the rights to two star systems, someone had just tried to put in for one of them. That put me on alert and even scared me. I ordered a call be made to the commander of the Sigur system warp beacon guard division.

"Space Corporal Valentin ton Osmun on the line!"

"Space corporal, I am calling to find out whether a request has come in to you from the Orange House Capital about appointing a sovereign for the system?"

"Yes sir, my Prince! Such a message just came in now. We haven't had time to answer it yet: **'Crown Prince Peres royl Paolo ton Mesfelle shall become the sovereign of the Sigur system. *Confirm? (yes/no)'***"

"I order you to say no! And write in the comments that the sovereign of your system is the Sector Eight Fleet commander, Crown Prince Georg royl Inoky, and usurpers are not welcome! If more of the same messages come in, ignore them. Is that clear, space corporal?"

"Yes sir, my Prince," he said, freezing for a few seconds, as if thinking about whether it was worth continuing, but then decided to continue nevertheless. "Your Highness, I must tell you about the discovery of an anomaly in the Sigur system. Perhaps it was this very anomaly that served as the scout ships' reason for installing a warp beacon here, in that there are no other objects of interest or planetary bodies suitable for settlement and development."

"What anomaly exactly?" I wondered aloud before receiving a clear answer from my subject:

"Approximately every eleven hours and seventeen minutes, the warp beacon from the Forepost-12 system becomes visible for a few minutes. The consistent pattern was noted by us yesterday. My people are studying this strange phenomenon now."

Geez. That really makes me wonder... I opened the star map of Sector Eight. Forepost-12 is an uninhabited system with an automatic warp beacon that serves as one of the linking nodes between the Swarm, the Kingdom of Fastel and the chameleon home-world. It seems that we have discovered the "back door" out of this dead end, which the pirates may have used to enter Sector Eight space undetected.

"So then, space corporal, you are to consider this information about the unstable warp beacon a state secret, and you are not to tell anyone about it. I order you to study this consistent pattern and turn off the Sigur system warp beacon while the Forepost-12 beacon is on. We already have enough uninvited guests coming in through the back way. But in general, excellent work!"

I signed off. So, I had basically succeeded in deflecting the claims of the various Orange House aristocrats on the systems I had conquered from the pirates. All that was left to settle the matter once and for all was to repeat the order to the Hnelle system soldiers not to activate their beacon for anyone other than ships from my fleet, and only after my personal sign-off. And then none of the four systems of the former Brotherhood of the Stars would be accessible to unwanted guests.

I was not able to finish my conversation with the Hnelle guards before the communications officer told me that the head of the Orange House, Duke Paolo royl Anjer ton Mesfelle, would like to have a talk with me. I sighed laboriously, imagining in advance how hard the forthcoming conversation would be.

"Georg, what do you think you're doing?!" from the first second, the Duke began to yell at me and I pressed the "End Conversation" button.

A minute later, he called back.

"For some reason the call cut off," said the Duke,

clearly not having understood what happened.

"That was me cutting off the call. I don't like it when people raise their voices with me."

"Georg, what is it? Are you drunk?" the head of the Orange House couldn't believe his ears.

"Not at all. I just would like to discuss these serious issues without unnecessary emotions or shouting."

The Duke furrowed his brow, went silent for a few seconds, then continued in a totally normal, business-like tone:

"What the heck, alright, straight talk. Georg, I will never give you my confirmation for the rights to the Sigur and Tivalle systems. It seems to me that you've already made quite the haul in the systems of the former Brotherhood of the Stars. So, it's time to practice some restraint. You got the captured ships and the Hnelle transportation hub and the rich planet Unatari-VII with all the pirate trophies that came with it. And that is why the remaining two systems will be given to someone else who has also done a lot for the Orange House and has long deserved such a reward."

"Duke, I will not inquire now what Peres royl Paolo and Sivir ton Mesfelle have done that's so great other than being born your son and nephew. I'll just state the facts: they will not become the rulers of these systems, because I will also never allow the local authorities to give their confirmation of that."

"You're forgetting your place, Georg!" the Duke raised his voice again, but after my reminder that I would hang up, he started speaking normally. "Peres and Sivir will arrive to their holdings with sufficient escort and all necessary documents, so anyone who tries to get in their way will be declared a traitor!"

"Duke, there's a simple thing you're not seeing: while your messengers are on their way, I could give these systems to any Kingdom, corporation or organization – it could even be a fictitious one or one that I just created myself. And the legal, responsible representative of that faction would confirm that those systems really are their property. So if you try to give my legally acquired systems to your relatives, the Orange House will be deprived of them entirely, simple as that."

The Duke practically roared back, his eyes burning with rage.

"You wouldn't do that! Doing something like that would be an extremely unamicable step in your relationship with the Orange House and the Empire as a whole! You'd be declared a criminal!"

"Why? Overdramatizing the situation and intimidating me is not advisable." I began smiling ostentatiously in reply. "The simplest option: I could give the Sigur and Tivalle systems to my legal wife, Princess Marta royl Valesy ton Mesfelle-Kyle. And why not? They would make a great gift and a sign of reconciliation at the same time. The two disputed systems would be given to the Kingdom of Fastel and would pay taxes to them, but I would remain at the helm nevertheless. And note, Duke, that this would all be done in full accordance with Imperial law. No one would be able to accuse me of even the tiniest infraction."

"We'll see about that," the Duke grumbled discontentedly in reply. "Georg, it seems you haven't understood that you're trying to cut yourself off too big a piece, and what's more you have the gall to be rude to an elder. What the hell? It's time to put you in your place. Know that until Peres and Sivir get the star systems promised to them, you will not be receiving a penny of financing from the Orange House. And I'll even tell you more – from this minute, not one dock in Sector Eight will sell you a single ship, and not one distributor will ship you a single ounce of metal for building new starships. Let's see how long you hold out and how quickly you run out of funds for fleet upkeep. I'm sure that in a few months you'll be apologizing to me and begging me to take these disputed systems from you!"

The Orange House head signed off. I let loose a string of curse words to the empty room. That old dude is trying to tie my hands with his embargo! And what? He provoked *me*. I was not prepared to let such impudence go so easily. So I pressed call:

"Bionica, transmit an order to all our financiers: all taxes and payouts to the Orange House treasury are to be temporarily halted. The funds are to accrue for now in a separate account until my personal word has been given."

How much was I supposed to pay in taxes to the Orange House just for what I'd found yesterday? I think it was one hundred fifty million. If the old man doesn't change his mind, this money will go to my fleet upkeep.

Over lunch, my daughter was complaining that she was bored – and that was probably true. The hurricane was still raging outside as before, though it had grown less strong, and Lika was still forbidden to go outside. She had no toys or playmates in the palace to speak of. I promised her that I'd come up with a way to have some fun. Lika had barely left for her room to watch some children's program when I called my secretary and another couple maintenance personnel from the castle staff. Pointing at random at one of the young men, I handed him a gold crown that I had found in one of the surviving safes:

"I want this gold band engraved with ruby letters. Make them pretty and intricate. They should say: 'True Pirate Princess.' Can you get it done in a couple of hours?"

The red-haired boy scratched his head thoughtfully and nodded yes.

"Great! Now you," I said to the other worker. "Scare up a miniature radio beacon and a direction finder. Ask the guards. They've definitely got a couple lying around. Set it up so the direction finder will pick up the beacon's frequency easily."

When the workers had left, I turned to the android. The blond girl was acting totally natural today. She gave no hint, in expression or gesture, to remind me of yesterday's craziness in the underwater cave. Yesterday, she was simply wonderful but, since this morning, with a sober mind, I was horrified. How much had I risked? If someone figures out that the Crown Prince has his fun with a robot, that'll be the end of my standing. No, they probably wouldn't revoke my titles, but the scandal that would result would still be horrifying. It would threaten a whole cascade of unpleasantries up to the point of it being forbidden for me to appear in polite society and me being officially reprimanded by the Emperor.

"Bionica, I hope you have enough discretion to not remind me further about what happened between us. And you must never tell anyone else about it under any circumstances. That is an order."

"Do not worry, my Prince. I'll be silent as the grave," the android girl whispered barely audibly, with a light bow.

I remained briefly silent, then changed the topic:

"The forecast says that the storm will be over in three hours. By that time, you should hide the crown given to you by the maintenance workers somewhere in the rocks. Place the little beacon next to the crown. As soon as the weather calms down, you'll call Lika to go swimming. I don't know how, but convince her to take a dive in the lagoon with the breathing mask. Lead her to the cave with the chest and pretend that you've just found it. Take out what's left of the drinks and hide the direction finder in the trunk. And put a sheet of parchment in there. Style it up to make it look old, and write on it that the most valuable treasure on the island can only be found by someone who is worthy and quick-witted. Well, and let Lika fiddle with the chest herself. She should open the lock. For a child, that's the most fun part. Let her take whatever valuables catch her eye. Don't worry, I'll compensate you for everything bought on your money. Well, and after make sure that Lika is able to find the crown using the direction finder, no matter what happens. Do you understand?"

Bionica began to smile and answered that she would do everything as I asked. I sent half a million credits to the android's account and went to my shuttle with a relieved heart. The pilot told me that the weather had cleared up enough to allow him to start. On the way, I was smiling, imagining the spark in my daughter's eye when looking for real treasure. I hope that my daughter will have something to tell her little friends about after the break. And then, this evening, Lika definitely won't be bored anymore.

The shuttle started off into the gloomy sky, packed with dark, thick clouds. But the experienced pilot had not been mistaken; I really didn't feel the wind anymore. We got out into orbit with no problems and were quickly approaching a belt of metal debris. The place looked surreal – there were twisted, melted structures, rotating pieces of ceramic metal, and a several-mile-long mess of cables.

"There's the temporary construction base," commented Admiral Kiro Sabuto, pointing at a bright spot in space far away from the drifting trash. "They've already begun cleaning up this chaos, and today a new platform for attaching hangars and construction girders was delivered. But the most interesting thing still isn't there. The battleship that was under construction has been cleaned of twisted hangar debris and pieces of superstructure that got blown apart in the explosion. The repair workers are living inside the battleship in sealed units. Two ship airlocks are in working order and, as it were, we are on our way to dock at one of them."

The shuttle turned sharply to the right and, without entering the cloud of debris, set off into the blackness of space. The huge ship appeared out of nowhere. I only spotted the mile-and-a-half-long goliath when it was less than a hundred yards out. I don't know how it was explained. Maybe the material the ship was made out of was bad at reflecting light, or maybe we approached from the dark side, but the sudden realization that you've just noticed such a huge titan so close to you has quite a bad effect on the nerves. Our shuttle seemed like a pitiful fly on an elephant's back.

Finally, our little ship was caught by the magnetic arms and pulled inside the larger starship. I was greeted by the leader of the repair brigade, Kul ton Fes, a man of practically square proportions with impossibly huge hands and the neck of a bull. Insofar as I understood, such a build was evidence that he was born on a planet with high gravity, and his swarthy skin spoke to the bright sun of his home.

"My Prince, welcome to our unfinished ship. I recommend that you attach magnetic pads to your shoes right away. Only one of our artificial gravity installations is working, and it is on reduced power − we're saving electricity."

I obeyed the man's advice and stuck the magnetic attachments on my shoes. We went down a long hallway and ended up in a round room with very bright lighting.

"This is something like our central office," Kul ton Fes explained with a snicker. "In reality, this is the distribution hub next to the future central elevators. From here you can reach many different sections of this giant."

The craftsman's assistant turned on a big screen on the wall and pointed to a map of the ship. Yes, the complexity of the forthcoming work made an impression. Most of the lines on the map were drawn in red, which meant these modules, sections, walls and partitions had not been built yet. Kul ton Fes turned on a laser pointer and pointed at a row of turrets on the ship's chassis:

"I'll begin with what's important. The hardest and most expensive is going to be scaring up high-power laser turrets. A battleship like this one needs gigawatt pulse lasers, a whole eight of them. We cannot get our hands on such equipment ourselves. Such things need special factories and a long calibration period, which is why they are made to order in the Imperial Core. One turret costs around seven million credits. Insofar as I understand, it was this lack of cannons that held the Brotherhood of the Stars back from finishing this ship. To purchase high-power laser installations, you need special permission from Imperial monitoring services, and getting that is no easy feat. Well, and obviously they had a deficit of materials. Here on Unatari, there is a heat-resistant tantalum alloy production facility, but its output is microscopic."

"You need tantalum alloy to complete the construction?" I clarified.

"Yes, my Prince. To build the chassis of any military starship, special kinds of alloys are needed, with certain characteristics. Usually, tantalum-based alloys are used. In addition, a great deal of these alloys are needed for building a frame, no less than three hundred thousand tons. If we can only count on the local production from Unatari, then we'll need seven hundred years before we have enough material. But if you can't get readymade alloys, then we could also work with tantalum ore concentrate. Then we could at least get started on making the armored plates on Unatari."

I turned and looked around for Admiral Kiro Sabuto. He was listening closely to the conversation and understood immediately:

"Yes, my Prince, I remember our conversation about the huge mountains of tantalum ore on the planet of the chameleons well. However, I must remind you that trading with the chameleon race is forbidden by decision of an Orange House court."

"Yes, I remember. Let's leave the issue of the battleship for now. How is the reconstruction of the docks coming along?"

Kul ton Fes shrugged his shoulders:

"It could be finished quickly enough. We've already ordered the equipment. As soon as it comes in from Tesse, we'll just need a couple days to put it together. But the problem is in cleaning up all this chaos. How can we talk about normal work when freight ships have to fly through a cloud of such abrasive fragments just to get here? And cleaning up all that dangerous garbage will take at least four weeks."

"I'm giving you a week. If needed, bring on more people and equipment from the planet, but it should all be working in seven days. My fleet, come what trouble may, has nowhere to go for repair. I can't keep sending them back to Tesse and asking my brother to fix them."

By the way, I was barely able to mention Tesse and my brother when... The communications officer told me that I was getting an incoming call from Crown Prince Roben royl Inoky. Well, I'll be! Has my brother come out of his multi-day drinking binge? I tried to get in touch with him a few times about various issues, but the Crown Prince's service answered that Roben wasn't available.

"What's up, little brother? I watched your parade, to be honest, on TV. You look good, but you've lost a very noticeable amount of weight. And Lika looked very classy. So grown up, and proud – she's really taken after our mother. But that's enough waxing lyrical. I, in fact, was looking for you for another reason. A whole Orange House fleet came unexpectedly to Tesse, two hundred ships. It's being led by that ghoul, Crown Prince Peres royl Paolo, who I've wanted to strangle since I was a child. He had the fortune to be born three months before I was. Just three puny little months is all it took for the line of succession to be not in our favor, that is, mine, yours and Violetta's. And so, that ghoul is interested in the Hnelle warp beacon. He wants to jump there with his whole fleet. I explained to him clearly that the beacon is turned off due to risk, but that caustic infection discovered some of your ships on Tesse and has expressed a morbid curiosity in them."

"Have they been there long?" I clarified.

"Ah no, ten minutes, or maybe fifteen."

"Have they started recharging their energy drives yet?"

"Not yet. Little brother, do you want me to refuse them service? Let them sit there for five or six hours charging their power from their own ship's reactors?"

"No need. Just hold them there for ten minutes. That will be plenty of time for my ships."

"Of course I'll do it, it's not an issue. I'm happy to

help you get the better of that ghoul."

"Thanks, Roben. And good health to your boy."

* * *

The first thing I saw after returning home was a whole mountain of jewelry on the floor of the entryway. The pirate chest was right there, though truthfully it looked pretty roughed up, as if someone had broken it with a sledgehammer. The happy Likanna, with the crown on her head and wearing a regal, red gown that was too long for a child, was jumping around the treasure and laughing in joy.

"Dad! You won't believe what you missed! You won't believe it! Me and Bionica got our hands on some treasure for you!"

"Why for me? You found it, it's yours," I chuckled, but the child wouldn't give up.

"No, that's not right. You said yourself yesterday on the stage that hunters will get twenty percent of the treasure. So I picked out what I liked – this crown here, and another pretty, ancient signet ring, but the rest you have to give to your planet. And all Bionica took was a thin gold chain. It was just lying there on the sand next to the chest."

A chain? I instinctively felt my wrist. It was true. The gold chain with a pendant depicting a scene from the Kama Sutra was not there. It must have slipped off yesterday. The clasp on that thing was pretty flimsy. I had already unlatched it inadvertently several times. I'll have to have a talk with Bionica about that before anyone else notices.

After dinner with Lika in an excellent family

atmosphere, I tended to my affairs. I had to sign and agree to a bunch of documents, confirm appointments to Unatari minister positions, sign off on the budgets of every city and the planet as a whole, and look over a plethora of information. Ugh, why did I get into politics? I am a fleet commander after all, not a ruler. How I understood Roben at that moment. I also needed assistants I could trust and who could take all this bureaucratic mess off my hands. Unfortunately, Bionica was not suited for that role. Conservative society would never accept a robot in such a high position.

The account balance change alert beeped. I opened the finance sheet. A deposit of three hundred and five million credits, the payout from my share of the confiscated pirate accounts, had come in! Awesome! Four hundred twenty million in my account. When would there be a better time to buy the expensive battleship cannons? And that was what I set about doing, as the risk absolutely existed that Duke Paolo might expand the embargo with time to include weaponry for my starships.

Eight gigawatt pulse lasers with delivery to Tesse. So, I had to additionally confirm my identity to get special permission for this purchase. The legality of the transaction was confirmed, and I transferred fifty-six and a half million credits. The order is supposed to arrive within five days. Great!

Global standing decrease. Current value -17

What was that? Why did that happen? What am I doing wrong? It couldn't be that a Crown Prince buying weaponry for his personal fleet could bother someone, right? Or were my purchasing cannons and my standing decrease two absolutely unconnected events that just happened to coincide? I hope that's it.

I looked at the clock. It was eleven at night. Weird that Duke Paolo royl Anjer wasn't trying to call me anymore. His son that he sent to be enthroned was probably starting to figure out that the Hnelle warp beacon wouldn't be turning on for him no matter how long he might wait around or curse. He probably had already complained to his influential daddy about my foul play. And it wasn't in the Duke's character to just let it go and forgive such an offense.

When a call did come in from the communications officer I reacted practically with relief – that old pecker finally decided to reach out. However, I was wrong. It wasn't the head of the Orange House at all. Who wanted to talk to me was an anonymous caller from the Obella system. Where is that? And why such mysteriousness? Before giving my permission to put them through, I took a look at the interactive guide.

Obella *is a small inhabited planetoid that orbits a gas giant. The star system bearing its name is located in Sector Three.*

Sector Three? The Green House??? I could not have been expecting to hear from anyone less. What could they have wanted from me? I prepared myself for a quarrel. On the screen appeared Katerina ton Mesfelle, my second cousin, who worked for the Green House.

"Hi, cousin! Why are you calling on an encrypted

channel and from an unknown number?"

"Georg, I have some very important information to tell you. The Green House intends to demand you make a report before the Emperor again."

"Again? What, was one time not enough for you guys?" I laughed.

"You don't understand, cousin. There's nothing to laugh about here. You've bruised the egos of many very influential figures, both from the Green House and other factions, and this time it will be much more serious. A whole office of lawyers is going through all the details of the great number of accusations, looking for precedents and preparing such a clever trap that even you won't be able to get out of it. You're being accused of high treason. Green House spies have found information that a Gamma Iseyek who marched in your group in the parade is an infamous and wanted terrorist, who is accused of a great many murders of Great House upper aristocrats. And they have witnesses who are prepared to swear that you were aware of that fact, but chose to have it covered up. The minimum is being charged with harboring a criminal; the maximum is high treason. And that isn't even close to everything. You're being accused of the murder of two members of the Green House. They're gathering a base of evidence and filing the motions as we speak. But the fact that you appointed a chameleon murderer as your authorized representative and head of your guard is already evidence of the fact that you approved of his actions and rewarded him with a promotion. You're being accused of ordering a double murder on Imperial upper aristocrats. That is a very serious charge,

Georg. The accusers could demand your execution. But that still isn't everything!"

The girl on the screen began coughing slightly, then continued.

"The most unpleasant thing is that the head of the Orange House, who is obliged to be present at the meeting and lead your defense, has actually just made a secret agreement with our new head, Duke Amelius royl Mast ton Lavaelle, which supports the accusations made against you!"

"Are you sure of that?" I clarified, and Katerina replied with a pre-prepared confirmation:

"Yes! I swear, Georg, that it is true! I was personally there next to Duke Amelius when the call came in from the head of the Orange House, so I inadvertently heard all their agreements."

I furrowed my brow. Duke Paolo turned out to be such scum! He decided to get me out of the way with another's hands!

"Is that all or are there some other accusations?"

"There are, of course. The list of accusations itself is so long that you could read it for days on end. Inhumane treatment of captives, illegal enrichment, tax avoidance, harboring pirates and slavers, illegal production of narcotic crystals, disrupting the unity of the warp beacon transportation network... But, to be honest, most of them don't hold water and could be refuted quite easily. They were added to the list just to make it look more impressive. And then there's the unnatural, for an Imperial Crown Prince, intimate relations with an android, which they could very well prove, and that would be especially telling given that earlier you swore that it wouldn't happen in the presence of the Emperor himself."

"What nonsense is this? What relations with an android?" I chuckled, internally hoping that my laughter would come across as less artificial than it felt.

"I'm not familiar with the details of that particular accusation. All I heard was something about system logs that are periodically sent by each android model to the manufacturing company. It isn't hard to understand that, as the manufacturer belongs to the Green House, your very android is being subjected to the most in-depth observation and messages it sends are studied thoroughly. Allegedly, a message came in recently that indirectly compromises you, and the technicians are hoping to soon get more clear evidence."

"Alright, we'll deal with it. Thank you, cousin!"

I opened the opinion change menu and improved my personal opinion of Katerina ton Mesfelle right away by ten points, informing her of it. I thought that Katerina would like it; however, my cousin's reaction turned out to be totally different.

"What are you doing?" she asked, looking clearly frightened. "Don't you know that faction heads can see these personal relationship numbers? I already get the stink eye in the Green House because of my last name, Mesfelle. But for having a record like that in my standing, they could even call on me to make a report before the Duke. At the upcoming meeting with the Emperor, your mother and I are supposed to read the accusations against you, and you're spoiling my standing with these data logs... Ugh, let's hope no one noticed!"

With these words, Katerina put an idea in my head. I realized I could use this to try to lure my cousin to my side.

"Katerina, what difference does it make? You're like a naive child with all your worrying. 'Will they notice me?' Dozens of spooks listen in on every conversation between Great House upper aristocrats and report anything suspicious to their faction head. Right now as well, our conversation is being listened in on. The very fact that you called me and helped me has made you a criminal in the eyes of the Green House. I'm sure everything will be reported on in no more than five minutes to Duke Amelius."

"Are you sure of that, Georg?" True horror could be heard in my cousin's voice.

"Of course. A hundred times I've noticed that Duke Paolo knew about my confidential long-distance conversations before he should have. That is why these kinds of meetings are normally held face-to-face, without exception."

"I'm dead! What should I do, Georg?"

"The easiest option is for you to come over to the Orange House. With your last name, even that brute Duke Paolo won't be able to refuse you. And fly at a relaxed pace to either Sector Seven or Eight, no one will dare stop you. You could come to Tesse. My brother, Roben, would be happy at your arrival. If you don't want to go to Tesse, I'd be glad to see you on Unatari. I'm in great need of sensible, reliable people to manage the planet. I swear that I will provide for your safety in Unatari. No one – not the Green House, not the Orange House, not even the Emperor himself – will be able to get you here. Just make your choice soon, before your security service apprehends you."

Katerina closed her eyes, sat like that for ten seconds, let out a sigh and said decisively:

"Alright. I'll fly to you in Unatari immediately."

The call cut off, and I mentally applauded myself. Having one of the main accusers come over to the side of the accused broke down the whole picture of my guilt in the eyes of an impartial observer. Because if I'm such a malicious criminal that the Green House wants to make me answer for my crimes, then why are their people fleeing to my side?

My conscious was tormenting me slightly. I had a good relationship with my second cousin, and I was sure that she needed to be together with me. And, who knows, maybe all long-distance conversations *were* overheard by the omnipotent special services?

There was just one important thing left to be solved. I pressed the call button.

"Bionica, are you far?"

"I'm in Princess Likanna's room right now. I'm reading her bedtime stories. Is it urgent?"

"No, no. When you're free, come to my office on the second floor."

While my secretary was away, I turned on the news. What I saw was worrying: there had been another alien incursion, once again in Sector Fourteen. The system we had just taken back from the aliens was lost again. The Red House fleet that had been defending it was well and properly crushed. Its losses were higher than seventy ships of various classes, including the battleship *Red Rage*. Again, it raised the question about the loss of connection with distant systems and the necessity of forming a united fleet composed of both Red House and Imperial forces for liberating the people there.

I listened carefully to the news and began to think. I had no idea why they hadn't turned off the warp beacon in the threatened system after the first attack. They could have at least turned it into "on request" mode like mine in the Hnelle system, right?

Ten minutes later, the blond android came into my office.

"Your Highness, Princess Likanna has fallen asleep. Did you have some questions for me?"

"Yes, there are a couple things. First, I'd like to know about the results of the second day of the pirate hunt."

Bionica smiled:

"It couldn't be going better. Another hundred thirty criminals were arrested, a few accounts that had slipped by were brought to light, and the funds in them were frozen to the tune of almost four hundred million. Two crystal manufacturing labs were destroyed. The criminal "King" Janis the First was discovered by shell collectors on an uninhabitable island and was killed by the police detachment they called. The reward will be split up between fourteen lucky people. The last "King," Velesh the First, has only used his card once. Yesterday, he bought a bottle of soda in a minimarket in the Astorimma airport."

"When did that happen?" I wondered.

"Immediately before the start of the ceremony. Literally a couple of minutes before our liner touched down. The police have already checked the security footage and discovered a tall, light-haired woman using the card. Clearly, this pirate King has an accomplice. We are trying to identify her as we speak."

"Can you show me that footage?"

Bionica came up to the screen on the wall, called up the service menu and entered a long set of abstract symbols into the command line. I opted not to mess with the strange options she had available, which it turns out could allow her to access police files on the other hemisphere of the planet directly from this terminal. All of my attention was directed at the screen where footage from a camera in a small minimarket began rolling. I carefully looked over the visitor, who, not trying to hide at all and almost purposely flaunting herself in front of the camera, walked up to the refrigerator, chose an item and handed over the card to pay.

"That's not a woman. The movement is too angular, the shoulders are too wide. That right there is Velesh the First in makeup, a wig and a set of fake breasts!" I said, expressing my hypothesis.

"Yes, the police also came to that idea. The likelihood of them being the same is eighty-four percent."

"Nevertheless, the cheek on that guy!" I said in admiration. "He doesn't look like he's dying of thirst at all. I suspect that Velesh intentionally showed up in front of the cameras just to show everyone that he was at the ceremony too. Alright, we'll leave Velesh for later. For now, I'm more interested in your logs and how often you send them to the android service company."

"I do not do that myself. My built-in BIOS automatically sends them all data about my location and status once a day. It's a built-in defense to prevent androids from being stolen and so competitors can't try to take an android apart for reverse engineering."

"And what information exactly is sent? I'm already none too pleased by the fact that my traveling through the galaxy is being monitored through my secretary. What else is in those logs?"

Bionica thought it over, clearly trying to find an answer to my question in some internal control and debugging programs.

"Uh oh!" the girls face grew long suddenly, while her eyes became round in horror.

And that "uh oh" was another thing that left me none too pleased...

FRIENDS AND ALLIES

BIONICA WAS lying on the table with her arms stretched out along her torso. The girl was conscious, and her blue eyes were staring up at the ceiling. She was giving instructions on her disassembly to the technicians bent over her. A chameleon from the bodyguard team put down the user's manual and picked up a screwdriver. He spent a long time reading an inscription on the android's temple, then confidently pressed one of the points near Bionica's earlobes with a surprisingly long finger. The upper part of the android's skull moved smoothly to the side, revealing computer chips, little flashing bulbs and rows of large, dark blue crystals.

"The internal computer jack for equipment diagnostics is located on the right side, slightly above my ear on the inside," commented Bionica in an absolutely normal, calm tone of voice. It was as if she wasn't bothered by the fact that her head was open and its contents were available for anyone to see.

Popori de Cacha gave his subordinate a flat tablet with a thin cable coming out. The chameleon confidently stuck the plug into the jack, and some lines of text ran across the computer screen.

"Menu, subsection Guaranteed Service, pick Settings there, and in the list that comes up choose Notification Settings," said the android girl, continuing to give instructions. In the menu there, you select History and see the time and contents of all logs sent."

"There it is!" shouted Popori de Cacha contentedly after a couple of minutes. "Sixteen days ago a command came in that significantly expanded the scope of the logs. Before that, this model would report only on the technical condition of its systems, once per day. But look here, the size of the reports sharply increased, and the sending frequency also went up to four times per day."

"Can you figure out who sent that command and what was in it?" I wondered.

Popori de Cacha asked his subordinate something. He spent a long time poking around in the settings and answered evasively:

"The command came in over normal service protocol from an android service center. There is one on every more-or-less developed planet. I could try to decrypt it, but that'd take time. And we probably wouldn't find anything out of the ordinary. The service center simply changed the settings of the service reports and the reporting frequency. Since then, the android has been sending its coordinates, reporting on highly complex decisions made by its artificial intelligence, which approach the limits of what its programming is capable of, and also about the use of the model's expanded set of functions."

Hmm, I thought, trying to digest this information. In normal words, the spies tracking Bionica had the technical ability to understand that, yesterday night, the android thought intensively and had sex. They could even determine the coordinates of the place, but no more. It seemed like not enough to accuse precisely the owner of the android of breaking generally accepted traditions and morals. Because there could have been someone else the girl used her "expanded set of functions" with, right? And what if I had delegated my super-administrator rights to an authorized representative? It wasn't coming together somehow...

"We're missing something. My enemies are sure that they can access a fuller picture. How would that be technically possible?"

"My Prince, it seems I've found something interesting." The chameleon stopped tapping his fingers on the virtual keyboard. Both of the creature's eyes were focused on the screen. "Approximately an hour and twenty minutes ago, a command came in to provide video recordings and all full logs from internal systems for a specific period of time yesterday. From midnight to twelve forty A.M."

I estimated in my head. As it were, at that time, I was swimming with Bionica, after which I got a bit too intimate with the android in the underwater cave. If my foes see that footage, it's over... Which is why I took the chameleon's next words as a gift from the heavens:

"The incoming command was declined by the android's system, because it contradicted another earlier order coming directly from the owner of the model. This plotter simply didn't have enough rights to carry out their mission."

"The Prince's order was clear," Bionica turned on the recording, and I heard my voice from the side. *"You must never tell anyone else about it under any circumstances. That is an order."* "To get the requested information, special rights were needed, which, at that time, the plotter did not have. However, my Prince, if the command really were to come in from an android service center, then next time your enemies could simply raise their privileges to service level and get around your order."

"Turn her off immediately!" I demanded.

Bionica did not resist, instead simply observing in resignation as Popori de Cacha pressed the hidden buttons near her collarbone with his fingers. The girl's eyes closed, and the little bulbs in her electronic brain went out.

"What shall we do, my Prince? The robot has become dangerous, and for your safety it must be disassembled and the memory banks destroyed."

I stood near the window in thought, looking out into the night sky. The risk of the information in Bionica's memory leaking was very great, and the consequences would be extremely unpleasant for me. But nevertheless, I was in no rush to agree to the leader of my guard's suggestion.

"Look, we'll leave destroying Bionica as a last resort. She has become my friend, and I do not abandon my friends, as you yourself well know. For now, let's try a different approach. The fact that agents of the Green House are living and working worry-free on my own planet is in no way amenable to me. Find out where the company's android service office is, and order everyone there arrested in my name – no exceptions. Let them be brought immediately to me on the island. On your way, you can even bruise them up and scare them. I need to make use of my fearsome reputation!"

I chuckled, and Popori de Cacha made a fairly good imitation of my smirk with his huge lips and rows of tiny, sharp teeth.

They were delivered at two in the morning. By that time, I was actually starting to nod off, which is why, when the reasons I was forced to stay up arrived, I received them with such a dissatisfied grin on my face that even the imperturbable Phobos and Deimos flinched involuntarily.

"There were three total employees of the *Bioengineering Corporation*, which services humanoid robots on Unatari," reported Popori de Cacha.

I walked up closer and looked over the arrestees. Hmm. Who do we have here? The company director was a tall, older man with a big forehead and a bald head that shone back at me in the lamp light. The technical specialist was a young man who looked athletic and had dark curly hair – probably a favorite with the women. And the android programmer had humanness settings set so low that even an unobservant person would never confuse it with a living human. The people were clearly in a frightened state and were totally silent, afraid of raising their eyes to me again. The android looked absolutely unshakable though, as if what was happening had nothing to do with it whatsoever.

"So, I'll ask you a couple questions, and you'll answer them honestly. If you do that, you'll be simply placed on a shuttle and sent back home. But if one of you tries to lie, the Beta Iseyeks can tell right away," I pointed to the two pill-bug looking creatures, which I had requested from General Savasss Jach for a few hours especially for this meeting.

I used the widespread legend that Beta Iseyeks could allegedly read thoughts. Actually, unfortunately, that was not the case at all. I asked General Savasss Jach about it and received a detailed answer that the majority of Beta Iseyeks have no psionic abilities whatsoever. And those who were found to have such talents were quite far from reaching Truth Seeker level. By the way, it was the human Truth Seekers that served as a reason for the Swarm to decide that one branch of the Beta Iseyeks would be bred for psionic abilities. Maybe eventually, after five or seven generations, the Swarm will be able to create mind-reading beings, but for now, the two pill-bug looking Iseyeks were only able to read the emotional background noise, no more. But that didn't mean that the interrogees had to know about that.

"I in no way advise you to lie. I normally feed liars to my praying mantis bodyguards."

I noticed scared faces inadvertently peeking up at Phobos and Deimos. Yes, the ten-foot-high insects looked terrifying as always. Even *my* heartbeat would speed up if I were to see the scary silhouette of either Phobos or Deimos at night in a dark hallway.

"So, listen carefully. I'm basically a paranoiac by

nature, and I really don't like it when someone tries to follow me." I pointed to Bionica, who was lying on the table with an open skull. "Can you explain to me how it happened that my android secretary suddenly began sending confidential information about me to my foes? I would also like to hear where the information your firm collects is sent to. And finally, the last question: who ordered you to download data from my secretary's memory banks? So, I await your answers."

The three exchanged glances, and the director stepped forward:

"Your Highness, androids are normally supposed to transmit information to service centers. How else could we catch a malfunctioning temperature regulator or that a particular joint is sticking?"

I interrupted his speech and said that I was already familiar with that information, and that I wouldn't have had a problem if my secretary had only been telling them about her technical defects. But I was interested in this particular case, when my android servant began transmitting a much greater volume of information and much more frequently.

"So then, we can easily figure out who gave that command and where it came from!" the young engineer lit up.

Popori de Cacha asked the young man to approach the table and pointed at the computer screen.

"Well, here it is. You can see it in the line. A technical command to change settings. To be honest, we'll need someone to decrypt it. Arcy, can you take a look at what was sent here?"

The android programmer approached the screen

and, after a momentary glance, said:

"Change in reporting settings. Frequency was raised to four per day, geographic location was added to report, signal intensity was increased, the spectrum of requestable parameters was expanded. Here there's a request for information on the use of cost-based processor logic – that's for living emotions and behavior as close to human as possible. Here there's a request to unblock a normally unused function set – infrared vision, crying imitation, heartbeat and breath stoppage, body temperature change, sexual functions, destructive behavior... The command came from station one hundred sixteen."

"Where is number one hundred sixteen?" the boss asked the android.

The robot's answer shook me to the core:

"The Throne World."

My elbow and shoulder suddenly began to itch, which made Doctor Nicosid Brandt's bugs kick into action. The Throne World. So it was from there that they were trying to follow me through my android secretary. Well, alright, it's not impossible. And what about yesterday's command?" On my request, Popori de Cacha showed another record.

"But this one here is from us, station two hundred thirty," said the director, after barely looking at the screen. "What's written there, Arcy?"

"It's not from us. Our station was merely an intermediary re-transmitter. Here it is: the command came from one hundred four, that's the Orange House Capital. It's requesting the surrender of records of the full spectrum of parameters and some video. And the information should again be routed through us to one hundred four."

I raised my eyebrows in surprise. Not the Green House, but the Orange? Strange, though very possible. But how did someone in the Orange House Capital find out how to issue a command to my android? It can't be that friendly acquaintances from the Green House told Duke Paolo royl Anjer's special services, right?

"These people are not lying. They really are not involved in the spying," said Popori de Cacha, translating the pill-bug's words.

"That changes everything," I said kindheartedly, turning to the three captives. "I am a complicated man. I am impulsive. I can even be harsh, but I *am* able to recognize when I've made a mistake. You will all receive compensation for your unjustified detainment. In addition, I am very satisfied with your answers. And I would be especially satisfied if you confirm your words with an official document from the android service corporation. And now the last, additional question: would it be possible, without breaking my servant or deleting anything from its memory, to turn off all these dispatch messages and at the same time guarantee that no one will be able to remotely control it ever again?"

The trio exchanged thoughtful glances again. The first to speak was the android programmer.

"Turning off log reporting is very simple, but blocking external control... In fact, that would mean giving the android total freedom. I've never heard of that happening."

"I not only have heard of it, I have seen it." I had to bend the truth a bit, but it really was just a bit. "The former head of the Green House, Duke Kevin royl Olefir ton Lavaelle, transferred his consciousness into an android body. As far as I know, that android was not reporting and was not controlled by anyone other than its own artificial intelligence."

The company director laughed happily:

"Well, that's because the head of the Green House was the owner of the android production corporation and had the ability to do such a thing. There are rumors that Duke Kevin is not nearly the only old aristocrat like that. He's just the first to have been brought to light. But then, how is that done? To do that, you have to break all corporate rules, open the sealed BIOS and fix it manually... If they find out though, you'll be sentenced so harshly that you won't be able to pay it off with five lifetimes. And if something breaks, no one will take that android in for repair."

I considered it for not very long:

"Rip out the seals! If anything happens, blame it all on me. Say the Crown Prince ordered it at the end of a blaster barrel."

The robot was finished only around morning. The programmed-in defense that limited the android's capability for independent living turned out to be quite complex, and taking it out was a long process. During it, a dispute arose on how to limit the receipt of remote commands to only those from the owner and no other external person, even if they have higher rights than the android's owner. They decided to turn off all remote commands, all the way. Other than that, some base limits were hardwired in, for example, the ones against violence and murder or lying to its owner. But I didn't insist on these; I was perfectly OK with a peaceful secretary that I could trust.

Finally, the plane took the satisfied and somewhat richer employees back home. In addition, the director also took with him a signed contract for the delivery of two thousand androids of various working professions for Unatari. He and I even drank to the occasion, and the easily-intoxicated, bald man said with feeling:

"My Prince, I'm still so happy that you conquered our planet! We'll finally have work. During the years of pirate isolation, there were only forty-three androids on the whole planet, including our Arcy. And now there will be thousands of them!"

Of course, I did not want to upset my accidental drinking companion by explaining that I didn't need these androids for Unatari-VII at all. No one knew about this project, which I had been mulling over the last few days, not even my closest and most reliable allies. The plan was a way to defend myself from Duke Paolo royl Anjer's pretenses and looked so shocking that it threatened me with a death sentence, if the information were to leak out before its time. On the other hand, if I am able to prepare everything and pull it off, then I'll have no more reason to fear threats from the Orange House head than I would a rainstorm out the window.

"Popori de Cacha, has your electronics specialist learned how to remove the protection and change the control settings on androids?"

"Yes, my Prince. If needed, we can now also carry out these operations on robot servants."

"That is great. I think such knowledge will soon come in handy for us."

Bionica was lying on the table, switched off. Of course, there was nothing stopping me from turning her back on, but for some reason I was putting it off. Finally, Popori de Cacha did it for me himself. The blond girl slowly opened her blue eyes, which were still fixed on the ceiling, and then her eyes acquired consciousness. Bionica turned her head and saw me.

"My Prince... This simply cannot be! I have turned back on, and I'm alive! And my memory is still working like before. But why? Because I was totally sure that you would turn me off forever. There just couldn't be another way. I don't understand. Why has this happened?"

I remained silent, observing my perplexed robot with tenderness. The head of my guard, Popori de Cacha, answered for me:

"A weak leader sacrifices others to save himself. A strong leader risks himself to save others. Crown Prince Georg royl Inoky is a strong leader. I realized that in the Throne World prison. It would have been much easier for him then to sacrifice me and keep himself out of it, but Georg acted differently."

Standing change. Popori de Cacha's opinion of you has improved.
Presumed personal opinion of you: +52 (trusting)

Standing change. Chameleon race opinion of you has improved.
Chameleon race opinion of you: +5 (warm)

The incoming messages were a pleasant surprise to

me. Because, I admit, I was expecting the head of my guard to have a negative view of all this fuss over the dangerous android. It seemed very simple: no robot, no problem! However, Popori de Cacha saw some deeper meaning in my actions and evaluated the situation in his own way. It's nice when others start to value you!

"Popori de Cacha, what you've just said is still just an advance, but I'll try to reaffirm your words with my deeds. But now, Bionica, that's enough lying around. We need to get ready to return to the fleet. Today we're holding the big full-capacity training sessions."

If you'd asked me just a few short weeks earlier, I would never have thought it possible to fall asleep on a shuttle while taking off into thick atmosphere. But I guess I learned something, despite the shaking and noticeable G-force. Clearly, it was the result of a sleepless night spent worrying.

"Here we go, finally! It's been a few days since I've been able to reach you," Mr. G.I. entered my dream and began to interfere with my sleep. *"At first, I thought you were also taking a crystal nap and so were unavailable, but it was taking too long, even for crystals. What do you think of crystals, by the way?"*

"I don't like them at all."

"You're a fool, Ruslan. Who takes crystals to enjoy themselves? They're a way of cleansing yourself of worry, taking a break from the world, finding a solution to your problems. Crystals are the best thing in the Empire. Everything else is schlock that you can easily

live without..."

He suddenly began giving a dumb laugh, then said it himself: "Pssst! Behave decently so no one will notice you," and began nervously laughing again.

Today Mr. G.I. wasn't himself. Perhaps he was actually in a drug trance or was extremely drunk. Today he wasn't even interested in how I was doing in the game, though I had a lot to tell him about my successes and new difficulties. Finally, Mr. G.I. finished snickering and said with pain in his voice:

"Miya has disappeared."

"What do you mean?" I asked in surprise.

"We had a fight, and she left me. It's been three days already since she left. She won't come home or answer her phone."

Georgiy suddenly began crying uncontrollably, then shouted out in rage:

"That bitch dragged me out here and left me all by myself! But Miya won't get far, because I've got her crystals! She'll come back for them! And then I'll really tell her, I'll..."

"My Prince, wake up, we're already under way!" Bionica woke me up at a very untimely moment, preventing me from finishing the conversation.

It seemed that, if I'd had another couple minutes, I could have found out something extremely important from Mr. G.I., who was in a less than fully conscious state, something that would explain to me all the details of how I ended up on *Marta the Harlot* and how I could get back home. Geez, why'd she have to wake me up at such a bad time?!

No, I did not try expressing my anger at Bionica or at anyone. This had nothing to do with them... And I even thanked the android for the firo nut drink she brought me. For some reason, Bionica sincerely thought I liked that drink. But really I couldn't stand it. No, it's tasty enough, if peculiar. What really bothered me about it was something else. It had a crazy coffee smell, which made you expect the taste of a nice mug of coffee, but instead you get something like sweet compote that was stirred with a broomstick.

"No, not to *Queen of Sin*," I said, stopping the pilot. "Let's dock at *Joan the Fatty.*"

The shuttle made a smooth turn and started off in the direction of the far-away, unmoving heavy cruisers. Through the porthole, I was able to see the three new *Katanas* reflecting the rays of the local sun back at me. On the side of the nearest *Katana*, there was some kind of clearly anime-inspired character like a donkey with claws and butterfly wings, and a huge, multi-color inscription was shining out in a jolly font: *Boydur the Hero.* I covered my face with my hands – how embarrassing!

My daughter had suggested the name, and I agreed to it rashly. First, because I promised. Second, I thought naively that Boydur, who I'd never heard of before, really was some great hero from human history that I'd missed out on. I called up the guide to assure myself of my error.

Boydur the Hero is a children's entertainment program and animated series of the same name. The main character is a kind but mischievous space creature from the fictional planet of Beide.

It was pretty bad, but it got "pretty worse" when I saw the second cruiser. *Jeanne the Star Traveler* was also not at all the fear-inducing scout or explorer I had supposed, but instead was a pink frog from some children's show or another. This created a special contrast between the first two and the third, which I had named myself, *Emperor August.* The thought to name a heavy assault cruiser after the Emperor seemed quite sound at the time. After all, August royl Toll had paid for the construction of this ship himself, and I wanted to underline my gratefulness and loyalty to the Empire. Mhm, a mutant donkey, a glamorous frog and... Emperor August. They make a great team. It'd sure be great not to be accused of defaming the ruler of the Empire.

The shuttle entered the dock, and I exited into my new flagship. Captain Oorast Pohl greeted me and, after a quick tour of the decks, showed me the new fleet headquarters with pride. The room had become a bit bigger, the number of screens on the walls had also increased, and there were clearly some more people in the headquarters as well. I noticed a few new faces and pointed that out to Admiral Kiro Sabuto, who was walking up to me. He reaffirmed my suspicions:

"Yes, we've added eight new people. Of the four officers your Highness sent to be reevaluated for combat ability, only Valian ton Corsa was able to pass the tests. The other three I sent to other ships, switching them out for more capable officers. And we had to add five more people to the staff – we needed a long distance communications operations group and a separate group for electronic warfare. Also, on account of the *Uukresh* coming out of repair soon, we've added a tactics officer who will monitor and support the effectiveness of the combat drones and frigate groups. All the officers we've brought on are far from amateurs and have combat experience."

"Great, where's my seat?" I wondered, and the admiral led me to a console in front of a huge stereo screen.

"Crown Prince Georg, you will have two personal assistants right away," said the admiral, pointing at the two chairs on either side of the main seat. "The proxy consoles can do all the same things yours can, so you can delegate part of your work to them if you're overloaded."

"Uhhhh. So, in any case I won't be able to get by without an Iseyek translator, so Bionica will be here to my right. And to the left... I'll have to think about it."

The officers were standing at attention. I gave them an "at ease" and walked around my command center, talking with my subjects and getting acquainted with the new faces.

"My Prince, I passed all disciplines honestly. You can have no doubts. Also, don't listen to the losers gossiping about the exam administrators allegedly not judging me based on my abilities so much as for my figure and other talents," said Valian ton Corsa with a happy smile, rushing to assure me.

I answered the girl in the same joking spirit:

"That's too bad... Because my royal friends are

always giving me a hard time for not having a pretty favorite in my retinue at state receptions. If you had failed the exams, maybe I could have taken care of that. But now I'll have to find another candidate, and you'll have to keep up with the hectic life of a highly skilled combat officer."

The officers around me began laughing, having well understood that it was a joke. A few seconds later, Valian also smiled, but it was somehow still an unassured and labored one. I realized too late that this girl, who really was quite pretty, could have been taking my words completely seriously.

But then, one of the new crewmembers really caught my interest. First, differently from most of the officers gathered, you could read about him in a popup, meaning he was a living player. Second, his having two Great House last names meant that the person before me was in no way just a normal person.

Angel royl Mauri ton Mesfelle-Miro, Viscount of the Blue House
    Age: 38
    Race: Human
    Gender: Male
    Class: Aristocrat/Military
    Achievements: Has been awarded the Silver Comet combat medal for participation in interspecies conflict.
    Fame: +2
    Standing: + 1
    Presumed personal opinion of you: Unknown
    Blue house opinion of you: -2 (indifferent)

You can only get combat medals fighting with the Imperial armed forces, not in Great House private armies. At some point, the Dukes and other aristocrats, competing among themselves to see who could have the most medals and orders hanging from their uniforms, brought the race to a completely absurd point, and the Emperor got fed up with all their useless window dressing. Seventy-three years ago, August issued an order saying that the only true medals were those officially issued by the Empire, and all others were meaningless jackstraw. No, it wasn't that the Emperor forbid the Great Houses from issuing medals, which they had invented a great many kinds of, but after that order, people began looking on anyone who had one with a sneer, and soon everyone stopped wearing them.

By the way, it was precisely the issuing of combat medals that was one of the topics I wanted to address with my officers after the end of the day's training. To my mind, the situation had changed slightly over the past decades: humanity had come across a worthy opponent for the first time and was taking serious losses. The soldiers risked their lives quite frequently, displayed their courage valiantly and were completely deserving of combat medals for their actions. And, in contrast to the phony imitation jewelry of the past, these orders and other signs of distinction really had a deep meaning, and their owners had indisputably earned taking pride in them.

I had a desperate need for my soldiers to be loyal to me in light of a potential forthcoming open conflict with the Orange House head, which is why the topic of combat medals seemed timely and useful. But first,

I'd have to morally prepare my officers so they would really have a chance to see these shiny pieces of metal as special symbols that one really could take pride in.

Suddenly, I realized that I had spent quite some time standing in silence in front of Angel ton Mauri, and I'd have to explain the fleet commander's excessive interest in the officer somehow.

"I can't decide for myself. Either I've been fabulously lucky and acquired an experienced combat officer, who I can entrust with important missions right away, or the person before me is a normal, high-born nobleman, whose influential parents succeeded at setting him up in officer's school at the right time. I mean no offense to you, Angel. I'm not at all familiar with your biography, which is why I can only judge you by your noble last name and your combat order. So, tell me about yourself."

The man answered unexpectedly:

"It's more the latter, your Highness. My parents really did give me away to officer courses in the Throne World when I was ten, and from there I was dragged along by fate to wherever the Empire was at war with someone. And it was at war practically all the time... Five years ago, on the way back from a deep expedition into Swarm territory, my cloaked frigate came out of warp unsuccessfully near Forepost-11, appearing around the debris of a recently demolished freighter. As my bad luck would have it, there was a pirate cruiser nearby, and it captured us. I spent five years in a pirate jail on the Hnelle station. In that time, I was declared MIA and discharged from the Imperial Space Fleet. A few days ago, I applied to be reinstated to the post of Imperial space captain but was refused. I applied to your fleet and unexpectedly was hired to work on the very same ship that captured my frigate five years earlier."

"This must be fate, Angel – which is why I won't be giving you a position here..." I said, not having ended my sentence before his face had already become perplexed and sour. "Because I am in desperate need of an experienced captain for a cloaked frigate, probably the very same frigate you lost five years ago. Because, as cloaked frigates are very rare, it's hardly possible that the Brotherhood of the Stars pirates could have acquired several of them legally."

I saw the eyes of this strong man fill with grateful tears. And I understood that I had just taken a man into my ranks that would never betray me and would remain loyal under any circumstances.

"I gladly accept your proposition, Crown Prince Georg royl Inoky!"

Standing change. Angel royl Mauri's opinion of you has improved.
Presumed personal opinion of you: +15 (warm)

Standing change. Blue house opinion of you has improved:
Presumed personal opinion of you: -1 (indifferent)

Standing change. Empire Military faction opinion of you has improved.
Presumed personal opinion of you: +4 (indifferent)

Now that's what I call a nice gift basket! No, honestly, I wasn't expecting it! Well, I could have foreseen that Angel would be glad at being given back his ship, but the rest was just a pleasant surprise. Especially the improvement with the military faction, given that a great deal was riding on their loyalty to me.

* * *

I repent! I slept through the first half of the training session in the most shameless fashion imaginable, just lounging on my yacht. I began watching the sped-up footage of what I'd missed to catch up before it ended. Under the terms of the training session, two evenly-matched fleets were to face off. I really had divided the fleet more or less down the middle, with five heavy cruisers on each side. One half was commanded by Admiral Kiro Sabuto, while the other was being led by Admiral Kheraisss Vej. In accordance with the rules, a ship with a shield that has fallen to ten percent is considered destroyed and is removed. Firing on it is also to stop. Frigates under a web within an agreed-upon radius from any cruiser, whether heavy or light, were also considered lost. I slept four and a half hours. In that time, the battle had come to eight to seven in favor of Admiral Kheraisss Vej.

"Alright, that's enough!" I brought an end to the practice battle in a confident, even tone, so none of the participants, I suspect, guessed that their commander had been getting some rest during their maneuvers. "Your forces are approximately equal.

Both sides' losses are as well. By the end, the frigates had learned how to orient themselves well in space, and there were no stupid, unjustifiable sacrifices. General errors we can discuss later. For now, take a half hour break, then we'll try to change the score with electronic warfare, frigate groups, shuttle docking at the closest possible distance, and also we'll test out our cloaker."

For the second half of the training session, I took turns leading both halves of the fleet, and I was opposed by my admirals, who were also taking turns. It was all as close to real space-battle conditions as possible. We weren't being stingy with drones, and the frigates were taking such fast corners and with such G-force loads, that you could hear the crews moaning on the public channel. No one was being cheap with rounds either. I had to hike up my socks so I wouldn't get dragged through the mud in front of my subjects. It didn't seem to go too badly: at the end of the battle, the score was nine to one in my favor. The only point for the other side was scored by Kiro Sabuto, in that he had a total of three *Pyros* "survive" on the battle field.

That evening, when I entered the large hall on *Queen of Sin*, where I had invited my fleet captains and their assistants, the officers stood up in concert and greeted my entrance with a long round of applause. I spent a few seconds basking in the rays of glory, but then I raised my arm, calling for silence.

I talked about a lot of things: about the role of the space fleet in the history of the Empire; about the fearless scouts, who had spent centuries expanding the boundaries of human-accessible space; about those heroes who cleared the way for the human race in the future by breaking the resistance of hostile species. I gradually led those gathered to the idea that a great feat deserves a reward. And so, when I said that I had made the decision to revive the tradition of rewarding fleet soldiers and officers who distinguish themselves in battle with combat medals and orders, the hall reacted with elation. I called Admiral Kiro Sabuto on stage. I couldn't think of anyone more deserving than the man who had distinguished himself in the battle with the aliens near the Vorta beacon, with the pirates in Himora, and also in the double battle near the Hnelle beacon. I personally pinned the badges to his uniform, and the reaction of the officers was quite positive.

Standing change. Empire Military faction opinion of you has improved.
Presumed personal opinion of you: + 5 (warm)

Lieutenant Nicole Savoia handled the issue of searching through the fleet archives for descriptions of past Orange House combat medals on my personal request. She then ordered the first shipment of the revived medals and orders to Unatari. The lieutenant herself had earned the "Silver Brooch," a four-pointed star with a longer point on the bottom. Inside the medal, the number of space battles participated in was engraved in gold. Nicole's medal showed the number four.

Our allies, the Iseyeks and the chameleons did not go without medals either. For example, the chameleon captain of the *Tusk-1* was given the "Order of the

Ruby" for bravery in the battle with the aliens. And an Alpha Iseyek, the senior gunner of *Vassar-3,* received a "For Service in Battle" medal. A detailed computer analysis of the battle in the Hnelle system had revealed that *Vassar-3* had destroyed seven enemy frigates, which was more than anyone else in the fleet.

When the rush associated with giving out medals had quieted a bit, I turned the microphone back on.

"And now, I ask for your attention. The issue I'd like to discuss with you is actually very serious. Right now, our fleet is nowhere near the largest in the Empire, but it is the single most battle-capable one. Since the skirmish with the aliens at the Vorta beacon, we have become stronger and we are continuing to grow rapidly stronger as we speak. That is necessary to withstand the threat of an alien invasion. But that increase in strength has upset some people in the Empire and even in our own Orange House."

"Why?" rang out a lone shout from the hall.

"Because a strong fleet, military glory, and victories against aliens and pirates have increased my authority and influence in the Imperial aristocracy, which threatens the established order. Other aristocrats perceive this strengthening of forces quite negatively, and so that causes a strong reaction from them. For our glorious victories, our fleet has already been deprived of Orange House financing, we've been forbidden from buying new ships, all space stations other than Tesse and Himora have been de facto closed to our ships for repair, we are forbidden to build ships ourselves, and an embargo has been put in place against the delivery of strategic materials..."

An outraged buzz broke out in the hall, and I called for silence again.

"That still isn't everything! We've already been accused of poaching the best and brightest Academy graduates, which is why we can see that our opponents' next step will be to place a limit on recruitment soon, which will make it difficult to hire new team members. But their most recent step already crossed all imaginable bounds – we were demanded to give up the territory we conquered from the Brotherhood of the Stars pirates to total strangers, depriving us all of the spoils of our victory."

The buzz in the hall grew simply deafening. I allowed my subjects to let out their pent-up righteous indignation, and began speaking again:

"To carry out our mission, to defend Sector Eight, our fleet needs resources, bases, and money. That is why I refused to give up the territory that is rightfully ours. And right now, there is a fleet in Tesse belonging to another aristocrat who wants to try to take our star systems by force."

Here I gave a jolly smirk, demonstrating my opinion of such an absurd attempt on the part of my opponents.

After a second's pause, the first laughs rang out in the hall, quickly growing into the laughter of hundreds of people and even nonpeople. The soldiers couldn't stop laughing for a long time, because of how absurd the idea seemed to them that we could be beaten in battle. My subjects' reaction made me very happy. They didn't even know the size of the enemy force, but nevertheless had no doubt that their commander would beat the enemy in any case.

"What I'm about to tell you must not leave this room. Today, we're going to leave for the Hnelle system. Tomorrow, we'll do another full-strength training session, then I will be flying to Tesse with a small part of the fleet. And if I'm not able to settle it diplomatically with the would-be usurper, we'll go back to the Hnelle beacon. And if our enemies are dumb enough to follow our ships, we'll meet them in the Hnelle system and give them a beating to write home to their mothers about!"

The enthusiastic roar of hundreds of throats reaffirmed that I had not been mistaken. My captains considered our mission just and, as such, were prepared to take on any enemy regardless of species or uniform color.

And Back to Tesse

I MISSED *Queen of Sin* coming out of the warp tunnel into the Tesse system. No, I didn't sleep through it, or forget; it's just that I was in the sick bay at the time. I sprained my left wrist. And it happened due to my own stupidity alone. I decided to, as they say, make the best of the flight time through the warp tunnel and set off for the gym. The twenty-four-hour gym was locked for some reason, but of course my privilege level was high enough to open the door. And there was no one to blame but myself here. As it turns out, the laws of physics can be quite variable in a warp tunnel. Everyone on the ship knew that and took preventative measures whenever we were approaching discontinuities in space. It would seem that I was the only one on the ship not in the loop. But at least it shed some light on why the gym was sometimes locked during warp jumps. There's not much to be happy about when an electromagnetic barbell that you've just managed to lift with extreme strain suddenly becomes four times heavier...

"Your Highness, the ambassador of the Kingdom of

Veyerde to the Orange House is requesting permission to visit *Queen of Sin.*"

Veyerde? It was probably something about their Princess again. Clearly, their ambassador wants to give me a note of protest for interfering in their King's daughter's personal life. Alright, it's not too hard for me to apologize. It won't cost a thing.

"Good, give it. How long will it be for that ambassador to reach us?" I wondered to a staff officer, receiving a very unexpected answer.

"Not long, my Prince. Their shuttle is just under two miles from us. They'll dock in a couple minutes."

Well, I'll be! I've got guests coming, and here I am on a hospital stretcher, naked as the day I was born, with a swollen arm. Then the doctor, having heard my conversation, forbid me to stand, as he hadn't yet finished the procedures. Finally, a few minutes later, I tore myself from the doctor's tenacious fingers and rushed to meet my official guest, buttoning up my tunic as I went.

The idea was that the figure of Captain Clay ton Avelle standing in the passage was supposed to put me on my guard, but I was in too much of a rush and didn't notice him standing there in confusion. After flying into the airlock hangar to meet the ambassador, I also stopped, stiff as a statue, next to the captain, because the picture that revealed itself there looked too unexpected.

I'll start with the fact that the Honorable Ambassador wasn't in the hangar, nor was his shuttle. Instead of all that, there was an elegant girl standing by the airlock door with her eyes timidly trained on the floor. She was wearing a magnificent blue dress, and her graceful gold crown was distinctly shining through her dark chestnut hair. Next to Princess Astra, and the popup hint confirmed my suspicions about my guest's identity, there was a whole mountain of cardboard and plastic boxes, like the kind normally used for storing clothes and shoes while traveling. Behind this heap of stuff, I somehow didn't even see right away that there was another guest: a humbly dressed and, you could even say, unremarkable girl, if it weren't for the clear resemblance in facial features with the beaming Princess in ceremonial attire. She was unambiguously a close relative of Astra, but who exactly I couldn't figure – there was no popup hint about the second girl.

"The shuttle arrived, hurried to unload, practically hurling boxes onto the floor, left the two girls and took off," said Clay ton Avelle, pointing out the obvious.

The captain and I spent some time just standing in silence and watching the Princess and her companion, who had arrived in such a strange manner. My guests also made no attempt to approach or start speaking. Princess Astra kept standing there with her head lowered, motionless like a porcelain doll. Finally, I decided to make a gesture of politeness and welcome this crown-wearing lady to my ship. Astra gave an elegant bow and answered my welcome in accordance with all rules of courtly etiquette, with all the long titles. After which, she added:

"My father, King Kant royl Pikar ton Veyerde, told me that your Highness, Crown Prince Georg royl Inoky ton Mesfelle, expressed a desire to converse with me."

She had more or less the right idea, but as far as I remember the conversation with the monarch, we discussed holding it long-distance. Was I misunderstood? Or was my promise to have a talk with Princess Astra perceived as sufficient reason to send his youngest daughter tens of parsecs away for a personal meeting with an Imperial crown prince? It was probably the latter option. Otherwise, they wouldn't have hurried to get off my ship, so that I wouldn't be able to send their daughter back in the same fashion she'd come in with just a quick apology.

"And how much time do we have to talk? When is the ambassador's shuttle returning?" Looking at the Princess's heap of boxes of things, I could already tell that the monarch, Kant royl Pikar, had bid his ambassador not to especially hurry to return, but all the same you need to dot your "i"s and cross your "t"s.

"The ambassador isn't coming back for me. He was in a great hurry to attend to urgent matters with the Orange House. He brought me here because it was on his way," the Princess as before wasn't raising her eyes, apparently preferring to study the floor tiles in the shuttle hangar.

So, it's clear. The aging monarch was stubbornly trying to set me up with his daughter. He even purposely burned bridges so the meeting would never end. His importunity was beginning to get on my nerves.

"Captain Clay ton Avelle, show Princess Astra to the shuttle that will take her back to the Tesse spaceport. And let your man help her acquire tickets for the next flight in the direction of the Kingdom of Veyerde. We've got a war with aliens here, a squabble with aristocrats, our systems are blockaded, and all kinds of great stuff, so I really have no time for a high-society discussion with a charming young creature such as the Princess."

"Prince Georg, I beg you to give me but a little of your time!" the Princess unexpectedly lowered herself to the floor, not quite bowing, not quite curtsying on her haunches; due to her magnificent, many-layered dresses, it was impossible to tell.

By the way, her skirts were laid out in totally perfect circles, as if they were drawn with a compass. I walked deliberately slowly around the girl who was sitting on the floor, then wondered:

"Have you been practicing long?"

The Princess didn't speak up, though her companion, a thirteen-year-old girl, answered for her:

"Yes, what's to hide? We've been rehearsing since we left home. With a whole team of directors, costume artists, make-up artists and psychologists working out in detail just how my sister should behave depending how your Highness received her. What you've just seen was scenario sixteen: 'He wanted to send Astra home without even talking to her.'"

I took a closer look at the talkative girl, whose speaking habits looked a bit too complex and correct for a thirteen-or-fourteen-year-old child. She says she's her sister? Well, why not? It could easily be. I noticed the family resemblance from first glance.

"Well, and who are you, young thing?" I wondered.

"That is my younger sister Florianna Blidge," answered Astra, and in the Princess's voice I detected distinct notes of shame. It seems it had gotten under the Princess's skin that I had begun speaking not with her, the bright, elegant beauty, but with her younger sister.

"Just Florianna, without 'royl' or even 'ton' in her name?" I asked in surprise.

"That's right, your Highness," answered the younger girl, looking me fearlessly right in the eye. "King Kant royl Pikar had doubts about my parentage, and the genetic test he had done proved his suspicions. Astra and I share a mother, but I have no rights to titles. Since six years old I've been living in the palace as a servant to my older sister."

I could see how unpleasant the topic was for the serious girl; however, she overcame her embarrassment and told me honestly about her situation. I even started to like the little squirt, but I stopped myself on the thought that her honesty and sympathy-inducing story were probably just the next speech thought up by the psychologists so I'd change my decision to send the sisters back.

"That is all very interesting, of course, and under different circumstances I would talk with you, but you've come at a very bad time. I have a few rather complex negotiations coming up, and my every minute is booked through..."

"Your Highness is not speaking the full truth in order to hide his true feelings. He really does have a lot to do and is very worried, but in fact, Astra, your unexpected visit has made him very happy," said the girl, looking me impudently right in the eye.

Huh, huh, huh... Now it's getting interesting. That little punk can't be reading my thoughts, can she?

"Flora has been a spontaneous Truth Seeker since childhood. Her abilities appear uncontrollably."

The incoming call signal interrupted our conversation:

"Your Highness, a message has come in from Crown Prince Peres royl Paolo ton Mesfelle. He is insisting on an urgent meeting in no uncertain terms. He calls us a 'gang of pirates,' 'impudent conquerors,' 'violators of order,' and other such epithets."

"Answer him that Crown Prince Georg is not able to receive him – he is busy with a pretty lady."

A minute later, the officer reported:

"That hasn't stopped him, he's still insisting on a meeting. Our radars have picked up a ship detaching from one Peres royl Paolo's cruisers and coming in the direction of our shuttle. Estimated time of arrival: ten minutes."

That's what I call a pesky guy. Only the Princess's presence held me back from swearing out my frustration aloud.

"So, ladies, you're in luck. Your being sent home has been set back for some time. Captain, give the sisters a cabin and send people to bring Princess Astra's things immediately." The time had come for me to play the rude, tactless pirate for a bit.

I called over the loudspeaker.

"Attention, team! Crown Prince Peres wishes to visit our ship – the very same highborn swine that had the gall to hang up on me and took it into his mind to take our star systems by force. He is behaving boorishly, calls me an impudent pirate, a chronic alcoholic, and an earthworm. Friends, I have a request of you. Let's give Crown Prince Peres exactly what he wants so badly: an uncontrollable, rag-tag horde of drunken cutthroats without the word 'discipline' in their vocabulary. So, if anyone has any empty bottles or bags of alcohol, take them out and throw them into the hallway – you can even break them. If there's some booze left in the bottles, I order you to drink it immediately. Admiral Kiro Sabuto, I know how reverently you treat the appearance of your subordinates, so I have an order for you: do not leave your chambers for the next few hours so you don't have a nervous breakdown. Everyone else, change your uniform to the most raggedy clothes or even rags you can get your hands on. This masquerade is very important so he won't take us seriously. And also, burn a couple mattresses with a blaster on the second deck. I want there to be smoke on the whole ship. Lastly, I'll need a pretty girl to sacrifice her good name for the glory of the whole Empire."

I haven't laughed that hard in a long time! No, honestly, you had to see it! I was watching on the monitor as Crown Prince Peres and his two assistants traversed the halls of *Queen of Sin*, giving a wide berth to the hordes of drunk, half-naked cutthroats. A den of iniquity, a scrapyard, an illegal immigrant detainment facility – these were the kinds of places that the scene brought to mind, not the chic yacht it actually was taking place on. It seemed to me that some crewmembers were overdoing it a bit, but the expression of horror and disgust on the face of the Crown Prince as he walked through the halls spoke to the fact that he earnestly believed that the chaos being acted out around him was real.

"Password!" Phobos croaked out threateningly in the hallway, pointing a bundle of stalks from his four upper appendages at the recent arrivals.

"What's the password, dummy?! They aren't even from our ship!" Bionica arrived just in time and dragged the praying mantis away from the scared-stiff visitors.

"Total strangersss? Eat!!!" the ten-foot insect displayed his aggressive nature with all his might.

"Phobos, shoo. We mustn't refuse what the devil brings us..." I said into the microphone.

The doors opened and a middle aged, but fit dark haired man came into the room wearing a dark red, expensive suit with golden epaulets. His companions remained in the hallway.

"Ah, Peres, my beloved relative, you could've knocked... Well, now that you're here, take a seat in any case. And you, scram!" The last sentence I had directed at Valian ton Corsa, who was sitting on the bed, under the comforter.

The girl, with disheveled hair, jumped up from the wrinkled bed sheets and, after hurriedly scooping up an armful of her scattered belongings, ran out into the hall. Peres's surprised gaze followed the naked beauty as she left, while he, I figured, read my "lover's" popup information. Oh well, there will be another portion of scandalous information for the news channels tonight. I hoped that this fresh information about Georg royl Inoky's new favorite would put the story with the android on the back burner.

"Do you know why I've come?" my uninvited guest wondered aloud gloomily.

"I have two guesses," I answered with a none-too-sober voice. "Either you've come to share a drink with a dear relative, or you've come to negotiate for the Sigur system, which has been promised to you. In the first case, here's a glass, here's a bottle, pour yourself as much as you like. In the second, my price is four billion credits."

"Have you lost your mind, Georg?!" he exclaimed. "The system isn't even worth that much!"

"To me it is. It is distant from the more heavily trafficked stellar routes, so there won't be strangers coming through. I can place bases, docks, and workshops there. I can train my fleet there and develop new tactics, and no one will see. You could even have a squadron of flying pigs there, and no one would find out. Also, it's a matter of principle – it is *my* system, and you want to take it from me. And what does a mere four billion mean to someone like you, the ruler of the rich Nessi system?"

"Sigur is not your system! The Duke declared to anyone that would listen that it belongs to me!"

"Well, then the price just went up to ten billion," I countered calmly. "In that, for you, it has become a matter of principle. You've been promised something, but you'll never be able to get it, and everyone knows it. What a shame, what a loss of clout... I'm offering you a great way out: ten billion to save face."

"Don't be stupid! My fleet is far superior to yours! I can take what is mine without spending a dime!" Peres rasped through his teeth. "There is no alternative!"

"Your fleet will never get through Hnelle. Are you hoping to sneak by my yacht? Not likely! Do you know what makes *Queen of Sin* special? She's a high-speed yacht, not a combat ship. She has the energy to make two warp jumps. That is precisely how I was able to set the speed record from Tesse to the Throne World recently. So your fleet isn't a threat to me. I'll go to Himora and jump to Hnelle from there. And the other ships – it's not an urgent matter, they can wait you out and jump after me when you're long gone."

"Not likely, Georg! I could even wait for a year. I would never miss the moment when you activate the Hnelle beacon. And then the question becomes whether the freight ships that are already backing up here in Tesse with goods intended for Unatari will share your patience."

I took a sip of my drink calmly and answered with a smile.

"Have it your way. I just needed proof that I tried to resolve the matter peacefully, and *you* were the one who wouldn't have it. If the Emperor should have to settle this later, I'll simply play back the footage of the conversation we just had. And now listen carefully and don't interrupt, so you'll really hear me: if your fleet enters the Hnelle system, as the legal holder, which I am until my daughter's coming of age, I have the full right to eliminate trespassers. Consider this your official warning. And now, do the nice thing and get off my ship. I haven't yet finished with sweet lady Valian."

Peres went back through the halls of *Queen of Sin*, and the first repercussions of our unsuccessful negotiation had already come in the form of system messages:

Global standing decrease. Current value -18

Global standing decrease. Current value -19

When the Crown Prince's shuttle had undocked from my yacht, I spent some more time in the command center silently watching the fear-inducing enemy fleet on the tactical screen as it seemed to hang in space not far from *Queen of Sin*. It was an impressive sight to be sure. There was a battleship, twelve heavy assault cruisers, twenty light cruisers, forty destroyers and two hundred frigates. As far as the enemy could tell, we had just twenty ships: *Joan the Fatty*, two *Legashes,* and a handful of support ships. Our forces looked clearly mismatched. Here in Tesse, with the protection of Roben and his fleet, I didn't have to worry about open aggression, but in Hnelle... The enemy was strong. Very strong.

* * *

In my visit to Roben, I took the two sisters. First, why not? Let the girls see the whole wide world, given that they had the chance to get out of their home system for once. Second, I was nursing the timid hope of leaving the both of them in my older brother's flying palace and not having to continue to carry the burden of responsibility for the Princess and her younger sister.

As before, Astra kept up the proud princess act. She didn't relax for a second, tried to maintain good posture, a straight back, an even head, hands on knees – that kind of stuff. With her short height, around five foot three, and wide ceremonial dress, somewhat inappropriate for a flight in a packed shuttle, the girl looked like a pretty, big doll, that someone sat up in a chair where she's stayed ever since, motionless. Her sister wasn't bound by such harsh restrictions and was spinning in place, like a top, looking at the belt of space stations, huge ore ships, and tiny shuttles that flew by overhead.

However, Flora's behavior changed sharply when it came time for our shuttle to land on the flying palace's landing pad. The girl suddenly narrowed her eyes and clenched her fists, as if preparing for a fight. I didn't figure out right away who she was reacting so angrily toward, but then I saw for myself. Millena Mayer was coming toward us through the bushes with a deadened gaze, clearly not caring to find a path. The eight-year-old girl's gaze was trained on Florianna, as if she didn't notice the others. The two Truth Seekers must have had something of a difference of opinion...

The bright blue sky suddenly began to quickly grow dark. A sharp cold wind began to blow. I noticed that Millena's eyes began to glow with an orange fire, and her hair was fluttering in the gusts of wind. The girl bared her teeth and hissed like a disgruntled cat. However, Flora didn't give way. She stretched out her hand in the direction of her rival and put the girl on the ground with an invisible blow. Millena answered by giving a sharp, ultrasonic shriek that made my ears close up.

"Hey, hey, that's enough!" Roben royl Inoky, who appeared from behind the bushes, broke up the attempt to establish dominance.

Millena lowered her hands, which she had been holding in front of her as if defending herself from an unseen force. Flora also immediately relented and fell down on the grass, drained of strength.

"Little brother, you've got to be kidding me! Have you completely lost your mind? Bringing a Truth Seeker here?!"

"Yeah, well, who could have known they'd go at it like that?" I answered, still not having shaken what I'd seen.

Roben walked up closer and gently rubbed his Truth Seeker's head.

"Millena here is still small and is very afraid that someone else will take her place. Truth Seekers need a strong, influential master. Only then do they reveal themselves, gathering their energy from the master's power or something – I don't know for sure. With me, the girl is progressing quickly. She's becoming more confident and strong. All the same, what a smart kid. She wasn't afraid to go against someone older than her!"

"Flora is self-taught. No one has trained her. Her abilities are spontaneous and unstable," I answered, observing as Astra, having taken a seat next to her sister, wiped Flora's nose, which was dripping with blood.

"Well, I see then. Millena still wouldn't have wanted to take on an experienced opponent; the girl understands her modest abilities. She wouldn't even risk getting near your Miya. She would give up immediately..."

My brother and I walked slowly along the garden

path. Astra stayed with her sister, and I told my other companions to stay near the shuttle. Roben walked laboriously with a wheeze and finally sat down on a bench, exhausted. I took a seat next to my brother.

"I have decided to sell my gladiator team," my brother told me.

"Why?" I exclaimed. Knowing about his many-year hobby, the decision looked beyond strange.

Roben stayed silent, looking at the pinkish evening sky, then answered:

"It's just that my cutthroats have stopped bringing me joy. Yes, to a spectator it looks impressive – blood, steel, battle, not for life but to the death. But I know that my players are pros and aren't really taking risks in the arena but, instead, just acting out for the audience. My son, now there's a real warrior! How he fights for his life! He's just passed his third month, but he's already been on the very brink so many times, balancing between life and death, something no gladiator would dream of..."

"How is the situation with your son now?" I wondered, not overly sure how my brother would answer.

But Roben perceived my question quite positively, in fact.

"The doctors say that the crisis has passed, and his health is on the mend. But since they said that two weeks ago, the kid practically died!" Roben cried out the last part of the sentence at full power.

We stayed silent for a little, then my brother, looking more at ease, added:

"Millena told me recently that she kind of felt an evil thought directed at my son. Someone really does want my son to die..."

Having noticed that I began trembling, Roben hurried to calm me down:

"No, no, Georg, don't worry. I know it's not you, little brother. But, to reassure my wife, send your Truth Seeker a bit farther away. Verena just isn't herself and has even begun looking sideways at every shadow, seeing a potential murderer in every visitor. But then a Truth Seeker, even if she isn't very experienced..."

I promised to have Florianna sent back to *Queen of Sin* before sundown, then suggested to Roben:

"Brother, I want to give you a present. To be honest, I am not sure how you'll react to it. Three invisible bodyguards who will protect your son's cradle day and night and stop any killer, even giving their own life to do so. Chameleons can't be bought. For them an oath of loyalty, once given, is sacred, which is why you can always be sure that they won't be bought off by some aristocrat."

Roben remained silent for a long time, looking at the sun as it slowly descended behind the horizon. But then answered, somehow immediately growing brighter in the face:

"Thank you, brother. Verena... yes, she was listening to our conversation and is grateful to accept your gift and also expresses her appreciation to you. Another thing... my son is also named Georg, just like you. Only my wife, myself and a very small circle of our closest contacts know that. And now you are also in on the family secret."

I opened the personal opinion change menu and raised my opinion of Roben by ten points. My brother answered in kind.

* * *

Roben and I were sitting in the very same alcove where we held our last meeting. This time, instead of more fruits I'd already grown sick of, I suggested we cook some marinated meat to go with our wine, right there in the fresh air. I even said that I'd cook it, so the servants wouldn't get in the way. For Roben, the idea of cooking something himself turned out to be, to put it bluntly, a novelty, and he simply sat next to me, slurping a light wine through a straw and enjoying the excellent weather and fresh breeze.

The conversation progressed, naturally, about politics. My brother was clearly nervous about the presence of outside combat starships in Tesse and was trying in every way to convince me to make peace with the Duke. I tried to convince Roben that there was no cause for alarm. My systems were well prepared to defend against an invasion, and Tesse was a totally neutral party in the conflict and was in no way under threat. The only thing I wanted from my brother was financial support, but Roben took a neutral stance on that issue as well.

"Georg, I want you to understand that I'm on your side in spirit. I have gone up against Duke Paolo's avarice before and know what a slimeball he can be. But you also must understand my position. I can't give you a billion, even on loan. The head of the Orange House has ordered that you be totally cut off financially, and I cannot disobey him. And now your systems are closed to incursion, but it would take just six hours to reach Tesse from the Orange House Capital. Just imagine it, little brother: just six hours and this place could be packed to the brim with the Duke's combat starships..."

"What if you also put your warp beacon in 'by request' mode? Then you wouldn't have to let anyone in unless you want them," I suggested, moving the coals around in the grill.

"What are you talking about?!" Roben even grew pale in fear. "For that the Duke would skin me alive!"

"Well, what if you turn it off altogether? Just for twelve hours... even for ten, turn off the Tesse warp beacon for equipment maintenance. I don't need any more time than that. I'm not asking you for ships, brother. I'm not asking for political support. I just need a billion credits and ten hours of your beacon being off. And I'll bring you Peres royl Paolo's head on a platter."

Roben, already far in the weeds, twirled his empty glass and immersed himself in thought, holding his head in his hands. While my older brother thought, I answered an incoming message.

"Good, give my permission. Yes, they can, they're on the list – five freighters from Tialla to Hnelle. Give them a window of time and turn on the warp beacon for five seconds."

I turned off the communicator and turned back to Roben.

"See, it's that easy. This whole blockade against me is coming apart at the seams. What's the sense in trying to block my ships from getting in from Tesse, when freighters with the shipments I need can easily get to Hnelle from Tialla or Himora, and from

Forepost-11...?"

Roben shuddered and answered decisively:

"Well alright, little brother. I promise you my beacon will be off for ten hours. But the billion is harder. No matter how you hide it, the Orange House financial control services will notice the money transfer. But there is a loophole: I suggest neither a gift nor a loan. How about I buy something from you for a billion credits? For example, I could buy your yacht. To be honest, I don't know the real price of *Queen of Sin*, but you must agree that it hardly exceeds half that amount, even including all the luxury items aboard."

Here began my turn to be immersed in thought. It was a good deal, but the meat was done, and we took a break to eat.

"This is some great stuff, little brother!" With clear satisfaction, Roben ripped into the smoky juicy pieces of meat with his teeth, interspersing bites with big gulps of wine. "We'll have to come out here in nature more often. Maybe something stronger? To me, wine seems a bit too weak. It doesn't get you drunk at all."

"Let's go stronger," I agreed.

Roben reached for the bottle, but suddenly tightened up, placed his hand on his left ear and asked me in surprise:

"Georg, are you expecting someone? It's just that Katerina ton Mesfelle is asking for you. She's just arrived on Tesse on an express line from the Core. Should I tell her you're here?"

"Yes, of course. And actually, send a high-speed shuttle out for her. She should join us for a get-together. I invited Katerina to join me in Unatari. She didn't have to think long; she hung right up and flew out. I already saw yesterday that our second cousin had made it out of the Green House to the Orange."

"I remember Kat well from when she was little," said Roben with a nostalgic smile. "When she was eight or ten, she visited me often on Tesse. If you look around, you'd even be able to find her old childhood playmates."

I put a new portion of meat to grill as the servants that Roben called brought in sparkling wine and all kinds of light appetizers for the lady who would soon be joining us.

"Well, so what have you decided about the yacht?" asked Roben, and I waved my hand decisively.

"Alright, I'll sell it. It's a shame, of course. I've grown accustomed to *Queen of Sin*. But right now, money is much more important to me. The only thing is that I'll be taking the crew with me for other ships!"

"Good, little brother, but only take your people. Leave all the valuables on the yacht. Because I know how you are. You pulled a good one on me with that *Uukresh*. By the way, what should be done with that ship? If you're clashing with the Duke, he'll want to confiscate such a valuable ship."

"You are, of course, right about that, Roben. I'll have to take the *Uukresh* with me. Its warp drives have already been fixed. I'll take it to Unatari and finish it up there. But, to be honest, I urgently need to start buying docks for it and shipping them in..."

I called Bionica, who was on *Queen of Sin*, gave her the equipment purchase orders and also told her about *Queen of Sin* changing ownership. The android promised that the crewmembers would all be transferred to *Joan the Fatty* within two hours.

I heard the crunching of sand. and saw Katerina ton Mesfelle walking toward us along a path. She was a beautiful, athletically-built brunette in a form-fitting traveling suit.

"So that's how it is! My cousins have started celebrating my arrival without me. It's not proper. Well, anyway, this lady is fresh off the road. Pour me a glass of something and get me something to eat. I haven't had a bite since this morning."

The account balance change alert beeped. A deposit of a billion credits! And, I wasn't able to turn off the screen before another billion came in! I took a look at the accompanying information. The first transfer, as expected, was from the sale of *Queen of Sin*. And the second had the note: "payout for breach of contract on the repair of the *Uukresh* carrier." I raised my eyes in surprise. Roben, sitting opposite me and pouring Katerina a glass of wine, gave me a wink. The three of us toasted to our meeting and had a drink.

"Ah, nice!" said Katerina, after draining her glass. "By the way, who was that sitting like a sad doll in the grass on the way here?"

I told her briefly about Princess Astra's arrival on my ship. The girl shook her head in reproach:

"Georg, you look so grown up, but you can be such a child! Allow me to give you my first piece of advice as your new assistant. In your difficult circumstances, that Princess is a life raft that you should be clinging to! If you were to appear with a girl as beautiful as her in high society, all conversations about the android would fizzle out on their own. That is why you should not be sending Astra home, but inviting journalists to flesh the topic out! And that's to say nothing of the fact that this girl is probably hungry..."

I went out after Astra and brought her to the alcove. Katerina slid the steaming and sizzling meat directly off the skewer onto her plate, and also grabbed vegetables and appetizers from the common dish with her hands, placing them on the plate next to the meat. Meanwhile, I asked the girl, clearly confused and not knowing how to behave, a question over the improvised table:

"Astra, tell me as honestly as possible: what were your parents' parting words to you?"

The girl didn't hide a thing:

"Your Highness, my father, King Kant, told me that a girl from a remote star system only gets the chance to speak with upper Imperial nobility once a century and that I should take hold of that chance with both hands. King Kant also said that he is simply not in a state to give a proper dowry for his fourteenth daughter, all the more so given that five of my older sisters have yet to marry. No one asked my opinion on the matter. My father simply ordered me to prepare for a trip and convince your Highness to let me stay with him at any cost, preferably forever, regardless of what role I'd take up – spouse, favorite, lover, or simply traveling companion. In any case, I'd be provided with the support I deserve. If I am not capable of charming your Highness, then I am to hold out at least for a few days in your company so I have the chance be seen in the company of an upper aristocrat. After that, it should be easier for me to select a groom. If, even with all of my effort, nothing is to come of this, I am to give a signal with this ring, and in three days I'll be picked up by a starship going toward the Veyerde system. But, if that does happen, I won't be able to count on a warm reception from my father. So, I am willing to accept whatever fate you give me... Oops! Just not that!"

The Princess, reaching for her glass, caught her wide sleeve on a meat sauce dish and tipped it over right onto her dress. It looked like an accident, but with these past "domestic fabrications," crafted carefully by directors, there was no way I could be sure. Katerina cleaned up the sauce as much as she could, though the dress was of course ruined. Astra's face had a very authentic look of being upset on it.

"It's alright, don't worry about it," I said, calming the upset Princess. "I'm not gonna promise you 'forever,' but consider yourself noticed. Katerina will try to get the whole galaxy talking about my new favorite. But meanwhile, invite your younger sister to our table. It isn't befitting for a child to go hungry."

The incoming call signal beeped. It was Admiral Kiro Sabuto on the line.

"My Prince, you asked me to tell you when this kind of thing happens. A large part of the enemy fleet has left on a warp jump toward Himora!"

"Great news, admiral. We've got them where we want them now!"

I signed off and reached for my glass of wine as my face lit up with a smile from ear to ear.

"Ladies and gentlemen, pour yourselves a glass up to the brim! Little Flora gets juice, everyone else gets something stronger. I offer a toast: to us continuing to allow our enemies to make mistakes!"

We clinked glasses and took a drink. Astra suddenly coughed, having choked on the wine.

"I beg your apologies," said the girl through welling tears. "The wine was stronger than I'm used to. At home they only gave me the watered-down stuff."

Katerina looked at me somewhat reproachfully:

"What did you pour her? Why are you trying to get a child drunk?"

"I gave her what everyone else was having. Well, alright, next time she'll get juice."

"No, no," Astra blurted out. "I'm no child. I'm already seventeen, which, according to Veyerdean law, makes me a legal adult. Also, it seems somehow strange to refuse wine to someone who's just been sent intentionally to fly across half the Empire to become a Crown Prince's lover!"

"Brave girl!" Roben began chuckling, but I did not support him in his mood:

"The wine just went to her head. But about this 'lover' talk, I'm almost three times your age, and if I say you get juice, you get juice." All I needed was another crime to be accused of. This time it'd be corrupting a minor.

"Actually..." Flora began, but I interrupted her immediately.

"And you, little lady, need to learn how to hold your tongue when no one is asking for your advice."

The two girls sat down, frowning and hurt, and I hurried to change the topic of conversation.

"How about I put some more meat on. In a few hours, I'll have to prepare my fleet to leave, but before that we'll have to haul this little 'lover's stuff to the yacht. Or have you reconsidered flying out with me?"

"No, I haven't. But you can leave the stuff if you want. Those boxes are all full of evening and ball gowns. As far as I understand, I won't be needing those on a combat cruiser."

* * *

"My Prince, *Oculus-3* is reporting that the enemy has arrived in Himora! A battleship, six heavy assault cruisers, ten light, lots of support ships. The frigates are in a five-hundred-mile-long straight chain from Tesse to the Himora station."

I laughed. Crown Prince Peres had taken everything I'd told him, allegedly in a drunken stupor, completely seriously. And now his ships were preparing to catch my yacht as soon as *Queen of Sin* makes the jump to Himora.

"Great, *Oculus-3*. Absolutely excellent data. Continue observation."

I took a look around. My head was still buzzing a bit, but the drugs Nicosid Brandt gave me had already chased the last traces of alcohol from my blood. All the staff officers were in their places waiting for my decision. My fleet's ships and seventy freighters came into the action from Hnelle, a little star barely visible from the Tesse system. The huge *Uukresh*, with holes gaping in its body, was also with us. Everything was ready for the beginning of the operation.

The historic moment had arrived. I decided I should probably say something to give future historians some material. I turned on the microphone.

"Ladies and gentlemen, as you already know, an

hour ago, I publicly stated my position clearly: the Hnelle star system is a zone for combat operations against the aliens and, as such, is closed. As the leader of the Sector Eight Fleet, I will not tolerate any other ships in the Hnelle system. Any fleet intruding here must be destroyed immediately, regardless of the color of their flag. However, some of the aristocrats were so greedy and stupid, that they decided not to listen to the voice of reason. We see that other ships are taking a course, with ours, to the Hnelle warp beacon. But what can we do? We warned them. Anyone who tries to stop us will be destroyed. That's how it was, that's how it is, and that's how it's gonna be. For the whole fleet! The warp beacon will be turned on in thirty seconds for exactly one minute! Countdown!"

I turned to the captain.

"Oorast Pohl, as soon the beacon turns on, don't rush to send *Joan the Fatty* through the warp jump. I want to see with my own eyes whether all of our ships go and whether our opponents will really dare jump into a closed zone despite the clear warning."

"Will do, my Prince! We'll make the jump after it's been on for fifty seconds."

Ten seconds, nine, eight... A few bright flashes went off. It was Katerina ton Mesfelle taking a couple pictures to remember the historic moment. Three, two, one...

"New beacon!" said Nicole Savoia, sitting to my left.

"All ships, warp!" I commanded, and around a hundred bright lines stretched out in one direction into the dark, starry sky.

Peres's ships stayed around us in space. It can't be

that they just decided not to risk it, right? But no, there goes the first, then another three, now a whole bunch of bright lines were stretching out from where Peres's fleet had been toward the Hnelle system.

"You've only seen part of my fleet, Georg. The rest are flying to Hnelle now from Himora! You're lost now, dummy!" The message came in from one of the enemy ships jumping into the warp tunnel.

That's all. There's no one left around us.

"You're the one who's lost, Peres," I said out loud for my subjects. "The jump from Tesse to Hnelle takes four and a half hours, but from Himora it takes a whole seven. Two and a half hours will be plenty of time for us to cut your fleet down several times over and turn it into a heap of twisted metal. Then, we'll wait for the second part and have a talk with the battleship. You didn't have any more ships. Not in Tialla, not in Forepost-11. We know that from our observers. The mousetrap has slammed shut."

The stars grew dark, the cosmos rolled up into a bright, glistening tunnel. *Joan the Fatty*, my flagship, hurried to take its place in the forthcoming battle behind the other ships.

It would seem that we just started a civil war in the Orange House.

THOSE WHO EXTINGUISH STARS

I WASN'T ESPECIALLY worried. What was more, I didn't feel any fear either. I knew very well that my fleet was stronger than Peres's group of starships that had left Tesse toward the Hnelle beacon. Yes, technically there were sixteen cruisers on each side. And yes, the total number of ships looked to be about even – ninety-three of mine against one hundred ten of the enemy's. However, my ten heavy cruisers to Peres's six meant that I had one and a half times his firepower in the main calibers.

Four and a half hours through the warp tunnel... So my officers wouldn't burn out too early, I ordered them all to get some rest before the battle, setting an example myself. My cabin on *Joan the Fatty* was quite spacious but of course, it wasn't even close to the chic apartments on my old yacht. However, it somehow wasn't right for me to complain about my fate. Many didn't even have a spare cot because there were temporarily two crews on *Joan the Fatty*, and instead of the recommended maximum capacity of four hundred, we had more than seven hundred souls on board.

I saw Bionica, frozen timidly near the stairs. It was clear that, once again, she had nowhere to sleep. I magnanimously invited the android girl to my cabin.

"My Prince, allow me nevertheless to refuse such a high honor," the synthetic blonde objected unexpectedly. "Such a decision could lead to a new wave of gossip, which would be quite untimely. Also, I've been promised a cot in an officer's berth on the second deck. But if you're looking for company, you really should be offering Princess Astra and her sister something more appropriate to their station than a bench in a common barracks with eighteen others."

"Ugh, Bionica... With you there I can just flop down into bed, even if I'm still wearing my uniform, and get a good night's sleep. But with this sophisticated Princess around, I'll have to worry that I've got a button on my collar undone, or not enough fresh fruit on the table, or her Highness has suddenly grown bored... Though sure, call the sisters to my cabin, but just warn them to be quiet and not bother me when I'm trying to concentrate."

They arrived in five minutes. First to come in was the slight Astra, who made the orange overalls she was wearing look even elegant, then her younger sister. They couldn't find a pair the right size for Florianna, which is why the sleeves and pant legs of her orange suit were rolled up. I pointed the sisters to chairs, a little couch, a refrigerator with drinks, and the shower, telling them to make themselves at home before I asked them not to bother me for the next three and a half hours. I really was able to lay forty minutes in silence, but then Flora called me in a timid, unsure voice:

"Crown Prince Georg, I beg your forgiveness for the trouble. I just wanted to ask if you needed any help winning this battle."

I opened one eye part of the way, took a look at the girl standing next to me and asked her with a smirk:

"I wonder, how are you gonna be able to help me?"

"For now, I'm a fairly weak Truth Seeker, but all the same I can try to attract luck, bring the enemy fear, and I might be able to cause some kind of malfunction on an enemy ship."

I sat up in bed and looked at the surprisingly serious girl. Apparently, she wasn't joking.

"Flora, I am not worried about this battle. We'll win unequivocally. But then two and a half hours later, it will get much more serious when the fleet comes in from Himora..."

"It isn't coming," Florianna suddenly interjected. "The second fleet, which is being led by Viscount Sivir ton Mesfelle, is still in Himora."

I shook my head. The things the girl was saying were too absurd to believe.

"You're wrong, little girl. The whole idea of Peres royl Paolo's tactic was to strike with two parts of his fleet. He understood that I wouldn't send my ships to Hnelle with such a dangerous opponent there and, allegedly, he sent part of his fleet away, when actually they were just preparing to strike from Himora. So the second part of the fleet is simply obliged to come; otherwise, they'll lose the first group for no reason without gaining a thing."

"Your Highness, I do not know why, but the enemy ships are still in Himora. Though the third fleet, the biggest of them all, is at full preparedness right now at the Orange House Capital. Duke Paolo royl Anjer is already on his flagship, a battleship called *Orange Splendor*, in order to personally bring more than a thousand ships into the battle."

The Orange House Capital? Damn, I hadn't thought to put my observers there, and it's turning out that was the wrong choice... I stood up and walked over to the Sector Eight map. Well, and why not? It's very possible. After a six-hour flight, the Duke's whole armada would be in Tesse. Then, they'd need an hour or two to recharge their energy at the station and, after that, make a fully-fledged strike on Hnelle. The mission of the first fleet, that of Crown Prince Peres, was clearly to get the beacon turned on. Perhaps the Crown Prince was really planning to get my ships tied up in the battle, then touch down with a one-or-two-starship landing party on the Hnelle station, and turn on the beacon, even if it isn't for long. And that was it. No matter how the battle with Peres's fleet turned out, I'd still lose. I, of course, did not have the forces to withstand the full might of the Orange House. But then Peres separated the fleet, and the situation became unclear – I probably *would* be able to destroy his fleet in two parts. But then, if a large part of the enemy's ships didn't jump to Hnelle... The Duke will clearly be unhappy with his son, who pissed away a victory that was already practically at hand.

I turned to the little Truth Seeker.

"Your abilities are intriguing. It's always good to know where your enemy's forces are. What else can you do?"

The girl became embarrassed and even blushed slightly.

"Pretty much nothing. That was my first attack of omniscience. But I'll learn everything and become useful. It's just that here on the starship, everyone practically worships their fleet commander, and a Truth Seeker has an easy time drawing upon the force of their delight, pride, and admiration – in other words, everything that surrounds a leader and is called 'power.' I only needed a half hour sitting with your crew in one room to feel that I had become a noticeably stronger Truth Seeker. I'd already be able to beat that little squirt in the flying palace."

Interesting observation. I pondered for a second. I'll have to try to keep this little girl here. What if I really can "level her up" into an honest-to-God Truth Seeker?

"Florianna, if what you've told me about the ships staying in Himora is confirmed, you can consider your usefulness confirmed as well, and you will be accepted into my retinue," I promised the girl.

"And my sister, Princess Astra?" the little girl clarified right away.

I shrugged my shoulders ambiguously. After turning around, I noticed that Astra was far from us. The girl had climbed into a chair and was sitting with her feet up, listening to music through headphones. In that the Princess wasn't listening to our conversation, I could speak freely.

"Hey Flora, can you tell me what's so great about your sister? Yes, she is a girl of rare beauty and, what's more, she's been raised well. But I'm a married man, and a Crown Prince can always find a great many other people to serve as his favorite or lover. Also, am I mistaken if I guess by your expression that you would not like me to allow Astra to stay with you?"

The youngster was noticeably startled. It seemed I was not mistaken. She quickly got her act back together and began laughing:

"In the Kingdom of Veyerde, I was always treated as a sponger and dirty bastard. So, I won't hide the fact that I would very much like to see the look on King Kant's face when he hears that the Crown Prince chose me as a companion and sent Princess Astra home. But that won't happen. You like Astra a lot. I can read it in your thoughts!"

I unwittingly became embarrassed. It's so hard to talk to a Truth Seeker! The little Florianna was clearly entertained by my embarrassment and began laughing. So I said ostentatiously strictly:

"There's no reason to get the Princess's hopes up too early. I really haven't decided on her yet. And, Flora, I haven't told anyone about my feelings, so whether I like Astra or not is of no importance. But digging around in my thoughts, especially for a little kid, is not recommended Some of the information in my brain is too dangerous, and you aren't old enough for the other stuff."

Joan the Fatty came out of the warp tunnel to a unified joyful cry on the fleet channel.

"There they are! Finally! Crown Prince Georg is with

us! We were afraid that you didn't make it before the beacon turned off! Well, now the enemy is screwed!"

"So, everything's ok. Let's get to work!" I hurried to announce my arrival to the fleet to calm my subjects down. "I need a tactical grid showing the location of every ship immediately. What is that debris around the station? Which one of you idiots broke off from the group?"

"*Tusk-4* entered the combat zone of an enemy light cruiser," reported one of the officers. "But the crew evacuated to safety."

"Was it so hard for *Tusk-4*'s captain to think to try the overdrive thrusters? Has he got an extra chromosome? He's under fire, and he doesn't even try escaping! I'd like to hand that captain over for organ donation as compensation for losing the ship... But that might spread the infection of uselessness! Who was it that split off? Where's the tactical screen, damn it?!"

Finally, after a few seconds, a three dimensional hologram came up in the hall showing where all the ships were. I studied our positions. The enemy ships had come out of the warp in a long spread-out cloud. There was no system to how they were arranged, as far as I could tell. Peres's ships that were closest to the Hnelle station were just 25 miles out, and the furthest were almost 400 away. Fifty miles from the station, at a slight distance from the line of the enemy fleet, our ships were waiting in combat formation. My fleet from Tesse was almost 200 miles away from the larger group. The *Uukresh* and freighters had come out of warp 2,000 miles from the battlefield, as I'd ordered. Just some idiot in a freighter – for some reason, I can't understand why – came out of warp 30 miles from the station in the very thick of the enemy fleet and had already been destroyed. I really hope that freighter wasn't carrying the cannons for my battleship...

"So, let's get started! This is an order for the whole fleet: defend the station, do not let the enemy get near it! Anti-support, target the frigates closest to the station! Main group *Pyros* and *Safas*, take point and place webs over there on those two marks. I've highlighted them on the map. Nicole, your mission is to bring the heavies out from Tesse to the main group..."

"This is *Warhawk-4*. I've got *Happy Dumpling* pinned down!" One of the two enemy light cruisers that was too close to the station was already under warp disruptor and stasis web.

"*Pyros*, put on more disruptors and webs. *Warhawk-4*, excellent! Remind me after the battle. You won't be just getting a medal for this; I'm throwing in an ass-whooping to go with it for falling out of formation. Heavies, focus on the *Dumpling*. Fire at will."

Several bright explosions streaked across space right away. Other than the *Dumpling*, two or three other enemy frigates had been destroyed in the very first phase of battle. The second light cruiser, unfortunately, was able to escape by jumping to its heavy cruisers.

In battle, after the spark of activity in the initial phase, a brief pause took hold. The opposing fleets went away from one another until more than two hundred miles stood between them. My starships from Tesse joined the rest of the group. The heavies joined the front group and slowly deployed out in the enemy's direction. The light cruisers, destroyers and frigates also took up their assigned positions.

"I need a loss report!" I demanded, and Admiral Kiro Sabuto sent a reply.

"We lost two frigates, *Tusk-4* and *Tusk-11*, as well as a non-combat starship. Based on the trade roll, the destroyed freighter was carrying robotic arms for the orbital docks. It's a shame, of course, but at least it wasn't the expensive battleship cannons. Automatic robotic arms can be bought again right on Tesse for two hundred thousand credits. The enemy lost a light cruiser and four frigates. In total, both sides' losses were insignificant and had almost no effect on the balance of forces."

Taking advantage of the pause, I demanded the Truth Seeker be brought to the headquarters, simultaneously calling my observer in Himora.

"*Oculus-3* on the line." One of the former pirates from the *Payoff* had volunteered to be my informant on the Himora station, and it took no more effort on my part to set him up in the long distance department.

"I need to know about the fleet in your system. Have they done anything? Did they jump to Hnelle?"

"No, my Prince. They're still here. Most of the ships are docked at the Himora station, including the battleship. As far as I understand, the ships didn't have enough time to recharge their drives, which is why they missed the short blink of the beacon. And now there's some infighting going on there. The Viscount has gathered officers on the battleship. An hour ago, there was a call made to the Viscount from Duke Paolo. They discussed something."

I thanked my agent and signed off.

"My Prince," said Admiral Kiro Sabuto, calling my attention. "The enemy's chaotic disorganization is coming to an end, and they are entering battle formation, trying to copy ours. There's a front group made of six heavy *Katanas*, thirty miles behind them are the light cruisers, and a bit further there are destroyers and frigates."

"Well, what can I say, dear officers...?" I watched on the big screen as Crown Prince Peres royl Paolo's ships tried to copy our fleet. "It's nice when someone sees you as an example to imitate. But, formation isn't everything. You also need to understand how to use it. We won't be stopping them from making yet another mistake. Is the cloaker on the field?"

"That's right," Angel's voice rang out. "I'm a hundred twenty-five miles from their heavy group."

"Let them get set up so you don't get revealed by accident. Then, get between the heavies and the rest of the fleet. How much time do you need?"

"Something like five minutes. Maybe four, if I take a straight line next to the destroyer group."

"Don't risk it, Angel. No reason to rush things. Just sneak through and give us the coordinates."

The enemy did not take active measures. Perhaps they were waiting for the second half of the fleet. Or maybe they were charging energy to flee back to Tesse or Himora. In any case, if they were waiting for the second part of their fleet to arrive, it was in utter vain, and, if they were expecting to escape, I was in no mood to allow that either. The officer sent after

Florianna brought her to me slightly afraid.

"Flora, tell me. Where is Duke Paolo royl Anjer's fleet? And where is Viscount Sivir ton Mesfelle's fleet?"

The Truth Seeker closed her eyes, spent five seconds in silence and answered:

"The Duke's fleet is still at the Orange House Capital. And the Viscount's fleet has also not left Himora, though they have received an order to go to Tesse."

"Thank you, Flora. You've been a big help. Long-distance communications group, send a message to Crown Prince Roben royl Inoky: 'Begin equipment maintenance.'"

Fifteen seconds later, I heard the surprised exclamation of one of my officers:

"The Tesse beacon has disappeared!"

"Don't worry. Everything is under control," I answered calmly. "Long-distance communications group, send the following transmission to the warp beacons in Himora, Vorta, Forepost-11, Forepost-12, Forepost-13, the Closed Laboratories, and Unguay: 'Code red. Extinguish star.'"

"The Forepost-11 warp beacon has disappeared!" Notes of panic could be heard in the officer's voice.

"That's alright. That's what we want. The fun and games are over. Now we start playing for keeps. If Viscount Sivir's fleet doesn't want to come to us, we will stop it from leaving and pay them a visit ourselves. But first, let's deal with the ships that are two hundred miles from us. Dear officers, does anyone know how to wipe out an enemy fleet right in front of us at full combat readiness without significant losses?"

No one answered me. The staff officers could only lower their eyes. Without having received an answer, I turned to my assistant sitting to my left:

"Lieutenant Nicole, we've got another question to check how much you really know. Heavy *Katana* assault cruisers. I'm interested in the distribution of cannon towers, as well as the thickness of the energy shield for both the front and back hemispheres."

The girl shuddered and answered loudly and confidently:

"The six main caliber cannon towers are capable of shooting at targets in the front hemisphere. Two of the towers are able to fire on the rear hemisphere. The forward shields of assault ships are eight times thicker than the rear ones."

"Very good, Nicole. And now a question to the ship captain. Oorast Pohl, how fast can a *Katana* heavy assault cruiser make a one-hundred-eighty-degree turn?"

The captain began coughing self-consciously:

"My Prince, I am not sure about the *Katanas*, but our *Flambergs* need one minute forty seconds to make a full turn with maneuver drives."

I turned everyone's attention to this:

"Memorize this: one minute forty seconds in a normal state. But with a stasis web? Or with ten stasis webs?"

"With ten webs, a heavy cruiser would take days to turn around," chuckled Kiro Sabuto, first to figure out what exactly I had in mind.

I took the microphone and turned it to the common fleet channel.

"Attention, everyone! All combat ships, make a

short advance toward the enemy. Maintain the same speed as the heavies. No one is to break out in front. I'll explain the mission: as soon as we get the coordinates, we jump to the enemy, behind their heavies. Frigates, as soon as you come out of warp, blast up to full speed and orbit the heavy cruisers. Hold them down with stasis webs and take down all the drones they release. Staff officers are to make sure the webs are laid evenly on all targets. All heavies, after exit from warp, do not pay attention to the enemy heavies and conduct focused fire on my command to eliminate their light cruisers. Our light cruisers, your mission is to fire on the destroyers and electronic warfare; deafen the enemy light cruisers. Attention! You will be the enemy's main target, so your shields are going to be being recharged by our heavies. If it all goes bad, don't be a hero. Just try to survive and escape the battle – that is an order. And finally, the destroyers. This battle is a holiday for you – ideal conditions! There's just going to be wagonloads of targets. The enemy frigates will have no choice but to try and break in to the combat zone. Split into groups of five. Show them your magic trick: one volley, one enemy ship down. Just don't stand around. Keep maneuvering all the time so you don't get your ass one-shotted by the cannon-fodder heavies. Is the mission clear to everyone? Has anyone not understood? Admiral Kheraisss Vej, have you understood what the android translator has been relaying to you?"

"My Princcce, stupid one among Iseyek no to be cap-i-tain ship. I understand all, and all mine understand all."

I sent the fleet ships a message with the jump coordinates from the cloaker.

"Alright then, five seconds to action! Four, three, two... Let's rip 'em to shreds! WARP!!!"

* * *

I don't know if I really have to describe everything that happened on the battle field. It was a shooting gallery, a football game with one end-zone. The only worrying moment came at the very beginning when the enemy destroyers and a whole swarm of frigates, taking heavy losses, was able to get into firing range. We lost a few frigates during that. But the first enemy ships to break in were soon destroyed, and the kindergarten chainsaw massacre went on. The enemy's resolve to continue the battle only lasted another five minutes. After that, the ships left on the battlefield gave up the second I suggested they do so. And no one could accuse the enemy captains of cowardice in in that moment. By that point, all that was left of their fleet that had numbered in the high hundreds was less than three dozen spaceships. I'm not sure that I could have acted differently in their position.

The overjoyed roar on the fleet channel was so long and enthusiastic that I even had to take off my headphones. But that didn't make it any better. The exact same noisiness and screaming was going in the hall, and I practically went deaf.

Standing change. Empire Military faction opinion of you has improved.

Presumed faction opinion of you: +6 (warm)

Standing change. Iseyek race opinion of you has improved.
Alpha Iseyek race opinion of you: +8 (warm)
Gamma Iseyek race opinion of you: +5 (indifferent)

Standing change. Chameleon race opinion of you has improved.
Chameleon race opinion of you: +6 (warm)

"Admiral Kiro Sabuto, report..." I wanted to demand an official record of the battle but cut myself off mid-sentence.

Florianna was writhing in very strong convulsions on the floor. The little girl was arching her back one moment, then curling up in the fetal position the next. What's going on with her? An epileptic seizure? That was the first thing that came to mind.

"Get a doctor immediately!" Scared shouts rang out, but the girl moaned out through her gritted teeth:

"I don't need a doctor... This... is totally different... I got carried away, not taking my strength into account... Agh!"

"I could be wrong, but to me that looked like a super strong orgasm," said Valian ton Corsa with surprise, looking down over the child.

"Probably," agreed Flora, trying to stand, but then falling to the floor again. "It's passing now... I beg your forgiveness for causing alarm. It's just that it was really hard to digest such a powerful flow of wild adoration and joy. My knees are still shaking..."

"Phobos, take the Truth Seeker away to my cabin and lay her on the couch. Let the girl get some rest and come back to her senses. Admiral, report on the results of the battle."

Kiro Sabuto called up a table on the wall and, using a laser pointer, he commented on the individual lines:

"We lost six frigates. Two in the initial phase of the battle, *Tusk-4* and *Tusk-11;* then another four during the active phase, *Tusk-7, Tusk-10, Safa-1,* and *Pyro-12* when the enemy destroyers got into attack range. The light cruiser *Umoyge-1* was damaged. When its shields ran down, it fled the battle and warped out. The enemy lost seventy-two ships of various classes. Twenty-nine starships have been captured: all six *Katana* heavy assault cruisers, in full working order, four *Thrush* light cruisers, four *Flycatcher* destroyers, and fifteen *Warhawk* frigates. In my opinion, it was a great trade-off. We lost six frigates, and in return we got ten cruisers, four destroyers, and fifteen frigates."

I shook my head. We should have suggested the enemy surrender a bit earlier. Then we could have avoided unnecessary victims and saved more ships for the fleet. But ok, if it happened, it happened.

"So, all ships, come to the station to recharge. We've got another enemy to take care of in Himora. Captured starships are also to dock for charging. Their captains and senior officers are to be brought to me. Crown Prince Peres royl Paolo ton Mesfelle is also to be brought, but observe all privileges appropriate to his title."

Global fame increase. Current value +10

Global standing decrease. Current value -20

Global standing decrease. Current value -21

Well then, it looks like my enemies heard about the results of the battle... To be honest, I was expecting much worse. Clearly, the information about the warp beacons being turned off had not yet reached them or at least hadn't yet been connected with Crown Prince Georg royl Inoky.

I received the Crown Prince in the large hall of the heavy assault cruiser, *Emperor August.* First, the name of the ship went well with creating an official atmosphere. Second, there were no rooms on my *Joan the Fatty* big enough for this kind of thing. The hall was lined with armed Beta Iseyek soldiers, standing like terrifying, silent statues painted in the colors of the Orange House. The chameleon bodyguards showed themselves to their high-placed guest for just a moment before camouflaging themselves again. Two rows of human soldiers, between which Prince Peres walked, were frozen at attention.

I met my relative in my severe, dark blue Sector Eight Fleet Commander's uniform with just one medal pinned to it – the Silver Brooch with the number five inside a four-pointed star. Next to me were my fleet's two admirals and three beautiful women: Katerina ton Mesfelle as my advisor, Princess Astra as my favorite, and Bionica as my translator. My forced guest gave a dignified bow, looked around and wondered:

"I don't get it Georg. Who are you really? Are you the drunk who has his fun with women of questionable virtue or who you are now?"

"I'm both at once," I chuckled back. "I can be flippant and silly but, if need be, I set all joking and eccentricity aside."

Peres royl Paolo spent some time in silence, then began speaking, retaining his dignity and appearance of tranquility.

"I've heard rumors that you're a good fleet commander, Georg. But I, I'll admit, couldn't believe them... Alright, let's be done with these empty words. I want to understand my status and what you are going to do with me. I warn you first: my father will not be paying any ransom for me if you're thinking about horse trading. I personally have no problem refusing my rights to the Sigur star system. Nessi is quite enough for me, and I have no use for an empty, remote system."

"To be honest, Peres, your agreeing to it is neither here nor there to me. You have no rights to Sigur whatsoever, so there's nothing for you to refuse. I want you to give an official order to all ships remaining in Himora. They must voluntarily join my fleet without resistance. As soon as you sign such an order, you can be free as a bird."

In reply, Peres royl Anjer burst into a malicious laugh:

"Is that all? You don't want anything else? You wouldn't like the Nessi system thrown in as a gift? I declare officially to you that I will not sign such an order. Those are my ships, and you won't lay a finger on them. Also, they have already left Himora to link up with my father's ships! There's no way you'll ever catch them!"

"Whatever you say, Peres. That's all I needed from you. What can I do? If you didn't want to give up your ships for your freedom, I'll have to send you to Roben royl Inoky. My brother has been dreaming for fifty years of having a discussion with you about the order of succession. Roben even bought all kinds of torture instruments from me that I found in the Brotherhood of the Stars palaces – the kind for the least talkative prisoners... So, maybe you'll rethink giving me the ships?"

To be honest, I just wanted to slightly spook Peres to make him a bit more pliable. I bent the truth a bit. Roben really had shown an interest in the pirate torture instruments, but only for the Tesse museum. However, what happened next was something I was in no way expecting:

Crown Prince Peres royl Paolo ton Mesfelle has resigned.

My jaw fell to the floor in surprise. My involuntary guest fixed his hair with his hand and wondered aloud in a calm voice:

"I would bet I'm not quite so interesting to Roben now. Can I go?"

"Of course, Peres royl Paolo. I wouldn't dare hold you here now. A ship will bring you to Tesse and further to Nessi as soon as the warp beacon is activated."

After Peres had left the hall with the same

unaffected look he came in with, Katerina ton Mesfelle said quietly but distinctly:

"I always suspected that Peres didn't care for politics or all these orders of succession deep down. But, Georg, you've just made a deadly, inconsolable enemy in the person of the head of the Orange House, who will never forgive you for his son's resignation. And you'll never convince Duke Paolo royl Anjer that Peres did it voluntarily."

I walked up to the table and poured myself a glass of mineral water for lack of something stronger at hand. Yes, what had happened was unexpected, and could hardly be called positive. I had no doubt that the Duke would be enraged. There was no conversation to be had about peace now.

"Alright, if it happened, it happened. You can't change the past; he can't take back his resignation. Call the captains here. I need the Truth Seeker immediately."

Ten minutes later, around a hundred people came into the hall – the captains and their senior aides from the ships captured in the last battle. Some of those who came in gave an ostentatious bravo, others were hanging back getting flustered after seeing the huge praying mantises. As I walked up closer, they froze in place. Most of them bowed respectfully or gave me a military salute. After I made sure everyone was together and listening carefully to me, I turned to the captains with a small speech:

"Dear officers, above all else, I want to express to you my respect and admiration. None of your ships fled the battle despite the unbalanced forces and big losses. And it isn't your fault that you were thrown wantonly into battle, like cannon fodder, tricked by a promise of reinforcement, and sent to make war on loyal representatives of the Empire just like yourselves. Your previous commander, Crown Prince Peres, has just given up on his unjust demands, having refused all pretenses toward me and even giving up his title. And now the question arises: what is to be done with you? I am offering you the chance to transfer to another fleet in the same old Orange House. All I ask is an oath of loyalty to me as your new commander. Given that, all your titles and positions will be retained. Your ships and crews will also remain with you. If any of you thinks that they are not ready or cannot transfer into the Sector Eight Fleet, just leave this hall. You'll be sent to Tesse on the next flight, and we will do you no harm. I am not considering forcing anyone onto my side. I'm only interested in volunteers, and I'll easily find a replacement for anyone not prepared to dedicate themselves to defending Sector Eight from alien invasion."

No one broke ranks. I waited for a few minutes to make sure, but no one stepped forward to refuse.

"Admiral Kiro Sabuto, swear in our fleet's new officers. I warn you in advance that a Truth Seeker will be reading you to check the veracity of your intentions. If any of you has changed your decision, this is your last chance to leave the hall."

I waited another minute, but no one stirred. The admiral waited for my signal, came out in front and began ceremoniously reading the oath. The officers repeated after him in concert. A minute later, when the oath had been accepted, I wondered to Florianna:

"What's your verdict, Truth Seeker?"

The little girl, who had been standing in front of the ranks until that point with a hood cast over her head, revealed her face, displaying her fiery orange eyes:

"My Prince, three of them were lying. That one, this one, and that lady over there. They all had the intention of fleeing at the earliest convenient moment, if possible with their ships. And that guy was drooling over Princess Astra during the oath swearing, so I couldn't tell if he really meant it or not."

After a couple of seconds, three decapitated corpses fell to the floor. The chameleons appeared for just a second and returned to invisibility. If the show execution of the traitors and oath-breakers had an effect on the other officers, they weren't showing it at all. No one budged or moved away from the dead bodies. Princess Astra and her sister also took the executions without hysteria or fainting.

I called the last of the named four over. The tall handsome brown-haired Corwin ton Ugar somehow resembled a hussar of centuries past. The little Truth Seeker walked up closer and observed his behavior attentively. I suspect that Popori de Cacha's chameleons were already holding their expertly-sharpened blades at the officer's throat, but he did not display any signs of fear:

"My Prince, this is simply more than I can bear. It's the first time I've seen such a pretty girl, and during the oath-swearing I really just forgot about everything in the Universe. All the same, my loyalty to you as a commander was never in any way in question."

I turned to Florianna. The kid shrugged her shoulders:

"This man is wheedling, trying to hide his feelings for my sister behind his truthful words. It is beyond a doubt that he will be loyal to you as a brave and experienced light cruiser captain. But given the slightest chance, he will try to take your favorite from you, Crown Prince Georg."

I looked at the captain. He was standing up well to my gaze and chuckled in reply. Not the slightest bit of fear or embarrassment could be found in Corwin ton Ugar's facial expression. The situation was, in fact, quite complex. There was nothing to punish my subject for; however, ignoring that episode without losing face was also not a possibility.

I tried to look at both of us from the point of view of an external observer: a young, tall, career soldier with an Imperial combat medal on his broad chest; and, on the other side of this young, dashing hunk, his rival for the heart of a lady, twice as old, shorter by almost half a head, fat and bloated... Hrmph... In literature and cinema, this situation has arisen hundreds of times. And even Tolstoy himself played on the theme in *War and Peace*, and the readers always sympathize more with the brave young man. But then, what do you do if you find yourself in the body of a rotund old Pierre Bezukhov? Solve the issue with force?

"What do you say, my commander? Will my head roll for sins I haven't yet committed?"

"It would be easiest to ask Astra herself." I found myself and turned to the Princess. "What do you say? Do you want me to give you this courageous officer?"

My favorite shook her head forcefully:

"No, no, Crown Prince. I am utterly satisfied in my current position, and I am not preparing to change a thing."

Apparently, the girl was totally serious about being afraid that I could make use of the situation to exclude her from my retinue. That was the exact reaction I was counting on.

"The lady doesn't want your company, Corwin ton Ugar. That makes the situation much simpler. Your impetuous head isn't the only part of you that could be cut off... Bionica, instruct Phobos and Deimos what part of this captain precisely needs to be ripped out if he gets anywhere near Princess Astra."

The android chirped something to the two bodyguards, and the two somewhat creepy Beta Iseyeks walked up closer and began looking over the man with interest, focusing their huge eyes on a spot somewhat below the captain's belt. Phobos even turned to look at his razor sharp upper appendage, apparently imagining what would be the best way of carrying out this mission. The smile slinked off Corwin ton Ugar's face, and he said distinctly:

"I have understood perfectly, my Prince. I will try to keep myself at a distance from your beauty."

On the way back to *Joan the Fatty*, walking through the halls of the Hnelle station, the little Truth Seeker seized the moment when all the others were quite far from me.

"Actually, my sister Astra told an untruth. In fact, she took quite the shine to the courageous officer. But I just didn't want to talk about it with strangers around."

"You're learning fast, Flora. If you had brought me shame in the presence of my subjects, I would have had to cut out your long little tongue."

The kid giggled happily:

"That's exactly what I read in your thoughts. It was the only reason I kept quiet."

There was fifteen minutes left before coming out of warp. I kept looking at the clock with increasing frequency. Time really was getting compressed. The Tesse beacon would turn on in twenty-three minutes, which is why my fleet had just eight minutes to wipe out the enemy in Himora or, at the very least, succeed in capturing the Viscount's most valuable ships and not letting them escape the trap.

"The Viscount's fleet is still next to the station, as before," Florianna announced confidently.

The kid yawned, making no effort to hide it. Her older sister Astra had gone to sleep a long time ago in a separate cabin, which had been split in two for the sisters. But Flora wouldn't, leave despite my admonishments.

"I really want to be here when your Highness achieves victory," said the little Truth Seeker, explaining her stubbornness. "Don't worry, Crown Prince Georg. What happened in Hnelle won't happen again. Back then, I just wasn't ready. This time I'll hold it together."

Katerina ton Mesfelle, sitting nearby with a mug of hot, firo-nut drink in her hands, turned to me and said:

"Georg, in any case, before you start shooting, try reasoning with the Viscount first. I already told you that we might be able to avoid this battle. Judge for yourself: Viscount Sivir openly disobeyed the Duke's order by not coming to help Peres. Going back to the Orange House to get severe punishments is something he definitely doesn't want. The fleet is only more or less loyal to him. He's just a temporary commander, appointed to the role of a Crown Prince that resigned. The surrounding warp beacons aren't on, and he doesn't know what to do. Even though the ships are still docked at the station, and they've had many hours to prepare, they still can't come to a unified decision. I'm telling you, Georg, there must be such chaos and scuffling going on over there that the combat structure of the fleet is simply unworkable. You just have to talk to them, not give them a common enemy to unite against."

"Alright, Katerina, we'll see. I'm not going to promise anything, but I'll try to resolve this peacefully. So, time... It's time for me to head to fleet headquarters."

To be honest, I strongly doubted my cousin's words. The picture was just too puppies and rainbows. However, reality fully affirmed what my new advisor said. You practically couldn't make out the Himora station. So thick was the layer of ships stuck onto it that they managed to look like nothing more than separate station elements. The docked battleship especially impressed with its size. It was a huge, terrifying ship called *Bride of Chaos,* which was twice as big as the space station itself. I turned on the public channel:

"Attention everyone! This is the Sector Eight Fleet Commander speaking, Crown Prince Georg royl Inoky ton Mesfelle. I order all ships to remain at the station, turn off maneuver drives and remove energy shields. Viscount Sivir ton Mesfelle and all captains are invited to a meeting on the heavy cruiser *Emperor August* in ten minutes. And yes, any ship that tries to undock or does not power down its shields in one minute will be immediately destroyed for disobedience."

I switched over to the internal fleet channel.

"To all ships in the fleet! Go out to the optimum shooting distance, but do not open fire and do not release drones! Remain at full readiness!"

"Now we'll find out whether there'll be a battle or not," said Admiral Kiro Sabuto, nervously tapping his fingers on the touch-screen table before suddenly exclaiming in joy, "Oh, look! They're turning off their shields! But the most important thing is what the battleship does... Yes! The battleship as well!"

That was just amazing. Now I needed to build on the success.

"General Savass Jach, make a landing on the Himora station. Resistance is not expected. Those on the station are our allies. You just need to show your power and maintain vigilance. Your mission is to turn off the station's warp beacon and also place a large enough group of soldiers on each ship to keep an eye on all key systems – cannon batteries, engine rooms, officer's decks, and so forth. Your order is only to protect. You are not to display aggression. Those are already our ships, de facto. All that's left is to back that up legally..."

And there I was again in the large hall of *Emperor August*. Another honor guard, terrifying praying mantises in formation, and the very same retinue, even if no one had woken up the wiped-out Princess Astra. But what a sense of déjà vu.

Viscount Sivir ton Mesfelle was a fairly young, blond man with long hair that fluttered freely. Instead of a military uniform, the man was wearing a form-fitting dark suit. He greeted Katerina like a close acquaintance, after which he daintily bowed to me in accordance with all court etiquette rules, given my seniority in title.

"Crown Prince Georg royl Inoky ton Mesfelle, I have come to your ship on your request and am prepared to hear your Highness out."

But instead of me, after getting permission first, Katerina began:

"Cousin, I see that your affairs have come to quite a bad state. You screwed Peres over, messed up a combat operation, upset the Duke and weren't even able to reach the Tivalle system, which was promised to you..."

"Ugh, Kat, tell me something I don't already know!" the Viscount said, waving it off in resignation. "The idea of splitting the fleet up wasn't even mine. But the Duke wants to put all the responsibility for its failure on *my* shoulders. At first, they trusted that I could give worthy command, but this has just been a whole cataclysm of bad luck... The crews revolted, saying I'm not a soldier and thus have no right to command. They flagrantly ignored Peres's order to jump to Hnelle. And then the warp beacons started disappearing from out of nowhere. The Duke yelled a horrible string of curses, demanding that I bring the fleet to Tesse. But how? All the beacons are off! I haven't been in such a truly sticky situation since we were in school together. Since that time, remember? When me and you decided to fix the test results and broke into the server room at night. We were trying to find the director's password for the terminal, but instead I accidentally turned off the financial department's security system and, that same night, some hackers stole a million and a half credits..."

"Alright, you can discuss your shared past with Katerina later," I said, interrupting the excessively talkative Viscount. "Sivir, I have an offer that you might find interesting. The Tivalle system, that was promised to you by the Duke, could really become yours. Endless fields of ice asteroids, rare isotope mines, billions in profits, glory to the 'Ice Viscount,' and guaranteed protection from Duke Paolo as well as any other foes. I need a viceroy I can count on. Someone who will develop production, increase output and provide me and my fleet with a constant source of tax income."

I suppose my offer surprised my distant relative, because Viscount Sivir, who must have already been thinking he was in a hopeless and abandoned situation, perked right up and exclaimed enthusiastically:

"I am ready, my Prince! What do I need to do to get that position?"

"As the deputy commander of the fleet in Himora, sign an official order transferring all your ships into the Sector Eight Fleet. That is all I ask. I'll deal with the captains myself. They're already waiting for the meeting. The contract on the Tivalle system and detailed production plans will be drawn up for you by Katerina ton Mesfelle. At the same time, you'll have all the time in the world to reminisce about your student years."

"Do you know who I am?" My well-earned sleep after such an action-packed day was interrupted by the voice of a young woman. It was a very pleasant and somehow soporific voice.

"I suspect that you are Miya," I answered, not overly confident.

"That's right."

She stayed silent for a long time, then spoke out reproachfully:

"Ugh, Ruslan, Ruslan... I wanted to talk to you about serious things, but I've discovered that you are not at all ready for such a conversation yet. It doesn't seem that you've fully realized the seriousness of the situation you're in. You've been entrusted with a frightening mystery, and you signed a contract to keep the personality swap a secret. And what do I find? Not only have you allowed a Truth Seeker to get close to you, you've already allowed her to uncover our shared secret. I have to interfere personally to avoid a catastrophe, the scale of which is hard to even imagine. At the same time, this will serve as a lesson to you. And in our next conversation, you'll give my words the attention they deserve."

* * *

The dream vanished as if by magic. I was sitting on

a huge bed. My heart was pounding in my chest, threatening to break out of my ribcage and fling itself as far as possible from the horror it had lived through. Had the lost Miya really spoken to me? Or was that just a dream? The most terrifying of my nightmares? Weird that I didn't see her face. She was speaking in a relaxed tone and at first glance revealed absolutely no cause for alarm. Nevertheless, the feeling wouldn't leave me that just now Death herself had been at my door and had just barely missed catching me.

Miya was talking about some kind of lesson that I need as an example to be more obedient. And she also talked about a Truth Seeker that I had brought too close to me. Florianna. There was no one else that came to mind here. According to Miya, Florianna had already figured out about Crown Prince Georg's change of personality. And that was why Miya was personally preparing to interfere and stave off a catastrophe. I threw on my robe and hurried into the hall toward the sisters' cabin.

Princess Astra was sitting on the floor in a pair of light fluffy pajamas, pressing the pale lifeless and limp Flora to her chest in terror. The little Truth Seeker's eyes were wide open and stationary. Blood was pouring out of her nose. Astra's pajamas were already soaked in her sister's blood. Flora's nightgown was also wet. A whole puddle had accumulated on the floor...

"I need a doctor immediately in cabin 2-18!" Popori de Cacha, who was standing next to me, said into his transmitter.

Astra looked at me. The girl's eyes were wide in

horror.

"Out of nowhere, Flora made a creepy scream and fell off her bed onto the floor," explained the terrified Princess. "I ran over, and when I got to her, she was already unresponsive."

The room quickly grew cramped as more and more people ran in. Several people and chameleons were hunched over the little Truth Seeker.

"She's breathing!" someone shouted joyfully.

"Let the doctor in!" Nicosid Brandt flew into the cabin with his assistants, immediately asking everyone else to go out into the hall.

A few minutes later, a hospital stretcher was carried past me, and I was able to see the tubes that had been inserted into the girl's mouth and nostrils. The terrified Astra was in fits of hysterics and was positively roaring. No one could calm her down. The girl was screaming that there was no way she would be made to stay alone in that room, because she was scared. I bid the Princess move into my cabin and reassured her that the chameleons would provide security.

Only a few hours later did the Princess calm down at all, before falling asleep on the couch. I covered her up with a warm comforter myself and left Phobos to guard her, as I went to the medical wing to see Flora for myself. Nicosid Brandt was sitting in a chair looking haggard and sorrowful. At that moment, his many years were especially noticeable. When I asked about how Florianna was doing, the experienced doctor shrugged his shoulders in confusion:

"My Prince, there is no way you will believe my diagnosis. The bilipid membranes in the girl's nerve cells have been severed and, as if all at once, the nerve cells have been burnt up in whole sections of her body. Such severe damage could only have been done by an infantry combat laser, but, if that were the case, then it isn't clear why no other types of cells were affected, only the nerve cells."

"Stop, stop. Can you say it again but in a language closer to the one I understand?" I asked the doctor. "What kind of injuries does Florianna have and what harmful effects could they cause?"

The doctor looked at me sorrowfully, as if my intellectual capabilities had just fallen sharply in his eyes, and said:

"To put it as simply as possible, she's paralyzed. The cells that transmit nervous impulses to the muscles are fried. Her legs, neck and shoulders suffered especially badly. The poor girl will never be able to move her arms and legs, hold her head up or turn her neck again. She cannot control many face muscles; smiling, frowning, moving her lips, swallowing food, or talking are all going to be impossible for her now. However, she can see and comprehend what she sees and hears. Her brain took no damage, no matter how strange that may be. I, despite all my knowledge and experience, cannot understand what happened to her or how it would be possible to be so precise when maiming a person."

But I, as it were, did know what happened to the kid and who did it. But I wasn't going to tell the doctor that. This information couldn't help him treat her, but it would raise a bunch of questions that I did not need right now. A call came in. I listened to the message and said with a sad smirk:

"Bad news never comes alone. I'd been called to the Throne World to the Emperor with the note *'immediately'*."

HERE, FISHY FISHY

I WAS STANDING in my headquarters next to a big table with a map of Sector Eight displayed on it. Captain Oorast Pohl, not hiding his aggravation, waved off yet another proposed route to the Throne World that I'd torn to shreds. Admiral Kiro Sabuto, sitting next to me, also couldn't contain himself:

"My Prince, where are you getting all this confidence that the Duke will definitely intercept the fleet in Tesse? It's not like we're any old criminals. Yes, there was a sticking point with his son in the Hnelle system, but Peres crawled in there himself, despite knowing it had been officially declared closed. Also, all footage of the battle with detailed time-stamping shows that it was Peres's ships that fired first. They destroyed our frigate first. What accusations could they possibly make?"

"Roben isn't answering my calls," I said, somewhat importunely. "That means that my brother is not at complete liberty. They won't let him talk long-distance. That means he's been given the works and is being pressed to get the information they need out of him. The only one who could imprison someone and conduct an interrogation of the ruler of a star system would be the head of the Orange House. But Roben is a neutral party that isn't engaged in this conflict, and look what he got. Just imagine how Duke Paolo would react if the people who actually fought with his son's fleet tried to come through."

The pair exchanged glances, then the captain of my flagship took a risk and spoke his mind:

"Crown Prince Georg, I mean no offense by this, but this wouldn't be the first time your brother didn't answer your calls for a few days..."

"But it wasn't in such a serious situation!" I interjected. "Yes, I have nothing to hide here. Roben used to get drunk pretty often and binge for many days. All the same, it's still very hard for me to imagine my older brother going on a binge with all this ruckus in the Orange House and fleets of opposing sides flying back and forth through his system. Also, every time I used to try to call Roben, his secretary would answer, but now even that's not happening. And the Tesse news channels are just showing fluff! Everyone well knows that in a system next to Tesse, literally just now, there was a battle between two huge Orange House forces. But even then, none of the many news channels on Tesse is commenting on these events, which are maybe a bit more important than a balloon blowing contest or the opening of a new pastry factory, as was being reported on."

The two had no choice but to agree that what was happening on Tesse was very, very strange. The impression was forming that all information coming out of that star system was going through very strict censorship. The admiral decided to try and get ahold of some acquaintances that lived on Tesse, just to check. At the same time, I tried to get information from my many business partners and suppliers. But, nevertheless, it was all in vain. No kind of interstellar communication was working.

"Let's fly to Hnelle," I decided finally. "Admiral, command the whole fleet to be at the ready in ten minutes! I'm gonna talk to some people to get the beacon turned on for a couple of seconds. We're gonna try to get to the Ulia system, which borders the core through Unguay. Yes, that way is significantly longer but going through Tesse, given how this situation has developed, would be rash."

All the past events poured down on me in one, packed, never-ending day that had begun fifty hours earlier with an arm injury in the gym and ended with a call to the Emperor. During that time, I had only managed to sleep in several-hour naps, so I was so tired that I was practically collapsing. I barely had the strength to throw off my uniform and crash down on the bed. Already dreaming, I might have heard Astra asking if she could lie down next to me because she was afraid to lie alone. It would seem I even gave my permission, but I'm not sure. Then, finally a well-deserved slumber washed over me.

I woke up from a bizarre sound in the room. Someone was cursing someone out at half-voice and even wised up and started swearing at a whisper. Before even cracking an eye, the first thing I did was call up the time panel. I had only managed to sleep five hours. What bastard woke me up?! I opened my eyes to see who this suicidally-inclined individual was. Bionica was sitting on the floor. Her light dress was splashed with something dark. Next to the android, there was a saucer and an overturned mug. Judging by the smell of coffee, my synthetic assistant had brought me my usual morning drink. By the way, judging by the time, on a normal day I would have been waking up at that exact time.

Next to Bionica, who was sitting on the floor, Astra was jumping up and down like an enraged fury. The only thing the Princess had on was a short, practically transparent tunic. Astra winced in pain and shook her beaten-up right fist. She also continued to whisper her complaints to the android. Bionica ran her fingers over the girl's left cheekbone in a very human-like gesture, checking for damage. At the same time, the artificial girl made no move to be quiet, and her language control filter was clearly off. All I had to do was sit up to make both sides of the conflict shut up and turn to me simultaneously. They even bat they're eyelashes at the same time.

"She started it! She came in without knocking!" came out as the reason for my being woken up so early.

I was in no mood to figure out who was at what level of fault and was preparing to simply throw the both of them out. But then, a clear voice rang out in my head.

Duke Paolo royl Anjer's fleet has just arrived in Nessi.

Hearing strange voices in your head is always a pretty bad sign, especially if you recognize who is speaking and realize with horror that it just can't be.

Probably, the expression of surprise and even fear showed on my face, because the quarrelers stopped trying to make appeals and trained their eyes on me.

"Bionica, bring me three more cups of coffee and some pastry to go with. Astra, change into something more appropriate," I ordered.

The android girl stood in silence, picked up the saucer and mug, and went out into the hall. Astra tried to act cute and declared that that was her normal night shirt.

"That's right, it's a *night* shirt. Night was over the second you two woke me up. And now someone from the housekeeping staff is coming to clean up after your fight, and I don't want you to give him a striptease."

I ordered the blinds to open, and the flexible metal bands crawled up from the huge picture-window wall. From this side of the armored glass, you could see flashes of lightening in the purple blackness. *Joan the Fatty* was going through the warp tunnel to Hnelle again. There weren't many windows on the combat cruiser, in that the priority when building the ship was a reliable chassis and not the comfort of its inhabitants. On the more modern *Katanas*, the body was solid and didn't have such obvious weak points as windows. But on the *Flamberg*, for the Crown Prince, they were able to find one of the few berths with nearly two-foot-thick glass.

"It's so beautiful! It's kinda eerie, but it's also just so awesome!" admired the Princess. She had already taken off her tunic and was holding the sealed packet with fresh clothes in her hands. "And where are we flying to?"

I looked from the corner of my eye at the naked, beautiful girl standing three feet away, though I didn't say anything about her appearance. But I did answer the Princess's question:

"We're flying to the Throne World, but we're taking the back way so we don't run into any trouble."

"The Throne World!" Astra clapped in joy. "I've always dreamed of going there! They say it's really pretty there, right? The White Palace, the Silver Palace, a living waterfall, a spinning city, a valley with millions of fires, an underwater tunnel at the bottom of the ocean... I've heard so much about these marvelous places!"

"It probably really is pretty there," I answered evasively. "But you won't be going to the Throne World if you're gonna attack Bionica. I saw a true princess in you – flawlessly neat, modest, and polite. But fighting with a peaceful robot secretary... That means you've still got some learning to do! Now I'm heading briefly to the medical wing to visit your sister and, when I return, I want to see a set table with breakfast and the two of you in a presentable state. Do you understand that, Astra?"

"Yes, my Prince," the girl answered with a slight bow, trying to get back the look of a porcelain doll, but given that she was in her birthday suit, it appeared comical.

"The patient has been sleeping for a long time, my Prince, but we can only know that thanks to the brain function diagrams and moving pupils," Doctor Nicosid

Brandt told me. "You can talk to her and ask questions. She understands them all and answers. I came to an agreement with the girl that closed eyes means 'no' and pupils pointing up means 'yes.' But, unfortunately, the patient was of little help in explaining how such an unusual injury took place. It happened in her sleep, and she woke up already paralyzed."

I asked him to take me into the hospital room. Florianna was lying on the bed, pale and motionless. There were suction cups attached to her arms, neck, temples, and forehead, with different colored wires coming from them leading to a medical device standing not far away. There was an IV stretching out into her arm. Based on what was written on the packet, she was on a glucose drip. I looked at the girl and paid attention to the eyes. They were deeply sunken, swollen and following me closely.

I took a seat next to the newly disabled girl and took her hand. Before all else, I asked her if she was in pain, but Florianna remained silent, not answering yes or no. Nevertheless, the girl made an effort to tell me something, casting her eyes to the side and repeating that motion several times. I looked in that direction. Over there was Nicosid Brandt, who was making some notes on a touch-screen panel at his desk. I asked the old doctor to leave the room briefly. The doctor had barely closed the door before I heard the voice in my head again:

Duke Paolo royl Anjer's fleet has arrived in Nessi. He has more than a thousand ships.

"Thank you, little helper," I said, expressing my gratitude to the girl that was still helping me, despite all the misfortunes that had beset her.

A tear drop suddenly rolled down Flora's face.

It's good that I can still be heard. My sister couldn't hear me, the doctor neither. I was really afraid that I wouldn't be able to talk to anyone... She told me that "my abilities as a Truth Seeker would not be harmed a bit," but if I weren't able to tell anyone about my visions, what would be the point of existing...?

"Hey there, don't cry. I can hear you perfectly, Flora. But now, tell me what happened in detail."

The only one guilty of anything in what happened is me. No one else. When the enemy fleet surrendered in Himora and began putting down their shields, there was another flood of admiration for the commander. It wasn't as mind-shattering as the one after the battle in Hnelle but all the same very strong. And I absorbed it. Not long before that, your Highness truly warned me that there was dangerous information in your brain and that the other part I wasn't old enough for. And out of pure curiosity, I decided I wanted to know what I "wasn't old enough for." But instead I found the "dangerous" stuff.

First, I only read the name "Ruslan." The rest was so incredible that I didn't believe it right away. Right after the new officers were sworn in, I went to my room so I wouldn't give away how overstimulated I was. I was just overcome by the desire to share my discovery with someone, but Astra was sleeping deeply and I didn't want to wake her up. Just imagine what would have happened if I woke my sister up. We'd both be dead at this point!

The girl went silent and closed her eyes. Huge tears streamed down her cheeks. I lightly caressed Flora's arm, but I wasn't sure if she could feel it.

"What happened next?" I asked her to continue her story.

She came to me in my dream. I heard a young woman's voice. That woman told me to wake up, because it wasn't befitting of her to kill someone who was sleeping. I woke up right away from the icy horror, wanting to call someone to help me, but I couldn't – my voice was gone! I was lying there with my eyes open in terror. I saw a room on the starship, and I saw Astra's cot, but I couldn't do anything. And I knew that I would die right then, as my heart had stopped. I really, really wanted to live though, and I don't know how, but I reflected the attack and started my heart again.

"Not bad, not bad. When I first noticed you a few days ago, you were a total nonentity. You learn quick," the woman said, having decided to speak to me again.

And suddenly the cabin disappeared, and I was on the shore of a calm sea on a white sand path. Above me, the bright yellow star of that world was sizzling. The sky was blue and cloudless. Next to me, in an alcove overgrown with vines, there was a young woman sitting in a rocking chair. She had long, straight, copper-red hair and very regular, defined facial features. I've never met such a pretty woman before. My sister is also an outstanding beauty, but Astra is like a brittle snowflake, and that woman is like a bright, beckoning flame. And even her big stomach couldn't spoil the overall impression, which reflected the natural beauty of a mother-to-be. The woman was painting her well-manicured nails bright orange and did not stop doing so, even while talking with me.

"And so, now that you're more than a nonentity, I'll give you a chance. If you answer my three questions correctly, you'll remain alive. Are you ready? Here's the first question. Whether you see it or not, I am very proud of the mental security I have provided Crown Prince Georg. The most admirable thing in my work is that you can't tell it's there. Any Truth Seeker, even with the most careful checking, would reaffirm that Georg royl Inoky's mind is completely open and accessible. In addition, I was sure that no one would be able to dig deep enough into his memory to find the parts I was really hiding. I see that you understand what I'm talking about. Well then, answer me. How did you do it?"

I told her about what happened in Hnelle, then Himora. The woman listened very carefully to my story, then replied thoughtfully:

"That means that Ruslan is defeating his enemies and is loved in the fleet. Everything is going according to plan. Ruslan is doing a good job in the role he was assigned. And even too good, given that a wild Truth Seeker was able to be uncovered so fast in his company. He has declared you his Truth Seeker and allowed you to take nourishment from his power. You are no longer an outsider, and the security let you in. And so, my second question: why does Ruslan want you around? Any old Truth Seeker can sponge off a strong master. But actually helping is something not everyone can do."

The question was unexpectedly difficult. I talked about how I'd located the enemy fleet. I talked about exposing the traitors, but my answers did not satisfy the red-headed woman for some reason. I realized that I wasn't answering the question right, and my life depended on it. Then I had a desperate flash of genius and shouted out that if I'm not around, then another Truth Seeker would be appointed to the Crown Prince, and she might not be as obedient as I.

"Now there's the real right answer. Crown Prince Georg really does need the support of a Truth Seeker and, if you've taken up that role, he'll never accept another. But look, I'm expecting you to continue helping Ruslan with all your strength. And now the third and most important question: how can we make sure that the secret you found carelessly will not be spread any further? I cannot allow any chance of complacency here, no matter how slight. I've got too much riding on this horse."

I promised to keep quiet and tell no one, but she did not accept my promise. She shook her head and answered that it wasn't enough. Then, she said:

"I'll save your life, and your ability as a Truth Seeker will not suffer a bit. But the rest, consider it a punishment for your excessive curiosity and a guarantee that the secret won't get out. Get ready, it's about to hurt."

And a second later, I was back in the starship choking on a scream from the horrible pain and fell on the floor off the cot.

I held the kid's hand. She was crying out of a sense of impotency and shame. Everything became clear to the utmost, but knowing all that couldn't help make Florianna better.

"How can I help you?" I asked, not able to bear the child's tears. "The doctor says that your body is paralyzed forever. So, if you want, you could have the contents of your brain transferred over to an android. You'd be able to walk and talk, and you'd become practically immortal, but you'd still be a robot. Or you could change out your appendages and body parts that have lost the ability to move with cybernetic prostheses."

No need. No need for now. If I acquire the ability to speak, that lady won't spare me a second time. Also, if I become an android, I'll lose the abilities of a Truth Seeker – the only thing that lady sees as valuable in me. Cyborg... sure, that's one option, but not now. Living your whole life as a thirteen-year-old girl without love or children is a curse, not a life. The only thing I'll ask your Highness is to allow me to be next to you in your moments of triumph, and my strength will grow. My worth, even in this motionless state, will continue to increase. And who knows? Maybe one day I'll figure out how to heal my own body.

"How far along is Miya's pregnancy?" I wondered.

That means the red-haired lady really was Miya, Crown Prince Georg's missing Truth Seeker. But alright, I could have guessed that myself if I hadn't been so afraid. I don't know how far along she is. I didn't talk to her long enough to determine the time by the size of her belly. But I can say one thing for sure: Miya is gonna have a girl, and whether she gets a "royl" or a "ton" depends exclusively on your Highness.

* * *

Breakfast went by in an atmosphere of pronounced, cold reconciliation between Bionica and Astra. Both of the beauties were obviously avoiding looking at each other and also were competing to see who knew more or was best at painstakingly following the most minor rules of table etiquette. On the backdrop of these ladies, I felt like an uneducated wild Pithecanthropus, who somehow ended up in the company of aristocrats. When I reached out for a pastry, both of my companions looked at me with such unabashed horror on their faces that it was as if I had at the very least jumped up on the table in dirty boots. Fortunately, *Joan the Fatty* was nearing the exit from the warp tunnel, so I found a plausible excuse and left the room.

The ships were charging their energy at the Hnelle station to be able to go quickly on the route from Tialla to Unguay to Ulia. I argued with the admiral about how to continue the route after the Ulia system through the Core, because Great House combat starships are utterly forbidden from traversing the Imperial Core. I no longer had a yacht, so the only options left were either to urgently buy some civilian ship to take the place of *Queen of Sin* or buy all the tickets on one of the luxury liners, seeing as how it was looked badly upon for an Imperial crown prince to travel in the company of other passengers.

Duke Paolo royl Anjer's fleet has just jumped from

Nessi to the Ulia system.

I cut off the conversation with the admiral and began thinking. The Truth Seeker's information was of critical importance. The head of the Orange House just blocked the only possible route to the Throne World with his fleet. It's done. Now, talking about how to get to the Core or choosing a civilian ship made no sense. In some way or another, my fleet would have to come up against the united forces of the Orange House. I wasn't feeling particularly suicidal, which is why I had dismissed such a path from the get-go. Of course, the option existed to break into the Core by sneaking past the enemy in a cloaked frigate; but, in that case, I would be threatened with severe punishment for entering the Core in a combat starship, a classification which includes cloaked frigates.

"We will not be flying to Tialla," I said, expressing my decision to the officers gathered in the headquarters before telling them that I needed to think alone.

I turned back to my berth and locked the door behind me, seeing as how concentrating in the headquarters – when you're constantly being distracted by people walking by or just officers looking in your direction – was not happening. The choice was a very serious one. What's worse: be late to a meeting with the Emperor and get a serious punishment, or lose a significant part of my fleet to make it there in time? I was tending to the first option, but it was no guarantee that a furious August wouldn't just order my fleet taken from me anyway.

Sitting in silence in the cabin, Princess Astra finally

couldn't bear it any longer and asked why I was so sad. I explained my dilemma to the girl – either be late to a meeting with the Emperor or fight my way to the Throne World.

"My Prince, I'd be totally fine if we just didn't fly to the Throne World this time," answered Princess Astra.

I snickered to myself. The girl was beautiful, but... No, the world "dumb" didn't fit Astra at all. She had a wonderful education; it was just that she was used to seeing the world from her egocentric point of view. She thought I was upset because I promised to show her the Throne World but was having problems following through. By the way, the Princess was an absolute authority on the subtleties of courtly etiquette...

"Astra, I really need your advice." I turned to my favorite.

"Yes, my Prince!" The girl was overjoyed at the chance to finally show her worth.

"Tell me, under what conditions can the Emperor change the time of a scheduled meeting or even cancel it, without giving any punishments to the person who didn't arrive on time?"

The Princess didn't have to think for long before she began fidgeting:

"First, in the case of death or severe illness of the individual called. Second, if the person called is a Mystic, took crystals before being called to the Emperor and is in a several-day-long crystal sleep. Third, if the individual called is under arrest or otherwise detained and cannot come to the Throne World. Fourth, if a war is taking place that the party called is taking active part in and cannot leave the front without upsetting order and causing heavy losses on his side. Fifth, if the call to the Emperor coincides in time with a very important event in the life of the one called – marriage, for example, or the birth of a first son. It seems that's all possibilities. In all other circumstances, said individual must immediately fly to the Emperor as quickly as possible."

War? I considered it seriously. Should I really start an open war with the head of the Orange House? For example, attack his capital while Duke Paolo royl Anjer's ships are God knows where... But I suppose not. No, not because I wouldn't get a pat on the head for it. Just because I wouldn't be able to conquer the Orange House quickly and turn off such a well-protected beacon in a capital station. Also, I am not sure how my subjects would react to such an order as attacking the Orange House Capital. But, nevertheless, there was something to Astra's words.

The solution came unexpectedly.

"Astra, you've been a huge help. If my plan is successful, I'll get in touch with your father immediately and thank him for raising such an excellent, smart daughter, and I'll name the battleship under construction in Unatari in your honor."

The girl went totally red in shame and lowered her eyes. I received a message about her personal opinion of me going up to +85. And when has the Princess had time to get her opinion of me up so high? I gave the girl a peck on the cheek and hurried to the fleet control room.

"This is the Sector Eight Fleet Commander! All ships! I declare that, this very minute, we will begin a training session at full capacity. In the first part, the new members of our fleet are to practice standard approaches to understand what I want from my fleet. In the second half, heavy and light cruisers will work on maintaining distance."

"My Prince, are we going to fight our way through after all?" the admiral clarified with a tremble in his voice.

"That will all depend on how training goes," I answered evasively. "There's no avoiding a fight, but where and with who is something I'll only know at the end of the day."

Katerina ton Mesfelle and I were sitting at a separate table in the officer's dining hall and discussing plans for the future over dinner. I told my trusted advisor honestly that I wanted to avoid such an untimely call to the Emperor, and it was precisely for that reason that I had ordered the Hnelle warp beacon turned on. My cousin, despite all her normal immovability, was simply in shock.

"Georg, instead of preventing an alien invasion, you're inviting them to come to Hnelle?!"

"Yes, that's exactly right, cousin. I, as the person entrusted with the defense of Sector Eight, am simply obliged to check whether the appearance of the alien ships the last time was a coincidence, or whether the aliens really are ready for an invasion. At the same time, if even one of their ships really comes to take a look at the switched-on beacon, I'll have an iron-clad reason not to fly to the Throne World. And then, Duke

Paolo royl Anjer's fleet can stay blocking the path to the Core 'til he's blue in the face. I still won't have to fight my way through his screen."

Katerina threw herself onto the back of a chair and began tousling a lock of her hair.

"Does anyone else know?" my advisor clarified a minute later.

"No one but you. I bet Admiral Kiro Sabuto is figuring it out, though. He gave me a really weird look when I gave the order to turn on the beacon. Though, it is possible that the admiral thinks it's some kind of bait for the Duke's fleet to get the Orange House ships out of the Ulia system."

"And what if the Duke really does send his ships here?"

"He won't have time. Also, my Truth Seeker is constantly following his fleet, and in Tesse I have an "oculus" – Angel's cloaked frigate won't let any combat ships get by unnoticed."

My cousin bent closer over me and said, barely audible:

"Admit the truth, Georg. Can you really hear the paralyzed girl? Or is that just a show for the public to highlight how exceptional you are to your subjects?"

Such mistrust actually made me somewhat hurt. I didn't start cursing, though, I just confirmed that I really could hear Florianna's voice. Then I added quietly:

"The poor girl! With me, her skills were growing too fast for someone without any experience. And she was not being careful enough. As a result, she accidentally detected the very thing Miya is trying to hide, and predictably, she suffered for her dangerous knowledge. Because it isn't for nothing that Miya is hiding. She is pregnant, and she thinks that too many people would want to take advantage of her weak point in that period and bring harm to her or the baby. But this is a secret, you understand that."

"Of course I understand. It isn't a small matter. So it was Miya that maimed her? Well, alright. It's a fairly predictable result for someone who was digging around in your Truth Seeker's business. Cousin, let's trade honesty for honesty, alright? Do you remember Viscount Sivir's story about our adventure in the institute? Well, there weren't any hackers. It was all me. As soon as the security went down, I transferred all the institute's money to one of my accounts. It was a huge scandal. Count Olberg paid the institute for all losses from his own funds, and the allegations against his son were dropped. No one even thought it could have been me."

"Come on. It looks like you're still that same scoundrel today!" I chuckled, hiding my surprise at her frankness behind a smile.

My second cousin snorted in offense:

"I just consider it my special talent to make decisions quickly. By the way, Georg, I just had an idea! Let's broadcast the alien invasion of Hnelle live! You lead the battle, and I'll set up a series of urgent broadcasts from the attacked system every fifteen minutes toward all systems in the Empire. You just have to win, and I'll try to make it so that the whole Empire will worry for us and keep their fingers crossed until the very end."

* * *

"Attention, all ships. Be at the ready in three minutes! The last time, the aliens appeared four hours and eight minutes after the beacon was turned on. Our mission is to check if that was just a coincidence. Heavies, get together more compact. Check your connections. *Hunchback's Heir,* you're falling out of formation. *Bride of Chaos,* you don't get away from the others either. *Tria,* stay at least twelve hundred miles out."

The seconds ticked by. The levels of stress in the headquarters grew to a fevered pitch. All unrelated conversations quieted down. People began looking at the big clock on the wall more and more frequently. One person prayed. Nicole Savoia, sitting next to me, got especially nervous. Her fingers were noticeably shaking, and she was fidgeting with her "Silver Brooch." I tried to distract my assistant with conversation.

"Nicole, what's your opinion? Will they come or not? And if they come, how many?"

The girl gave a start:

"I think they'll come. And not two like last time, but a lot. Five."

"Do you think five is a lot?" I said in surprise, even beginning to snigger. "We could grind five of them into dust and not even feel it. The main thing is that they come. I wouldn't like to fight with ships from our very own Orange House."

"Ready in thirty seconds!" said the officer.

I placed my hands on the console and took another look at my subjects that were gathered around me in my headquarters. No one was confused or lost. Everyone knew what they were supposed to be doing. The team had made good progress. They were sure of themselves and their commander. Everything was how it should be.

"Five, four, three..."

"Here, fishy fishy!" I exclaimed loudly.

In response, I got a cry of surprise in unison with notes of distress. The aliens did come. And it was even somehow an unexpectedly large number. Many more than I thought...

END OF BOOK ONE

ABOUT THE AUTHOR

Michael Atamanov was born in 1975 in Grozny, Chechnia. He excelled at school, winning numerous national science and writing competitions. Having graduated with honors, he entered Moscow University to study material engineering. Soon, however, he had no home to return to: their house was destroyed during the first Chechen campaign. Michael's family fled the war, taking shelter with some relatives in Stavropol Territory in the South of Russia.

Having graduated from the University, Michael was forced to accept whatever work was available. He moonlighted in chemical labs, loaded trucks, translated technical articles, worked as a software installer as well as scene shifter for local artists and events. At the same time he never stopped writing, even when squatting in some seedy Moscow hostels. Writing became an urgent need for Michael, driving him to submit articles to science publications, news fillers for a variety of web sites and a plethora of technical and copywriting gigs.

Then one day unexpectedly for himself he started writing fairy tales and science fiction novels. For several years, his audience consisted of only one person: Michael's elder son. Then, at the end of 2014 he decided to upload one of his manuscripts to a free online writers resource. Readers liked it and demanded a sequel. Michael uploaded another book, and yet another, his audience growing as did his list. It was his readers who helped Michael hone his writing style. He finally had the breakthrough he deserved when the Moscow-based EKSMO - the biggest publishing house in Europe - offered him a contract for his first and consequent books.

Want to be the first to know about our latest LitRPG, sci fi and fantasy titles from your favorite authors?

Subscribe to our NEW RELEASES newsletter:
http://eepurl.com/b7niIL

Thank you for reading *Sector Eight!*
If you like what you've read, check out other LitRPG
novels published by Magic Dome Books:

Dark Paladin LitRPG series by Vasily Mahanenko:
The Beginning
The Quest

**The Dark Herbalist LitRPG series
by Michael Atamanov:**
Video Game Plotline Tester
Stay on the Wing

The Neuro LitRPG series by Andrei Livadny:
The Crystal Sphere
The Curse of Rion Castle

**The Way of the Shaman LitRPG series
by Vasily Mahanenko:**
Survival Quest
The Kartoss Gambit
The Secret of the Dark Forest
The Phantom Castle
The Karmadont Chess Set
The Hour of Pain (a bonus short story)

Galactogon LitRPG series by Vasily Mahanenko:
Start the Game!

Phantom Server LitRPG series by Andrei Livadny:
Edge of Reality
The Outlaw
Black Sun

**Perimeter Defense LitRPG series by Michael
Atamanov:**
Sector Eight
Beyond Death
New Contract

In order to have new books of the series translated faster, we need your help and support! Please consider leaving a review or spread the word by recommending *Sector Eight* to your friends and posting the link on social media. The more people buy the book, the sooner we'll be able to make new translations available.

Thank you!

Till next time!

Made in the USA
Middletown, DE
07 January 2018